midnight
CALLER

leslie TENTLER

midnight CALLER

MIRA®

MIRA®

ISBN-13: 978-0-7783-2934-3

MIDNIGHT CALLER

In memory of my mother, who taught me the thrill of a rainy day and a good book.

ACKNOWLEDGMENTS

There are so many people
to whom I am indebted. Many thanks to
my agent, Stephany Evans, at FinePrint, and
to Susan Swinwood and Linda McFall at
MIRA Books for their wonderful guidance and
support. Thanks also to my husband, Robert,
for his unending patience and handling of all
things in our lives not book-related,
and to my friend Michelle for being
my reader and constant sounding board.

1

Trevor Rivette waited in autopsy room three in the basement of All Saints Hospital, aware the conversation taking place in the corridor was centered on him. The door had been left ajar, and he listened intently as he looked around the windowless space that held the sharp odor of antiseptic.

"The FBI man's in there with the body. Says he just got into town."

The heavy drawl belonged to Douglas Semer, medical examiner for the Orleans Parish, whom Trevor had met a short time earlier. A pale, older man with thick glasses that gave him an owlish look, he'd greeted Trevor's arrival with a hint of suspicion.

"How long's he been waiting?" another male voice asked.

"Half hour, maybe."

A third man spoke. His voice was gruffer, as if he'd been smoking cigarettes for most of his life. "He say why the feds are interested in our dead body?"

"Nope. I told him I'd have to wait for the NOPD to get here before I could give a rundown on the gross exam." Semer's reply held a tone that suggested *we local boys stick together.*

Trevor returned his gaze to the stainless-steel autopsy table that held the victim's nude body. The girl's lips were blue and slightly parted, and her reddish-blond hair fanned out behind her head. A body block had been used to position the corpse for autopsy, and the telltale Y-incision that ran from each shoulder before extending into a single line down to the pubic bone indicated Semer had completed his job.

She was sixteen at best, years younger than the other victims so far. The fact that she was barely more than a child made this particular death seem even more pointless and brutal. Releasing a breath, Trevor stared at the engraving on the room's wall. The words were in Latin, but he made the translation easily.

This is the place where death rejoices to teach.

When it came to dead women lying on tables, he felt as though he'd already learned enough to last him several lifetimes.

The door to the autopsy room opened, and Semer entered with the two men he'd been conversing with in the hallway.

"Detectives McGrath and Thibodeaux, this is Agent Rivette with the FBI." Semer made the introduction, and Trevor stepped forward to shake hands. The first, McGrath, was middle-aged and heavyset with a balding pate and a mustache, and Thibodeaux was a lanky African-American with hair that had begun to gray at the temples. Like Trevor, they both wore holstered guns on their hips.

McGrath made a point of squinting at the guest pass clipped to Trevor's suit lapel. "So, Special Agent Rivette, Semer says you're from up north. Does that mean you're from the field office in Mobile?"

Trevor smiled faintly at his joke. "A little farther north than that. D.C., actually. I'm with the Violent Crimes Unit."

"VCU, huh? That's big time." McGrath's expression, however, indicated he was unimpressed.

Trevor continued, "I was on my way to your precinct to

get a look at the crime scene photos, but I wanted to stop by here and see if the autopsy report was ready."

"Only an unofficial one," Semer stated. "Nothing's typed up yet and the toxicology results won't be back till tomorrow—"

"Rivette's a local name." The other detective, Thibodeaux, cut in. Leaning against the front of the built-in refrigeration unit where bodies were stored, he looked at Trevor with interest. "Genealogy's a hobby of mine. If I'm not mistaken, your last name's Acadian, isn't it?"

Trevor nodded faintly. "I've got some family here."

When he offered no further details, Thibodeaux moved his attention to the corpse. "This girl somebody special, Agent? You've come a long way."

"It's not so much the victim as the way she was murdered." A microphone used for recording the medical examiner's notes hung over the autopsy table. Trevor moved it out of the way so he could lean over the body and point out a puncture wound behind the tip of the jaw. "The jugular and carotid artery were severed in a single slice. The manner of death, along with the rosary used to bind the victim's hands, fits a pattern of murders in other cities over the past eighteen months. ViCAP kicked out your victim as another possible match."

McGrath tapped the notepad he was holding with a ballpoint pen. "You're saying we've got a serial murderer working New Orleans?"

"I doubt this is coincidental. The M.O. is too similar, which is why I flew down."

"To take over our case."

Trevor stared at an open cabinet that contained tools of the trade, including a rib spreader and handheld bone saw. He was prepared for resistance. "Look. I know local police and the FBI have a reputation for not getting along—"

"Like atheists at the Vatican," Thibodeaux muttered.

"That doesn't have to be the situation here," Trevor emphasized. "I'm not interested in who gets credit for what—I just want to find this guy. We can work this murder together, share information, or we can work it apart. But this is New Orleans, and I'm guessing you guys have a backlog of cases that need to be moved into the black."

Thibodeaux narrowed his eyes. "So it's a *help me help you* kind of deal?"

"Something like that."

Rubbing his jaw, McGrath asked, "How many victims?"

"Five, counting this one."

"Where?"

"D.C., Atlanta, Memphis and Raleigh. Now here. The good news for you is that he seems to have a one-vic-per-city policy. He may have already moved on, which means I will soon, too."

"And if he hasn't?" Thibodeaux inquired.

"Then we got a bigger problem than one dead body." McGrath scratched behind his ear with the pen. "The media give this prick a name yet?"

Trevor crossed his arms over his chest. "The press hasn't connected the murders yet due to the widely dispersed locales, and because certain identical facts have been kept confidential. Internally, he's being referred to as the Vampire, based on the method of killing and because several of the victims have been tied to the goth club scene in their respective cities."

"Well, this one was found in an abandoned shotgun on Tchoupitoulas, nowhere near any of the nightlife," Thibodeaux said. "'Course, lividity suggests she was relocated several hours after death. The amount of blood at the crime scene also doesn't match the severity of the vic's injuries."

McGrath turned to the M.E. "Speakin' of, we got an ID on her yet?"

"Still a Jane Doe," Semer said, taking his c
to the autopsy table and clicked on the overhead
snapped on a pair of latex gloves. "You boys rea
full tour?"

The harsh lighting made the dead girl's ashen skin look nearly transparent, and the body cavity sagged along the closed autopsy incision due to the removal of internal organs.

McGrath blanched. "Jesus, Semer. What you do with the stuff you pull out of 'em, I don't wanna know."

"Then I won't tell you." Semer shifted his eyes to Trevor. "But Agent Rivette is correct—the cut to the throat was the fatal strike. It was basically an exsanguination. Approximate forty percent blood loss."

Using his gloved hand, he indicated other incisions on the body. "All these other cuts, mostly superficial, were made antemortem."

He pushed his glasses up the bridge of his nose. "If you want my opinion, I'd say the son of a bitch took his sweet time with her before she died."

What had once been a working-class neighborhood had taken a distinct turn for the better, but the house in New Orleans's Faubourg Marigny District still looked familiar to Trevor Rivette. Changes had been made, of course, so that the house was a better fit with the BMWs and Volvos parked along the tree-lined street, vehicles of the upwardly mobile families who now inhabited the area, pushing up the homes' value. Like the neighboring houses, the West Indies-style cottage was no longer a staid white. Painted a vibrant raspberry, its gingerbread trim was well cared for and accented in pink. Wrought-iron picket fencing bordered the yard, and rattan rockers sat on the covered front porch next to green ferns in clay pots. From his vantage point on the sidewalk,

.evor heard children's laughter coming from somewhere down the street. A wind chime on the house's porch tinkled in the warm zephyr of the early evening.

If he didn't know better, he might think this had been a good place to grow up.

He opened the fence gate and walked the short distance up to the porch. As Trevor stood on its whitewashed, wood-planked flooring, his hand rose from his jeans pocket to rub briefly at his forehead. This was Annabelle's house now. The ghosts were still here only if he let them be.

She must have been waiting for him, because the door opened before he knocked. Annabelle Rivette smiled as she pulled her brother into her arms. When she finally released him, Trevor stared into the face that was ingrained in his memory. Annabelle had changed little. Her wavy, brunette hair and sky-blue eyes were exactly as he remembered.

"It's been a long time, Trevor," she said.

"Too long," he admitted. He was regretful of how much time he'd allowed to pass. It had been three years since he was last in New Orleans. He'd returned for their mother's funeral, but even then he'd arrived only a short time before the service and left soon after. There had been a justifiable reason—a double homicide in Richmond had pulled him away. But they both knew that even without the responsibilities of his career with the FBI's Violent Crimes Unit, he'd have found it difficult to stay.

A child's thin voice called from inside the house, and Annabelle led Trevor from the porch into the front room. Nearly everything here was different. The high-ceilinged space was painted blue and beige, and an area rug covered the wood floors. Plantation shutters had taken the place of heavy curtains over the windows. The stiff antique furniture was also gone, banished in favor of an overstuffed couch and matching chair with an ottoman. Even the fireplace mantel, which was original to the house and hand carved from cypress wood, had lost its dark stain. It was repainted white, and the antique mirror that had once hung over it was replaced with a cheerful painting of a French Quarter scene.

"There you are," Annabelle said as a little girl came into the room. "Haley, this is your uncle Trevor."

Haley stared up at him unabashedly. A stuffed animal, a purple angora cat that looked as if it had seen better days, dangled from her grasp. Tendrils of curly hair had escaped from her ponytail, and she brushed them out of her face with a slight frown of annoyance.

"I haven't seen you since you were a baby," Trevor said.

"I'm not a baby anymore. I'm five years old." She held up one small hand with all her fingers outstretched.

He smiled as he knelt down, putting himself at eye level with his niece. "What I meant was that your mom sends me photos, but I didn't realize how big you'd gotten."

Haley swung the frazzled cat back and forth, her eyes still fastened on Trevor. "You look like Uncle Brian."

His chest tightened at the mention of his brother's name. He thought of Brian's dark hair and blue-gray eyes, so much like his own. "Yeah, I guess I do."

"Mommy says you have a gun, like a policeman. Did you bring it?"

"I left it at the hotel." He didn't mention the compact off-duty gun, a .380 Beretta semiautomatic he was carrying concealed in an ankle holster. "They're not safe, you know."

"Then why do *you* have one?"

Trevor looked at Annabelle. The grin on her face seemed to say, *See what I put up with?*

"Dinner will be ready soon, sweetie," she said to Haley. "Why don't you go play for a while. Uncle Trevor and I are going to talk about grown-up stuff."

"Can I watch cartoons?"

"Knock yourself out," Annabelle replied, and Haley disappeared down the hallway.

"Thank God for television." She looked at Trevor, who had stood back up and was glancing around the room. "Do you want something to drink?"

"Just a soda, if you have one."

He followed her into the small kitchen. Trendy Mexican tile had replaced the worn linoleum, and there were new appliances in eggshell white. A pot of something savory bubbled on the stove, filling the air with the scent of tomatoes and spicy peppers. A gourmet coffeemaker sat on the counter, instead of the old-fashioned percolator Trevor recalled from his childhood. Like the parlor, everything about this room was fresh and new. It was as if Annabelle thought she could transform the house's karma by ripping out enough fixtures and flooring, and covering the walls with a coat of paint. The image of a hulking man with a swinging fist clutched at him, stealing his breath before it disappeared as swiftly as it came. Trevor touched the scar that ran along the base of his chin. His proof the past existed.

"You okay?" Annabelle handed him a soda from the refrigerator.

"Yeah." He nodded, aware that despite their time apart, his sister still had the ability to read his face.

Annabelle had also gotten out a soda for herself, and they sat down across from one another at the table. He took a sip from the can that was already slick with condensation and stared out the window into the small backyard bordered by an ancient brick wall. A massive, moss-draped live oak provided a canopy for nearly the entire patio area and farther back, a child's swing set. Looking up through the tree's outstretched limbs he could see slivers of sky as daylight faded into the gathering dusk.

"Sawyer Compton says hello," Annabelle said. Sawyer was

an old friend who'd grown up a few streets over. He'd played football at Louisiana State University before attending law school, and Trevor knew he was serving as assistant D.A. for the Orleans Parish.

"How is he?"

She smiled as she lifted the soda can to her lips. "Maybe you should stick around and find out for yourself. He's having his annual crawfish boil in a few weeks."

"You know why I'm here, Anna."

Her expression turned serious. "Your job. It's the only thing that could make you come home, short of a family crisis. How many days are you here?"

"I don't know yet."

"But no longer than you have to be?" When he didn't answer, Annabelle relented. "You look tired, Trevor..."

Her words trailed away as he reached out and took her hand. His eyes fell on her wrist, which had become visible at the sleeve of her cotton blouse. Annabelle said his name softly, but he held on to her, his fingers tracing the raised edges of the scar. He knew there was a matching one on the other wrist, which she'd discreetly hidden under the table out of his view. Trevor's brow furrowed.

"You ever see him, Anna?"

"Dad?" She shook her head. "No."

"Does Brian ever see him?"

"I doubt it."

Trevor nodded but didn't speak. Annabelle slowly pulled her fingers from his and went to the stove, stirring the pot's contents with a wooden spoon. She opened the door to the oven, peering inside at a loaf of French bread and turning on the broiler to brown its top.

"Don't let me forget about that." Closing the door, she moved around the kitchen, pulling out dishes from an overhead cabinet. In that instant, she reminded Trevor of their mother, during the better times when she hadn't been drinking.

Annabelle turned around, leaning against the counter as she spoke. "You're surprised I'm still living here, aren't you?"

"Yeah, I guess I am."

"There were some good memories here, too. It took me a long time to remember that. You, Brian and I were still together."

Annabelle returned to the table with plates and a stack of paper napkins. Trevor stood and took the plates from her, putting one in front of each seat while she went to retrieve the silverware from a drawer next to the sink. When she came back, she said, "When Scott and I split up, the truth is I didn't have anywhere else to go. Haley and I needed a home, and Mom left this house to all of us."

"You've done a great job with it."

"Brian and Alex have been a big help. They painted the house, put in the new kitchen floor and rebuilt the porch."

"Anna, the bread."

Using a dish towel as an oven mitt, she withdrew the plump loaf and dropped it on top of the stove. "One-third of the house belongs to you, you know. With the prices they're getting in Marigny these days…"

"I don't want anything. It's enough for me if you and Haley are happy here. I'll sign my share of the house over to you, if that's what you want."

"Brian said the same thing, but I'd prefer it if we all still owned a piece of it." She paused, running her hands along the top of her jeans. "You don't have to keep sending me checks, Trevor. I'm back on my feet now, and I'm working at the gallery four days a week, handling the bookkeeping. In fact, I want to pay you back when I can."

He shrugged. It had been only a few hundred dollars a

month, but he thought his sister could use the money, with Haley to care for. He knew the child-support payments arrived sporadically at best. "Don't pay me back. Just put the money in my niece's college fund, okay?"

Annabelle's eyes filled with emotion. She walked to Trevor and hugged him.

"It's good to see you," she whispered. He held his sister in his arms.

When they pulled apart, she tried to hide the glimmer of tears. "Dinner's ready. I'll go get Haley. She doesn't wash her hands if you don't stand over her."

Trevor's gaze moved to the table. He'd already noticed it had been set for only three.

"Brian flew Alex's Cessna down to Naples," she explained. "Some pain-in-the-ass client keeps changing his mind about the artwork for his beach house and Alex couldn't go in his place. He said to tell you he's sorry, and that he'll call you tomorrow."

"I hope they're giving drug tests to private pilots these days, too."

Annabelle looked at him. "He's been clean for nearly two years now. And he really does want to see you."

He merely nodded, watching as his sister left the room. He thought of the last time he'd seen Brian and the hurtful things they'd said to one another. Trevor hadn't meant a word of it, but he'd been frustrated and angry. He'd also been terrified Brian's problems were his fault.

He's been clean for nearly two years now.

More than anything, Trevor realized, he wanted Annabelle's declaration to be true.

2

Despite her urging, Trevor didn't stay with Annabelle, preferring to sleep somewhere that didn't hold his history within its walls. Instead, he'd booked himself at a nearby inn on Esplanade Avenue, at the edge of Marigny bridging the French Quarter.

Annabelle was right, he conceded as he unpacked his clothing from his travel bag. If his job hadn't demanded his return, he wouldn't be here, save for a family emergency. Trevor thought of the house his sister now inhabited and wondered how she managed to commune in seeming comfort with the ghosts of their shared past. The scars on her wrists proved the ability hadn't always come so easily.

He looked around the room, which was clean and affordable enough to be on the FBI's approved-expenditures list. It had worn dark carpet and a television that sat on the dresser across from the double bed. A single French door led to a balcony overlooking the inn's courtyard and pool. Trevor walked out onto it and stared into the gently lapping waters below.

Five females, tied up and tortured, their throats methodically cut. He rubbed his hands over his face, knowing his failure to catch this psychopath had resulted in another death.

Special Agent in Charge Johnston, head of the FBI's Violent Crimes Unit, had assigned Trevor to look into the so-called Vampire Murders occurring in different states as a special VCU project. The protocol had become almost routine: sometimes with or without a partner, Trevor went to the city where a murder fitting the pattern was found, gathered information and worked the case, then passed it on to the local FBI field office in each respective city when the leads ran cold.

And so far, that was pretty much all he had—cold leads. There had been no witnesses, no DNA match in the ViCAP database, and the widely dispersed locales meant the deaths were considered by local authorities to be isolated cases. Only the VCU had noted a unifying modus operandi, which was why it had gotten involved.

In the meantime, while Trevor still didn't know the unsub, the unsub had gotten to know him. The perpetrator had established contact—hand-written notes, souvenirs from kills sent through the mail—so far all of it untraceable and meant to prove the Vampire was far superior to his hunter.

Unable to shake off his frustration, Trevor went inside and changed into running shorts, a gray T-shirt and tennis shoes. His iPod was on the fritz, so he'd brought a small transistor radio with earphones to accompany him on his regular five-mile run. Trevor picked it up from the dresser, hoping the device could drown out his inner monologue of doubt and self-recrimination. Closing the door to the room behind him, he went down the stairs, stretched in the faint glow of the swimming pool and took off toward the French Quarter. As he ran, he kept a steady pace despite the city's humidity that lingered well after dark. The music from the radio strapped to his upper arm was the only sound he heard.

Inside the Quarter, the throngs of tourists had thinned from earlier in the day. But there were still people out on the narrow streets, many of them with go-cups in their hands as they strolled between the bars and strip clubs in the timeworn buildings. As he turned the corner of Chartres onto Dumaine, Trevor toggled the radio's dial without breaking his stride. The classic-rock station he'd located at the inn was becoming static filled, the Rolling Stones's "Sympathy for the Devil" fading in and out of white noise. He skipped over jazz, blues and Cajun zydeco stations that weren't coming in much better, then stopped dialing when a teenage female voice emerged clearly over the airwaves.

"Who is he to tell me what I can or can't do with my body? He's not even my *real* dad."

"How old are you, Shayla?"

"I'm fourteen, almost fifteen."

"I see." The other voice was that of a woman, laced with a soft Southern drawl. "What kind of tat did you have in mind?"

"I wanted an ankh, not too big, on my shoulder." Trevor knew what the symbol was, a cross topped by an oval loop, an Egyptian symbol for eternal life popular within the goth subculture.

"Well, that sounds pretty tame. What does your mom think?"

"She doesn't care about me or what I do."

There was a lull in the conversation, as if the woman was actually considering the caller's dilemma. *Of course, she was too young to have a tattoo,* Trevor thought, ignoring the sweat that stung his eyes. *Why doesn't the woman just tell her that?* People on the street looked like blurred watercolor images as he ran past.

"Here's what you *could* do. You could get one anyway, without your stepfather's permission."

Great idea. Trevor shook his head, sprinting in front of

a horse-drawn carriage carrying a group of cup-sloshing revelers.

"But if you do," the woman continued, "you're going to deal with some major grief when he finds out."

"Tell me about it." He could almost hear the teen rolling her eyes.

"There's one thing I want to mention. You said your mom doesn't care about you. I have no idea if that's really the case, but maybe your stepfather is saying no because he doesn't want you to do something you'd regret later in life. Tattoos are permanent, and he wants to be sure you're ready for a commitment like that. Misguided or not, it sounds like he cares."

The girl was quiet for a moment. "Maybe."

"Take my advice, Shayla. Take the money you'd spend on a tattoo and get an ankh pendant, an expensive one. Consider it a wardrobe investment. Wear it, and when you're eighteen, if you still want the tattoo, go for it."

The call ended, and the woman said, "You're listening to *Midnight Confessions* with Dr. Rain Sommers on WNOR, New Orleans's alternative radio."

The station switched to a jingle for low-carb beer. With a sickening jolt, Trevor became aware of where his subconscious had guided him. Dauphine Street. Mallory's was only a short distance away, where his father was either pouring liquor behind the bar or drinking away his paycheck on the other side of it. He stopped running, bending at the waist with his hands on his thighs as he caught his breath. He closed his eyes, his indecision frustrating him, but the magnetic pull of the bar finally won out.

I won't go in, he vowed. All he needed was to see the bastard through the window and confirm for himself that God in all his injustice hadn't yet seen fit to strike him down. The talk-show host returned to the air as Trevor wiped his face with the damp cotton of his T-shirt and set back out.

"Our next caller is Daniel from the French Quarter. What do you want to talk about tonight, Daniel?"

"I want to talk about you, Rain. About your legacy."

There was a moment of dead air. "Sorry. We don't talk about me, that's one of the rules. Do you have a problem I can help with tonight?"

"You're my problem, Rain. I can't get you out of my mind."

"That sounds like a pick-up line. A clichéd one."

Just as the woman's voice was sultry, the caller's was deep and hypnotic. Trevor forced his muscles to work harder. The street seemed to be giving off waves of heat, the air around him heavy, and any hint of a breeze had disappeared.

"It's true, Rain. I've become quite interested in you."

"My star must be rising. I have my first bona fide stalker." Her tone was edged with sarcasm. "Look, Daniel. We're busy people around here, so worship me on your own time. Now, do you have something to talk about or not?"

When the caller merely laughed, she added, "So, how old are you, Dan? You sound a little more *mature* than our regular callers."

"You could say I'm a little older."

"How much?"

"Older than you can *possibly* imagine."

Trevor was lost in the conversation, oblivious to the speed at which he was running. The bar, a shabby dive where James Rivette worked, sat across the street. A Budweiser sign blinked in its darkened window.

"And Rain? My name isn't Daniel. It's Dante."

Trevor ran into the street just as the speeding Cadillac turned the corner against a red light. The car slammed on its brakes and screeched as it tried to stop. His body contacted with the fender, spun once and thudded on the car's hood before dropping onto the oily street. Pain shot through his skull as the black Louisiana sky closed in around him.

3

"Why the hell did you hang up on him?"

Rain glanced up as David D'Alba's voice came over the intercom at WNOR. She could see him through the window that separated the production room from the on-air studio where she sat. He stared at her, his headphones around his neck and his hands on his lean hips. When she didn't answer, he tossed the headphones onto the console and strode toward her.

"The guy was a creep, David."

"Which is why you should've kept him on the line." He went to the monitor to check the playtime left on a song track being used during the show's break. Then, moving her microphone out of the way, he parked himself on the desk's edge and stretched out his long legs on either side of her chair.

"So his questions were a little out of line," he remarked. "It was making for a good show."

"He asked me about Desiree."

David shrugged. "Everyone asks you about Desiree."

"He wanted to know if I liked rough sex, among some more perverse things I'd prefer not to repeat."

"What can I say? We've got some sick puppies out there."

"I'm a psychologist, David. I'm used to all types of topics, but the rule is that we discuss the caller's problem. I don't talk about my personal life, especially my sex life, on the air."

"Maybe you should." He reached out to toy with a strand of her red-gold hair. "It could boost our Arbitron ratings."

Rain pushed away from the desk. She stood and paced the small studio. "It wasn't so much what the guy was saying. It was just—"

"The *way* he said it?"

She ignored the smirk on David's handsome face.

"Okay, the guy was a jerk. We've established that." Growing serious, he shifted his weight on the desk and folded his arms across his chest.

Rain stopped pacing and leaned against the wall's soundproof padding. In the production room, David's assistant, Ella LaRue, was tidying up. She wore a tight, cropped T-shirt with D'Alba Enterprises printed across its front and an even tighter pair of denim shorts. Seeing Rain's gaze on her, Ella offered a smile that was syrupy sweet, but her espresso eyes were cold. She leaned forward, her raven hair spilling over one shoulder as she pressed the intercom button.

Ella's honeyed voice flooded the room. "Thirty seconds and counting, David."

"Run an ad spot. We're not done in here." He looked at Rain pointedly.

"My listeners are primarily teens and young adults," Rain said. "And yes, at times they say things for shock effect. But that man sounded much older."

"Now you're an ageist?"

"That's not what I mean and you know it." She shook her head, unsure of how to explain the feelings the caller had provoked. Normally, she had the ability to blow off the freaks who occasionally got onto the airwaves, but Daniel or Dante or whatever he'd called himself had rattled her.

"There was just something insidious about him," she said quietly.

"I still haven't heard a reason for disconnecting a caller during a live show." David rubbed a hand over the stubble on his jaw, a sign of his increasing impatience. "You left me with dead air, and that's unacceptable."

"Then you need to do a better job screening callers."

"Hold on." Rising from the desk, he closed the small distance between them. "I'm the producer and you're the talent, remember? Who gets through to you is my decision."

Rain kept her words controlled. "This show is supposed to offer advice, not pander to the lowest common denominator. This isn't what I had in mind, David. You convinced me nine months ago that if I did this show I could reach more kids than I ever could through private counseling. And I believed you."

Her eyes slid closed. *And I did this for you.*

She wanted to add that she'd agreed to the show to help out the career of the man she thought she'd loved. Until *Midnight Confessions,* Rain had managed to live her life in relative anonymity. She'd never sought out the spotlight that was in many ways her birthright as Desiree Sommers's daughter. But she had no one to blame except herself. She'd compromised her principles because she'd been too infatuated with David to deny him, or to think rationally about what he wanted her to do.

"You *are* reaching them, Rain." David put his fingers under her chin and lifted her gaze to his. "They're listening to you."

Before she could react, his thumb brushed her bottom lip. His head dipped lower, his intent clear. Rain stiffened and placed her hand against his chest.

"Don't," she whispered. In her peripheral vision, she saw Ella storm from the production room. David took a step back, acknowledging her rebuff with a few sharp nods of his head.

"I know I screwed up with you," he admitted. "But I won't have you damaging this show."

"What does that mean?"

"It means you need to get the stick out of your ass, *Dr. Sommers.* So this guy wasn't some spoiled teenager, whining because Mommy doesn't love him enough to buy him a sports car. That's good. It means we're broadening the audience. And if it takes some kinky-sex talk to get listeners tuning in, so be it."

David raked a hand through his hair, which shone nearly blue-black under the studio's recessed lighting. "Was this guy a nutcase? Absolutely. But this show's about ratings, and it's your job to keep guys like him on the line. I've got a lot riding on this, Rain."

He looked up as the on-air sign began to blink above them. "We're back in thirty seconds."

"David—"

He turned at the doorway. "There's another caller waiting in the queue. A sweet fifteen-year-old whose boyfriend is pressuring her to have unprotected sex."

A flicker of indignation remained in his dark eyes. "See if you can handle this one without a meltdown."

He drove her home once the show had ended. David's Jaguar stopped in front of the Greek Revival house in the Lower Garden District, its powerful engine idling as Rain searched on the floorboard for her handbag.

"I could come in for a while," he suggested. The rest of the show had gone off without a hitch, and David's foul mood had given way to his usual charm. "Just to talk?"

Rain shook her head and reached for the door handle. "It's

late and I have a private counseling session early tomorrow morning."

"I'm sorry about tonight. The guy spooked you. I should've been more understanding." He stared out the windshield before speaking again. "I've been under some pressure lately."

"It's okay." She gave him a vague smile. "Good night, David."

His hand returned to the leather curve of the steering wheel. "I want you back, Rain. I'm not giving up on that."

Their eyes met before she closed the door and walked the short distance from the sidewalk to the house's veranda. The Jaguar remained out front until she was inside. She watched from the foyer as David made a sharp turn in the street, the car's headlights briefly illuminating the scaffolding on a neighboring house that was under renovation.

As David drove away, Rain wondered if he would go to his own French Quarter apartment, or whether he'd seek out some other female companionship. David was a sexual creature, she'd always known that. It was part of his attraction. But she hadn't expected him to cheat on her.

They'd been together for only a few months when Rain had walked into David's office at WNOR on a night she wasn't supposed to be there. He had looked remorseful as he struggled to get dressed, but Ella hadn't bothered to cover herself. Instead, she'd remained sprawled across David's desk, her skirt hiked up around her hips and her blouse discarded on the floor.

He'd called it a slipup. A moment of weakness that wouldn't happen again. Still, despite David's pleading, Rain had ended their relationship with the exception of her contractual obligation to *Midnight Confessions*. Time had passed and they'd managed to maintain a loose friendship for the show's sake, but she continued to deflect his attempts at reconciliation.

The truth, she thought as she laid her handbag on the

antique table that sat just inside the door, was that at least in her mind it was indeed over. She no longer loved David, if she ever really did.

Before David, there hadn't been anyone in Rain's life for a long time. She'd been busy completing her doctorate in psychology at Tulane, and then later, building up her private practice while caring for her beloved, ailing aunt Celeste. David had filled the void in her life that had become so much deeper after Celeste's passing. He'd convinced her to do *Midnight Confessions,* banking on her public persona as Desiree Sommers's daughter.

The radio show had been a mistake. Once her contract was over in three months, she didn't intend to renew. Rain had procrastinated in telling David, but after tonight, she knew it was something she'd have to do soon.

She stepped farther into the house. The Greek Revival on Prytania Street held significance to her that went beyond its listing on the New Orleans's historical society register. She'd lived there her entire life—the first two years with her mother and then later, with Celeste. She smiled faintly, aware the house's dark history did little to neutralize the strange legacy surrounding her. But it was where she belonged. Rain walked from the parlor into the remodeled kitchen and poured a glass of red wine. She was comfortable here, and the trust fund her mother's estate provided ensured her ability to keep up the residence.

Rain took a sip as she decided whether she was hungry enough to make something to eat. Dahlia, a black cat she'd adopted as a stray, leaped onto the counter. Rain jumped as she caught the quick movement of the feline in the corner of her eye, splashing wine onto her silk blouse.

"Dahlia," she scolded, wiping at the delicate material with a napkin. The cat padded across the counter and offered her head to be scratched. As Rain complied, a fat moth bumped against the kitchen window, drawn by the interior light.

It's true, Rain. I've become quite interested in you.

Her thoughts turned to the show's caller and the intrusive questions he'd asked. She'd felt intimidated by him even through the distance of the airwaves.

Putting out a dish of food for Dahlia, she gave the cat's head one last scratch. Then taking her glass of wine, she set the security alarm and went upstairs.

She flipped a switch, and the bedroom filled with soft light. The room had the same high ceilings and hardwood floors as the rest of the house, and a marble fireplace graced the wall at the foot of the four-poster bed. A painting of Desiree hung over the mantel. In it, she wore a black gown with a plunging neckline that revealed an expanse of porcelain skin. Desiree's almond-shaped hazel eyes, so much like Rain's, stared out from the canvas.

Dante had wanted to know what it was like to share the same blood as Desiree Sommers. Although Rain was used to being asked about her famous mother, his particular wording struck her as peculiar and faintly alarming.

She went into the bathroom to prepare for bed, returning in pajama pants and a camisole top. A television was hidden in a highboy armoire. She clicked it on, then turned back the bed's matelasse coverlet to reveal blush-colored sheets. Rain sat against the plump cushions and throw pillows that were piled against the headboard with one leg curled beneath her. As she took another sip of wine, her eyes fell on a silver-framed photograph on the nightstand. She put down the glass and picked up the photo, tracing its image with her finger.

Desiree and Gavin Firth looked happy together. The photo was taken thirty years earlier by an amateur's camera—in 1981, the same year in which they'd both died. Gavin was smiling broadly, his arms wrapped around the petite redhead. Confusion filtered through Rain's mind.

She'd been only two years old at the time of their deaths. All she knew about them were the memories that Celeste, Desiree's older sister, had shared with her and what she'd read in the tabloids about her parents' passionate but tragic love affair. Her eyes focused on Gavin, the man who was her father and who'd taken away the one thing that mattered most to a child.

He'd murdered her mother in cold blood before killing himself.

Rain fell asleep that night thinking of her mother and wishing she'd been given even a brief time in which to know her. A ringing phone woke her a few hours later, but when she answered in a voice husky with sleep, there was no one on the other end of the line.

4

"Dr. Patel, he's waking up again."

Trevor felt someone squeeze his hand. Slowly, he opened his eyes and squinted into the room's severe brightness, finding it hard to focus.

His sister leaned over him. She stood next to a white-coated man who appeared to be of Indian descent. Trevor flinched as the man flashed a penlight into his eyes, holding first one of his eyelids open and then the other as he waved the torturous beam back and forth.

"Pupil response is still a bit sluggish." The doctor flipped off the light. "Can you tell me your name, sir?"

Trevor uttered his name. His throat felt as if it had been scrubbed with sandpaper.

"And what is today's date?"

He attempted to swallow before speaking again. "May eighteenth."

The doctor smiled. "We'll let that one pass. But it's after midnight already, so you're a day off. You've been down for the count, as they say."

Trevor tried to sit up, but a firm hand on his shoulder held him back.

"Not so quickly. You've got a head laceration and a

probable concussion, although your CAT scan rules out intracranial bleeding. You're lucky you didn't break any bones. Regardless, you're going to be our guest for the next twenty-four hours." The doctor scribbled on a clipboard, then hung it in a compartment at the foot of the gurney. To Annabelle he said, "We'll be moving him to a private room shortly."

Pushing back the curtain to leave, he added, "In the future, Agent, I recommend looking both ways before crossing the street."

Once they were alone, Annabelle poured water from a plastic pitcher into a cup. She put a straw into the liquid and helped him take a sip. The water felt cool against his dry throat.

"You're at All Saints Hospital, in case you were wondering."

Trevor touched the small bandage near his hairline. He felt sluggish and sore. "How long have I been here?"

"An hour, maybe. You've been in and out of consciousness. You were dehydrated, too." She frowned at the IV line attached to his forearm. "Do you even remember what happened?"

Trevor fell silent. He'd been running in the darkened French Quarter. But it was as if the rest of his memory was cloaked in heavy fog.

"You ran out in front of a car," Annabelle supplied, a faint tremor in her voice. "You were in front of Dad's bar, at Mallory's. Trevor, what were you doing there?"

The staccato bursts of pain in his head intensified. He closed his eyes and tried to stop thinking.

Sleep was broken into intervals by the night nurse. Routine procedure for a head injury, she came by to check his pupils and assess how easily he awakened. Each time Trevor was prompted to open his eyes, he saw Annabelle in the vinyl recliner next to the bed. At one point when she shifted uncomfortably, he recalled mumbling something to her about going home, that Haley needed her. When he awoke again to the early-morning sky outside the room's window, she was gone.

The acetaminophen had only slightly eased his headache, but at least his double vision had cleared. He located the button that raised the top of the hospital bed. As he sat up, Trevor realized he was being observed from the doorway. True to Annabelle's words, Brian looked clean and sober. Although he was still thin, he'd lost his formerly gaunt appearance.

"How's the patient?" he asked, sounding uncertain.

"The patient wants the hell out of here." Trevor couldn't remove his gaze from his younger brother. Brian came into the room and sat in the recliner Annabelle had vacated, his expression serious.

"You didn't have any identification on you. If the accident hadn't happened outside of Mallory's, no one would've known who you were."

Bits of Trevor's memory clicked together. He recalled the neon beer sign in the bar's window, its orange glow casting a reflection on the sidewalk below. Then seconds later, headlights blinding him as he started across the street.

"Dad was there last night, at the bar," Brian continued. "There were people gathered and he came out to see what was going on. He recognized you."

Trevor said nothing. He didn't like to think of James Rivette standing over him on the filthy French Quarter street.

"He called the loft. I wasn't home, so Alex talked to him. Alex went to stay with Haley so Annabelle could come to the E.R." Brian's lips thinned and he studied his hands before speaking again. "He called Alex a faggot, of course. He also said he wanted a hundred dollars for making the 911 call to report your accident."

Trevor nearly laughed at Brian's statement. He'd think it incredulous if he didn't know his father. Still, his hands tightened on the sheets.

"Were you going to the bar to see him?"

"No," he lied. The truth didn't make much sense, either.

"Trevor—"

"You wouldn't understand."

"I wouldn't understand," Brian echoed softly, his voice edged with disbelief.

Brian hadn't even attended their mother's funeral, too high to show up. The last time they'd seen one another, it had been a few months before Sarah Rivette's death. Since then, loving, forgiving Annabelle had been the only connection between them.

"I'm sorry about rehab," Brian said, as if he could sense the direction of Trevor's thoughts. "I know that place cost you a lot of money. I guess I just wasn't ready."

Trevor didn't reply. An orderly in green scrubs and Air Jordan sneakers entered, carrying a food tray that he deposited on a mobile table before leaving.

"You want some breakfast?" Brian stood and moved the table closer.

"Annabelle says you're clean."

His gaze didn't waver. "Almost two years."

"You're working again?"

He nodded. A space of silence hung between them. After a few moments, Trevor said, "I'm glad you came by, Brian."

Brian walked a few steps from the bed. He looked out the window, its metal blinds bending under his fingers. "I didn't just *come by*. I've been here most of the night, like Annabelle. I came straight from the airport."

Had he been so out of it he hadn't noticed Brian's presence? Trevor remembered seeing Annabelle and the night nurse. But at times he'd been vaguely aware of others in the room, disembodied voices and shifting gray shapes against the monochrome walls.

"You've been here?"

"Does it surprise you that much?" Brian shook his head. "You got hit by a car last night, Trev. Knocked out cold. You could've been roadkill."

"Well, I'm not."

"Your radio wasn't so lucky. The paramedics wanted me to tell you it's toast. They didn't even bother turning it in."

Another piece of the puzzle snapped into place. Trevor had been wearing a slim silver radio on his bicep, attached with a Velcro strap. He'd been listening to a talk show, and one of the callers had put his senses on high alert.

You could say I'm a little older.

How much?

Older than you can possibly imagine.

The man had called himself Dante. The name fit with the goth undertones of the killings. Perhaps even more significant, the taunting notes Trevor had received over the last several months were signed with the letter *D*. It was a distinct possibility he was grasping at straws, but he was driven by the need to find out what else the caller had said. Pushing back the sheets, he lowered his legs over the side of the bed.

"What are you doing?"

"I have to go talk to someone." Wincing, he pulled the IV needle from his arm. A drop of blood splashed onto the tile floor. He stood, feeling shaky, but Brian blocked his path.

"You haven't been discharged. You're not going anywhere."

"I have to. It's important." Trevor sidestepped him and found the running clothes and sneakers he'd been wearing the night before inside a closet next to the sink. "Are you going to help me or not?"

"Only if I want Annabelle to flatten me. What's so important?"

Trevor ripped off the hospital gown and began getting dressed. "Not what. Who. A radio-show host. I was listening to her last night when I ran in front of that car."

He searched his slowly returning memory. "Her name was weird—something like Storm Showers."

Brian suppressed a smile. "You mean Rain Sommers."

"You know who she is?"

"Yeah, I do. But why can't this wait?"

"Because I think she might've been talking to my unsub."

5

Sunlight spilled across the four-poster bed. Rain groaned and buried her face against the pillow, then raised her head to squint at the clock through a haze of red-gold hair: 7:45 a.m.

Shit.

She threw back the covers, causing Dahlia to scurry from the mattress. Oliver Carteris was her standing Friday-morning appointment, and Rain wanted to be dressed and have had her coffee by the time the teenager arrived. With Oliver, she'd learned it was crucial to be on her toes.

An empty wineglass sat on the nightstand. After the phone rang in the middle of the night, Rain had been unable to go back to sleep. Unnerved by the silence on the other end of the line, she'd gone to the kitchen and poured another glass, then stayed up watching late-night television. *Some psychologist,* she thought. *Trying to solve the jitters with an expensive Pinot Noir.*

She'd just stepped from the shower when she thought she heard the faint creak of a floorboard.

"Is anyone there?" Rain was aware of the sounds old houses made. Feeling foolish, she wrapped a towel around herself, then opened the bathroom door and peered into the bedroom. It was unoccupied except for Dahlia, who'd returned to the rumpled coverlet and was basking in a fat streak of sunlight. The door to her bedroom that led into the hallway was half-open, but Rain couldn't remember if she'd left it that way. A drawer in her dresser bureau hung agape as well, with silk undergarments in various shades draped over its edge like strands of Mardi Gras beads.

Get a grip, she told herself, and went back into the bathroom to dress.

Standing on the staircase twenty minutes later, she realized it hadn't been her imagination. Oliver Carteris lounged on the chintz sofa in her parlor, sipping from one of her Wedgwood cups.

"I made coffee." His voice held a faint British accent, and his dark eyes reflected intelligence. "I needed the caffeine."

"You're early," Rain pointed out. *A half hour early.* It unnerved her greatly that Oliver had managed not only to get through a locked door but also to bypass her home security system. She gave him a hard look as she came the rest of the way downstairs, then walked to the sideboard in the dining area, where she poured a cup of chicory-laced coffee from the thermal French press.

"You don't wait to be let in?" She sounded tense as she came back into the room.

Oliver gave a practiced shrug. His longish hair was glossy black, and today, shot through with streaks of red. Despite the New Orleans heat, he had on dark jeans and a long-sleeved black T-shirt that advertised an industrial-metal band. Scuffed leather boots were on his feet. Since he didn't seem interested in moving from the sofa, Rain sat in the armchair across from him.

"Want to tell me how you got in here?"

"Old houses." He nodded toward the glass-paneled door. "Piece of cake to snap the locks."

Rain knew about Oliver's background of B and Es that were part of his sealed juvenile record. Now that he was eighteen, however, the predilection was causing considerable concern for his father, a respected cardiac surgeon.

"And my security system?" she asked.

"You keep the pass code taped inside a cabinet door in the kitchen."

"You've been going through my cabinets, too?"

"Just looking around."

Despite the casual discussion, she felt furious that Oliver had sneaked into her house and had been snooping. But she'd spent months trying to build a rapport with him, and she was hesitant to lose the progress they'd made.

"We need to have a discussion about boundaries, particularly when it comes to my home, Oliver. Did you take anything from my bedroom?"

"I wasn't in your bedroom." Avoiding her gaze, he picked at the black polish on his fingernails.

"If you were, just tell me—"

"I *said* I wasn't there." He glowered at the chandelier that hung from the parlor's high ceiling. "This is bullshit."

"What is?"

"These lame counseling sessions."

"I'm sorry you feel that way." Rain placed her cup on the end table. "I was under the impression our sessions were helpful. Regardless, your attendance is court-ordered—"

"Who's David?"

The question came from out of the blue. "Why?"

"Go look for yourself." Oliver pointed to the kitchen. Rain stood and walked through the arched entrance. On the counter, under the iron pot rack that held Celeste's prized copper cookware, was a bouquet of lavender roses. It lay on its side, wrapped in tissue and tied with a large bow.

"They were on the doorstep." He stood closely behind her, watching as she took a crystal vase from a shelf and filled it with water from the sink. "Don't you want the note?"

Rain turned to see the opened envelope he waggled.

"He wants you to forgive him. What did the bugger do?"

She felt her anger flare again as she reached for the note. "That was personal correspondence."

"So?"

Rain sighed heavily. "It's an invasion of my privacy. Just like coming into my home without my knowledge or permission. And it needs to stop."

"I'd say it's fair exchange. Your job is to invade *my* privacy. You ask me questions so you can report back to my father."

"We've been through this before, Oliver." Untying the bow, she removed the flowers from the tissue and plunked them in the vase, which she'd moved onto the counter. "Anything you say here is confidential. It's between us alone."

"Is anything that happens here confidential, too?" he asked in a low voice most likely meant to be seductive. He towered over her, and Rain had already noticed his eyes were red and glassy.

"I could send flowers, if that's what you want."

"What I want is for us to get started on our session," she said calmly. "I'd also like to know if you're high."

His smiled slipped. Muttering under his breath, he started to walk away, but Rain laid a hand on his arm. Oliver's behavior was irrational this morning, even for him. "Something's clearly bothering you. Why don't we go into my office—"

"And talk?" He let out a bitter laugh. "Do you really think I tell you anything that matters?"

She looked him in the eye. "I hope you do, yes."

"Then you're the one who's high."

"Oliver—"

He jerked his arm away from her with such force that he knocked the vase with the flowers onto the floor. It shattered into pieces. Oliver stood with his hands clenched into fists at his sides as he stared at the mess. Rain's stomach turned a small somersault, but she held her ground.

"It's okay. It's just an accident." She took a step closer. "Whatever's going on, let me help you."

The broken glass made a minefield of the floor. It crunched under Oliver's boots as he left the kitchen. A moment later, she heard the front door slam.

The doorbell rang as she finished cleaning up the glass. Rain assumed it was Oliver returning to apologize, but when she opened the door there were two men standing on her veranda. One she recognized immediately as Alex's partner, Brian Rivette. But the other, a dark-haired man with a small bandage on his right temple, she'd never seen before.

"Brian, it's good to see you." Rain greeted him with a warm embrace. "But what brings you here on a Friday morning?"

"I better let him explain." Brian indicated the other man. He was dressed in slacks, a dress shirt and tie, although his jacket had apparently been discarded in deference to the heat. A holstered gun sat on his hip.

"This is my brother, Trevor Rivette. He's with the FBI."

Rain knew Brian had a sister, but she'd never heard mention of a third Rivette sibling. Especially not one who was a federal agent.

His expression was earnest. "Dr. Sommers, I'd like to have a word with you about your show."

She opened the door wider. "Please, come in."

As they followed her inside, she glanced at her wristwatch. "I have a therapy session with a patient at ten."

"I'll try not to take up too much of your time."

Rain gauged Trevor Rivette to be three or four years older than his brother. She'd noticed that unlike Brian, he didn't speak with the slower, lengthened vowels of a Deep Southerner. There was, however, a family resemblance in the strong cheekbones and slightly squared jawline.

"Could I get either of you some coffee?" she asked.

"No, thank you."

"I'll have some," Brian spoke up. "But I'll get it myself so you two can talk." He headed off toward the dining room.

"Why don't we go into my office." Rain led the agent through a set of French doors that separated her workplace from the rest of the downstairs. In addition to a desk, there was a barrister's bookcase in the room, as well as two matching wing chairs with a small table between them. Hanging above the desk was a black-and-white photograph of an ornate gate in an aboveground cemetery, a stunning image of one of New Orleans's famed Cities of the Dead.

"I wasn't aware my brother knew you so well," he said once Rain closed the doors behind them.

"Alex Santos, Brian's partner, is one of my oldest friends," she explained. "That's one of his photos on the wall. It's a fairly well-known print."

He regarded it briefly before moving his blue-gray gaze back to her. As curious as she was about Trevor Rivette, she was more perplexed as to the reason for his arrival. She wondered if *Midnight Confessions* had broken some sort of on-air indecency rule.

"If this is about the subject matter of my show, you really should take it up with David D'Alba, my producer. I know we walk a fine line regarding regulations."

"I'm with the FBI, Dr. Sommers. Not the FCC."

Rain sat in one of the wing chairs, and she studied him as he stood in front of the window. He'd loosened his tie, and she noticed how the smooth cotton of his dress shirt fit his chest. He appeared extremely physically fit. But his face was pale, and his right temple looked abraded and bruised under the bandage. She wondered what had happened.

"You had a caller on your show last night," he said. "A man who called himself Dante?"

The name caused Rain's heart to jump a little. "Yes?"

"I'm looking into the murder of a teenage female here in New Orleans. The killing has similarities to murders committed in other cities over the past eighteen months."

"And you think this Dante person is linked somehow?"

"I don't have anything to go on but my instincts, but I believe it's a possibility. Would you mind taking a look at a snapshot from the M.E.'s office?" he asked. "The victim's currently a Jane Doe. Brian says you specialize in adolescents and young adults—"

"So I might recognize her?"

"Maybe." When she nodded her consent, he reached into his back pocket and retrieved the snapshot. Rain looked at the grim photo, a close-up of the dead girl's face. She was obviously lying on an autopsy table, her skin waxen and eyes closed. A sheet covered her shoulders and neck, concealing her nearly up to the chin.

Rain gave a faint headshake. "I don't know her."

Taking the snapshot back, he walked to her desk, indicating the framed cemetery photograph she'd pointed out earlier. "That's a rather gothic image, don't you think?"

Rain looked at him. "I think that's open to interpretation."

"One of your callers last night was talking about an ankh tattoo. Would you consider your show to have a special appeal to the goth community?"

"May I ask where you're going with this?"

He crossed his arms over his chest. "Several of the victims

have been associated with a goth lifestyle, or were known to have frequented goth clubs in their areas."

"And the girl here in New Orleans?"

"We're not sure yet."

Rain rose from the chair, aware he was watching her intently.

"You haven't answered my question, Dr. Sommers."

Brian's avoided gossiping about me to his brother, she thought. "Some of my listeners consider themselves goth. Speaking of which, how did it happen you were listening to my show last night, Agent? You're hardly our demographic."

"I went for a run, and needed something to listen to on my radio."

"And you chose a talk show that caters to teens and young adults and features alternative music?"

He shrugged. "If you're asking if I'd have preferred some classic rock, the answer is yes. Yours was the only station I could pick up in the Quarter."

Rain accepted his honesty with a slight smile. He closed his eyes and rubbed his right hand over his face.

"Are you all right?"

He disregarded her question, although discomfort was evident on his features. "I need to know exactly what the caller said to you last night."

"I thought you were listening."

"Not to all of it."

She reached for the phone on her desk. "Our shows are digitally recorded. I'll call the studio and have them make you a dub—"

Rain stopped speaking as his hand covered hers, keeping her from picking up the handset. Up close, she could see the scar that ran across his chin, the only detraction from an otherwise nearly perfect masculine face.

Although his tone was gentle, it carried an urgency. "I will need that recording. But right now, just tell me what he said to you."

Rain hesitated.

"He asked if I enjoyed being tied up during sex." The slight quaver in her voice belied her directness, but she didn't look away. "He said he wanted to watch me bleed. I hung up on him."

Something darkened in the depths of his eyes. "Your show airs again tonight?"

"Tuesdays through Fridays. Tonight's the last one for the week."

"I'd like to be at the radio station, in the studio with you. If he calls again, I can try to have the line traced."

A car alarm went off nearby, its electronic shriek causing Rain to turn her head toward the window. Then she looked at him again and slowly nodded her agreement. "I'll speak to my producer and let him know."

"Thank you."

Unable to stop herself, she raised her hand and gently touched the bandage at his temple.

"You should get some rest," she said softly. Her eyes held his for several moments, and then she walked to the French doors. Through their glass panes, she could see Brian waiting in the parlor. Dahlia had found him and was perched in his lap.

"How does he kill the victims?" Rain asked, aware her question was born of morbid curiosity. When he didn't answer, she turned back to him, her hand remaining on the door handle. "I'm a trained psychologist, Agent Rivette. I'm familiar with psychotic criminal behavior."

His voice was impassive. "He ties them up, tortures them and then he cuts their throats. The killer considers himself a sanguine vampire, although in reality he's more likely a sado-erotic blood fetishist who's spiraled out of control."

Her grip on the handle tightened. "You think he drinks their blood?"

"It's possible, yes."

Rain swallowed hard. "Are these instincts of yours ever wrong, Agent?"

"Sometimes."

"Then maybe the man who called my show isn't who you're looking for."

His gaze was direct. "This psychopath has already killed five women. Are you sure you're willing to take that chance?"

6

"You could've told me you knew her," Trevor said from the passenger side of the silver Audi. He studied Brian's profile as his brother shifted gears and accelerated the sports car.

"I did tell you."

"You said she was an *acquaintance*. Not someone you know well enough to rummage through her refrigerator looking for milk for your coffee. Even her cat knew you, Brian."

"Rain's really more Alex's friend than mine," he replied. "Back in his starving-artist days, he rented a room over the carriage house. Celeste sort of adopted him."

"Celeste?"

"Rain's aunt. She died of cancer last year."

The Audi approached Coliseum Square, the focal point of the Lower Garden District. People were walking their dogs on the lush grass or jogging on the pathways under the shade of moss-draped live oaks. A teenage boy stood alone at the edge of the park, capturing Trevor's attention. Garbed in jeans and a long-sleeved T-shirt too hot for the season, he glared at their car as it passed.

Dante had said he wanted to watch her bleed. Trevor felt it in his gut—the caller to *Midnight Confessions* wasn't just some garden-variety pervert. He leaned his head against the headrest and tried to ease the throbbing behind his eyes. The headache had worsened since he'd left the hospital, but there was little time to recuperate.

"You're going to get a ticket," he warned as Brian accelerated again. They were outside the residential area now, and Brian had chosen to take the business 90 in lieu of the quieter side streets.

"Relax." Brian looked over at Trevor, although it was hard to see his eyes through the dark tint of his sunglasses. "I'm a pro at avoiding cops."

For Brian, there had always been an attraction to speed. It was evident in the car he drove, the small plane he'd learned to fly, and not so long ago, in an even faster, potentially more dangerous lifestyle of drugs and random sexual partners. Trevor's gaze traveled to the gold band his brother now wore on his left hand, symbolic of a monogamous commitment.

Annabelle had said Brian was painting again. She'd shown Trevor some early reviews that had appeared in the local arts paper. He wanted badly to believe in the transformation and forget about those years of Brian at his worst.

Brian turned his head under the weight of his brother's stare. "What?"

"Nothing." Trevor shrugged, not wanting to ruin their companionship. Instead, he shifted his thoughts to Rain Sommers. The petite redhead was nothing like he'd expected. She was polished and feminine, with delicate features and striking amber eyes. Not to mention, he'd noted the Ph.D. after her name on her business card. It confirmed the title *doctor* had been earned and wasn't just some affectation for the show's benefit.

"What the hell kind of name is Rain, anyway?" Trevor massaged his forehead. "What were her parents, hippies?"

"You really don't know."

"Know what?"

"Ever heard of Desiree Sommers?"

A small, slender woman with a mass of coppery hair and eyes rimmed in dark makeup flashed in Trevor's mind. "The singer? That's her mother?"

Brian nodded. "They're dead ringers, aren't they?"

Desiree Sommers had been part of the avant-garde music scene in the late seventies and early eighties. Half whiskey-voiced torch singer and half rock diva, she'd only begun to receive national attention when she'd been murdered in her New Orleans home. The tragedy had become a rock legend, a *True Hollywood Story* that made Desiree larger in death than she'd been in life.

"That's the house where she was killed, isn't it?"

"Rain's father murdered her mother and then killed himself," Brian recounted. "Rain was asleep in the next room. She was two years old. Celeste, Desiree's sister, moved in and raised her."

They rode in silence while Trevor digested the information, not speaking again until they turned off the freeway and entered the Marigny neighborhood where Trevor's hotel was located. Brian parked on the street across from the building with black-shuttered windows and geranium baskets hanging in the breezeway. He left the car idling so the air conditioner remained on, and removed his sunglasses.

"You okay? I saw you rubbing your forehead."

"I'm fine."

"Signing out against medical advice wasn't a good idea. You look like hell, Trevor."

"I just need something for my headache, that's all."

"I should take you back to All Saints."

"Don't worry about it." Trevor released the seat belt. "You've done enough, driving me here from the hospital to shower and change, then taking me to meet Dr. Sommers."

"She's going to want you to call her Rain," Brian commented. "And I drove you because you shouldn't be driving yourself. If you were listening, the doctor said someone needs to stay with you. Why don't you come back with me to the loft. Just for the afternoon."

"I've got a lot to do. Some calls to make, for starters."

The car filled with quiet tension. "You don't even want to meet him, do you?"

He looked at Brian. "That's not true."

From a young age, Trevor had understood Brian was somehow different, in a way their cop father would have only raged against. As the older brother, he'd made it his job to deflect and buffer, for as long as he could.

"I know I made things harder for you," Brian said quietly. "But I never asked you to fight my battles."

"I wanted to protect you."

"You didn't have to—"

"Yes, *I did*," Trevor countered almost angrily. "He would've destroyed you."

"Christ, Trevor. What do you think he did to you?"

Silence lingered between the two men, creating a chasm filled with painful memories. Trevor opened the door, allowing a wave of oppressive heat to enter the vehicle's interior. He got out and stood there for a moment before leaning back inside, one hand on the car's roof.

"I *will* meet Alex," he promised. "At your art reception Sunday night. Annabelle already told me about it."

"You'll be there?"

"I wouldn't miss it."

Brian's eyes searched his brother's. Then he nodded in acceptance. "Just take it easy, okay?"

Trevor closed the door and watched Brian drive away, the car a blur of silver metallic on the narrow street. Once it disappeared, he ground the heels of his hands against his eyes. His entire body was feeling the impact with the Cadillac.

Inside his hotel room, Trevor went into the bathroom, ran some water into a tumbler that sat on the counter and downed two Tylenol tablets. When he looked in the mirror, his own pale reflection stared back. The bruising around the cut on his forehead was the only wash of color in his face.

Christ, Trevor. What do you think he did to you?

Brian's pointed question came back to him, and he wondered again at the impulsiveness that had led him to Mallory's bar. Maybe the Cadillac was some kind of cosmic warning to stay the hell away from his past.

He turned off the bathroom light and went back into the bedroom. He placed several calls, including one to the local FBI field office to check in, and another to Eddie McGrath at the NOPD. There was still no ID on the Jane Doe found in the shotgun house on Tchoupitoulas, the detective told him. In turn, Trevor informed McGrath of the possible lead he had at the radio station, and his plan to sit in on the talk show that night. His final call was to SAC Johnston at the VCU offices in D.C. Johnston was a gruff character, bald and built like a brick shithouse, with the hard glint of a former military man.

"Resources are spread thin right now—I've got your partner working on a child-murder case in Maryland," Johnston said over the phone, referring to Special Agent Nate Fincher. "He's not going to be able to make it down there."

He thought of the type of investigation Nate was handling. "Tough case."

"Aren't they all."

Trevor filled Johnston in on the Jane Doe autopsy and the caller to *Midnight Confessions*.

"Desiree Sommers's daughter, huh?" Johnston's deep voice held a hint of nostalgia. "I used to listen to her as a teenager.

Keep me posted, Rivette. I think the caller's a long shot, but it's worth looking into. Some of these guys are so full of self-importance, it's impossible for them not to brag about their accomplishments. Who knows—maybe this asshole's looking for a forum."

Afterward, Trevor removed his firearm still inside its holster and placed it on the nightstand. He had a lot to do, but he lay down and waited for the Tylenol to kick in. Squeezing his eyes shut against the light that filtered through the window, he thought again of Rain Sommers. Although she'd done her best to hide it, he'd seen the flicker of fear in her hazel eyes.

She had reason to be afraid, he realized.

The sign on the window advertised a blue-plate special along with the city's best shrimp étouffée. It was early evening, the dinner rush ended, and only a few tables in the small diner on Frenchmen Street were occupied. Trevor entered with the strap of a computer case over his shoulder. He'd just completed a meeting at the FBI field office with the local SAC and had a little time left before heading to WNOR.

"Take a seat anywhere you want, chère," a platinum blonde called from behind the counter. Her eyes gave him the once-over.

He selected a booth in back and the waitress followed him over, placing a glass of ice water on the table while he powered up the laptop. He ordered the étouffée along with a cup of coffee and handed back the laminated menu.

While he waited for his food, Trevor ran an Internet search on Desiree Sommers, his curiosity piqued. The query returned dozens of hits, so he began working his way down the list. The first was a fan-operated Web site with a distinct gothic theme, and it included a gallery of photos of the singer. He clicked through the images, lingering on a scanned reproduction of

Desiree's debut album. The cover was a scratchy black-and-white photo, of Desiree wearing a revealing cocktail dress and torn fishnet stockings. Her porcelain complexion had been made to appear even paler with makeup, and her eyes were rimmed in dark liner. She stood alone in a room surrounded by candles.

The album's title was *Decadent Soul*. Trevor read in the caption beneath the image that it had been released in 1979, two years prior to her death.

Trevor sipped the coffee the waitress had brought him and continued to study the image. The resemblance between Desiree and her daughter was evident. Both women were beautiful, although Rain Sommers had an understated elegance compared to her mother's overt sexuality. He clicked through several more Web sites, reading sensationalized accounts of the murder-suicide that ended Desiree's life.

"I can't figure out if you're a businessman, a cop or a tourist." The waitress broke into his thoughts as she set a plate of the Creole stew and rice in front of him. He pulled his gaze from the laptop's screen and glanced up at her.

"Pardon me?"

"Well, you're wearing a suit and you've got a laptop, so I thought maybe you're catching up on some work from the office." Her eyes traveled to the bandage on Trevor's forehead. "But most businessmen don't look like they came off the losing end of a bar fight."

Trevor scooped a mound of the étouffée onto his fork and took a bite. Although his headache had eased, he'd eaten little since the previous night at Annabelle's. He felt almost instantly better as the food hit his stomach.

"The sign don't lie, best in New Orleans," the waitress proclaimed. She took some extra napkins from her apron pocket and laid them on the table.

"Anyway, when you took off your jacket, I saw that." She

nodded toward the gun on Trevor's hip. "So I figured you were a plainclothes detective. Only thing is, you're dressed too nice for the NOPD. They usually favor short-sleeved dress shirts and polyester clip-on ties."

Trevor swallowed more food. "Why'd you think I could be a tourist?"

The waitress slid onto the bench across from him. He estimated her to be only in her late thirties, and although not unattractive, she looked as though she'd already lived a hard life. But her penny-brown eyes sparkled.

"You're looking up Desiree on the Web. I thought you might be sightseeing. Of course, you're not the type usually looking for her place."

Trevor wiped his mouth with his napkin. "What type is that?"

"You know, ghouls. We get them spooky kids in here all the time, the ones with the dyed black hair and eyeliner. After Anne Rice's old house and Trent Reznor's place, Desiree's is next on the freak-show tour."

Leaning forward, she tapped a lacquered nail on the table. "Here's one thing they don't tell you in the tabloids. After that British guitarist cut Desiree's throat, he wrote the word *whore* on the wall in her own blood. They say the wall's been painted over a dozen times, but it still shows through. How's that for a bedtime story?"

"Or an urban legend."

"Maybe." Her hand curling under her chin, she changed topics. "Anyone ever tell you that you've got beautiful eyes, chère?"

From the open kitchen, a man sporting a stained T-shirt cleared his throat and gave her a warning stare. The waitress slid from the booth. "So, you gonna tell me? Businessman, cop or tourist?"

Trevor reached for his wallet in the back pocket of his suit pants. "Let's just go with someone needing his check."

"I love a man of mystery." The waitress grinned as she rummaged in her apron pocket for his bill. Scribbling on the paper, she laid it on the table.

"That's your lagniappe. Your little something extra." She winked and pointed at the name Crystal with her telephone number scrawled next to it. "You come back anytime."

As Trevor finished his food, he sent an e-mail to the NOPD records office, using his federal badge number to request the files on the murder of Desiree Sommers, if they even still existed. Leaving cash to cover his meal and a tip, he returned the laptop to its case and walked outside.

The sun was beginning to set over the tops of the ancient, pressed-together buildings. Although it was outside the Quarter, Frenchmen Street was nearly as commercial, lined with smoky bars and casual restaurants. The vibration of a bass guitar came from one of the music clubs, the instrument sounding as if it was being tuned for the night. Trevor checked his watch and estimated the time he needed to get to the WNOR studios in the Central Business District.

His car, a rented Ford Taurus, was parked in an alleyway behind the diner. As Trevor turned the corner, he noticed its interior light was on and the driver's-side door ajar. He slowed, setting the computer case down and withdrawing his gun as he looked around the isolated alley.

Nothing. He appeared to be alone.

Approaching the vehicle, he slid cautiously into the front seat and removed the black cross that hung on a leather cord from the rearview mirror. Studded with rhinestones, the gothic, fleur-de-lis pendant glimmered dully. Trevor felt his heart speed up. His guess was that it belonged to the Jane Doe.

It wasn't the first time the man he was searching for had

given him a trophy, just to remind him that he was one step ahead. But it was the first one delivered personally.

It also meant the killer was still in New Orleans.

over, with a deepy mug to identify that that he was
placed. But it is the FBI's new to deaver's freeman.

It also means she rules away this measure. Colonia.

7

"Where were you tonight?" David wanted to know as Rain entered through the doors of the radio station. He stood at the chrome-and-glass reception desk, going over the evening's playlist. "I came by to give you a lift."

"I'm sorry. I had some errands to run." Rain hoped he wouldn't ask for details. The truth was, she'd avoided him when he'd come by her house earlier that evening. She'd hidden as David knocked on the front door and then peered inside through the parlor windows. Finally, he'd returned to his Jaguar and driven away.

Admittedly, it wasn't adult behavior on her part. But the past twenty-four hours had unsettled her, beginning with last night's caller to *Midnight Confessions*. Then Trevor Rivette had appeared on her veranda with a gun on his hip and a grim theory about the caller's identity. She didn't need David stepping on her already frayed nerves.

Rain attempted to walk past him, but he blocked her path. "Did you like the flowers?"

His face bore the look of a hopeful puppy. When she'd called him that afternoon to let him know about the FBI's interest in the show, she'd forgotten to even mention the bouquet.

"Yes, thank you. They're lovely."

David's eyes traveled over her, taking in her ivory raw-silk blouse and tailored black slacks. "I meant what I said in the note—"

He stopped midsentence as Ella appeared from the hallway.

"David, I've got the dub of last night's show." She glided into the reception area with a compact disc and pretended not to notice Rain's presence.

"Please take it to Agent Rivette," he replied dismissively. Rain didn't miss the annoyance that shone in Ella's eyes. She pivoted on one high heel, the heavy scent of perfume accompanying her retreat into the studio's interiors.

"Where is he?" Rain inquired once Ella was gone.

"The FBI agent? Waiting in the production room. Why does the name Rivette sound familiar?"

"He's Brian Rivette's brother. You remember meeting Alex's partner?"

"Ah, Alex." He bobbed his head. Rain pursed her lips, aware of the mutual dislike between David and her friend Alex Santos.

"I see the resemblance, now that you mention it. So, is this Agent Rivette a homosexual, too?"

"Why don't you ask him?" Rain suggested. "Worst case, he'd think you were coming on to him and shoot you."

Ignoring her sarcasm, he went to adjust the lighting on the WNOR logo that hung on the wall behind the reception desk. "Well, it looks like your concerns about this Dante character were on target. You must feel some vindication in that."

Rain would have preferred to be off base. She was reminded that in less than an hour, she might be talking to Dante again over the airwaves. Although she'd studied criminal behavior during her doctoral program, her exposure had been mostly academic. Dante added an element of realism she'd neither expected, nor wanted, to experience firsthand.

"This could work to our advantage, you know."

She realized David was still speaking, and she'd missed whatever else he'd just said. "Excuse me?"

He shrugged his shoulders under his Hugo Boss shirt. "All I'm saying is that if this lunatic calls back, don't worry about how risqué the conversation gets. We're cooperating with a federal investigation. Surely that gives us leeway in what's being said on air."

He patted his shirt and trouser pockets. "I wrote some barbs and double entendres that might be interesting. Maybe you can work them into the conversation, if I can remember where the hell I put them—"

"They're on your desk." Ella had returned, holding a WNOR mug brimming with caramel-colored coffee. She smiled at David. "Just the way you like it, with lots of steamed milk."

Ella even made the words *steamed milk* sound suggestive. She pressed the mug into David's hands, which was so full, hot liquid sloshed over its rim.

"Damn it, Ella!"

As Ella snatched tissues from the desk and brushed at the spot on David's trousers, Rain slipped from the reception area. She found Trevor in the production room, finishing up a call on his cell phone with his back to her. When he closed the phone and turned around, his eyes met hers. Like earlier that day, his tie had been loosened, and the sleeves of his dress shirt were rolled up to reveal the lean muscles of his forearms. Although the bandage remained on his temple, much of his color had returned.

"Dr. Sommers."

"Rain," she corrected.

"Rain." There was a brief silence as he looked at her. "I

have an FBI field technician standing by to help with the trace. If the call's made from a landline, it should be an immediate process."

"What if he uses a cell phone?"

"We can triangulate the call using cell towers to pinpoint its origin. The process takes longer, but if the call is made from an urban area with multiple towers, it's possible to narrow the caller's location to a few hundred feet." He placed his hands on his hips, wedging his right one above his holstered gun. "Are you going to be able to do this?"

Rain let go of a nervous breath. "I'm going to try."

"I'll be sitting across from you, right here in the production room. You'll be able to see me through the window. Your producer's run an additional feed into your headset so I can talk to you while you're on air without the caller being able to hear me. Do you want to try it out?"

Going into the broadcast booth, Rain picked up the headset and put it on. She could see Trevor, who'd remained in the production room and wore a similar device. "Agent Rivette—"

"It's Trevor," he replied, his voice coming through clearly. He must have sensed her anxiety, because he added, "Remember, this might not be the guy. He might not even call back."

"But you don't believe that, do you?"

He gazed at her through the window. "No."

A promotional poster for the goth band Raven was pinned to the wall inside the booth. Rain stared at the grainy image of a stone staircase with a winged female descending the shadowed steps. Was the ethereal figure a vampire or an angel? She'd never paid much attention to the poster before, but tonight she found it nearly as unsettling as the clock on her desk announcing the time in bold green digits. It was a quarter to ten, fifteen minutes before *Midnight Confessions* went on air.

Rain paced the booth, the space feeling suddenly confining and cagelike. Then she walked briskly down the hall and into the ladies' restroom. Avoiding her reflection in the mirror, she ran some water in the basin and wished she could follow it down the drain. The smell of pine-scented cleanser caused her stomach to roll. Could she do this? What if she said something that tipped off the caller about the trace?

She wasn't certain how long she'd stood there trying to get her bearings, but a knock sounded against the door. Trevor's voice was uncertain.

"Rain? Are you all right?"

She opened the door halfway.

"There's something you should know about me," Rain said quietly. She let several beats of silence pass before making her confession, but it was something he had to be told. She sighed and felt a sense of shame. "I can't drive."

His forehead creased. "I don't understand."

"It's a phobia. I'm a therapist with a completely ridiculous, unmanageable fear. Does that give you confidence in me?"

"What does that have to do—"

Rain shook her head, frustrated he was unable to follow her logic. "If I can't do something as basic as drive a car, how am I supposed to keep a possible serial killer on the line long enough to trace his location?"

"You talked to him last night, Rain. Nothing's changed."

"I hung up on him," she reminded. "And that was *before* I knew who he might be."

Trevor studied her face. "Are you coming out of there or am I coming in?"

She hesitated before stepping back and allowing him inside. Once she'd closed the door behind them, she leaned against the wall's cool porcelain tiles.

"I don't even have a driver's license," she admitted. "Counseling sessions, hypnotherapy, nothing's helped. Thank heaven for the St. Charles Streetcar Line or all my money would be spent on taxis."

"Rain—"

"I don't think my patients respect me, but why should they?" She frowned at the stall's metal door. "Just this morning, one of my teenage patients broke into my house. I think he stole my underwear. He denied it, of course, but there's a pair of blue silk panties missing from my lingerie drawer. I don't even want to know what he might be doing with them…"

Realizing she was babbling, Rain felt a flush creep onto her cheekbones. She closed her eyes. "God. That was TMI, wasn't it?"

"It's okay."

"I just thought you should know I might screw up your investigation."

"You won't." Trevor held her gaze. "Try to remember that he can't touch you through the airwaves. It's just a voice."

"But that's not really true. That it's just a voice?"

He bent his head closer to hers, his voice low. His hand touched her arm. "I've heard you on the radio, Rain. Just treat him like a normal caller. You can do this."

He started to say more, but the click of the door handle drew their attention. David gawked at the two of them together in the intimate space. "What's going on? Why aren't you in the booth?"

"I needed a moment to pull myself together." Rain tucked a strand of hair behind her ear and evaded his stare.

"You're on air in three minutes." He left the door open and headed back down the hall.

Trevor looked at Rain. "You okay?"

"Do you mean am I done freaking out?" She nodded, still

mortified. "Thanks for not laughing about the car thing. Or the stolen underwear. I can't believe I told you that. You must think I'm nuts."

"You've got a case of the jitters, that's all. You didn't ask for any of this."

"If the caller is who you think he is, why would he call *me?*"

"Maybe he needs a medium to share his fantasies, and your show fits the bill." He paused, his eyes somber. "It's also possible he feels some connection to you through your mother."

So he knew about Desiree, after all.

Rain felt the butterflies in her stomach kick up again.

More than two hours had passed. Rain had taken a half-dozen calls, none of them from Dante. One caller was a teen-age female seeking advice about an unplanned pregnancy. Another, a male in his early twenties, was pondering dropping out of his senior year of college to play in a rock band. Several others had called in to discuss various sexual topics. The last one, a female, mostly wanted advice on losing weight.

Rain looked at Trevor through the window separating them. If he was concerned Dante might not make an appearance, he gave no indication of it. Instead, he sat quietly in the production room, listening to the on-air conversations.

"We've got less than an hour. He's not going to call," she said once a spot for Dixie Voodoo beer began running in the commercial break.

"There's still time," Trevor replied.

Uncertain if he was offering hope or a warning, she glanced away.

A few minutes later, as the last strains of a song track played over the airwaves, David stood from the console where he'd been screening calls. The excitement on his face caused Rain's pulse to spike.

"This is it. We've got Dante on line two."

Trevor extracted his cell phone and pressed it to his ear. Through her headset, Rain heard him request the trace. At nearly the same time, the on-air sign in the broadcast studio sprang to life.

Keep it together, Rain. She pressed the blinking button on her own console.

"We're back with *Midnight Confessions*." Tamping down her fear, she added, "I'm Dr. Rain Sommers, and our next caller is Dante from the Quarter."

His words settled over the airwaves like heavy velvet. "Do you remember me from last night, Rain?"

"You're not someone I'd forget," she admitted.

"You hung up on me."

"Well, you're back on the air now."

"So all is forgiven? Perhaps my choice of topic was too provocative?"

Rain took in a tight breath. "Refresh the audience on your topic, Dante."

"We were talking about bondage and bloodplay, and whether you found the idea of it erotic. I merely offered to induct you, to show you the ropes?" He chuckled softly. "No pun intended."

Trevor's voice came through her headset. "You're doing fine, Rain. The call's being made from a cell phone. It's being triangulated now, but you're going to need to keep him on the line."

Rain steeled her nerves as she returned her attention to the caller. "You'll have to forgive me, but the words *blood* and *play* don't go together in my dictionary. Care to elaborate?"

"I'm surprised you're claiming ignorance, my dear. After

all, you have your own link to the goth community. Blood games are hardly a novelty in those circles."

"Are you part of the goth scene?"

"When it suits my needs," he replied. "For the most part, I find their gloomy atmosphere tiresome. All those dour wannabes walking around in black clothing."

"So you *don't* identify yourself as goth?"

"Do *you?* Your mother was the prototype, Rain. She was goth before there was such a thing. A pity she died while you were so young, and in such a brutal manner. But then, her death has made you a bit famous, hasn't it?"

Rain wanted to tell him to go to hell, but she was mindful of the need to keep him talking.

"Not all goths are into blood," she pointed out.

"Not all," he agreed. "But you've failed to answer my original question. *Blood,* Rain. Does the idea of bleeding for your lover excite you?"

The titillation in his voice made her hands shake. "No, Dante, I can't say it does."

"You're certain?" He went on, undeterred. "Bloodplay is an erotic exploration, one that blurs the boundaries between physical pain and pleasure. I expected you to be more sexually adventurous, considering your lineage. Desiree's sexual pursuits, well, they're quite legendary."

"What you describe not only sounds painful, but dangerous. Have you thought about AIDS or hepatitis?"

"Those are purely mortal concerns."

Rain was unable to keep the incredulity from her words. "You're implying by that statement you're immortal?"

"Blood is a life force. Our ancient civilizations knew that. In many ways, they were much wiser than we are today." He spoke as if educating a child. "Blood offers the promise of eternal youth."

"And I thought you had to go to a plastic surgeon for that."

A hush erupted over the airwaves. For a moment, Rain thought Dante had hung up. But when he spoke again, his tone morphed into something churlish and threatening. "Mocking me can be very dangerous, little one. I'd take great pleasure in disciplining you."

He can't touch you through the airwaves. Rain repeated Trevor's statement in her head like a mantra.

"I meant what I said last night," he whispered. "You'd be lovely, tied up and bleeding for me."

"You're insane." Her comment was swallowed up in dead air. Dante was gone. David cut to a block of ad spots, and an upbeat jingle for the Clean Cajun car wash began playing over the station's intercom. Rain felt the last of her courage desert her. She shut off the speakers that fed into the broadcast booth, cutting off the absurdly happy lyrics about clean, shiny cars.

"I think I pissed him off," she said as Trevor appeared in the booth a few moments later.

"You did fine," he assured her. "We've narrowed the caller's proximity to a five-block radius. The call came from somewhere on North Rampart, near Armstrong Park. I'm working with the local police on this—they've got squad cars en route."

"He wasn't in the Quarter?"

"No." His cell phone rang, and Trevor spoke with whoever was on the other end of the line. She listened as he gave a description—white male, late-thirties to mid-forties, well educated. The image seemed pedestrian to her, as if Dante might be her balding optometrist or the bookish accountant who did her taxes. It didn't match the freak she'd been conversing with on air, a man who'd clearly had some psychotic break with reality.

"Tell the units to ask around, see if anyone saw a man matching that description in the area," Trevor instructed. "That's a predominantly black neighborhood. A white male, probably driving a luxury sedan or SUV, might be remembered."

He closed the phone and went to where Rain sat at her desk. Dropping down beside her, his eyes sought hers. "I've got to get over there. Are you going to be all right?"

"We're going to have to do this again, aren't we?"

"This is the guy, I'm even more sure of it. He's going to call again."

A chill swept over her, and she realized she was grasping his hand. "You gave a description of the killer. Someone's seen him?"

Trevor shook his head. "It's a profile of the unsub—"

Seeing her confusion, he added, "Unknown subject of an investigation. The profilers at the VCU are good at what they do, but there's a lot about this one that doesn't add up. Based on his voice, the race and age sound right, as does the level of education. It's just…"

His words trailed away. Rain realized he was censoring what he told her, shading and erasing the things he didn't want her to know. They both became aware of David's presence in the doorway. Discreetly sliding his fingers from hers, Trevor stood.

"There's another twenty minutes in the show, but we can play music if you're not up to it," David offered, looking at Rain. "You'll need to queue out at the end of the segment."

She nodded. "Thanks."

Trevor spoke to David. "Could we have a word?"

The men went into the hall, but Rain could still hear their voices in fragmented conversation.

Would like to station a uniform in her house… Not necessary. I'll be staying with her tonight… Then at least have a unit conduct regular drive-bys…

How afraid should she be? Rain was certain Dante had known she was lying when she claimed to be unfamiliar with bloodplay. As a psychologist, she understood the term's sexual connotation, as well as its categorization as edgeplay due to the high risk involved in participation. Bloodplay, by definition, was the cutting of a consensual partner in order to cause bleeding. If Trevor was right about the caller's identity, the word *consensual* had little bearing on Dante's practices.

She looked up as David reappeared.

"The phone lines are tied up with callers trying to get through," he said, his expression as giddy as a child at an amusement park. "Not to mention the message board on the WNOR Web site. Everyone wants to talk about the psycho who just called in. The traffic's going to shut down the server."

"You sound pleased."

"Pleased? I'd like to offer Dante his own contract. He's fucking gold."

He leaned against the door frame. "I've got to admit, you surprised me. After the way he rocked you last night, I didn't think you'd be able to keep him on the air."

She decided not to voice the truth. She'd been scared out of her mind.

"I'm spending the night at your place." He raised a hand to squelch her protest. "This isn't negotiable. I'll sleep in the guest room, or downstairs on the sofa, if that's how you want it."

"Does Trevor—" Rain corrected herself. "Does Agent Rivette think I'm in danger?"

Although David's voice was soft, his dark eyes pinned

hers. "You need to understand something, Rain. You're a case number to him. A file he needs to close, that's all."

His Bruno Maglis echoed down the hall as he walked back to his office.

8

The guidebooks to New Orleans encouraged tourists to avoid North Rampart after dark. Looking down the shadowed street, it was easy for Trevor to understand why. He stood in front of a closed pawnshop protected by a drop-down metal cage. Nearby, overflowing trash cans hunkered in front of a faded billboard touting Big King malt liquor. A rat, startled by the beam of Detective McGrath's flashlight, scurried from the garbage into an alleyway.

Things were odd here, Trevor thought as he walked to the other side of the shop. For starters, the street was mostly deserted. The squad cars dispatched to the area had only served to scare away the junkies and thugs who typically patrolled the locality at night. He glanced at his wristwatch and tried to make out the time in the dark.

"This is a waste of time," McGrath muttered beside him.

A light flared up ahead as Thibodeaux lit a cigarette. "Wanna know what I think? I think that hit on the head last night rattled your brain, Rivette. The uniforms already covered this area twice over. What do you expect to find out here?"

"I'll let you know when I find it." Trevor walked a little

farther, uncertain himself as to what he was actually looking for. He stopped in front of a tavern, its neon sign droning on the quiet street. Beyond the grimy windowpane, a stoop-shouldered bartender leaned against the counter, drinking a draft beer and watching ESPN.

"What about that guy? Anybody talk to him?"

McGrath gave an affirmative grunt. "Claims he hasn't seen a thing all night unless it was on the flat-screen."

Trevor sidestepped a puddle of water. He wasn't willing to give up, not yet. He slowed at a line of pay phones on the corner, their metal casings battered and scrawled with graffiti. They were relics, out of place with the current landscape. Everyone right down to street grifters had cell phones these days. There were even prepaid ones bought with cash, popular with drug dealers and others with unscrupulous business to conduct. A short while ago, the wireless carrier had confirmed the caller to *Midnight Confessions* used one of those phones, making it impossible to trace it back to a subscriber.

So why had he made the call from *this* area?

The bronze glow of a street lamp lit the corner. Every now and then it flickered and buzzed, as if it had a short circuit and might go dark at any moment. But it still illuminated the flyer taped to the side of the first phone's hooded exterior.

Give Us Red, We'll Give You Green. Orleans Parish Blood Bank Pays Donors Cash.

"Bring that light over here, will you?" Trevor asked.

McGrath shone the flashlight over the area as Trevor pulled on a pair of latex gloves. He squatted in front of the first phone and peered under its base as he felt inside the darkened partition intended to hold a phone book. Rising, he dipped his index finger into the coin-return slot and plumbed its hollowed depth. Empty. He continued down the line, repeating the process on each pay phone.

Thibodeaux snickered in the background. "You looking

for pocket change, Agent? Thought you feds were paid better than that—"

His taunt died as Trevor made contact with something wedged into the slot of the last phone. He retrieved the piece of paper folded so it was small enough to fit inside the compartment.

"Fuck me," McGrath intoned, staring over Trevor's shoulder at the note. It was written on heavy stationery, and Trevor recognized the dull brown of what he'd first thought to be ink.

Welcome back to New Orleans, Agent Rivette. Looks like we've both finally come home.

The note was signed with the letter *D*. McGrath raised the flashlight. "Is that blood?"

All business now, Thibodeaux extracted an evidence bag from his trouser pocket. He held it open so the note could be dropped inside. "Forensics can dust this for fingerprints and see if the blood matches our vic. Not much point in going over the pay phones, though. Every skell in New Orleans has most likely had their hands on 'em."

"I've got something else that needs to go into evidence," Trevor mentioned. "A necklace that probably belongs to the Jane Doe."

"Yeah? Where'd you get it?"

"Someone broke into my car earlier and hung it from the rearview mirror."

"This psycho's reached out to you *twice* tonight?" Thibodeaux blew smoke from his nostrils before tossing his cigarette onto the sidewalk and grinding it out with his shoe. "There's a voodoo shop 'round that corner, Rivette."

Trevor shrugged. "It's New Orleans. There's a voodoo shop around every corner."

"Well, this one's the real deal. None of that lame-ass tourist shit. You get over there in the morning and tell the high priestess Hélène I sent you."

"What for?" He expected another of Thibodeaux's wise-cracks, but his expression was serious.

"To get you a gris-gris for protection, son. All the cops here carry one—probably some FBI agents, too. Seems to me this vampire's got a real jonesin' for you."

"Drink this."

David handed Rain a crystal tumbler as they stood in the kitchen of her house in the Lower Garden District. His eyes watchful, he gulped from his own glass and waited while she took a sip.

"I hate bourbon," she confessed.

She set the drink on the countertop, walked into the parlor and sat on the sofa, placing one of the striped throw pillows onto her lap. Sighing tiredly, she looked around the familiar room and tried to distance herself from the night's events.

It was widely rumored the old house had ghosts. A tour bus, its signage proclaiming it as part of the Official Haunted New Orleans Tour, even drove past several times a week. On more than one occasion, Rain had heard the bus operator over a loudspeaker, recounting Desiree's murder to photograph-snapping tourists. But whatever spirits inhabited her home, she'd grown comfortable with long ago. She'd never felt unsafe here. At least not until tonight.

"What's going on with you, Rain?"

She looked up, realizing David had followed her into the parlor.

"I guess this Dante thing has me a little on edge," she admitted.

"I'm not talking about Dante." He sat down next to her, contemplating the amber contents of his glass before speaking again. "I'm talking about us."

She closed her eyes. "David—"

"What was up with you and the FBI agent tonight? Or was that all for my account?"

"Please don't do this," she implored. "Not tonight."

"Don't do what? Ask you where I stand?"

"Are you still sleeping with her?" Rain interrupted, unable to stop herself. A part of her wanted to know if he'd thrown away their relationship for more than a one-night stand.

"Would it matter to you if I was?"

Rain paused for a long moment. Then she shook her head and replied with honesty, "No. Our relationship is over."

She'd turned on a single lamp in the parlor, and its muted light silhouetted David's profile. He had angular, chiseled features, and his olive complexion and black hair hinted at his Creole lineage. Rain knew he'd been linked to several New Orleans socialites in the past, as well as to one internationally famous runway model. In the beginning, she hadn't understood his fascination with her. She was too small, definitely not leggy and far from exotic. She wasn't his type, although Ella LaRue certainly was.

"I still want you, Rain."

"You want *Midnight Confessions.*"

"I thought that was something you wanted, too." He tossed down the rest of his bourbon.

Now or never, she thought. It was time to tell him the truth.

"We need to talk about the show, David. I'm not sure I want to renew my contract when it runs out."

He set the glass down on the table in front of him and wiped his hand over his mouth. Unable to bear the silence, Rain got up and walked across the parlor's floral rug. His voice made her turn back around.

"Listen to me." He'd risen in front of the sofa, and he gestured with his hands, throwing them wide before dropping them back down to his sides. "Now is not the time for you to run out on *Midnight Confessions.*"

"I'm sorry—"

"I haven't told you yet, but they're considering us for syndication. The show would have to expand to a full five nights a week, but we could be airing in six major markets by fall."

He walked toward her and clasped her arms. "We could go *national,* Rain. Do you know what that means?"

"Why didn't you tell me about this before?"

"I'm telling you now. I've been shopping dubs of the show around for a while. Our Arbitrons are solid. I thought you'd be pleased."

"We should've discussed this."

He let go of her. "Christ. I need another drink."

Snatching up the tumbler, David stalked back to the kitchen. She found him with his palms planted on the granite counter, a fresh glass of bourbon in front of him.

"I need this syndication deal." He lifted the glass and swallowed. "I'm behind on some loans. I could lose everything."

Rain fell into stunned silence. She thought of his luxurious French Quarter apartment, his expensive car and the beach home on St. George Island. David was known as a successful entrepreneur. She'd assumed producing *Midnight Confessions* was merely a complement to his partial ownership in the radio station. And that the radio station, in turn, was just one of several other business ventures. She'd had no idea things weren't going well.

"What about the restaurant?"

David's was a Creole-style dinner spot tucked into the Shops at Canal Place, an upscale mall on the edge of the Quarter near the four-star Wyndham Hotel.

"It's bleeding money," he confessed. "Everything's going to shit."

"I didn't know."

"Of course you didn't. Do you think I wanted you to know what a mess I've made?"

"If there's anything I can do—"

"You can renew your contract," he said tightly. "You can forgive me for fucking Ella."

There was desperation in his eyes as he waited for a response. Hearing none, he drained his glass again. As he did so, Rain searched his face for some glimpse of the charming man she'd imagined herself in love with only a few months earlier, but he'd all but disappeared. After a short while, he reached for the decanter and splashed in another drink.

"You're pleased with yourself, aren't you?" he asked.

"What do you mean?"

David's eyes glinted like a knife blade. "You shut me out of your bed, and now you're holding my financial future in your hands."

"That's not fair."

"National syndication means a lot of money." The tumbler hit the counter with a sharp rap. "If the show takes off, it could mean a publicity tour, maybe a book deal, guest spots on TV talk shows—"

"You certainly have this all figured out."

"I do. At least I *did*." His face suddenly loomed near hers. "Damn it, Rain! How could you not want this? How could you not want *us?*"

He pulled her to him, his hands cupping her bottom so that she was drawn fully against his hips.

"Tell me we weren't good," he challenged huskily.

"Stop it." Rain tore herself from his arms and took several steps back. Normally she could handle David, but she wasn't used to him drinking so much. "I think you should go."

"I'm staying," he stated flatly. "You shouldn't be here alone tonight."

"I'll be fine." Rain walked to the wireless phone that hung on the kitchen wall. "You shouldn't be driving, either. I'm going to call you a taxi."

He bridged the distance between them and yanked the phone from her hand, replacing it roughly in its cradle. "I don't need a goddamn taxi."

She trailed him to the front of the house. David stared onto the darkened street. The cicadas' chant from the garden had grown louder with the door open, and the moist heat of the New Orleans night filtered in and clashed with the house's air-conditioning.

"Just tell me you'll think about *Midnight Confessions*," he said.

"David." Rain's voice was soft. "I'm pretty sure my mind's made up."

His eyes carried the weight of his words. "Whatever happens between you and me, Rain, I can deal with it. But the show is my last hope. I won't let it go. I'll do whatever I have to."

He walked to the Jaguar and drove away. Rain continued standing at the window long after she'd closed the door and locked it. Outside, a squad car rolled past. Its spotlight swept over the lawn as it conducted a safety check, ensuring nothing looked amiss.

I won't let it go. I'll do whatever I have to.

Whether David's words were a threat, she wasn't sure.

9

The ringing cell phone shattered Trevor's sleep. He fumbled on the nightstand for the offending device and managed to flip open its cover.

"Rivette," he mumbled hoarsely.

"It's McGrath. Thought you'd want to know we got an ID on the Jane Doe."

Trevor scrubbed a hand over his face at the sound of the detective's voice and sat up. "Who is she?"

"Her name's Cara Seagreen. She was a sophomore at St. Vincent Catholic in Jefferson Parish." He paused, and Trevor heard a young girl talking in the room with the detective. "Hold on…"

There was a muffled sound that Trevor assumed was McGrath covering the mouthpiece with his hand.

"Tell Momma I'll be down in a minute. I'm making a call." His voice became clear again. "Sorry about that. I'm at home. Anyway, it turns out the vic's parents were out of town and thought Cara was staying at a friend's house, a classmate named Simone Bausell. This friend, and I use the term loosely, never told anyone Cara had disappeared while they were out clubbing. Both girls are underage and Simone didn't want to get into trouble. So she lied to her mother, told

her Cara's parents were back and the girl had gone home. Meanwhile, the vic's parents return from one of those ocean cruises last night to find out their daughter's disappeared. They called the police."

"Which explains why no one was looking for a missing teen." Trevor looked at the clock next to the bed. It was just past 7:00 a.m. Light leaked into the hotel room under the drawn curtains.

"I got the M.E.'s toxicology report in my e-mail this morning, too," McGrath continued. "The vic had a shitload of Ecstasy in her bloodstream."

"Did the friend say which club Cara disappeared from?"

"Apparently, Simone was pretty baked herself that night. Says she visited a string of clubs, as well as an illegal rave in one of the old mansions upriver. Really gettin' her party on, if you know what I mean. She can't seem to recall at what point she and Cara were split up, or where."

"You believe that?"

"I don't know."

A creaking sound came through the phone and Trevor envisioned McGrath shifting his large frame in his chair. "I've got three girls myself, Rivette. My oldest is almost the same age as the vic. It scares the hell out of me what kids are into these days."

"I'd like to interview the friend myself."

"Thought you would. The mother's bringing her into the precinct this afternoon. They've lawyered up, so they won't be alone."

Trevor wasn't surprised. "What about the vic's parents?"

"They're pretty upset, as expected. I met them at the morgue at five-thirty this morning for the ID."

"You should've called me."

"We're working on this together, right? No point in nobody getting any sleep. I didn't call Tibbs, either. He's positively cranky without his beauty rest," McGrath replied. "By the way, the cross left in your car belongs to Simone Bausell. She let the Seagreen girl borrow it, along with the trampy clothing found at the crime scene."

"Nice friend."

McGrath snorted. "Wait till you see her. She's what Courtney Love probably looked like as a kid."

The roar of the room's air conditioner kicked up, forcing Trevor to press the phone harder against his ear to hear the detective.

"Has this been a pattern with the other vics?" McGrath was asking. "This lunatic leaving you trophies from the kill?"

Trevor pinched the bridge of his nose. When his cell phone rang, he'd been dreaming, more a nightmare, really, and it was beginning to return to him in pieces. He worked to shut out the familiar images so he could concentrate.

"Rivette?"

"I'm still here. And no, it's not the first time. I work with a partner sometimes, but the letters and packages have all been addressed to me. We're lucky all he left behind last night was a necklace. The last time I got a ring through the U.S. Postal Service. It was still on the vic's finger."

"Jesus." There was a brief silence before the detective spoke again. "Look, it's Saturday. My youngest has a soccer game this morning at City Park, but I'll meet you at the precinct this afternoon. Around one."

"Yeah. Thanks, McGrath." The phone went dead. Trevor peered into the shadows. The adage "No rest for the wicked" ran through his mind, and he wondered what Dante was doing right now. Stalking his next victim? If he was a resident of New Orleans as the note suggested, was he at home in one of the quiet suburbs? Trevor thought of him mowing his Bermuda lawn while his wife and children looked on, unaware Daddy liked to cut up women for kicks. Whatever his current activity, the multijurisdictional aspect of the crimes suggested the unsub was someone who traveled frequently, such as a salesman or business executive. But what did it mean that he was now playing on his home court?

Not to mention, the note meant the unsub had done his homework. He knew Trevor was from New Orleans, too.

Dragging a hand through his hair, Trevor felt the need for coffee to push away the residue of sleep. He stared at the darkened screen of his laptop that sat on the small desk. At the least, he needed to get his report filed with the VCU before meeting up with McGrath to interview the Bausell girl that afternoon.

After pulling on jeans and a T-shirt, he walked to the coffee shop across the street to purchase a cup and a copy of the *Times-Picayune*. Trevor was returning when he saw him, loitering by the line of vending machines inside the hotel's breezeway.

"Hello, son."

For a man approaching sixty, James Rivette was sturdy-looking. He was an inch taller than Trevor and heavier by thirty pounds. Although his thick hair had grayed and deep lines bracketed his mouth, he still cut an imposing figure. His presence had served him well as a police officer working some of New Orleans's toughest neighborhoods. The last time the two men had seen one another had been three years ago, across Sarah Rivette's casket. There had been no words exchanged then, only glares that were thick with challenge and meaning. Trevor realized his entire body had tensed, an ingrained fight-or-flight reaction that not even his years of training as a federal agent could alter.

"I came by to see you, Trev."

Trevor kept his voice flat. "You've seen me."

"Seems like you wanted to see *me*, too." James indicated the cut on Trevor's forehead. "I called 911, you know. What the hell, boy? Don't they teach you to watch for cars at that fancy training academy in Quantico?"

Trevor looked away, squinting at the sunlight that reflected off the courtyard's pool as he tried to regain his equilibrium.

"What were you doing outside my bar the other night?" James had been leaning against the breezeway wall. Now he straightened and walked closer. He took a drag from his cigarette as he waited for a response.

"I was out for a run."

"Got to keep in shape for the FBI." His tone mocking, James's gaze roved over his son. Trevor noticed his eyes were bloodshot, his nose mottled where the spiderlike vessels had ruptured from years of alcohol abuse.

"Guess you've been to see our Annabelle," he commented.

Trevor's jaw tightened. "You don't have the right to say her name."

James merely smiled at the fierce statement, revealing strong-looking teeth that had yellowed only slightly despite the heavy use of nicotine.

"Always the protector, ain't you, Trev? Too good to be a beat cop like your old man, though." His eyes broke away to follow a swimsuit-clad young woman headed toward the chaise lounges alongside the pool. "You don't even sound like a Southerner no more. Guess I can thank your aunt Susan for that, uppity bitch."

Trevor's grip tightened on the disposable cup, causing its plastic lid to buckle. He barely felt the trickle of hot liquid as it made contact with his skin.

"So," James said. "You here for business or pleasure?"

When Trevor didn't answer, his father chuckled. "I'm just trying to make small talk. I know why you're here. I've still got a few friends left at the NOPD."

"I doubt that."

James moved toward him, and Trevor caught the odor of whiskey on his breath. "That smart mouth used to get you into trouble—"

"The playing field's more level now, *Dad*."

"You think you're something, don't you? With your big-time law degree and your Department of Justice badge to shove in people's faces—"

"I'm better than you. I know that much."

"You don't know shit." James flicked the cigarette to the ground at Trevor's feet. Turning to saunter away, he tossed off one last statement. "Tell Annabelle to make you some of her biscuits while you're in town. That gal's a better cook than your momma ever was."

Trevor remained rooted in place until James had rounded the corner and disappeared. Then he went up the stairs and let himself into his room, hating the tremor in his hands as he swiped the security card to open the door. Leaving the coffee and newspaper on the desk next to the laptop, he grabbed his gun and left the hotel.

It was still relatively early, but the temperature had already begun to build, sending up heat from the concrete in rolling waves. He'd watched her leave her house that morning, making her way on foot and then taking one of the St. Charles streetcars to the French Market on Decatur Street.

He knew her destination, based on her routine and the wicker basket she carried. He found her again easily once she'd departed the streetcar. She was browsing through the market stalls and picking out goods. Her selection consisted of fruit, cinnamon-dusted pecans, cheese and large olives— the good Italian kind marinated with herbs. She picked up a loaf of rustic-looking bread, lifting it to her nose and sniffing its freshly baked scent before dropping it into her basket, as well.

She wore denim shorts and a green tank top with thin spaghetti straps. Braless, her nipples were faintly visible through the tank's material. He rarely saw her dressed like this, and the unintentionally provocative outfit left him transfixed by her simple beauty. She wore no makeup and her red-gold hair had been pulled up into a loose twist, a few tendrils escaping to frame her face.

She looked so much like Desiree. He felt something dark and hot move in his veins.

After she made her purchases, she sat at a café table protected from the sun by a brightly colored umbrella. She drank coffee and leafed through the pages of a psychology magazine she'd brought with her from home. He was close enough to make out the details—the silver bangle bracelet on her wrist, the graceful curve of her slender neck, the frosted pink of her painted toenails in the flat sandals. Her skin was pale, as if it rarely saw the sun, and he could see the faint sprinkle of freckles across her creamy shoulders.

A man in blue running shorts and white T-shirt stopped at her table. Smiling, she stood and embraced him, her small hand threading through his salt-and-pepper hair. He wondered who the intruder was. It wasn't the Creole bastard he'd been certain she was bedding. Another lover? He didn't like the thought of that because it made her seem less worthy of his devotion. He wanted—*no, needed*—to believe that while she possessed her mother's looks, she didn't share her lack of morals.

She conversed with the man a while longer, then lifted on tiptoe and hugged him again before he went on his way. As she returned to her magazine, a breeze ruffled her hair so that she had to push it out of her eyes.

Once they were together, he'd have her grow it out long,

nearly down to her hips the way her mother's had been. He imagined his fingers slipping through the strands that were the color of fire and felt like spun silk. He'd run her baths that smelled of lavender, and in their bed, he'd leave a scattering of rose petals on which they'd make love.

A barking dog being dragged on a leash interrupted his fantasy. Rain looked up at the intrusion as well, and he stepped back behind a stall filled with canary melons. He watched as she bent to pet the dog. The homely mongrel was as thin as its owner was fat. It lapped up the attention she gave, its scraggly excuse for a tail wagging furiously.

He reminded himself that he had to be careful. It was still too soon to reveal himself.

He had a schedule to keep.

10

The sound of the sidewalk jazz band rose to the loft apartment in New Orleans's revitalized Warehouse District. Standing at the window, Brian Rivette took in the bustling scene below him. Tourists tossed change into the musicians' open instrument cases while a little farther down, a man in a flowing white tunic and dreadlocks paced the street, carrying a bible and a hand-painted sign. The man raised the sign over his head, and Brian had to squint to read the words:

Armageddon Is Approaching. The End Is Near.

Turning back from the window, his eyes scanned the apartment he shared with Alex Santos. The loft was open and spacious, with hardwood floors and exposed-brick walls that had at one time comprised the frame of a textile mill. Synapse, the art gallery and studio Alex owned, was on the ground floor of the building, but Brian preferred working here in the sun-filled loft. He returned to the sketch pad he'd laid on the coffee table when he'd heard the music outside. The drawing didn't look like much yet, just a series of grayed lines and shadows. It was the bare bones he put on paper first, and in his mind's eye he could see how the drawing would take shape.

Before he'd met Alex—before he'd gotten clean—his

artwork had been harsher and unrefined. Thirteen years his senior and already a successful, nationally renowned photographer, Alex had been his mentor. He'd guided Brian's raw talent and forced him to challenge himself on both artistic and personal levels. When Brian had finally decided to stop using for good, it was Alex who'd been there for him.

The door to the loft opened. Alex entered, his gray-flecked hair wet from his morning run in the humid climate. His cocoa-brown eyes fastened on Brian, who now sat on the leather couch with the sketch pad on his lap and a charcoal pencil in his left hand. Alex walked over to press a kiss on top of his head.

"You're dripping on my sketch."

"Sorry." He grinned and headed toward the well-equipped kitchen. Alex was a stellar cook, another thing for which Brian realized he was fortunate.

"Guess who I ran into?" Alex called. Brian heard him removing what he assumed was the pitcher of freshly squeezed orange juice from the refrigerator.

"Who?"

"Rain, sitting at a table in the French Market." Alex returned to the living area. He selected a chocolate croissant from a basket on the table to have with his juice. "I reminded her about your opening tomorrow night."

Brian looked up from the sketch. "Don't you think that might be a little weird? I mean, Trevor's going to be there."

"Why would it be weird?"

"She's part of his investigation."

Alex shrugged. "It's not like they have to talk shop."

Brian had told Alex in confidence about taking Trevor to meet Rain, and about the possibility that one of her show's callers was responsible for a string of murders, including one committed recently in New Orleans.

"Remember, they're trying to avoid any mention of a serial

killer getting out to the press," he said. "I hope you didn't tell anyone."

"Well, now, you tell me. And I just got off the phone with the bureau chief at the *Times-Picayune*."

Brian rolled his eyes at Alex's sarcasm and returned his attention to his work. Putting his breakfast down, Alex studied the drawing.

"That's good," he said, watching as Brian worked.

"Good enough for Synapse?"

Pride was evident in Alex's voice. "I know talent, Brian."

"I'm a little freaked about the show."

"You're worried about the critics who'll be there, waiting to malign your work? Or the fact that your big brother will finally be meeting me?"

"Alex…"

"We've been together for almost two years. I just think it's odd I haven't so much as laid eyes on the guy, that's all."

"He doesn't come around much," Brian said quietly. "You'll meet him tomorrow night."

"He won't like me. He's a homophobe, and I'm hardly in the closet."

When Brian gave him a look, Alex raised his eyebrows. "What? You said as much yourself."

"That's definitely *not* what I said." Brian put down the sketch, unsure of how to explain his complicated relationship with his brother. Restless, he went to look back out the window. The musicians were making out like bandits, their instrument cases filling with coins and paper bills. The doomsayer had wandered off, replaced by a street artist who'd set up his easel not far from the band, hoping to glean business from the gathering crowd. For a while, Brian had supported his habit doing pencil drawings of tourists for cash. He would avoid getting stoned until he'd made enough money, then head out to the edges of Storyville to score. At his lowest, he'd even turned a trick or two in order to buy heroin or cocaine, his drugs of choice. But that had been before Alex and it was part of a past he wanted to forget. He stared at the gold band on his left hand. All that seemed like someone else's life now. Brian knew how lucky he was to be alive and healthy.

"I don't think it's about me being gay," he said, still gazing out the window. "It's about me being an addict. Trevor tried like hell to get me clean."

Alex came to stand behind him, and Brian drew a breath before speaking again. "It was before I met you. Trevor took a leave from work, came down here and literally kicked my ass. He dragged me kicking and screaming into a rehab facility, a private one in Baton Rouge that cost him a lot of money."

Alex's arms went around his waist, and his chin rested against Brian's shoulder. "What happened?"

"I bailed on the program the first chance I got. When I was high, nothing mattered but staying that way. After I ran away from the center, Trevor kind of gave up on me. I don't think he knew what else to do. The last time I saw him, we said some pretty awful things to each other."

"Like what?"

"It doesn't matter now."

Framed photos sat on an end table—pictures of Alex's parents and sister in Puerto Rico, images of Annabelle and Haley, and one of Brian's deceased mother, Sarah. Brian picked up a recent shot Alex had taken of him with Annabelle. They stood together at a street fair in Annabelle's Marigny neighborhood. Trevor's absence was like a physical pain, a yawning hole in their family that had been left unfilled. There was so much Alex didn't know, things Brian was unsure he'd ever be able to share with him.

He replaced the photo. "Can we talk about something else?"

"Sure." Alex took Brian's hand and looked down at his charcoal-smudged fingers.

"But this brother of yours. Is he half as hot as you?" His smile was mischievous, and Brian knew he was trying to lift his somber mood.

"Because if he is…"

Alex left the statement hanging and Brian graced him with a halfhearted laugh. He pulled his hand away and went off in search of his other art supplies.

"I'd be careful. He carries a gun."

"And handcuffs? Please, God, let there be handcuffs."

He barely dodged the croissant Brian picked up from the table and launched in his direction before leaving the room.

If you looked at it long enough, the West Indies-style cottage could take on human qualities. The two large windows in front were like eyes, the vertical slash of the door a nose, and the wide porch a mouth with even, white-planked teeth. It was something Trevor and Annabelle had discussed often as children, their young imaginations ripe.

Trevor knocked on the door, then turned the handle and found it unlocked. He went hesitantly inside, intending to call out for Annabelle and Haley. But his throat felt constricted, his nerves still jangled by the unexpected run-in with his father.

The interior was more cluttered than the night he'd been over for dinner. Toys were scattered around the front room and a worn, crocheted afghan lay bunched on the sofa. A half-empty juice glass and a cereal bowl in a ring of milk sat on the coffee table. Haley's breakfast, no doubt.

This house had secrets. Every corner revealed some part of his life Trevor had worked to push from his mind. His eyes traveled to a closet in the hallway. *Don't think about it,* he told himself, but the images were closing in. He'd put Annabelle and Brian inside that closet, warned them to stay quiet as James Rivette's thunderous voice filled the house. The rest of the memory came flooding back. His mother's pleas from the kitchen, and the sound of fist hitting flesh. He'd run then, wedging his own thin body between his parents and bracing himself for the hurricane force of his father's rage.

Trevor ran his hand over his forearm. He felt the slight ridge in the bone where the break had healed. That time, he'd been eight years old.

He went down the hallway and past the bedroom's half-open door. The shower ran in the bathroom, although he barely heard it. His concentration was on the memories that tugged at his mind.

James and Sarah's bedroom had been on the main floor, the children's located upstairs. The boys shared the larger room and Annabelle had the small, atticlike space with a ceiling that leaned in under the slant of the house's gabled roof. Unable to stop himself, Trevor climbed the narrow staircase. When he reached the top, he saw that his and Brian's old bedroom now appeared to be inhabited by Haley. Their bunk beds were replaced by a single twin with a patchwork quilt and eyelet dust ruffle. A braided-rag rug covered the hardwood floor, and a bookshelf sat against the far wall, lined with stuffed animals and dolls.

It all looked so normal.

Trevor turned, seeing the closed door to the room that had once belonged to Annabelle. Gathering his courage, he moved closer. He slowly twisted the glass knob and pushed open the door.

The room was mostly empty now, used for storage. Boxes bearing his sister's neat handwriting were stacked inside, labeled as Christmas decorations and Haley's baby clothes.

The image came at him instantly, stunning him like a physical blow. His father turning to look at him, still in his uniform, his eyes like twin stagnant pools. Annabelle, her face hidden behind her hands.

Don't you know how to knock, boy?

He closed the door, his heart hammering.

"Trevor?" Annabelle stood in the hallway behind him. She wore a thick bathrobe, and her hair was damp and curling around her face. "I got out of the shower and saw your car outside—"

Her voice halted and her eyes flickered to the closed door before moving back to his face.

"Did he come here?" Trevor demanded. "Don't lie to me."

"You're trembling." She reached for him. "Let's go back downstairs."

He shrugged off her touch and paced the hall. "He was at my hotel this morning, Anna."

Sliding her hands inside the pockets of her robe, she sighed in resignation. "He came by yesterday, looking for you. But he's never been here before, I swear. He leaves us alone."

"Why didn't you tell me? Are you all right?"

She nodded. "I didn't want to upset you. Haley answered the door, and I didn't want to make a scene. He was here for only a minute and then he went on his way."

"Keep your doors locked from now on, you hear me? I was able to just walk in here."

"Haley forgets sometimes. We'll be more careful."

"That's not good enough. You're going to file a restraining order when the courthouse opens on Monday."

"He isn't a threat anymore. He's older, and all those years of drinking and smoking—"

"Christ. And you feel sorry for him?"

"Of course not," she answered, defensive. "I just refuse to let him—*what he did to us*—rule my life anymore."

She gazed at him, her eyes soft. "Can't you see? He's stolen enough from all of us already. I'm not going to let him show up here and disrupt my life. I won't give him that power."

Trevor felt a pressure on his lungs that made it hard to breathe. His presence had brought James Rivette back to this house. That thought alone was enough to justify his years of staying away.

"Trevor, he stole *you*," Annabelle whispered.

"I should've stopped him from hurting you."

"You did. I promise, he never touched me again."

He shook his head. "I should've known sooner."

It was the reason Annabelle rarely bore the burden of their father's wrath. He'd thought it was because she was so good, so innocent, that even a bastard like James Rivette couldn't bring himself to harm her. He'd been incredibly naive.

Annabelle took a step closer. "He nearly killed you."

He looked again at the closed door. What he'd been told about that day had been in opposition to the splintered memories that had resurfaced, whip-shot images that were too brief to hold on to but still left behind questions he couldn't shake.

"It's okay," Annabelle said gently. She put her arms around him. Trevor flinched and tried to pull away, but she held tight, refusing to let go.

He felt dampness on his cheeks and realized he was crying.

11

A black easel sat in the foyer, bearing a placard with a single statement in elegant typeface:

Synapse Introduces the Art of Brian Rivette

The strains of a jazz piano floated above the conversation as Rain entered the gallery, impressed as always by its gleaming hardwood floors and high ceilings. A tuxedoed waiter stopped alongside her with a tray of champagne glasses. She selected one and took a sip, her eyes scanning the stylish crowd. Rain wore a simple slip dress of gray silk with a matching wrap that drifted around her bare shoulders. A square-cut amethyst hung on a delicate chain around her neck, and she touched the pendant absently as she stopped in front of Brian's first piece. It was an oil on canvas entitled simply *Woman,* painted in a loose style that added a suggestion of movement and voluptuousness.

"What do you think?" Alex appeared next to her, dressed in dark slacks and an open-necked white shirt.

"It's beautiful," she said. "I've always loved Brian's pencil drawings and watercolors, but I can see he's equally gifted with oils."

"It's a new medium for him, but his style is exquisite. I

couldn't resist putting a few into the show." He smiled, his dimples deepening. "Of course, I could be biased."

"You? Never."

She gave her friend's arm an affectionate squeeze as they studied the painting together. After a few moments, Alex added, "You look lovely, by the way. Dolce and Gabbana?"

"St. Peter Thrift Shop," Rain corrected wryly. "I think the fashionable term is *vintage.*"

More guests arrived, and Alex, always the exuberant host, went to greet them. He returned to Rain's side as she made her way to another of Brian's pieces, a somber watercolor that captured the fogged blues and grays of a rainy New Orleans street. Entitled *Monday on Dauphine,* the work was exceptional, with the storefronts reflecting back the luminosity of the rain in their windows and the puddles on the sidewalk acting as mirrors to the scene.

"Where's David?" Alex inquired. "Parking the beloved Jaguar?"

Rain caught the contempt in his voice. "We broke up several months ago."

"That's what you keep telling me, but I don't think he got the memo." He glanced suspiciously around the room. "Wherever you are, I swear he's lurking nearby. I think he considers you his property, as much as that damn car."

"Speaking of cars, I saw the Audi Brian was driving. That's quite a birthday gift."

"Don't change the subject."

She decided to spare Alex the details of her confrontation with David two nights earlier. Instead, she took another sip of champagne, her eyes drawn to the other side of the gallery. Trevor Rivette stood close to an attractive, dark-haired woman. His companion said something to him, and her hand rested on his shoulder.

Rain lowered her eyes. She'd expected him to be here,

but she was surprised by how disappointed she was that he'd brought a date. He wore dark slacks and a V-neck summer sweater he'd pushed up on his forearms, a different look from the conservative business clothes she'd seen him in previously. The sweater displayed his athletic build, and his thick hair looked burnished under the gallery lights. He was drinking only Perrier, and Rain watched as he tilted the bottle to his lips and swallowed. She blushed when she realized Alex had caught her appraisal.

"I hear you've met Brian's brother?"

Rain nodded without giving further detail, since she wasn't sure how much information Alex had been privy to through Brian. She and David had been instructed not to discuss the possible connection between *Midnight Confessions* and the serial murder investigation.

"He's different from Brian," Alex mused. "Gorgeous, obviously, but a little intense for my tastes."

"What do you know about him?"

"He's thirty-four, single, he has a law degree from Georgetown, and he's been with the FBI for seven years," he recounted. "Brian seems to worship the ground he walks on."

"Do you like him?"

"I actually just met him."

When she gave him a surprised look, he added, "Apparently, big brother doesn't make it back to New Orleans often. He's a bit estranged from the family."

"Why?"

"I'm not sure," he admitted, frowning. "My understanding is that he went to Maryland to live with an aunt and uncle there when he was a teenager. Brian won't talk about whatever happened."

She followed Alex's gaze. He looked at Brian, who was in discussion with a silver-haired, goateed man Rain knew to be a serious art collector.

"All he's ever said is that their father was an abusive son of a bitch, and Trevor took the brunt of it," Alex continued. "Their mother died a few years ago. She was drunk and fell down a flight of stairs."

Rain stared into the golden liquid in her glass. "How terrible."

"Annabelle doesn't say much about the situation, either."

"Annabelle?"

"Brian's sister."

Rain glanced again at the woman standing next to Trevor, the resemblance dawning on her. She knew through Alex that Brian had a sister who did the bookkeeping at Synapse, although they'd never met. She had a young daughter, too, if Rain recalled correctly.

"Enough of this depressing talk," Alex proclaimed, taking her arm. "Tonight is about having fun. And making Brian rich and famous, of course."

Guiding her toward a group of art patrons, he whispered, "Be warned, I'm not above using your celebrity to impress a few checkbook-carrying guests."

"I'm not a celebrity," Rain protested, although she knew Alex was like a runaway train she was unlikely to derail.

As he made introductions, Rain smiled and engaged in small talk, but her thoughts remained on Trevor Rivette. She'd thought about him for most of the weekend, although she realized it was probably due to the anxiety she felt about the caller to *Midnight Confessions*. Her psychologist's mind reasoned that as a federal agent, he represented security and protection, and she'd been feeling vulnerable.

You're a case number to him. A file he needs to close, that's all.

She reminded herself of David's words, and tried to push Trevor Rivette from her head.

* * *

As the night wore on, it became clear Alex had invited the entire Orleans Parish to Brian's opening. Despite the gallery's impressive square footage, it was overflowing. For Alex and Brian, however, it meant the show was a success. Already, nearly a dozen of Brian's pieces had gilt-edged cards beneath them, subtly announcing them as sold.

Rain worked her way through the crowd, trying not to make eye contact. She'd never gotten used to the attention that came with her job as host of *Midnight Confessions*. Several people had asked for her autograph, which she'd given, and another had inquired what it was like to be Desiree Sommers's daughter. There was an obvious interest, and Rain did her best to answer such questions as politely but as vaguely as possible. Worse, only a short time ago, she'd found herself cornered by a writer for *New Orleans Trends* magazine. The man was eager to do a profile on her and was ignoring her request not to be interviewed during the reception. When they'd been momentarily interrupted by another guest, she'd taken the opportunity to slip away.

Her purse and wrap were in Alex's office. She'd retrieve her things and then discreetly make her way outside to hail a cab.

Rain let herself into the office. It was furnished in dark cherry wood and burgundy leather. A desk lamp cast the space in a golden glow, and framed art in various sizes leaned against the walls, having been removed from the main exhibit area to make more room for Brian's work.

But the photograph was there, as always.

Alex had the ability to work magic with the camera, and it still surprised Rain that the image hanging over his desk was actually her. Years earlier, before Brian even, she'd joined Alex at a restaurant in the trendy Bywater neighborhood. They'd gotten buzzed on rum hurricanes and Rain had finally agreed to be photographed. Afraid she'd change her mind when she sobered up, Alex hadn't wasted any time. He'd walked her to the gravel path atop the levee overlooking the Mississippi, where he'd pulled his camera from his ever-present shoulder bag, and started snapping photos. Rain wore jeans and a lace camisole, and the winds coming in from the river had blown strands of hair across her face. Even she had to admit the effect was evocative, her resemblance to Desiree made clear through Alex's lens.

Rain heard the door open behind her. It was Trevor, another refugee from the din inside the gallery. Their eyes met in the room's soft lighting.

"Art showings really aren't your scene, are they?" Rain asked as he closed the door behind him. She felt her heart flutter at the realization they were alone.

"Is it that obvious?"

"I'm not much for crowds, either," she admitted. "But I wanted to be here for Alex and Brian. It's a big night for them."

"I thought celebrities loved this kind of thing."

"I'm hardly a celebrity," Rain clarified for the second time that night.

"Your fans out there say otherwise. You've had people milling around you for most of the evening."

She followed his gaze to the image of herself over Alex's desk.

"Not to mention, regular people don't have posters made of them," he added, walking to her.

"That's not a poster. It's an original photograph."

The arch of his eyebrows indicated he didn't see the difference. Rain picked up her purse from the desk, attempting to make light of their situation. "I was going to come by and say hello earlier, but I decided not to, considering the circumstances. I mean, what would I say? 'Nice to see you, and how's that hunt for a serial killer going?' Conversation like that tends to ruin the party atmosphere."

"With all the noise out there, I doubt anyone would have heard you, anyway." He glanced at the clutch purse she held. "Are you leaving?"

"In a little while."

Trevor's sweater was a deep slate color that set off his eyes, and she noticed the injury to his temple had faded a bit and was covered only by a small butterfly bandage. Rain had the urge to reach up and gently touch the tender area as she had two days ago in her office. But instead, she simply smoothed her hands over the fragile silk of her dress.

"I've been wondering about the trace on the call. Were you able to find out anything?"

He shook his head. "The caller was gone by the time we got units into the area. No one claimed to have seen anyone matching the profile."

Rain peered at him, aware of something in his guarded expression that told her he knew more than he was willing to divulge. "Is there something else I should be concerned about?"

"Anything you need to know about the investigation, Rain, I'll tell you."

She tilted her head speculatively. "Is this the part where you do your Jack Nicholson impression and tell me I can't handle the truth?"

He swallowed a sigh, his hand rising to massage the back of his neck.

"If you're expecting my cooperation, Agent Rivette—"

"It's Trevor," he reminded. "And some aspects of the case need to remain confidential."

"If it relates to me in any way, I have a right to know." Rain added softly, "After all, you're using me to get to this man, aren't you?"

His jaw tensed, letting her know she'd hit a nerve.

"Dante left me a note at the location where the call was made, welcoming me back to New Orleans," he said. "We also found the disposable cell phone he used in a trash can. It was wiped clean of fingerprints, and any DNA residue won't match previous offenders in our databases—or at least that's been my experience so far."

It took only seconds for Rain to connect the dots. "If he left you a note, then he knew you'd be out there looking for him. He knew about the trace?"

"My guess is that he's been watching you. Or me. Maybe since the moment I got into town." He gazed at the amethyst that hung around Rain's neck. "He left a necklace in my car the same night I came to your radio station. He took it from the victim."

"Why would he do that?"

"He wants me to know he's one step ahead."

Realization settled over her. Until now, she'd held on to the possibility that Trevor was somehow mistaken, that Dante wasn't the man he was looking for but was just another pervert who'd gotten onto the airwaves. The note he'd left at the location on North Rampart proved otherwise.

"I didn't want to tell you because I didn't want to frighten you further." Trevor studied her face. "I left your producer a voice message yesterday morning, alerting him to keep a close eye on you."

Absently, Rain ran her hands over the gooseflesh that had risen on her arms.

"You're cold." He went to the couch and retrieved her wrap. But instead of handing it to her, he stepped closer, leaving little distance between them. Trevor slid the silk around her bare shoulders, his fingers warm and lingering on her skin. His touch caused a delicious shiver to run through her.

"I could get D'Alba for you," he offered, voice low. He'd

let his hands fall but hadn't yet moved away. "Tell him you're ready to go."

Rain stared up at him, her breathing made shallow by his nearness. "He isn't here."

Trevor scowled. "He let you come alone?"

"David doesn't *let* me do anything. He's my producer, that's all. Besides, I doubt that Dante is milling about somewhere in Synapse, waiting to snatch me from the crowd."

"It's after you leave here that concerns me more." He finally took a reluctant step back. "The NOPD's in on this. There's a squad car conducting drive-bys on your street as a minimal precaution. I wanted to have a uniform stationed inside the house, but D'Alba said he was staying with you."

"David's not staying with me," Rain replied.

"Then I'll have someone over there tonight."

"That's not necessary."

"I really think—"

"No," she stated firmly. It was true Dante had unsettled her, but what Trevor couldn't possibly understand was how much she valued her privacy, due to the intrusions she'd dealt with over the years as Desiree's daughter. There'd been fans of her mother's who'd invaded the wrought-iron fencing around her home, attempting to snap photos through the windows. They'd even pried bricks from the garden walkway to take as souvenirs. Despite her apprehension, she didn't want a stranger taking up armed guard in her house. In fact, she didn't want a firearm in her home at all. The house on Prytania had seen enough violence. Considering Trevor's career choice, if she told him that, he'd probably accuse her of staunch liberalism. Which wouldn't actually be too far off the mark.

"I have a home-security system. I'll keep it engaged," she said, sounding braver than she felt.

Trevor rubbed a hand over his jaw, the action making it clear he didn't agree with her decision. "I'll have a unit swing by here and take you home, at least. An officer can escort you to the door and check out the house before you go inside."

Rain nodded, relenting to that one suggestion. Trevor went to Alex's desk and picked up the phone. She listened as he called the precinct, giving his federal badge number and requesting a squad car. He hung up after providing the gallery's address.

"They'll be here in a few minutes."

Rain touched his arm, which was all hard sinew under warm skin. "Thank you."

As he looked at her, she felt an almost magnetic pull between them. Finally, she let her hand fall away and he moved to the door.

"Trevor?" Her voice caused him to turn around. He'd opened the door slightly, and a thin slant of light from the hallway spilled across the floor.

"What I said about you using me to get to Dante. What I meant was—"

"I didn't lead Dante to *Midnight Confessions*. He came there all by himself. He'd still be listening to your show even if I'd never heard him call in that night."

Rain realized he was right. "I want to help the investigation in any way I can. But I have to know the truth about what's going on."

Trevor shifted his weight in the doorway and she saw the same internal struggle as earlier appear in his eyes.

"We got an ID on the victim," he said. "Her name is Cara Seagreen. She was a fifteen-year-old from Kenner, out clubbing with a fake driver's license. I spent most of yesterday afternoon interviewing the girl Cara was with that night."

"What did you find out?"

"Nothing more than the general vicinity of the Quarter the two girls started off in. Cara's friend admits to taking Ecstasy, and as you're probably aware, a common side effect is memory loss. She isn't even sure at what point of the evening Cara disappeared, or which club they were in when she saw her last. But they'd definitely been to several of the goth hangouts in the city."

Trevor opened the door wider, letting the rumble of conversation from the gallery filter inside.

"You've got my card, Rain. If you need anything, or if you change your mind about having a guard inside your home, just call. In the meantime, I'm going to put a unit on the street outside your house permanently. If you're alone, the drive-bys aren't nearly adequate."

He bid her good-night and left the office, but Rain remained inside a while longer, still struck by the physical attraction she'd felt to Trevor. She also collected her thoughts. Dante had known about the trace. She considered the possibility that he'd seen Trevor arrive at her house that morning, and put two and two together.

Which also meant he'd been outside somewhere, watching her all along.

12

As the Taurus turned onto the Canal Street Wharf, Trevor saw a half-dozen patrol units, their blue lights cutting through the mist rising from the Mississippi River. He shifted the vehicle into park, then turned off the engine and glanced at the illuminated clock on the dashboard: 2:52 a.m.

McGrath had called Trevor's cell phone a half hour ago, letting him know another victim had been found in a storage facility near the water. He calculated the distance between the wharf and where Brian's art reception had been held just a few hours earlier.

It was less than five city blocks.

Flashing his shield at the uniforms, he lifted the yellow crime scene tape and stepped under it. The officers who nodded him through were drinking coffee from disposable cups and speculating on the upcoming season for the New Orleans Saints. As Trevor approached, bursts of light came from inside the metal warehouse, indicating a forensics photographer was on the scene. Frustration washed over him, and he stared out at the moored ferry that traveled back and forth to Algiers Point during the day. Water lapped rhythmically against the boat's sides as it floated in wait for the dawn.

It occurred to him the victim inside the building would never see another sunrise.

It was the first time the unsub had struck twice in the same city. In each location previously, there'd been only one murder. Then weeks or even months would pass before another body was discovered, and in another city altogether. But this latest victim had turned up only a few days after Cara Seagreen, in the same general locale, suggesting the killer's M.O. was changing, his bloodlust escalating. Trevor would call SAC Johnston in the morning, let him know his stay here would be extended.

Welcome back to New Orleans, Agent Rivette. Looks like we've both finally come home.

The message penned in blood two nights earlier, directed to him, gave him a chill. Trevor wondered if all the time he'd been following the killer's trail of bodies, the ultimate destination had always been here.

A warm breeze swept in from the river, carrying the water's rich, fecund smell. The low blare of a foghorn came from somewhere in the distance. He entered the building, the hard soles of his shoes echoing off the concrete floor. The victim had been left just inside the structure, in front of a section of worn-looking passenger seats that had been removed from the ferry for repair. Like Cara Seagreen, it appeared to be a female teenager.

Detectives McGrath and Thibodeaux were already there, along with the photographer and several technicians wearing bright yellow overalls with N.O. Crime Scene Unit emblazoned on the back.

"Thanks for the call," Trevor said, approaching the group.

McGrath was down on his haunches examining the body. "Same M.O. as last week, including the approximate age of the victim."

The scene was another variation of the one he'd grown to know too well. Duct tape covered the victim's mouth and her wrists were bound in front of her with the beaded rosary. Pulling on latex gloves, Trevor dropped down next to McGrath and looked at the girl more fully. She was thin, so much so that her hip bones protruded and her ribs were clearly visible. Her small breasts were almost nonexistent. The girl's eyes, now staring blankly toward the ceiling, were rimmed in dark makeup. The mascara had run in black rivulets and dried on her cheeks. A gash to her throat indicated rapid exsanguination, and her nude body revealed a dozen or more additional cuts. While the corpse was streaked with blood, there wasn't enough of it staining the concrete underneath. Its dearth pointed to the likelihood that the killing had occurred elsewhere.

"The M.E.'s office rolled her over earlier. There's lividity. Decedent's body temperature also indicates postmortem of about three to five hours." McGrath scratched the bridge of his nose. "Oh, yeah. She's got a tattoo at the base of her spine. Some kind of fancy cross."

"One thing's for sure." Thibodeaux jotted notes into a spiral pad. "Curtains don't come close to matching the carpet."

Gently, Trevor brushed the vibrant, too-red hair back from the girl's forehead. The color was unnatural looking and definitely a dye job, but its hue still reminded him of Rain. He looked over the body, finally focusing on the back of the victim's right hand.

"Anybody recognize this?" The lucent skin covering the fine bones bore an ink mark, an outline of a bird in flight, although the image was smeared and barely visible.

"Forensics already got a photo of that," Thibodeaux said. "I'm pretty sure it's an ink stamp from the Ascension. I recognize it because we had some problems with drugs there when I was in Vice."

"Ecstasy?"

"Among other stuff. That's probably where our vic met up with the Count."

"Goth club?" Trevor studied the blurred ink.

"Yeah, but it's not one of the places Simone Bausell thinks she visited with the Seagreen girl." With a grunt, McGrath forced his girth to a standing position. "Which puts yet another nightspot on the radar."

Trevor asked one of the technicians for an evidence bag, then carefully covered and sealed the hand. "Who called in the body?"

Thibodeaux withdrew a pack of Marlboros and a lighter from his pocket. He tapped a cigarette from the carton. "A security guard was cruising the area in one of those tricked-out golf carts and saw the door cracked open. He decided to have a look inside—"

"Tibbs, you always gotta smoke around me?" McGrath interjected. "You know I quit."

"And you've got no willpower." Lighting the cigarette, Thibodeaux inhaled nicotine into his lungs with a show of satisfaction. "Consider me an example of behavior not to emulate."

McGrath ignored his partner's antics. "Anyway, this rent-a-cop was puking by the edge of the docks when we got here. We're gonna go talk to him now."

Trevor still knelt next to the body as the two detectives walked away.

"Trevor Rivette?"

He looked up to see a tall, solidly built man in khakis and a golf shirt. Sawyer Compton's blond hair was cut so short it nearly stood up on top of his head. Even in the bright lights of the crime scene his skin held a golden tone that suggested California surfer dude, not assistant district attorney for the Orleans Parish. After all these years, Trevor still recognized him immediately. He stood, and despite the latex gloves, shook Sawyer's hand warmly.

"Annabelle said you were in town, but I didn't realize it had anything to do with business." Sawyer grinned at his childhood friend. "Been here long?"

"A few days."

He surveyed the dead girl's body. "So, what's going on here, Trev? And more specifically, why does it interest the FBI?"

Trevor answered with a question of his own. "The ADA always show up at crime scenes in the middle of the night?"

"Only when I get calls from reporters, fishing for information."

It wasn't unusual for a beat cop working a scene to make a few bucks by tipping off the media. "How much do they know?"

Sawyer shielded his eyes from the portable lights set up around the area. "The reporter asked about a connection between the murder tonight and one that took place last week. A female teen found in a crack house on Tchoupitoulas? The murders were similar."

Trevor looked at a drain in the center of the concrete floor. Its metal grate was rusted. From somewhere outside the building, he heard male laughter. A response to a crude joke being told by one of the uniforms, he guessed.

"You still working serial murders with the VCU?" Sawyer inquired.

"I've been following this guy state to state for a year and a half now. New Orleans is his latest stop."

Or his ultimate destination.

"It's not that I'm not glad to see you, Trev." Sawyer scrubbed a hand over his wheat-colored hair. "But hell, you're like having a van from the Weather Channel pull up in hurricane season. You know it's gonna be bad news."

Heather Credo sat in Rain's office and picked sullenly at the dark polish on her nails. Dressed in black jeans and a cropped top, her arms displayed faded scars and new, fresher scabs that were angry horizontal stripes against her skin.

"I'm a cutter." Her tone was defiant as she glared at Rain, who sat in the armchair beside her. "So fucking what?"

Rain offered no reaction to the girl's outburst. "Well, your parents are worried about why you're doing this to yourself. That's why they sent you to see me. They thought maybe you'd like to talk about what's bothering you."

Heather tossed her dark hair over one shoulder. Her Cupid's-bow mouth twisted. "Mom's just worried my arms are going to be scarred up at my sister's wedding in September."

"Do you care how you look for your sister's wedding?"

"I'm ugly. Who cares if my arms are cut? They're just scared I'm going to embarrass them and ruin perfect Lauren's perfect day."

"You're not ugly, Heather." The girl was tall and willowy, and underneath the pinched, churlish expression were delicate features and large brown eyes. "And I think you know that."

When she shrugged, Rain added, "Do you think you might be depressed? Because a lot of times hurting yourself goes with being sad or anxious about something."

Rain peered at the teen. Cutting was often a way of coping with feelings that otherwise couldn't be easily expressed. Heather had been through a lot recently, including her parents' divorce, brought on by a very public affair her father had engaged in with a much younger woman.

"Anything you say stays right here between us."

Heather bit her bottom lip. "What if I don't want to say anything?"

"That's okay, too." There was a long silence. Heather bounced one knee as she looked out the office window and into the house's courtyard garden. Her breath hitched. Rain reached out and covered the girl's hand with her own, feeling a small victory when she didn't pull away.

The session was hardly a breakthrough, but it was the closest Rain had come in getting Heather to talk. Their previous appointment had been spent with the teen staring at a spot on the wall, her responses to Rain's questions terse, if they were given at all. But this time Heather had actually shown an emotion besides anger, even if she still hadn't divulged much about what was going on inside her. Rain thought of the girl's self-inflicted wounds and was aware of the pain she must be internalizing. At least she'd begun to establish some trust between them. It was a slow process, but eventually Heather would open up to her.

She was entering her notes into the computer when the phone rang.

"Rain Sommers." She spoke into the receiver, her fingers slowing on the keyboard long enough to tuck the handset between her shoulder and ear.

"It's Trevor Rivette. Can we speak for a moment?"

She stopped typing and looked at the clock on her screen. "I'm expecting a patient in fifteen minutes—"

"This won't take long. Another girl was murdered last night. The body was dumped a few blocks from Synapse."

Rain took off the glasses she wore for computer work and laid them on the desk, momentarily shocked into silence.

"The *Times-Picayune* broke the story online this morning, including the possible link to the serial-murder investigation," he continued. "It'll probably make it into the evening print edition. I didn't want you to be surprised."

She could hear the tense edge to his voice. Now that the media was onto the story, she guessed the pressure to make an arrest would increase, as well.

"What about *Midnight Confessions?*"

"There's no mention of it at this point. No one in the media has made any connection between the caller to your show and the murders. I'm hoping to keep it that way as long as possible." Trevor paused before speaking again. "Rain, I need you to go to a dance club with me."

"A dance club?"

"A place called the Ascension."

The Ascension was located on a derelict portion of Claiborne Avenue in Mid-City. The converted cathedral lent itself to the club's heavy goth vibe, although the dance floor was just as likely to be inhabited by thrill-seeking tourists or students from the universities. But it was infamous for its private rooms, including the basement, which those who considered themselves true goths preferred to frequent.

"I'm familiar with it," Rain said softly.

"The victim hasn't been identified yet. Our only lead is an ink stamp on her hand that came from that club. I'd like to check the place out."

Rain had seen the stamp on more than one of her patients. "You can get into the main area of the club if you're eighteen. But they stamp anyone under the age of twenty-one so they can't buy alcohol. Unfortunately, it doesn't keep them from sampling the illegal drugs that get passed around."

"So I've heard," Trevor replied. "The homicide detectives I've been working with checked with the club's management already. They don't have any security cameras or closed-circuit-TV monitoring. We were hoping to catch the girl on tape, see who she might've been talking to."

Rain pressed her fingers against her temple as she listened, not surprised the club was lacking in security measures. "Trevor, what do I have to do with this?"

"You're accepted by this group. If I'm with you, I'll have more credibility than if I go in there alone, looking for information." He lowered his voice. "It would just be the two of us. The NOPD detectives would stick out even worse than me, and the same goes for any of the local FBI field agents. You said you wanted to help, and I know you have contacts. I need to use them."

Rain thought of Trevor with his conservative haircut and suit, flashing his shield and attempting to get cooperation in a place like the Ascension. The goth community was a closed group. He was right—without her he didn't stand a chance. "When do you want to go?"

"Tonight. Around ten o'clock. I'll pick you up."

After he'd hung up, Rain held the phone for several moments before placing it back in its console. Then she used her computer to access the *Times-Picayune* Web site. News of the second murder was listed in the headlines, and she clicked on the link for the brief article.

Discovery of Second Victim Suggests Serial Killer May Be New Orleans's Latest Tourist

An unidentified female was found by police in a maintenance building on the Canal Street Wharf early this morning. Apparent cause of death is stabbing, although an autopsy has yet to be conducted. The murder is similar to that of another New Orleans female last week, and an NOPD spokesperson confirmed that a member of the FBI's Violent Crimes Unit is involved in the case, investigating ties to killings in other cities, including, most recently, Raleigh and Atlanta…

Rain read the rest of the article, relieved at least there was no mention of her or her show.

The Ascension. She'd been there several months earlier, for a publicity appearance David had set up for *Midnight Confessions*. Much about the club had disturbed her, from the barely lit back hallways to some of the clientele who'd seemed overly fascinated by her presence. One of them had gotten close enough behind her to cut away a lock of her hair. She'd felt the man's presence, recognized the faint tug on her head and the snip of scissors near her ear. But she'd seen only his broad shoulders retreating into the roiling sea of dancers before David had pulled her toward the cordoned-off VIP area near the bar.

Rain touched her hair, recalling that David had merely laughed about her off-kilter fan base. A thread of unease wrapped around her. If it was true the latest victim had been at the Ascension, couldn't Dante be there tonight, as well?

13

"You're lucky you haven't been around," Nate Fincher, Trevor's partner at the VCU, told him over the phone. He was referring to the child-murder case in Maryland to which he'd been assigned. "The parents are high-profile—the father's some megamillionaire software entrepreneur and the mother's a former model. The media's all over it and Johnston's getting heat from the Bureau's higher-ups to find the unsub."

Trevor knew the drill. "Which means you're getting heat, too."

"The kid was just four years old." Despite his normally professional demeanor, anger tinged Nate's words. "The nanny took him to the playground, turned her back for a minute, and claims he was gone. There was no ransom demand. His body turned up twelve hours later in a drainage ditch off the highway. Strangled to death."

"Are you looking at the parents?"

"We haven't ruled it out."

As Nate filled him in on his case, Trevor stared at the television, the sound on low. It was dark outside, and he'd brought a fast-food meal back to his hotel room so he could eat and shower before picking up Rain Sommers to go to the Ascension. The day had been a long one, spent canvassing the area around the Canal Street Wharf, trying to find someone who might have seen anything remotely suspicious in the hours leading up to the body's discovery. He had also been back to the morgue at All Saints Hospital to witness the autopsy firsthand.

"Sorry you're down there working this alone—"

"Not a problem."

"You getting any help?"

"I've been working with the two local homicide detectives who initially caught the case," Trevor said. "The Bureau field office is providing some help, too. More, now that the body count here is at two. A couple of agents helped with the canvas."

"Has the unsub made contact with you again?"

Trevor told him about the necklace that had been left in his car, and the note from the pay phone near Armstrong Park indicating the killer might be a resident of the city.

"Maybe that's why he's fixated on you," Nate ventured. "You're both from New Orleans. He thinks you have the Big Easy in common."

The problem was, Trevor thought after the call had ended, his New Orleans heritage wasn't something most people knew about. For all intents and purposes, he was from Bethesda, Maryland—he'd relocated there as a teenager out of necessity. Few people outside his own family knew much about Trevor's past. Even Nate had been told only the bare, unemotional facts and not the full story.

And that was the way he wanted to keep it.

He had a little time before leaving, so he got out the photos from the M.E.'s office taken that afternoon. Trevor flipped through the grim, sterile shots to find one he might be able to use at the club to hopefully get an ID.

Another Jane Doe. The Vampire investigation was a special VCU project, but it wasn't high on the priority list of cases since a single victim in a single city didn't attract a lot of attention. Trevor wondered how that might change, especially if a third body turned up in New Orleans.

He hoped he didn't have to find out.

Rain had styled her hair so that it was sleek and glossy. She'd also taken a more liberal hand with her makeup, accentuating her eyes with a kohl pencil and black mascara, painting her mouth a deep red. The low-cut, black halter top wasn't exactly goth attire, but she knew the look was dramatic. In the mirror, it was Desiree who stared back at her. Rain's expression was composed, but inside she felt as fragile as glass.

She jumped at the chime of the doorbell. Extinguishing the lavender aromatherapy candle she'd lit in a vain attempt to calm her nerves, Rain went downstairs.

Trevor stood on the veranda. Opening the door to him, her gaze traveled over his jeans and dark T-shirt. "You look like a college student."

He offered a faint smile. "Hardly, but it's the best I could do. Black leather isn't exactly part of my wardrobe."

"Where's your gun?"

"In an ankle holster. Less conspicuous."

As he followed her into the parlor, Dahlia darted past them and up the staircase. Rain started to make a comment about a black cat crossing one's path, but thought better of it and remained silent. She stood by as Trevor stared up at the elegant, crystal chandelier, dimmed so that it gave off a murky glow.

"Is that the original?"

"Restoring the house was my mother's dream," Rain told him. "After she died, my aunt Celeste took over the renovation. She preserved as much of the original house as possible, including the light fixtures."

He nodded, and she wondered how much he already knew about the house and its dark past. If she had him pegged right, Trevor had already done his homework on Desiree, the house on Prytania and her. He'd probably read the horrific details of her parents' murder-suicide right down to the thirty-year-old police report.

"It happened in the first room upstairs on the right," she said quietly. "In case you were wondering."

He gazed at her. "I wasn't."

Rain felt instantly contrite. "I didn't mean that the way it sounded. I'm just used to people being curious—"

"The way you're dressed tonight. Are you trying to look like her?" he interrupted her, his blue-gray eyes as direct as his voice. Rain stared down at her hands. Although she normally left her nails bare, tonight she'd painted them blood red. Only now did she realize the irony.

"I thought I might be able to help you," she explained awkwardly. "At the club, I mean. Some of the people there are really into Desiree."

Trevor took a step closer. He studied her necklace, which rested in the delicate space where her collarbone dipped in at the base of her throat. It was the same amethyst pendant she'd worn to Brian's reception. He touched it with his fingertip, causing her heart to beat harder.

"Help me get into the Ascension, or use you as bait for Dante?" Apparently, he hadn't forgotten the comment she'd made the previous evening.

"I trust you," Rain said simply.

A weighted silence fell between them, until Trevor dug into his back pocket and handed her a photograph, warning her first. "This was taken by the M.E. at the autopsy this afternoon. It's the second victim."

Rain looked at the snapshot. Once again, the girl was covered nearly up to her chin by a sheet, and she lay on a stainless-steel table with her eyes closed. She was waif thin, and her hair was a bold shade of red that looked as if it had been dyed in raspberry Kool-Aid.

"She's so young." Disturbed, Rain handed back the photo.

He replaced it in his pocket. "What do you know about vampire goths?"

"Well, they do exist. They're a small subculture within the goth community. But most of them limit their involvement to role-playing."

"That's all?"

"Some of them take it a step or two further," she admitted. "A few claim to drink blood from animals, or willing human donors."

"What about not-so-willing donors?"

"I'd prefer not to think about that." She went to the end table and picked up the small purse she planned to carry with her. It contained lipstick, her cell phone and a few other personal items. When she turned back around, she found Trevor watching her.

"There's a possibility Dante will be there tonight. If he is, he's going to be interested in getting close to you." His eyes remained on her as she walked back to him. "You need to be careful."

"I will."

"You do look like her, you know," he said softly.

He waited while she set the house's security system, and then he led her outside to a waiting sedan. The scent of night-blooming jasmine hung in the warm air as Trevor opened the car's passenger-side door and she slid inside. Across the street, an NOPD squad car sat in the shadow of a gnarled pecan tree. Although Rain couldn't see the occupants inside, they were another reminder that she was a woman who needed protection.

* * *

The Ascension was like a blasphemous fantasy come to life. Housed within the structure of a large stone-and-brick-work church, its dance floor thrummed with a synthesized beat as bodies flailed under a two-story-high vaulted ceiling. Massive iron chandeliers hung from heavy chains, and spotlights swung around the cavernous space, illuminating arched, stained-glass windows. An ornate cross hung over the cathedral's pulpit, now in use as a live-performance stage.

Rising on tiptoe, Rain leaned close to Trevor. She put her hand on his shoulder and her mouth against his ear so she could be heard above the synth-pop music. "Is it what you expected?"

"I think Sister Clarice, my third-grade teacher, just rolled over in her grave. What are the confessionals used for?"

"You don't want to know."

While the atmosphere was undeniably gothic, the club's main area catered to an eclectic crowd. Trevor held on to Rain's hand as they worked their way through the revelers. Above them, a balcony indicated a second floor where a lounge area was located. People leaned over the railing, tossing glittering diamonds of black confetti onto the crowd.

Rain pointed to a stone archway veiled with heavy red curtains.

"There's a room in the basement. It might be the best place to start." A male with spiked wristbands and multiple piercings jostled her in an attempt to get past. Trevor caught her waist and pulled her to him.

"You okay?"

Nodding, she lifted her gaze to his. Her stomach flipped at the sensation of being held against the hard muscles of his chest.

"I don't want you out of my sight," he reminded. He took her hand again as they headed toward the archway, but a hulking man in leather pants and a shirtless black vest blocked the entrance. Dark makeup framed his eyes.

"Private club." He glared at Trevor, who looked poised to pull his shield from his pocket and push his way through. But as the man glimpsed Rain, recognition flared in his eyes. He stepped back and bowed his head with near reverence.

"Forgive me, Dr. Sommers. Please go ahead."

"We're expected?"

"Armand says you're always welcome." He continued to regard Trevor with a hostile expression, but he didn't stop him as he followed Rain inside.

"Armand?" Trevor asked as Rain parted the velvet curtains.

"He owns the Ascension," Rain said. "He's also a huge Desiree fan."

They walked into a dimly lit, tunnel-like corridor that was degrees cooler than the overheated dance floor. The sounds of the live music faded as they traveled farther, until they reached a stone staircase that appeared to drop directly into hell.

The stairs were steep, ending in a shadowed foyer that opened into a larger room. As their eyes adjusted to the darkness, forms took shape—black-clothed humans with pale faces. Rain had been to the Ascension before, but not into this private area. The furnishings were simple, with couches lining the windowless walls and a wood-paneled bar located in the far corner. The place smelled dank and musty, a reminder they were below street level. She felt eyes turning toward them as the whispered name Desiree floated in the air.

A woman latched onto Rain's arm as she went past. Her black hair hung into mascara-caked eyes. "You're supposed to be dead, sugarplum!"

"I'm not *her,*" Rain said coldly, but the clawlike grip tightened.

"They worship you here, but I know the truth! You're a little whore! You deserved what you got from your old man—"

Trevor disengaged the woman's hold. "Touch her again and deal with me."

She sneered at him, but sank back into the shadows.

"A fan?" he inquired. His arm slipped protectively around Rain as he moved her toward the bar.

"More like a stalker." Rain peered at the half-moon imprints the woman's nails had left in her skin. "I've seen her before, outside the WNOR studios."

"And I thought I only had Dante to worry about."

At the bar, Trevor ordered a soda for himself, and Rain requested red wine. As he handed her the stemmed glass, he said quietly, "Back in my day, these were just punk rockers."

She took a sip of wine. "Actually, by most accounts goth *is* an offshoot of the punk movement of the seventies."

"Was that what Desiree was part of? The punk movement?"

"Desiree defied categorization. She was more of a torch singer, really, but her vibe was goth. She gave off that sort of creepy, sensual New Orleans attitude in buckets." Rain stared into the burgundy liquid. "My father, however, was definitely on the edges of punk. I think Desiree's association with him, along with the way she died, is the real reason goths have embraced her as an icon of sorts."

"Gavin Firth was your father," Trevor recounted. "The British guitarist for the Dreads."

"Yes." She grew quiet, realizing he hadn't posed a question but had made the statement as fact. It was confirmation he'd done his research just as she'd expected. She looked at the soda he held. The previous evening at Brian's reception, she'd seen him only with sparkling water.

"You don't drink, do you? Not even off duty?"

"No." He didn't elaborate. Instead, he gazed at a tall male garbed in a frilly shirt and black coat who appeared to be squeezing through the crowd toward them.

"Rain!" Armand Baptiste called from a distance. He had flowing black hair and eyes rimmed with dark eyeliner. Although he was older than the others frequenting the goth-only area of the club, his face still held the visage of slightly androgynous good looks.

"Who's that?" Trevor asked in a low voice.

"Armand." Rain lifted her hand in a slight wave. "In addition to the Ascension, he owns a successful antique business. He's also on the Orleans Parish Council."

"You're kidding."

"Goths are all ages, and they come from all walks of life," Rain said. "Armand is an elder in the goth community. He dresses normally during the day, for business and council meetings, but…"

Her voice trailed away as Armand arrived. He bowed and genteelly placed a kiss on the back of her hand.

"You look lovely, my dear. And so much like Desiree it hurts. I'm pleased you've finally accepted my invitation to join us." His silvery-blue eyes traveled appreciatively over Trevor. "Do you have a new lover, Rain?"

She felt herself blush. "This is Special Agent Trevor Rivette. He's with the FBI."

Armand's eyebrows lifted, and Trevor removed the photo from his pocket. "Do you recognize this girl?"

"Should I?" Armand asked with disinterest.

"You tell me. Her body was found last night. She had a stamp on her hand from your club."

Rain attempted to soften Trevor's response. "We're just

trying to find out who she might have spoken with, or if she left with anyone."

"Two detectives were here earlier today asking my club manager the same thing. I'll give you the same answer he gave them. I've never seen her before."

"Look again," Trevor instructed. "Unless you want me to start asking questions about the absinthe you're serving, which is illegal, or the underage kids who are down here with drinks in their hands."

Armand sighed. He lifted a pair of bifocals he wore on a chain around his neck and perched them on his nose. Taking the photo, he said, "Pretty, I suppose. But if she was around here I wasn't paying attention."

"Then you won't mind if we talk to your patrons."

"Suit yourself." He gave back the photo and pointed to a group of teens in the corner.

"Baby bats," he muttered. "You can start over there."

Trevor leaned forward. "Excuse me?"

"Kindergoths. They're here almost every night. Our clan does its best to indulge them, but they can be a rowdy bunch. They'd be of more use to you than the older clientele. If the girl was here, she was probably with them."

"Thank you, Armand," Rain said.

"I'm at your service." He smiled, but the affection he'd expressed for her earlier appeared to have drained from his eyes.

"You're making friends," Rain commented once Armand had left the bar.

Trevor finished his soda. He returned the glass to the bar top, his eyes on the teenagers who stood together like a leather-clad herd. Then he laid a few bills down to pay for their drinks.

"Let's go talk to the Lost Boys."

14

The sickly-sweet smell of clove cigarettes hung in the air as Trevor and Rain approached the teenagers. A few of them held beer bottles or plastic cups filled with what was most likely alcohol, despite the stamps on their hands marking them as underage. *This place would be a wet dream for an ATF agent,* Trevor thought. He considered busting both the bartender and Armand for serving to minors, but reminded himself it wasn't why he was here.

It didn't take long for one of the teens, a petite Asian girl with piercings in her lip and nose, to recognize Rain. She came over and asked timidly for an autograph on a paper napkin. Several others soon followed. Trevor stayed back a step, allowing Rain to interact with the group. She held up the photo he'd given her.

"Do any of you know this girl?"

A male with a bad complexion and a T-shirt that read Fuck the Mainstream snatched the photo. "Shit. Is she dead?"

"Do you recognize her?" Rain repeated.

He grinned slyly. "Yeah. She blew me in the bathroom last night."

A few of the teens burst into laughter.

"Watch your mouth." Trevor made his presence known.

At his stern expression, the kid's smile faded and he handed back the photo.

"Her name's Rebecca." The voice came from the edge of the crowd. The girl had ink-black hair plaited into two thick braids. She wore a miniskirt with torn fishnet hose and platform Mary Janes.

"You know her last name?" Trevor inquired.

She shook her head. Moving closer, she took the photo. "God. What happened to her?"

"She met up with the wrong person. When did you see her last?"

"Last night, I think. She's only been coming around the past few weeks."

"Was she with anyone?"

"Besides this jerkoff?" She rolled her eyes at the male who'd been showing off earlier. "Ethan hit on her. She told him to get lost."

"Bite me," he retorted.

She clicked her teeth like a snapping dog. "You wish."

Trevor looked over at Rain. The throng around her had grown, and she was signing another autograph. He drew the girl to a nearby table, pulling out a chair for her and locating himself so he could keep an eye on things. "Sit. What's your name?"

"Aurelia."

"Is that your real name?"

She nodded toward Rain. "Is that *her* real name?"

When Trevor continued to stare at her, she sighed. "It's Marcy. Marcy Cupich."

"How old are you, Marcy?"

She frowned suspiciously. "I thought you wanted to know about Rebecca."

Underneath the severe makeup, Marcy had unremarkable, although not unpleasant, features, and Trevor guessed her natural hair color was ash blond to light brown. When she spoke, she had a lisp, and he'd noticed her tongue was pierced with a silver ball stud.

"Just tell me what you know," he instructed.

She took a nervous sip from her cup. "Are you a cop?"

"I'm a federal agent. And you're too young to be drinking."

"Are you going to arrest me?"

Trevor took the cup. "Not if you start talking."

"Like I said, I saw her last night." Marcy fiddled with one of her braids. "She was talking to some guy for a while. He was kind of tall, with dark hair."

"What time was this?"

"Around nine or ten, maybe."

"Was he goth?"

Her forehead wrinkled thoughtfully. "A little, I guess. I didn't get a real good look at him."

"Could you tell how old he was?"

She shrugged. "Not really. Maybe in college?"

"You sure he wasn't older? My age at least?"

"I don't know. I think he was younger."

Trevor rubbed the back of his neck. What the girl was telling him didn't match the FBI profile. He considered the likelihood that whoever the victim had been seen with was just another horny teenager looking to get laid. "Did you see if Rebecca left with this guy?"

Marcy shook her head. Trevor asked a few more questions, including whether she could give a description to a sketch artist.

"I told you, I didn't get a good look at him. His back was to me most of the time."

"But you could try." He gave her his card, along with a number to call the next morning to schedule some time with the artist. As his eyes fell on the small glass vial she wore on a chain around her neck, she touched it self-consciously.

"It's not blood. It's just corn syrup with red food coloring."

"This vampire stuff isn't something to play around with," he told her. Marcy nodded, although he doubted his warning carried much weight.

She left the table and went back to her friends. The young people were still crowded together, but Trevor no longer saw Rain. Apprehension snaked through him. He stood and scanned the basement. Where was she?

A man in black leather leaned against the wall on the far side of the room. His eyes met Trevor's in an unspoken challenge, and his cold smile revealed incisors sharpened into fanglike points. The man motioned for him to follow.

As Trevor pushed through the horde, the goth opened a door behind the bar and disappeared. Had he taken her? Trevor stopped to withdraw the gun strapped to his ankle. Then he traveled through the same door into an unlit hallway.

Cautiously, he moved forward with his weapon braced in both hands. Farther down the passage, shallow light spilled across the stone floor, indicating an interior room. But he made it only a few more feet before the light went out. Trevor crept closer, until he stood outside the now-darkened doorway. He took a breath and quickly turned its corner, peering into the nearly opaque blackness as he made a sweeping arc with the gun's barrel.

Nothing. It was as if the man had disappeared into thin air.

Trevor made out the shapes of cardboard boxes stacked shoulder high against the walls. He was in some kind of supply room. A rotating fan hummed in one corner, moving the musty air around in warm bursts. Taking one hand off his gun, he felt along the wall for the light switch.

The vicious blow caught him between the shoulder blades and dropped Trevor to his knees. A second later, another jolt of pain shot through him as the square toe of a boot made hard contact with his side. He sprawled to the floor, the gun skittering from his grasp.

The man was large, with a shaved head, and not the one he'd trailed inside—which meant there were at least two of them. His boot aimed again for Trevor's ribs, but this time he rolled out of reach. Using his feet, Trevor struck at his attacker's ankles and was rewarded with a heavy thud as the man fell with a curse. But there was little time to recover his gun that was lost somewhere in the darkness. He recoiled at the shift of shadows and the flash of a knife as a second attacker approached. It was the man who'd enticed Trevor to follow him earlier.

"Get up and hold him!" the man barked.

The first assailant rose and lunged again at Trevor, who was now standing and prepared for another attack. Although the man was hulking and thick-shouldered, Trevor was faster. He sidestepped his blow and hit him with a fist to his face. Blood poured from the man's nose. Sputtering, he crashed back down like a stone.

The knife-wielding accomplice was on him with catlike speed. He took Trevor off balance, slamming him against the wall and shutting off his windpipe with a forearm across his throat. His stringy black hair swung from his head.

"You're dead, pig," he hissed.

Trevor caught the goth's other arm as it poised in the air for a downward strike with the blade. The man grinned savagely. Even in the darkness, Trevor could see his animalistic teeth. They struggled, their muscles straining as he held the knife at bay. The first attacker was back on his feet and lumbering toward them. Panic slid over him. He wouldn't be able to fight them both at once.

"Trevor?"

It was Rain's voice, calling from what seemed like a long distance away. The man clutching the knife looked around, his hair whipping into his face. Using the distraction as an opportunity, Trevor shifted his weight and jerked his knee into the man's groin. There was a howl of pain as the knife clattered to the floor. The hard pressure on his throat was gone and Trevor gasped, filling his lungs with air.

Rain called out again, closer this time, and the two assailants receded into the darkness as if it had gobbled them whole.

He bent forward with his hands on his knees, coughing. Light flooded the room. Rain stood with Armand Baptiste, his fingers on the light switch.

"Trevor!" Rain rushed to him. "You're hurt!"

He held his side. "I'm okay."

"What're you doing in here?" Armand demanded. "This area is employees only!"

"Tell that to the two freaks who tried to gut me." Panting, he stared at Rain. "Where'd you go? I thought they grabbed you."

"One of the girls wanted to show me something. You were busy with—"

"What part of *stay with me* did you not understand?"

He spotted his gun wedged between two stacks of cardboard boxes. Grimacing, Trevor walked over and picked it up. He looked around for the assailant's knife, and found it under a shelving unit that held bar supplies. Taking a paper napkin from one of the shelves, he retrieved the weapon, being careful not to smudge any prints on its handle. As he did so, he noticed another doorway in an L-shaped alcove in back of the room. It explained how the men had exited without running into Armand and Rain.

"Where does that go?"

"To the alley—"

"Those ghouls work for you, Baptiste?"

"I've no idea who you're talking about," the other man replied.

Trevor opened the door. The stairwell was narrow, with steps that had settled unevenly with age. He climbed them with his gun drawn only to find himself at street level, next to a metal Dumpster. The alley was empty.

It was as if nothing had ever happened. He wouldn't have believed it himself if not for the ache that inhabited his side.

"Are you okay?" Rain stood at the top of the stairs. Her red-gold hair lifted in the warm breeze that had worked its way into the gap between the buildings.

"I'm fine."

"If you describe these men to Armand, maybe he can—"

"Your *friend* doesn't want to help. Can't you see that?" The look on her face made Trevor instantly regret his harsh words. He walked to her.

"I told you to stay with me," he repeated, although this time the admonishment came out more softly. He didn't want to think about what might have happened if those men had confronted her instead.

"I'm sorry," she whispered. "And Armand is *not* my friend."

He pushed back an errant strand of hair the wind had blown across her face. "When I couldn't find you, I thought…"

"I shouldn't have left," she admitted, touching his wrist. "But there's something I think you should see."

The unisex bathroom was tucked into a corner of the church's basement. Trevor flashed his shield at the half-dozen patrons who waited in line for use of the room, causing them to scatter.

After knocking but getting no response, Rain turned the knob and found it unlocked. She opened the door. A female with an Annie Lennox crew cut leaned over the sink, snorting a line of white powder with a rolled-up bill. Tattoos covered her arms. She rubbed her nose and looked up with a glaze of irritation across her pale face. "Occupied. That's why the door's closed, bitch."

Her eyes widened at the sight of Trevor, appearing behind Rain and holding up his shield. "Get lost. Unless you want me to run you in for possession."

She brushed hurriedly past them. Inside the bathroom, there were no stalls, only a single toilet and washstand. The small room was dirty and poorly lit. Graffiti covered the plastered walls.

"One of the girls brought me in here to show me." Rain walked inside and pointed to a spot next to a rusted paper-towel dispenser. Written among the obscenities and crudely drawn, nearly pornographic cartoons was the name Rebecca, along with a telephone number. "Apparently, she saw Rebecca writing this on the wall several nights back. If you run the number, you'll probably find out who the girl is."

Trevor stared at the number, then shifted his gaze to a long-stemmed rose that lay forgotten on top of the dispenser. Nearly hidden behind beer bottles, it had withered and turned brown, as if it had been there for at least a couple of days. He was no longer certain whether he was tracking a killer or simply following a path Dante had laid out for him.

Rain continued peering at the wall, at a second sequence of numbers and letters written in bold marker just below Rebecca's name and phone number.

"Any idea what this is?" She looked at Trevor, who'd

already pulled his cell phone from his pocket and flipped it open.

"Yeah. It's my federal ID."

By the time they returned to the house in the Lower Garden District, it was after 1:00 a.m. Trevor escorted Rain up the sidewalk and onto the veranda. He stood, his hands in his jeans pockets as she unlocked the door and disarmed the security system. She turned to him in the doorway.

"How badly does it hurt?"

"What?"

"Your side. You were holding it while we were waiting for the forensics team." She drew him far enough inside to close the door behind them and gain some privacy from the patrol car that sat on the street. Before he could refuse, she eased the bottom of his T-shirt from the waist of his jeans.

"Rain…"

"Let me see." Carefully, she lifted the shirt's hem. Her breath caught as she saw the faint discoloration at the bottom of his rib cage.

"We should take you to the hospital." Her fingers felt cool against his skin. "You could have a broken rib."

Trevor lowered his shirt. "I've had busted ribs before. Trust me, you know if you've got one. All I need is an ice pack and I'll be good as new in the morning."

"This is my fault. If I'd stayed put—"

"In case you haven't noticed, I have a habit of getting *myself* into trouble." He indicated the scabbed cut on his forehead. "It's a safe bet I'd have run into those guys on my own."

His casual comment didn't seem to appease her. She shook her head. "The killer wrote your ID on the wall. First the necklace in your car and the note he left you after Friday's show, and now this?"

"He's baiting me. It isn't unusual for the unsub to maintain contact with law enforcement. It increases his feeling of superiority. Dante figured I'd end up there sooner or later." Trevor only wished they'd been able to learn more from the teenagers. But after another fruitless hour of questioning clubgoers, he'd called it a night. At least they had a first name and phone number that would most likely allow them to identify the victim.

Rain's hazel eyes were questioning. "What took place at the club tonight—is it typical of your job?"

"You mean do I get my ass kicked every night?" He attempted a smile. "No. But what happened means my being there made someone uncomfortable."

"You were attacked with a *knife*. The fact that you're taking something like that in stride tells me it's not the first time."

"I'm a federal agent working violent crimes, Rain. Getting into scrapes is part of it sometimes."

"Regardless, it has to affect you."

"Is that your psychologist's opinion?"

Rain gazed up into his face, her expression concerned. "That's an opinion from someone who cares."

They stood close together. Trevor studied her pretty features, fairly certain she could hear the heavy beating of his heart. He was mindful of the physical attraction he felt to her—he'd been attuned to it, in fact, since nearly the first moment Brian had introduced them.

"I do what I have to."

Her voice remained soft. "Then you should make sure it doesn't get the better of you."

Rain's hand lingered against his shirt. He thought of earlier that night, when he'd brushed the silken strands of hair from her face. And before that, the way his fingers had curved around her small waist as he pulled her against him on the dance floor. Both gestures had been spontaneous, nearly on instinct, but they'd left him feeling a little dazed. For a fleeting moment, his brain had pushed away the responsibility that came with his job. The way she was looking at him now, he believed she felt the same intense chemistry between them.

"You're part of this investigation, Rain," he said quietly, a reminder as much to himself as to her.

"I know," she murmured.

"Then you understand why—"

Rising on tiptoe, she kissed him tentatively. Trevor stood frozen as desire warred with his self-control. Her body pressed lightly against his, and her palms slid upward to rest against the solid line of his collarbone. Silence passed between them as Rain pulled back finally, her lips slightly parted and her eyes liquid and uncertain. Trevor let go of a breath. Then he cupped her face in his hands and gently tilted her head back before covering her mouth with his own. She responded in a way that sent his pulse racing faster. He deepened the kiss briefly before reluctantly breaking contact. His eyes held regret as they stared at one another.

"I'm going to check the house before I go," he managed to get out in a hoarse voice. Rain nodded. When he returned to the foyer a few minutes later, she stood in the same spot, but her eyes were distant.

"Set the alarm after I leave."

Outside, Trevor spoke to the uniforms in the squad car. Then he climbed into the sedan. He waited until the parlor light was extinguished, leaving the house's bottom floor dark.

Trevor felt shaken, and not by the confrontation at the Ascension. In an investigation of this magnitude, Rain was a complication he couldn't afford. With the taste of her still sweet on his lips, he started the engine and drove away.

15

His mouth full of oyster po'boy, McGrath glanced up from his computer screen as Trevor exited the precinct's interview room.

"Find anything out from the roommate?"

"Not yet. She's pretty upset." Trevor felt tired down to his bones. Despite the late night at the Ascension, he'd been going full speed since just after seven that morning. The number from the club had been traced to an apartment a few blocks off the Tulane campus, identifying the victim as Rebecca Belknap, an eighteen-year-old freshman from Memphis. For the past half hour, Trevor had been trying to get some useful information from the dead girl's roommate, who the NOPD had picked up from a college classroom and brought into the station house.

Thibodeaux left the interview room behind Trevor. He swung the door open to briefly reveal the girl, who sat red-eyed and sniffling with a pile of crumpled tissues in front of her.

McGrath shook his head once the door had closed. "In my day, girls weren't allowed to live off campus. They lived in dorms with dorm mothers. They had curfews, too."

"Times have changed." Thibodeaux swiped several French

fries from the glistening heap boated in a paper tray on McGrath's desk. The food reminded Trevor that he'd agreed to meet Brian for lunch that day, something he now regretted, considering his schedule.

Chewing, Thibodeaux pointed a fry at Trevor. "So what do you think, FBI man? That girl in there one of them goth kids, too?"

"She doesn't seem like it," he said.

Little had turned up inside Rebecca Belknap's apartment, which the roommate had given permission to search. In Rebecca's bedroom, there were some goth-style clothes mixed in with the otherwise normal college attire of jeans and sweatshirts, tank tops and shorts, but not much else was out of the ordinary. An FBI field tech had gone with Trevor and confiscated Rebecca's laptop, which he hoped might give some insight into who she had been in communication with, perhaps through deleted e-mails, or a MySpace or Facebook account.

He walked to the watercooler and filled a paper cup, but a call from McGrath regained his attention.

"Hey, we got a hit on your knife prints, Rivette."

Trevor joined Thibodeaux in peering over McGrath's shoulder at the computer screen. An olive-skinned male with scraggly hair and black eyes stared back at them from a mug shot. Even without the goth makeup, Trevor recognized his knife-wielding attacker. McGrath switched the screen to a second photo that revealed the man's sharpened incisors.

Thibodeaux let out a whistle. "You weren't kidding about the teeth. You think he filed those himself?"

"Let's see who we have here." McGrath adjusted his bifocals and read aloud from the screen. "Maurice Girard. Age thirty-five. Most recent conviction for possession with intent to distribute. He's been out since January, early release from Angola State Prison for good behavior."

"I'm bettin' he's a regular choirboy now," Thibodeaux quipped. "I'll put an APB out for him."

The information precluded the possibility of his attacker also being Dante, Trevor realized, since a number of the murders had occurred during the time Girard was in prison. Nor did Girard match the FBI profile. Of course, neither did the male who'd been seen with the victim at the Ascension prior to her murder. Marcy Cupich, the girl he'd talked to at the club, was scheduled to come in later that afternoon to meet with a sketch artist.

He continued scanning the on-screen information. "Do you know Girard's parole officer? Marvin LaRoche?"

"Marvin the Roach, we like to call him," McGrath said. "We'll pay ol' Marv a visit, see if he knows where Girard's hanging out these days."

He pulled a piece of paper from the stack in his in-box and handed it to Trevor. "We got the full autopsy report back on the Belknap girl, too. Toxicology indicates Ecstasy, as well as Rohypnol."

Trevor looked at the report. "The date-rape drug? That's new."

"Maybe this one didn't go along so willingly."

"Hey, Rivette. You gonna sit in on that shrink's talk show again tonight?" Thibodeaux settled on the edge of McGrath's desk and snagged another fry.

He nodded. "You want to come along?"

"And listen to that touchy-feely crap? I don't think so." The detective wiped grease from his fingers with a paper napkin. "Besides, the Belknap girl's parents are flying into Louis Armstrong tonight. McGrath and me are the lucky bastards who get to go meet 'em."

"Lieu's orders," McGrath grumbled. "The father's a big-time contributor to the university. You know what that means?"

He pulled a roll of antacid tablets from his desk drawer and popped a pastel-colored wafer into his mouth before answering his own question. "It means we need to find this vampire son of a bitch."

Returning to the interview room, Trevor sat across from Rebecca Belknap's roommate and placed the water on the table in front of her.

"Thanks," she said quietly. Melanie Cantella was mousy-haired and bookish, with a round face and lackluster brown eyes hidden behind thick glasses. Slightly overweight, she wore shapeless denim overalls and a blue T-shirt with the Tulane University seal.

"Feeling better?" Trevor asked.

"I'm sorry for…crying," she stammered. "It's just that I can't believe Becca's…dead."

"I know it's a shock. But we need your help if we're going to find out who did this. Any information you have could be useful."

"I'll try."

"Let's start over. We already know Rebecca visited a club called the Ascension the night she disappeared. Can you tell me anything about that?"

Melanie sniffled and wiped her nose with a tissue. "She only started going there lately. She was really into the clothes. She got a tattoo a few weeks ago, too. I warned her that when her parents saw it they'd have a fit."

Trevor recalled the ink cross at the base of the victim's spine. "Did you ever go to the club with her?"

"No."

"What about Rebecca's friends? You didn't meet anyone new recently?"

"I already told you and the detective, I didn't really know a lot of her friends. I already gave you a list of the ones I knew about from phone messages and stuff. She never brought them to the apartment."

"Why not?"

Red splotches infused her face. She pushed her glasses up the bridge of her nose and avoided Trevor's eyes. "I think she was embarrassed of me. We were roommates only because we're from the same hometown. My dad works for Becca's dad, and her parents thought I'd be a good influence on her, make sure she studied. I'm sort of an A student. They said if she got an apartment off campus, it had to be with me until she brought her grades up."

Trevor felt as if he was hitting a dead end. McGrath and Thibodeaux had gone to meet with Girard's parole officer, but he'd stayed behind to finish the conversation with the roommate. "You don't remember her mentioning any guys? You shared an apartment, Melanie."

"Becca didn't tell me much. She thought I was spying on her for her parents." She shredded the tissue with her fingers. "The only way I knew she'd hooked up with a guy was if she didn't come home for a day or two. That's why I didn't report her as missing. I just thought—"

She stopped speaking and tears glinted behind her glasses. Trevor nudged the cup of water closer, encouraging her to take a sip.

"Melanie, do you know if Rebecca ever listened to *Midnight Confessions?*"

She nodded dully. "All the time. Becca liked to brag about knowing a celebrity."

He looked up, uncertain he'd heard her correctly. "You're saying she *knew* Rain Sommers?"

"She used to. Becca's parents were making her see a therapist. She had bulimia, you know…make herself throw up to lose weight?"

Trevor pondered the revelation, confused. Rain had given

no indication that she recognized the dead girl. In fact, she'd gone with him to the Ascension to circulate the morgue photo and try to get an ID.

"Do you recall how far back it was that she was seeing Dr. Sommers?"

Melanie shrugged. "It was a while ago. Last fall. Rebecca only went a couple of times."

"Why'd she stop?"

"Her parents sent her to someone else. They're real strait-laced, and when they found out who Dr. Sommers's mother was, they canceled her sessions. I remember Becca was pretty mad about it. I think she dyed her hair that red color because she wanted to look like her."

A tear rolled down Melanie's plump cheek. "Becca wasn't always nice to me, but I never wanted anything bad to happen to her."

"I know," Trevor said understandingly.

"We were both going home for the summer in a couple of weeks." Her shoulders shook as she began to sob again. "What am I going to say to her parents?"

Trevor watched through the plate-glass window as a police-woman guided Melanie into the back of a squad car to drive her home. He stood in the sixth-precinct lobby, still trying to wrap his mind around the information that Rebecca Belknap had been one of Rain's patients. It made it a strong possibility the selection of the latest victim hadn't been random, and it also created another link between Dante and Rain. But how was it possible that she hadn't recognized her former patient? Trevor retrieved his cell phone from his pocket. He was about to call her when he saw someone approaching. It was Brian. And he looked pissed.

"I lost track of the time," he explained when his brother reached him.

"I've been waiting at Zombo's for over a half hour."

"I got tied up. We got an ID on the second victim this morning."

"You know that thing you're always carrying around with you?" Brian pointed to the phone in Trevor's hand. "Ever think of using it? Or at least checking your messages? I've called you twice."

"I said I forgot. I'm sorry."

Heaving a sigh, Brian relented. "So you identified the body. That must be good, right?"

"It'd be a hell of a lot better if I caught this psycho before another one turns up." Trevor stared onto Royal Street, where a television-news van had arrived. The *Times-Picayune* article the previous day had kicked off media activity, making the likely presence of a serial killer a top story on the local news. In response, Trevor had been put in charge of formalizing a task force between the FBI, NOPD and the district attorney's office. He was aware the media attention would only increase when the identity of the second victim was released that afternoon.

"Have you eaten yet?" Brian asked.

"No."

"Spare me a half hour, then. It's not the fried catfish at Zombo's, but there's a deli near Riverfront Park that makes a good muffuletta."

Trevor shook his head. "I can't—"

"Half an hour," Brian urged. "We can watch for paddle wheelers like we did when we were kids."

A short while later, seated on a bench next to a waxy-leafed magnolia, Trevor and Brian dug into their sandwiches. The river stretched in front of them like a sea of butterscotch under a cerulean-blue sky. People strolled on the park's brick promenade, most of them tourists, judging by the shopping bags and cameras. Trevor watched as, farther down, several small children waded in a public fountain. He checked his watch—he was expected at the FBI field office near Lake Pontchartrain at one-thirty.

"Sorry I gave you hell for forgetting about lunch." Brian took a sip from a sweating bottle of root beer. "I know you've got a lot on your mind."

Trevor merely nodded. He didn't want to ruin Brian's meal with the grim details of the case. Instead, he took another bite from his sandwich.

"The truth is I wanted to talk to you," Brian said.

"About what?"

"Annabelle. She's worried about you." Brian squinted against the sunlight. "Actually, so am I."

Trevor said nothing. He returned his gaze to the group of children. A young mother supervised them from the fountain's edge. She squealed as one of them kicked out a spray of water, dousing the front of her sundress.

"Annabelle told me she found you outside her old room. She said you were upset." Brian paused. "She thinks you were having some kind of flashback."

Trevor wadded up the wax paper holding the remains of his sandwich. He tossed it into a receptacle next to the bench.

"Have you ever talked to anyone, Trevor? About what happened?"

"It was a long time ago. Let's leave it in the past."

There was a lapse of silence and then Brian said, "The past is never dead. It's not even the past."

Trevor laughed faintly. "Now you're quoting William Faulkner? *There's* a guy who knew something about tragic Southern families."

"Trevor." Brian's voice was soft.

"Let it go, Brian. I'm already on overload with the case. I got about three hours' sleep last night. I can't handle a conversation like this right now."

Looking out over the park, Trevor's vision was drawn to a row of crepe myrtle trees, their limbs weighed down with pink blossoms. Heat shimmied up from the brick walkway, and he felt a drop of sweat roll down his back underneath his dress shirt.

A child's wail came from the fountain. Trevor saw the mother wading in after one of her charges. It was then that he noticed the man on the pavilion's periphery. Despite the heat, he wore a long black trench coat. His hair looked unwashed and stringy, and his pale face held mocking dark eyes. He'd been watching them have lunch, of that much Trevor was certain.

He barely heard Brian still talking beside him. He stood and began winding his way through the tourists. But the man was moving as well, shrinking farther from his line of sight as he slipped between the trees at the edge of the promenade and headed back toward the French Quarter. Trevor broke into a run after him, barely aware of Brian calling after him. He cut through a chain of shrubs and sprinted across the street at the edge of the park. A car blew its horn, but he kept going, his eyes on the figure's flapping dark coat a block in front of him.

The man went around the corner, disappearing behind a crumbling stone wall nearly obscured by primrose jasmine. Trevor followed his path into a gated courtyard.

He turned around once, twice. There was no other way out.

Where the hell had he gone?

The air in the courtyard felt heated and sluggish. Trevor's hair was damp with perspiration, and the pain in his side from the previous evening seemed to radiate through his body. Overhead, the tops of the courtyard's banana trees ruffled in the breeze brought in by the river.

Trevor was unaware as to exactly when he'd pulled his

gun, but he whirled when he heard someone approach and pointed the weapon. Brian took a step back, raising his hands in front of him.

"Whoa! Take it easy, Trev! What's going on?"

He lowered the gun and used the sleeve of his shirt to wipe his forehead. "You saw him."

Brian's face was flushed as he attempted to catch his breath. "I ran after you all the way from the park. I didn't see anyone."

"He came in here!"

Concern filled Brian's eyes. "Trevor, there's no one here."

Trevor looked around again, refusing to believe it had only been his imagination.

16

The patio at Jezzabel's was cool, thanks to overhanging shade trees and several outdoor fans. Rain followed the maître d' to a table next to a display of ferns and potted ivy, then took a seat in the cushioned rattan chair he pulled out for her.

"Will you be dining alone this afternoon, ma'am?" he inquired.

"Someone's joining me." She unfolded the cloth napkin and placed it on her lap. "I left his name with the hostess."

The maître d' nodded. "I'll direct him this way as soon as he arrives."

Alex had called Rain the morning after Brian's art showing, and they'd agreed to meet that Tuesday for lunch at the popular restaurant on Magazine Street. Acquainted with Alex's tendency to run late, she settled into the comfortable chair and ordered an iced tea with mint while she waited. But it didn't take long for her thoughts to travel to the previous evening and the kiss she'd shared with Trevor Rivette.

She was thirty-two years old and not once in her life did Rain recall making the first move. Not until last night. Still, she recalled Trevor's reaction. His lips had been warm and firm as they explored hers. When he'd finally pulled away, she was certain it was sexual attraction that had darkened his eyes to a stunning midnight blue.

You're part of this investigation, Rain. His words echoed in her memory. Lost in reflection, she ran her fingers through the condensation on her water glass.

"Dr. Sommers?"

Rain looked up at the man standing next to her table. Although Dr. Christian Carteris had never attended a counseling session with his son, she recognized him from the portrait of the board of directors in the lobby of All Saints Hospital, as well as the photos that appeared regularly in the society column of the *Times-Picayune*. Dr. Carteris appeared to be in his early to mid-forties and, like Oliver, he was tall and dark-haired. His steel-framed spectacles glinted in the sunlight.

"Dr. Carteris." Rain offered her hand in greeting. "So nice to finally meet you in person."

"I hope I'm not disturbing you. I just finished lunch and saw you being seated. Could I have a word? It's about my son."

"I'm sure you understand I can't discuss what's said in therapy—"

The surgeon patted the air as if to ward off her concern. "I appreciate the need for confidentiality, and I'd never expect you to divulge anything Oliver might have told you during his sessions. The truth is, there are some things I feel compelled to share with you. It might be pertinent to his treatment."

His eyes fell to the unoccupied chair. "May I? At least until your guest arrives?"

"I think that would be all right."

Pinching up the knees of his tailored suit pants, he sat across from her. "I'll get right to the point. Oliver's conduct at home has become increasingly erratic. So much so that I searched his room last night after he'd gone out."

He adjusted his eyeglasses, his expression grave. "I found

marijuana, as well as a white powder the hospital's pharmacist informs me is crystal methamphetamine. I'm particularly concerned about the latter."

He had good reason to be worried. Rain recalled Oliver's behavior during his last therapy session—the crystal meth would explain his paranoia and hostility.

"Have you talked to Oliver about what you found?"

"I tried to this morning, but he shoved me against the wall and stormed out. He was furious I'd gone through his things." He hesitated briefly, appearing sheepish. "I was actually a bit fearful of him. My own son."

There was a break in conversation as the iced tea Rain ordered arrived. Once the waiter retreated, the surgeon continued. "I worry Oliver's problems are my fault. I tried to compensate for the loss of his mother at such a young age, and I realize now I overindulged him. I looked the other way when the behavioral problems started."

Rain was privy to Oliver's records. Although Dr. Carteris was American, Oliver's mother was European. She'd been killed in a car accident in a Pacific Rim country where the surgeon was conducting private research. Oliver had been nine years old.

"As you know, I returned to the States two years ago to accept the position of chief of cardiac medicine. My hope was for Oliver to complete his education here."

Rain felt a tug of sympathy. Christian Carteris was at the top of his field. She could imagine the high expectations he must have had for his son.

"Oliver's very intelligent." A note of pride entered his voice. "Did you know he's fluent in three languages? He also has a gift for the violin. He was on a music scholarship at Loyola before he was expelled."

Rain nodded solemnly. "Yes, I'm aware of that."

"Now he works at a video store in Bywater, earning

minimum wage. Just enough to pay for his recreational drugs, apparently. I'd be lying if I said I wasn't disappointed."

"You're a very successful man, Dr. Carteris. Perhaps Oliver feels an undue amount of pressure to achieve and he's rebelling against it?"

"I expect only what my son is capable of, nothing more." He looked pensive and shook his head. "Regardless, I only wanted to let you know about the drugs, as well as the change in behavior. I thought it might be important."

"It is," Rain agreed. "I wish there was something I could say to alleviate your concern. But if his drug use is escalating, as the crystal meth suggests, there might be a need to consider in-patient rehabilitation. There are some excellent programs. I could make recommendations."

"Oliver despises me already," he replied sadly. "Can you imagine if I put him in a facility? But I'll do what I have to, of course."

"It's a difficult decision, but Oliver might eventually thank you for caring enough to do what's best for him."

The surgeon's gaze was direct. "I have to be honest with you, Dr. Sommers. You came highly recommended. I'm discouraged Oliver's therapy sessions haven't resulted in a better outcome."

"Psychotherapy is a long process. I've only been seeing Oliver for a few months."

"You're right," he conceded. He laced his fingers together on the table in front of him. "And I'm trying to be patient. But I love my son. It's the reason I've tried to overlook, even defend, his behavior. At least until now. He's getting mixed up in a lifestyle that could destroy him."

"Talk to him," Rain urged. "Without accusations or judgment. You're his father and it's important you keep a line of communication open."

"The last thing he wants is to talk to me."

She reached across the table and touched his hand. "Just let him know you're there if he needs you."

"Yes, I'll try."

Her eyes shifted to the patio's entrance. The maître d' was leading Alex toward their table. He waved at her with an apologetic grin on his face. Dr. Carteris pushed his chair back and stood.

"I see your guest has arrived, and I've taken enough of your time. Thank you. I'd be grateful if you'd forward me information on the treatment programs."

"Of course. Whatever I can do to help."

He gave a cordial greeting to Alex as they passed one another.

"Look what happens," Alex teased as he slipped into the chair. "I'm a few minutes late, and you're picking up men in the middle of the afternoon."

"He's the father of one of my patients."

"He wasn't wearing a wedding ring." He unfolded his napkin with a flourish. "And I thought you only had eyes for Trevor Rivette."

Rain felt color rise in her face, which only made Alex's grin broaden. "Oh, my. You *do* like Brian's brother, don't you?"

She managed a small laugh, although she evaded his stare. "We're not in grade school, Alex. What should I do, pass him a note?"

"That depends on what the note says," he replied wickedly, then glanced at Rain's beverage. "Please tell me that's a Long Island."

"Sorry. Just regular iced tea. I have another patient session in a few hours and the radio show tonight."

"Spoilsport." With an exasperated sigh, Alex signaled the waiter.

Thoughts about Oliver continued to plague Rain after she'd left the restaurant and taken the St. Charles Streetcar to its stop near her home. The marijuana Dr. Carteris had found was hardly a surprise to her, although she was taken aback by the crystal meth. Oliver's drug use was more hardcore than she had suspected.

His next therapy session was scheduled for the following morning. Rain wondered whether he'd show up after his outburst the previous week. If he missed an appointment, she'd have no choice but to report his absence to the courts. Hopefully, it wouldn't come to that, since Oliver would view the action as a betrayal. Trust was key to her relationships with her patients—with anyone in her life, Rain realized. Once that trust was broken it was nearly impossible to regain. Which brought her thoughts to David. They'd had no communication since she'd told him of her intention not to renew her contract, but she'd have to face him at the radio station that night. Rain considered this inevitability as she climbed the steps onto the veranda of her house. She nodded politely to the officers who sat in the squad car across the street, their presence becoming as certain as the humid New Orleans climate.

Her cell phone began ringing while she entered her pass code into the security system. She retrieved it from her purse and answered it.

"You were talking to him."

"Oliver?"

"I *saw* you. You were touching him."

Rain felt a tingle of nerves. He must have been spying on them from somewhere in the restaurant.

"It's not what you think. We ran into each other by accident," she stated calmly. When he said nothing, she added, "I didn't tell him anything about our sessions. I only listened to what he had to say. He's very concerned about you."

She ignored his bitter curse, her desire to reach out to him overcoming any trepidation she felt. "I'm at my house, Oliver.

Do you need to talk? I have another appointment scheduled this afternoon, but I'll cancel it if you want to come over."

For a few moments, she could hear his breathing, harsh and tinny sounding through the phone. Rain ran her hand through her hair, her nape damp from the time spent outdoors. She tried to think of what else she could say to convince him.

"I didn't break our therapist-patient confidence. I need for you to believe that—"

Rain exhaled as the phone went dead. Oliver was gone.

17

The door to David's office at the radio station was closed. Rain passed it quietly, grateful for the temporary reprieve. Oliver's accusatory phone call that afternoon had left her drained, a feeling that had only increased as daylight faded into evening and she prepared herself to deal with another live show.

She slipped into the small studio and kept her mind occupied with selecting the recorded voice tracks that would be used between the live advice segments. A few minutes later, however, it wasn't David but Trevor who knocked on the door. Rain removed her headset as he came inside.

He laid the morgue photo on the console in front of her. "We got an ID this morning. The victim's name is Rebecca Belknap."

Rain's mouth went dry as she studied the photo of the dead girl again, mentally changing the hair color from siren red to honey blond. *My God.* The image fused with her faint recollection of the girl who'd sat in her office months earlier. Becca Belknap had made it to only two sessions before switching to a different therapist. She'd had an eating disorder. The girl's pale skin in the photo stretched tightly across her cheekbones. She looked as though she'd lost another ten to fifteen pounds off her already thin frame in the time since Rain had seen her.

"She was one of your patients?"

Still looking at the photo, Rain tugged at her lower lip. "I can't believe I didn't recognize her. She looks... different..."

"Different how?"

"She had blond hair before. She's thinner, too." Reflectively, she touched the delicate bridge of her own nose. "I think she might've had some cosmetic surgery. I'm pretty sure there was a bump right here before."

Although he remained silent, Trevor studied her. Rain pressed a hand against her stomach as she rose from the chair. "You think I knew who this girl was and didn't tell you?"

"I didn't say that."

Moving away from him, she stopped in front of a cork message board on the studio wall. Rain stared at the random photos tucked between the station's daypart schedule and office memos. What kind of therapist didn't know her own patient?

Walking up behind her, Trevor clasped her shoulders. His touch caused her to release the breath she hadn't realized she'd been holding.

"People can look different in death," he offered. "Along with the physical changes in her appearance..."

She turned to face him. "I should have known. She was my patient—"

"A while ago. You see a lot of kids. It happens, Rain. Don't be so hard on yourself."

"You don't understand. They're not just numbers to me." Her voice trembled. She'd expected awkwardness after their kiss last night, but she hadn't dreamed of being faced with what he'd thrown at her. The now-recognizable face of Becca Belknap seared itself onto her brain.

"I need you to focus, Rain. What do you remember about Rebecca?"

Her memories of those two brief sessions were like an out-of-focus slide show. Rain closed her eyes and tried to concentrate.

"She was referred to me by a general physician. She had symptoms of anorexia-bulimia, which would explain the weight loss since the last time I saw her. Especially if she failed to get treatment after she left my care or if it was unsuccessful."

"Anything else?"

She shook her head. It had been so long ago. Without consulting her notes, it was difficult to recall anything beyond the bare facts. "You think her being my patient means something, don't you?"

Trevor didn't answer. Instead, he regarded her thoughtfully before speaking again. "Do your patients ever come into contact with one another? Maybe while one is leaving a session and another is coming into your home?"

"I try to schedule buffer time between appointments so that doesn't happen."

"But it's possible?"

"Maybe," Rain acknowledged.

"What about group therapy?"

"I do pro bono group counseling through the Louisiana Department of Social Services one afternoon a week. But Becca Belknap was a private patient. She came to my house."

She'd been expecting Trevor's next words, but they still jarred.

"I need access to the files of any male patients you were seeing in the same time frame as the victim."

"I can't do that."

Trevor dragged a hand through his hair. He looked as tired as she felt. "Even if you're protecting a killer?"

Rain tried to squelch the uneasy feeling in her stomach. "As you know, I specialize in adolescents and young adults. My male patients are all in their teens or early twenties. No one even comes close to matching your profile of the killer. Dante isn't a kid, Trevor. You've heard him on the phone. Even if he's using a voice synthesizer—"

"I still have to eliminate any possibilities, even the remote ones."

She met his gaze. "I can't give you my files. And you don't have probable cause for a warrant. You're simply trying to cover all your bases."

"I'm *trying* to do my job." He massaged his eyelids tiredly with his fingertips and sighed. "I'm sorry. I've been talking to the victim's friends since late afternoon. They all seem pretty harmless."

Rain moved closer to him. "What do you really think this is about, Trevor? Why Becca Belknap? There are a half-dozen girls I'm counseling right now. Why not pick someone…"

Her words died as Trevor's hands slid through her hair. The sensation sent little jolts of awareness along her skin.

"*This* is the connection," he murmured. The certainty she saw in his eyes made her heartbeat quicken. "Dante picked this girl because she was a redhead, Rain. The fact she knew you was just another bonus. He's escalating, and he's looking for ways to get closer to you."

She blinked as a knot settled in her throat. "That's your gut instinct speaking again, isn't it? You're saying you think Becca Belknap is dead because she was some sort of substitute for *me?*" She backed away. "I won't accept that."

"Rain." Trevor caught her arms and drew her closer. "Try to stay calm. You may still have to face Dante on the air tonight."

She attempted to laugh, but it ended on a note of hysteria. Her body hummed with nerves and exhaustion. All she wanted to do was go home, take a hot bath, have a glass of wine and fall into a mindless sleep. Too tired to fight, she pressed her hands over her face and leaned against his chest.

"It's okay," Trevor said. "We'll get through this. I'm right here with you."

"I have the playlist." Rain looked up to see David in the doorway. Dividing a hard stare between the two of them, he laid the document on the table and went back down the hall.

At 1 a.m., Rain signed off with her listeners. Her eyes met Trevor's through the glass window. Frustration was visible on his features as he stood and reached one hand behind his neck to massage the muscles there. She felt as tense as a coiled spring herself after spending the last three hours in nerve-racking anticipation of a phone call that never came.

David was in the production room with Trevor. She'd been cognizant of his unbroken gaze despite the few terse words he'd said to her all evening. He sat with his elbows on the control board and his fingers templed pensively in front of his face as he regarded her with cool eyes. He raised one hand and motioned for her to join them. Feeling as though she'd been summoned by the executioner, Rain stood and walked to him.

"You were off tonight," he remarked. He adjusted a dial on the board as he spoke. "About as witty as cardboard."

"That's a matter of opinion."

"I'm your producer. *My* opinion's the one that matters." The superiority in his tone left a stinging silence in the air. Rain lifted her chin, knowing his annoyance had more to do with what he'd witnessed earlier than it did with her performance.

She waited for his next jab as he fished a silver Mont Blanc fountain pen from his shirt pocket and began turning it absently in his fingers.

"You came off like an amateur. Ella could have done a better job tonight."

"Then let her," Rain replied evenly. "I'm sure she'd love a break from getting your coffee and manning the reception desk."

He glared at her. "Ella isn't under legal contract. You are."

A contract that was about to expire. Not wanting to give more fuel to David's ire, Rain kept the thought to herself. She glanced over at Trevor. So far, he'd remained silent, but she'd recognized the subtle change in his posture as David continued raking her over the coals. Rain silently willed him to stay out of it, but David seemed intent on drawing him into the fray.

"Looks like your killer stood us up tonight, Agent Rivette." He swiveled the leather executive chair in Trevor's direction. "Maybe he was as bored with the show as the rest of New Orleans."

"He'll call again."

"And when do you think that might be?"

"Give it time."

David let out a laugh. "At the expense of my ratings? I have news for you. If this little surveillance project continues to be a distraction to the talent, I'm going to have to end it."

Trevor crossed his arms over his chest and shifted his stance, although his tone remained casual. "So far your participation has been voluntary, but it doesn't have to be."

"Meaning?"

"I can be here by invitation or by writ. And you can be charged with interference with a federal investigation if you cause problems."

A flush crept up from David's collar. He'd begun tapping the pen on the console, the rapid staccato a giveaway to his growing fury. The pen gave a sharp crack as he threw it down and pushed away from the board.

He pointed a finger at Trevor. "Fuck you."

David stalked from the room. A few seconds later, the door to his office slammed shut with a force that vibrated the studio's glass panels. Rain went to the doorway and looked out into the hallway. But all she saw was Ella, sitting at the reception desk with a smug expression on her face.

Rain turned back around. The expensive pen now lay under the control board, its broken casing bleeding indigo ink onto the oat-colored carpet.

"That went well, don't you think?" Trevor smiled faintly, but his eyes told her he was feeling anything but playful.

18

For years, he'd been unable to remember the details. Now it seemed they were returning with breathtaking clarity.

Trevor pushed the sheets back and sat up in bed. He ran a hand over his face and shivered as the cold air being pumped out by the air conditioner made contact with his sweat-dampened skin. This time, the memory had been so vivid his heart still pounded. He'd felt the cold steel of the gun barrel pressing against his forehead, heard the bullet's metallic clink as it dropped into the hollow chamber. Worse, he'd heard Annabelle's breathless sobs as she begged for his life. The badge on James Rivette's uniform glinted in the sunlight squeezing in through the small attic window.

You think I won't do it, Trev?

He'd told his father to go to hell. The images had stopped there, wrenching him awake.

Several days earlier, when he'd stood in the threshold of Annabelle's old room, his brain had allowed him only a small glimpse of that scene before slamming the door shut. Tonight, while he'd existed in the nothingness of sleep, it had returned to him freely.

Trevor slid his feet over the edge of the bed and squinted at the digital clock on the nightstand: 2:00 a.m. In the clock's glow, he could make out the Glock 9mm handgun he'd left next to it, within easy reach.

Dante's latest gift also lay on the nightstand. That knowledge grounded him back to the present, as surely as the wail of the squad car that roared past the building before fading into the distance. After he'd taken Rain home, he'd gone straight to his hotel, yearning for a hot shower and some badly needed sleep. But a note on the door of his room informed him there was a package waiting for him at the front desk. This time, the token was an emerald ring, mailed to him in a plain white envelope with no return address.

Trevor turned on the lamp and picked up the clear baggie holding the ring, along with a short note written in blood like the last time.

She was a pretty girl. Where were you, Agent Rivette?

He'd tell Rebecca Belknap's parents about the ring tomorrow, confirm with them it had belonged to their daughter. But then it would go into evidence until the investigation was closed. Right now, that day seemed like a long way off.

A knock sounded on the door and Trevor instinctively reached for his gun. Slipping against the wall next to the room's window, he lifted a corner of the curtain and released a breath at the sight of Rain standing alone.

He slid on his jeans and opened the door, still holding the gun in his right hand although he'd reengaged the safety. Rain wore tan shorts and a scoop-necked top, her hair pulled into a ponytail. The fact that she wore no makeup, not even lipstick, made her appear somehow even more vulnerable to him. He scowled as thunder rumbled overhead.

"What the hell, Rain," he said softly, wondering what she was doing here. They were on the hotel's second floor and across the street below them, he could see a taxi pulling away from the curb.

Trevor took a step back and let her inside. Rain's gaze

moved from the unmade bed and back to him as he stood bare-chested in front of her. Although she didn't remark on it, her eyes drifted to the faint bruise on his abdomen from his run-in with the two men at the Ascension.

"I couldn't sleep," she admitted. "I have to see the rest of the victims. What if I knew them, as well?"

"So you came here alone in the middle of the night? Did nothing we talked about get through to you?"

"I need to see the other photos. All of them." The lamplight brought out the gold in her amber eyes, and he thought he saw the glimmer of unshed tears.

Trevor dragged a hand through his hair. Taking in Rain's grief-stricken expression, he didn't have the will to scold her further. The discovery that she'd actually known Rebecca Belknap had obviously upset her, perhaps more than he'd realized.

"You've already seen photos of both victims in New Orleans," he reasoned. "The chance of you knowing one of the victims in another city—"

"Please."

Taking the time to pull on a T-shirt, he went to the desk near the window and picked up a thick folder that lay next to his laptop.

"Some of these are disturbing," he warned, handing it to her.

"How many victims in all?"

"Six. Each in a different city, with the exception of the last two here. We think the unsub has a white-collar job that requires him to travel, which explains why the murders have been geographically dispersed."

Rain opened the folder. The photo on top of the stack was of a young female lying on the cold steel of an autopsy table. The girl's eyes were open but unseeing, their corneas clouded, and her lips were tinged blue. Cuts made by the killer covered her breasts and abdomen, and the deep gouge in her neck gaped open.

Trevor heard the waver in Rain's breathing. The previous photos she'd seen had been easier to deal with, he knew, since they'd been taken specifically for the purpose of getting an ID. These photos were raw, the camera concealing nothing.

"This is the same girl you showed me when Brian brought you to my house?"

Trevor nodded. "That's Cara Seagreen, the first victim in New Orleans. She was also the youngest."

He studied Rain's profile as she sank onto the edge of the bed and concentrated on the photo. She took her time, staring at the snapshot for what seemed like an eternity. Then she shook her head. "She was never one of my patients. I've never seen her before. I'm positive."

Rain went through the rest of the morgue photos of the other victims, looking at image after image of their bodies postautopsy, the closed Y-incision a shared brand on their skin. When she was halfway through the stack, Trevor sat beside her and placed his hand over hers. He knew the order of the photographs by heart.

"The rest are the crime scene photos. I don't think—"

"I *want* to see them."

A flash of lightning illuminated the dark edges around the closed curtains. A half second later, thunder exploded and the hard fall of rain outside enveloped the room.

"Maybe you should," he said finally. "Something might stand out to you."

He removed his hand and allowed her to continue. The morgue photos were sterile compared to the ones from the crime scenes, the bodies left behind like broken, bloodied dolls. Even after seven years' working with the FBI's Violent Crimes Unit, Trevor was still haunted by the damage inflicted by the killer's knife. He could only imagine what Rain must be experiencing.

"You okay?" he asked once she'd made it through several of the photos.

She nodded, although her face had paled. "Their wrists. They're bound with a rosary?"

"It's part of the killer's signature, one of the details we've kept from the press," Trevor explained. "We haven't been able to trace the maker, although we think each of the rosaries is handmade and fairly expensive. A jewelry expert believes they're Italian imports. They're made with—"

"Black crystal beads with mother-of-pearl and a Celtic silver cross." Rain finished the statement for him, her voice barely audible. "The rosary medal is an image of Saint Agnes, the patron saint of chastity and virgins."

He looked again at the photo, making sure. It simply wasn't possible to glean that level of detail from the images. "How do you know that?"

"Because I have the same rosary. It belonged to my mother. It was used as part of a photo shoot."

Electricity ran along his skin. "Photo shoot?"

She took a breath before continuing. "A series of photos ran in *Blue Moon* in which the rosary was used."

Trevor recalled the defunct publication, which had been likened to *Rolling Stone* but had failed to build a mainstream following. After a decade of operation, the magazine closed its doors in the mid-eighties.

"Desiree used the rosary in provocative ways." Rain smoothed the rumpled bed linens, avoiding his eyes. "At the time the photos were published, they were considered highly controversial. Some religious leaders labeled them sacrilegious soft-core pornography. The magazine was pulled from shelves all over the country."

"Are the photos on the Internet?"

"I'm not sure. Copies of the magazine issue are rare." Rain hesitated. "If not, I know someone who has several as part of his memorabilia collection."

Trevor had gone to the laptop and was powering it up. "Who?"

"Armand Baptiste."

He sat in the chair in front of the desk as the computer screen came to life. Clicking the browser icon, Trevor returned to one of the fan-operated Web sites he'd bookmarked earlier. This time he dug deeper into its photo archive using the keywords *Blue Moon*. With Rain watching over his shoulder, he went to two other sites before locating the images.

Although the quality of the scanned photos was poor, they still delivered a sensual impact. Desiree wore a sheer negligee that left little to the imagination. As Rain had described, a rosary was used in each of the darkly dramatic photos— one in which it was worn as a necklace, resting between the well-displayed curves of Desiree's breasts, and another in which she sat in a chair with her legs spread apart, the string of prayer beads dangling suggestively between them. But it was the third photo that caused Trevor to lean toward the computer, his pulse speeding up at what he saw. In what was staged as an obvious bondage scene, Desiree was lying on a stripped mattress, her wrists bound with the glittering black rope of the rosary. Her eyes were wide in mock fright, and her painted, luscious mouth was gagged with a strip of cloth.

Rain's voice came softly from behind him. "God. He's trying to re-create that photo, isn't he?"

"Have you seen these before?"

"Only once, a long time ago. Aunt Celeste was very protective of me. But I was curious and…"

There wasn't a need to state the obvious. The photos inexplicably connected Dante to Desiree and by extension, to Rain herself. She walked to the French door that led onto the balcony and stared out. Trevor traced her footsteps until he stood directly behind her, and he felt her flinch as lightning lit the black sky. It was followed by a roar of thunder, and the room's light dimmed before brightening again. Jewel-like beads of water ran down the door's glass panes.

"Rain." At the sound of his voice she turned to him. Her head and narrow shoulders were framed by the light emitted from the swimming pool below.

"I've tried to respect your wishes." Reaching out, Trevor touched her face. "But it's time you started taking more serious precautions."

"There's a patrol car outside my house practically around the clock—"

"With two apparently inept cops sitting in it. Were they *asleep* when you took off in the middle of the night?"

"They didn't know," she confessed. "I went out the back and met the taxi a couple of blocks over, at Coliseum Square."

"Why would you do that?"

"Because of what happened between us last night." Rain looked at the worn carpet. "You were so concerned about protocol, about me being part of the investigation. I didn't think you'd want those officers knowing I was going to your hotel."

"I want a post in your house, Rain. The only reason I didn't push the issue in the first place was because D'Alba told me he was staying with you."

"I didn't think that would be a good idea," she countered. "David and I haven't been together as a couple for a while now."

"But he wants you back."

She didn't answer, but her eyes told him it was true. She walked to the nightstand and picked up the baggie containing the note and emerald ring.

"It belonged to Rebecca Belknap," Trevor said. "Dante sent it to me through the mail."

Blanching, Rain laid it back down. She thoughtfully bit her lower lip before speaking again. "The victims in New Orleans were just teenagers. But the ones in the other cities—they all looked older in the photos, maybe by ten or fifteen years. Do you know why?"

He shook his head. "There's a lot I don't know."

"What about Marcy Cupich?" she asked, hopeful. "The girl who saw Rebecca talking to someone at the Ascension?"

"She came to the precinct to meet with the sketch artist. Unfortunately, it was a waste of time. It turns out Marcy wears glasses, but she's vain and doesn't bring them with her when she's clubbing. Other than a dark-haired male, her description was pretty vague."

Thunder vibrated the room, and Rain looked as if she might jump out of her skin. Trevor approached her.

"I'm going to drive you home. And the cops outside your house are going to come *inside*. They'll stay downstairs. You won't even know they're there."

"It's only a few hours until morning. Could I stay here?" She must have anticipated his refusal because she added quietly, "We won't do anything, just sleep."

He looked at her in the lamplight. "Rain…"

She bowed her head. "The truth is, I'd really like you nearby."

The storm was in full force outside. Rain's eyes remained downcast, hidden beneath a veil of thick lashes. At least this way he'd know she was safe, Trevor rationalized. She wouldn't be out roaming the streets, by taxi or on foot.

"Starting tomorrow night, there's going to be a muscle-bound cop standing guard in your foyer. Agreed?"

Rain nodded. Gathering the soft cotton of his T-shirt in her fingers, she anchored him to her briefly before letting go.

He went into the bathroom. When he came out, she was wearing one of his shirts she'd taken from the armoire. Its sleeves were turned up and its hem skimmed the tops of her slender thighs. The ponytail was gone and her coppery hair hung around her face. Shaking his gaze from her, Trevor walked across the room to peer out the window from behind the curtain. But the downfall obscured his vision so that only a circle of light from a street lamp below was visible.

"Which side of the bed do you want?" she asked almost shyly.

"The one near the door." He waited until she climbed under the covers. Then Trevor went to the bed and turned off the lamp on the nightstand. Still dressed, he lay down but stayed on top of the sheets. The hard beat of the rain outside slowly lulled him to sleep.

When he awoke later, the downpour had receded. The sky, visible through a gap in the curtains, appeared iron gray and barely tinged with light. Rain was snuggled against him, her body warm, soft. Trevor was holding her, a realization that caused his heart to beat harder. Every part of him was touching her, it seemed. Rain's small, soft breasts pressed into his chest, and she'd kicked the sheets away in her sleep, her slender legs now wound with his. His hand had found its way under the shirt she wore, and his fingers splayed over the silken skin of her lower back. He swallowed hard. Trevor thanked God he was wearing his jeans. Still, his male response to her closeness must have awakened her.

Rain's face lifted to his. Her eyes were sensual, heavy-lidded with sleep.

Unable to fight the impulse, Trevor bent his head, his lips touching hers. He felt her hand thread through the hair at his nape, and his stomach somersaulted at the way Rain's mouth parted so willingly under his. His tongue mingled with hers, exploring, his body weight shifting so that he lay partially on top of her. Trevor's hand stroked over the gentle curves of her body as their mouths remained joined, tasting one another. Rain's bare thighs were incredibly soft, and invitingly open.

He could get used to this, he realized. The feel of her, having her near.

And it was that one thought that stopped him. He broke the kiss with reluctance, breathing heavily as he stared into her face. Rain's lips appeared full and slightly swollen from their kisses. Her eyes shimmered with desire. He was attracted to her so very much, but it wasn't what he'd been sent down here to do.

"That shouldn't have happened," Trevor said softly. He rose and sat on the edge of the bed facing away from her. "It's light enough now. I'm taking you home."

As morning revealed itself in a misty hush, he angrily paced the parlor. He'd been outside the hotel last night, watching from his vehicle as the light faded from the second-floor room.

He had followed her there—in fact, he'd watched the taxi pick her up—and all along he'd had the sickening suspicion she was going to him. *Like mother, like daughter,* he thought bitterly.

Whore.

Staring out from between heavy velvet drapes onto the rain-wet street, he wondered what crack in the universe occurred when one's lover and one's enemy united. His hands clenched into fists as he envisioned what they'd been doing together in the darkened room, their bodies writhing, their sweat slick and glistening. *She was his.* He wouldn't allow anyone else to have her. Agent Rivette's energy was strong—his heightened senses told him so—but he would still pay for his thievery, and pay hard.

Slowly, he shook his head, his need for revenge nearly as strong as his bloodlust. He could have taken her last night as she waited alone on the barely lit sidewalk near Coliseum Square. The little fool. It would have been so simple and so satisfying. He felt a tightening in his belly at the prospect of finally possessing her. But he'd always been one to delay gratification.

He reminded himself he wouldn't have to wait much longer.

19

Baptiste Antiques was located on Royal Street, within walking distance to Jackson Square and St. Louis Cathedral. Trevor entered the lavish showroom filled with hand-tooled mahogany furniture and paintings in gilded frames. The interior smelled of wood oil, and the sound of his dress shoes was absorbed by the deep pile of Aubusson carpets.

An exotic-looking woman with black hair pulled into a chignon appeared from behind an Oriental screen. "May I help you?"

"I'm here to see Armand Baptiste."

She eyed him as if trying to determine his buying power. "I'm afraid Mr. Baptiste is occupied. Perhaps I can be of service?"

Trevor held his shield out for inspection. "Let him know Agent Rivette with the FBI is here."

The woman went to a lacquered table and picked up a telephone handset. Looking at Trevor suspiciously, she spoke into the receiver. A moment later she indicated a door in back of the showroom. "He'll see you now."

Trevor crossed the room to the closed door. He didn't knock but went directly inside. The office was furnished with the same if-you-have-to-ask-the-price-you-can't-afford-it decor as the showroom. Baptiste sat behind an enormous mahogany desk with an inlaid-teak design. The financial section of the *Wall Street Journal* lay spread across its top.

"To what do I owe the pleasure, Agent Rivette?"

"I have a few questions."

"Ah." Baptiste paused to sip a dark espresso. "But do I have the answers?"

He wore a tailored suit and solid-color silk tie, and his hair was slicked back into a neat ponytail behind his head. Rimless bifocals sat on his nose. Baptiste bore none of the theatrical makeup he'd been wearing at the Ascension, making his transformation from goth elder to New Orleans businessman complete.

Trevor slid Maurice Girard's mug shot across the desk. "This is one of the men who attacked me at your club two nights ago. His parole officer confirmed he works for you."

"That's possible." Baptiste regarded the photo. "I have interests in several businesses, and dozens of employees. I can't be expected to know all of them personally."

"Interesting, because the P.O. says Girard was hired specifically by you. I'm wondering whether his job description extends to assault on a federal officer."

Baptiste removed his bifocals and laid them on the desk. He pinched the bridge of his nose. "What's the man's name?"

"Maurice Girard. His fingerprints matched the partials from the knife recovered in the supply room at the Ascension."

"You're welcome to check with Human Resources," he offered. "Even if this *Girard* does work for me, I didn't order him to attack you. If you don't believe me, why don't you pick him up and ask him yourself."

"Good idea. Only, Girard didn't make his parole meeting this morning. His apartment also appears to be vacated."

"Then what can I do for you? I'm a busy man."

Acting as if he had all the time in the world, Trevor examined a paperweight on Baptiste's desk. He turned the cobalt-blue orb around in his palm a few times before tossing it into the air and catching it in one hand. Baptiste followed the movement with his eyes.

"That's very expensive. It's centuries old, imported from Budapest."

"No kidding." Trevor gave it another casual toss. "What other things do you import?"

"Baptiste Antiques has specialized in fine European artwork and furnishings, as well as major estate sales in the southern United States, for three generations. If you're interested in something in particular, Miss Takura in the showroom—"

"As a matter of fact, I am interested in something." Replacing the paperweight, Trevor dug into the pocket of his suit coat and withdrew the black prayer beads and silver cross. He laid them on the desk.

"A lovely piece." Baptiste picked up the rosary and examined it. "Excellent craftsmanship. The semiprecious stones make it somewhat valuable. But I hadn't figured you for a religious man, Agent."

"Ever import anything like that?"

"I'm sorry, but no."

"Ever seen anything like it before?"

"Perhaps…where did you run across this item?"

"It belonged to Desiree Sommers. Rain gave it to me this morning."

"Is she interested in selling it?" he inquired. "I can make her a generous offer."

"That's nice to know, since I have a half dozen more identical to it. They were used in the commission of six murders."

Recoiling, Baptiste put down the beads. "I wouldn't

know anything about that. I only want it for my memorabilia collection."

"So you recognize the rosary?"

"I do," he admitted. "I believe it's from the *Blue Moon* photos, circa 1978. If you look at the images carefully, you'll notice a voluptuousness to Desiree's figure. She was twelve weeks pregnant with Rain at the time."

Trevor returned the rosary to his pocket. He'd hoped the religious object would rattle the other man somehow, but so far he remained unflustered. "Rain tells me you're on the parish council, Baptiste."

"As were my father and grandfather," he said proudly. "One might say civic leadership is in my blood."

"What about dressing up like Marilyn Manson and hanging out with pretend vampires all night? That kind of thing run in the family, too?"

Baptiste picked up a silver letter opener from his desk. He tested the sharpness of its pointed end against the pad of his index finger. "What makes you so certain these vampires are pretend, Agent Rivette?"

"I don't believe in vampires. Delusional psychotics are a different matter."

Chuckling, Baptiste stood from behind the desk. He went to look out the office window, which provided a view of the cathedral's Spanish facade and rounded spires. Outside, the clouds were burning away to reveal blue sky.

"There are plenty of role-players in the goth community," he said. "But make no mistake. There are real sanguinarians among us. However, those I've become acquainted with use *willing* donors. These donors are erotic masochists who are as excited by giving blood as those who take it. There's nothing illegal about that."

"What about the drugs and underage drinking in your club? I'm pretty sure that's illegal."

Baptiste turned from the window. "Is that a threat? Because you should know I have some very important friends—"

"I don't care if you play golf with the mayor, Baptiste. All I'm saying is that the Ascension puts you in a position to know things. If you're hiding something—or someone—now would be a good time to come clean."

"You're quite certain of yourself, aren't you?"

Although he said nothing, Trevor's gaze soaked into the other man's. Baptiste paused as he brushed several imaginary specks from his lapels.

"I suppose you *are* to be admired, considering your family situation." He shook his head in mock sympathy. "Very troubling past."

Trevor felt his guard rise. "My family's none of your business."

Baptiste smiled at the sharp response. "Your father really *was* the worst kind of bastard, wasn't he? And as one of New Orleans's finest, he was virtually untouchable. It must bother you that he never paid for what he did to you."

His pale eyes gleamed with knowledge. "Tell me, Agent Rivette, how many days were you comatose? They say one's mind is never the same after an event like that. Yet here you are, and looking quite virile if you don't mind me saying so."

Trevor walked to where Baptiste stood. Surprise and anger reverberated through him. "Don't fuck with me."

Baptiste held his hands out in an innocent gesture. "I'm only expressing admiration for your resilience—"

"If you're involved in these murders in any way, I *will* take you down."

"I can only assure you I'm not," he replied mildly. "Now,

if we're done here, I'm expecting a client. You'll give Rain my warmest regards?"

For several seconds, Trevor met the man's self-satisfied stare. Then he turned and left the room.

20

"Uncle Trevor!"

Haley darted toward Trevor when she saw him standing inside the main gallery at Synapse, her shoes squeaking on the polished wood floor that reflected the late-afternoon sun. Trevor's niece had warmed up to him quickly, and her grin was enough to temporarily distract him from the thoughts that had been crowding his head for most of the day. After leaving the antiques firm, he'd sat in on a VCU conference call, then met with two other task force members to look into what had turned out to be a cold lead. But he still couldn't shake the revelation that Armand Baptiste had somehow known about his difficult past. For the past half hour he'd driven around the city, trying to make some sense of it.

"What're you doing here, kiddo?" he asked, scooping Haley up for a hug before returning her to the floor.

"I'm painting." Her small hands went to the paint-splattered smock she wore over her T-shirt and shorts. "Uncle Brian and Uncle Alex have a pretzel and paints for me."

"Not a pretzel. An *easel*," Annabelle corrected, trailing Haley from the hallway. "It keeps her out of my hair while I'm working on the books."

Embracing Trevor, she added, "I'm surprised to see you. Are you done for the day?"

"Is Brian here?"

"He's just finishing up with a client—"

"Is that your gun?" Haley interrupted, staring wide-eyed at the holstered firearm Trevor wore. "Do you shoot people?"

"Not unless I have to," he answered honestly. "And only bad people."

"Is everything okay?" Annabelle asked, frowning as she peered at him. She looked pretty in a floral-print dress, her dark hair pulled back in a low ponytail.

"I'm fine," Trevor replied, although it wasn't how he felt. There was no denying Baptiste had thrown him.

How many days were you comatose? They say one's mind is never the same after an event like that.

Haley tugged at his pants pocket. "Uncle Trevor, do you wanna see my painting?"

"Haley, let him be."

"It's all right," Trevor said. Haley reached for his hand and led him from the gallery to Alex's office. A child-size easel had been set up near the desk where Trevor presumed Annabelle was working.

"I'm impressed." He studied Haley's artwork with a serious eye. She'd painted a square house with bright flowers in front of it and a smiling yellow sun overhead. The drop cloth under the easel was even more colorful, protecting the floor from a kaleidoscope of splatters and drips. "You're as talented as Uncle Brian."

"It's the house where Mommy and I live."

"I recognize it." He looked up, his eyes meeting Annabelle's as Haley chattered about the finer details of the painting. His sister's face appeared hopeful. The cheerful interpretation of their family home seemed to declare the darkness was gone from it now, the bad times faded and replaced with better ones. Memories pulling at him, Trevor glanced away and nodded at the arrangement of spring blossoms next to the computer.

"Nice flowers."

"They're for Mommy," Haley said. "They're from—"

"A friend," Annabelle interjected. She blushed and looked on the verge of saying something more, when Brian appeared. He stood in the doorway with one hand braced casually on its frame as he greeted Trevor.

"Alex is cooking dinner for everyone," he said. "He's making a half ton of paella. Why don't you eat with us, Trev."

Trevor hesitated. "I'd like that. Thanks."

"I'm almost finished with these guys. As soon as they're gone, we'll go upstairs."

Brian left the office, and Trevor slid his hands into his pockets and turned around. The photograph of Rain hung over Alex's desk. It had an artistic style, as if a special lens had been used to soften the focus and give it a dreamlike quality. Rain's eyes in the photo were alluring, their color like sunlight filtered through a jar of honey.

"I saw you watching her at Brian's reception," Annabelle said as she stood beside him.

"I thought we were talking about who sent you flowers."

"I saw her watching you, too, whenever she thought you weren't looking."

Trevor glanced at Haley, who'd picked up her brush and was humming to herself as she placed the finishing touches on her painting.

"She's directly involved in the case," he said, as if that fact was all that was required to negate his feelings.

"I just want you to be happy, Trevor." Annabelle's blue eyes stared into his. "What's wrong? I can see it in your face."

"Nothing's wrong."

"Is it why you came to see Brian?"

He shrugged. "I just thought I'd come by, that's all."

Annabelle looked skeptical. From the gallery, they heard the front door shut. Brian called to them, announcing he was closing up for the night. Trevor went with Annabelle and Haley back out to the front, where Brian was lowering the recessed lighting that illuminated the artwork around the room.

"We're all set," he announced. "Let's go."

With an exaggerated grunt, Brian hauled a giggling Haley up in his grasp, holding her like a football while he set the security system with his free hand.

"If you don't want to talk to me, talk to Brian, okay?" Annabelle urged quietly. She slipped her arm inside Trevor's as they walked to the building's interior lobby to take the elevator upstairs.

Rain lay on the padded mat, attempting to focus on the relaxation pose of *savasana*. But her thoughts remained elsewhere. Not even the monkish chants playing over the yoga studio's intercom could deter her from thinking about what had happened between Trevor and her that morning. Waking up in his arms, being kissed by him like that—the thought of it still sent a spiraling sensation through her. It was a memory she carried with her throughout the day, long after Trevor had driven her home and taken Desiree's rosary with him.

They'd nearly made love. She didn't want to cause more trouble for him, but the passion between them had been undeniable.

Unfortunately, Trevor had left her with her own problems to deal with, including the fact that Oliver Carteris had failed to show up for his scheduled appointment that morning. The yoga class ended, and she rolled up her mat and retrieved her personal belongings from the studio's shelved wall. Rain noticed the blinking light on her cell phone. Had Oliver returned her call?

She checked her messages. But it was from Trevor, reminding her of their bargain. No more watches on the street outside—he'd arranged for a policeman to be stationed directly inside her home beginning that evening. The message was disappointing, since she'd hoped he might take on the task himself. She didn't want a stranger guarding her. But she also understood the heavy responsibility he had, and that her convenience wasn't his first priority.

Rain said goodbye to the regulars in the class. Then she placed the strap of her mat bag over her shoulder and began the short trek home through the Lower Garden District. The sun's intensity had faded as the day turned into evening and a faint breeze stirred the warm air. The broad leaves of banana trees peeped over the houses' private courtyards, and lively zydeco music played from someone's patio.

As she turned the corner onto Prytania, a squad car drove slowly up beside her. The driver's-side window rolled down.

"Everything okay, Dr. Sommers?"

Rain nodded. "Are you the officers staying in the house tonight?"

The young policeman who was driving had auburn hair with long sideburns and a Cajun accent. He shook his head. "No, ma'am. Officer Dumas will be staying with you. He'll be here when you get back from your show."

Rain recognized the two policemen. They were the ones who watched her house during the afternoon. Their cruiser was usually parked underneath the pecan tree on the opposite side of the street.

"Would you like something to drink? Some iced tea or lemonade?"

Both men lifted their cans of soda simultaneously.

"We just made a run to the market around the corner, but thanks," the young man said. "We're gettin' ready to head out for shift change, anyhow."

The second officer who sat on the passenger side was gray-haired, with a mustache and a slight paunch. He touched the bill of his uniform cap in a cordial nod before the vehicle rolled forward.

Rain walked up the short set of stairs to the house's white-columned veranda. As she unlocked the beveled-glass front door, an unfamiliar object caught her eye. An elegantly wrapped box sat against the wrought-iron railing, hidden from street view by an azalea bush. Rain recognized the signature silver wrap and blue satin bow of Mélange, a gift boutique tucked into an exclusive area of the Quarter.

Taking the box inside, she set it on the Queen Anne table in the foyer and removed the bow. The lid lifted off easily. Underneath a lining of tissue paper was a beautiful crystal Lalique vase. A card was also inside—a note from Dr. Carteris offering the vase as a replacement for the one his son had shattered. If Oliver had told his father about the vase, then at least the two were talking, Rain surmised. She hoped Oliver would contact her soon to reschedule his missed appointment before she was forced to report him.

Carrying the vase into the kitchen, Rain set it on the counter and went about making a simple dinner. She took a copper pot from the hanging rack and placed it in the basin, then turned on the faucet to fill it with water for cooking pasta. She clicked on the small kitchen television set to catch the evening news.

Rain didn't hear the creak of the floorboard behind her until it was too late. Her heart lurched as a gloved hand clamped over her mouth and yanked her back against a hard chest. A sinewy forearm locked around her waist, practically lifting her off the ground.

Frantic, she tried to pry the leather-clad fingers from her lips as she was dragged through the arched opening that led from the kitchen. Rain clutched at the doorway, but the man easily broke her hold. In the foyer, she kicked at the Queen Anne table, hoping to knock it over and make some noise the officers might hear, if they were still outside. But the table merely wobbled at her efforts.

He headed with her toward the staircase. To the bedrooms? Cold terror tore at her insides.

As they reached the first step, Rain grabbed onto the banister, gaining enough leverage to wrench free of the man's grip. She bolted, but only got a step away before he was on her again. Her cry for help died abruptly as he fell with her to the parlor's hardwood floor, knocking the air from her lungs.

He flipped her onto her back. Through glazed eyes, she saw a male figure wearing a ski mask so only his eyes and mouth were visible. His irises glowed red through the slits in the mask. Rain stared in disbelief. Images of the dead women in the photos, their necks brutally gouged and their bodies slashed, flashed in her mind. She imagined her own throat filling with blood.

This can't be happening.

She was pinned to the floor under his weight, her shoulder wedged painfully against the door frame at the foot of the stairs.

"Scream again and I'll kill you." His fingers tightened around her neck. He straddled her, his breathing shallow and harsh. He smelled of sweat. Rain knew only one thing—he was going to kill her anyway.

His free hand moved to her yoga pants. The leather gloves were cold against the damp skin of her stomach as he got a strong hold on the waistband and began to tug hard. Sucking in a weak breath, she clawed at him like a trapped animal.

He swore viciously as her nails left angry lines down the side of his neck.

"You fucking bitch!"

He backhanded her across the face. Her vision dimmed and she feared she was about to lose consciousness, then wondered if that might be a blessing, after all. He put a finger to his lips, warning her to be quiet, then went back to work on her clothing. Rain lay stunned as she heard the stretch fabric of her halter top tear.

God, please. No.

Helpless, she turned her head, hot tears leaking from her eyes. Her watery gaze fell on the cast-iron doorstop that kept the mudroom open where Dahlia's litter box was located.

Slowly, Rain inched her hand toward the heavy object shaped in the silhouette of a reclining black cat. The man grunted as he groped her breasts, obviously aroused. She stretched farther, her fingers clumsy with fear before finally closing over the feline's curled tail.

Rain swung the object at the man's head. He must have seen it coming, because he raised his arm to deflect the blow at nearly the same second. He howled as the weight hit his elbow and fell sideways, giving Rain opportunity to push him off and crawl away. Her scream pierced the air as he leaped on her again, slamming her back down to the floor. The man spat a stream of curses. Putrid saliva flowed from his mouth onto her skin. The gloved hand was back around her throat, ending her cries for help.

Rain struggled for breath as his fingers squeezed like iron bands. *She was going to be the next victim. Her house would be the next crime scene.*

Darkness reached out to her, and she went into its arms.

21

"I can do it." Haley looked determined as she attempted to toss the green salad with two wooden paddles.

"I don't know," Trevor said. "That's a pretty big salad."

The bowl was nearly as large as the child. Haley stood on a chair next to the dining room table so she was better positioned for the task. Her tongue darted out from the corner of her mouth in concentration, and Trevor braced his hand against her back so she didn't topple over.

"Great job, sweetie," Brian exclaimed as, job finally completed, she climbed down to the floor. Smiling, she scampered into the kitchen where Alex and Annabelle were preparing the rest of the meal.

"I think there's more salad on the table than in the bowl," Trevor commented once Haley was out of earshot.

Brian scooped up the errant vegetables. "She likes to help. Thank God the table's clean and we're all family."

Over the Latin rhythm coming from a set of wall-mounted speakers, Trevor could hear Annabelle pressing Alex for his paella recipe. His sister's laughter rose musically to the loft's exposed-beam ceiling. He had an empty feeling inside his chest. *This is the part of life I've missed out on.*

Brian handed him a bottled water, interrupting his thoughts. "I've been meaning to ask. What do you think of Alex?"

"I like him," he answered truthfully. He twisted the cap from the bottle. "You seem good together."

"We are. I owe him a lot."

Trevor looked at him for several seconds. "You're really okay this time, aren't you?"

"I'm not going to screw up again, Trev."

He thought of the night he'd taken Brian to the facility in Baton Rouge. He'd returned home at Annabelle's urging to try to talk some sense into his brother. After a day spent looking, he'd found Brian at a friend's apartment, passed out with a needle still stuck in his forearm. Trevor had hauled him into a cold shower, terrified by his recklessness. Then he'd physically forced him into the car and driven straight out of New Orleans. He cringed inwardly at the brutal statements they'd exchanged.

"What I said the night I put you in rehab," he began uncertainly, searching for the right words. "It's no excuse, but my anger got the best of me. I couldn't stand…seeing what you were doing to yourself. You're a talented person, Brian. You were throwing it all away."

"We both said things we didn't mean that night." Brian sounded sincere. "I'm not that person anymore. I hope you can believe me."

By all appearances it was true. In the space of time since Trevor had last seen Brian, he'd somehow managed to turn himself around. If Alex was to thank for that, then he was eternally grateful to him.

"Do you want to tell me what happened at Riverfront Park yesterday?" Brian asked. Trevor rubbed his neck. As far as he was concerned, the subject was closed.

"I know what I saw." He glanced toward the kitchen to make sure Annabelle and Alex were still occupied. "He was there, watching us. It was the same guy who tried to knife me at the Ascension."

"I didn't see anyone," Brian insisted. "That courtyard only had one way in and out—"

"You think I'm seeing things?"

"I think you're under a lot of stress. You said as much yourself. This crazy vampire case you're working, combined with coming back here and seeing Dad again. Maybe it's too much."

Trevor left the bottled water on the table and went to stare out the loft's floor-to-ceiling windows. The sun was setting over the rooftops of the buildings, and in the distance he could see tugboats and steamers as they floated on the Mississippi like ghost ships.

"You've stayed away from here for so long." Brian's reflection appeared in the glass as he stood behind him. "Maybe you're on some kind of sensory overload."

Trevor continued looking out at the panoramic view. "I had a suspect tell me this morning he knew what Dad did to me."

Brian walked up to the window. "How's that even possible?"

He shrugged. He'd been searching for that answer himself. "Maybe he paid off someone in the records room at the NOPD. This guy is some kind of elder in the goth community. Creepy as hell. However he found out, he was obviously trying to rattle me, and it worked."

"That makes no sense. The police records don't say a damn thing about what really happened that day. You know that."

Trevor merely nodded. It was difficult to be around Brian or Annabelle without his mind hurtling back to the shadowed events that had pulled them apart. Even now, he struggled with the decisions he'd made, and their subsequent impact.

"I left you and Annabelle alone," he admitted, finally ready to broach the topic. "But I just couldn't come back here."

Brian's gaze was steadfast. "You didn't have a choice. You were in no condition—"

"I got *better,* Brian. If I'd been here, maybe I could've—"

"What could you have done? Kept me from using? You did come here, and you tried. Several times, in fact. I threw it in your face."

He swallowed a sigh, but his brother wasn't finished. Brian lowered his tone.

"What about Annabelle? Think you could've kept her from slicing her wrists? Or stopped Mom from having that last drink and taking a header down the stairs?"

Trevor closed his eyes, the questions as familiar as his own skin. "I don't know."

"Well, I do. You're just not that powerful, Trev," Brian said softly. "What happened in that house messed all of us up. We've all had to face our own demons."

Annabelle called to them over a clatter of china and silverware, announcing that dinner was about to be served, buffet style from the kitchen. From where Trevor stood, he could see Alex carrying a pot heaped with steaming seafood and rice to one of the marble-topped counters.

"All you ever tried to do was protect us. And we betrayed you for it."

"You told the police exactly what Dad told you to. You were ten years old."

"We let you believe a lie—"

The shrill of Trevor's cell phone cut into Brian's words. With a halfhearted curse, Trevor answered it.

"When?" He clapped a hand over his ear in order to hear the caller above the music and conversation spilling from the kitchen. The words coming through the phone made his heart pound. "Is she okay?"

He asked a few more questions and disconnected the call. "Tell Alex I'm sorry. I can't stay."

"What's happened?"

"It's Rain Sommers. She was assaulted in her home. They've taken her to All Saints."

"God! Alex and I will come, too."

"No. Stay here. I'll call you as soon as I can." Before Brian could ask anything else, he strode across the apartment and let himself out the door.

22

The smell of antiseptic was strong, overpowered only by the noise and rush of activity inside the E.R. Nurses in scrubs called out names and escorted patients to exam bays, and rows of chairs held people waiting for treatment. As Trevor sidestepped an orderly pushing an EKG cart, his gaze fell on a stern-looking African-American woman behind the admissions desk. She was trying to obtain information from a man wearing bib overalls and speaking in a frantic Cajun patois.

Trevor went up to the desk. "I'm looking for a woman brought in earlier—"

The nurse held up a hand, the gesture making it clear she expected him to wait. Her eyes remained on the flustered Cajun. "Sir, I can't understand a thing coming out of your mouth."

Frustrated, Trevor slammed his shield onto the counter. "Rain Sommers. Early thirties, assault victim. Where is she?"

Giving him a wary glance, she adjusted her eyeglasses and consulted the computer screen. "Exam room eight. Follow the markers down the east corridor."

"He's looking for someone, too. His daughter-in-law." Trevor returned the shield to his pocket as he indicated the other man. His grandmother had used the same bayou dialect that was in essence a bastardized French, and he was surprised he could still pick up enough of it to translate. "She was flown here by helicopter after a car accident in Houma. He doesn't think she had identification with her."

"Merci." The man pointed to the screen and looked hopefully at the nurse.

Trevor didn't wait to see if the relative was located. He took off down the hall, scanning the windowed exam rooms as he passed.

"Agent Rivette?" A uniformed officer with graying hair and a mustache spoke to him. Trevor recognized him as one of the policemen assigned to keep watch in Rain's neighborhood during the day.

"What the hell happened?"

"Looked like she was on her way back from yoga class. Even talked to her before she went in the house. He must've already been inside—"

"Did it occur to you to check the house *before* letting Dr. Sommers enter?"

The officer's thick eyebrows clamped down over his eyes. "That wasn't our assignment, Agent. We're only supposed to sit outside and keep an eye out for anything unusual. Look, it was shift change and the only reason we were still out there is that I got a call from central. She's lucky we heard her scream."

After a moment of staring at the officer, Trevor blew out a breath and redirected his anger onto himself. He'd finally gotten Rain to agree to a guard stationed inside the house, but he hadn't scheduled the first shift until that evening. He should have gotten someone over there sooner.

"The perp must've fled out the back door when he heard us coming in through the front," the officer recounted. "We didn't get a look at him. Units are still cruising the area, but he's probably long gone."

"How badly is she hurt?"

"She's a little banged up, but she seems all right." A young auburn-haired officer joined them. "We got inside before too much happened. She might've blacked out for a few seconds, so we brought her in to get checked out, just to be on the safe side."

"Where is she?"

He pointed to an exam room at the end of the hall. "The detectives are with her now."

Trevor walked toward the room, cold fear still balled up inside him. He was all too aware of what could have happened if the officers hadn't forced their way inside when they did. He stopped outside the door, where he could see Rain through a slit in the window's closed curtains. She sat on the thin padding of an exam table, her legs dangling over its side. He swallowed hard at the faint bruises shadowing the slim column of her throat. Trevor passed a hand over his face, trying to keep his emotions in check.

With heavy feet, he moved into the exam room. McGrath was busy lobbing questions at Rain while Thibodeaux scribbled in his ever-present notepad. She lifted her eyes to him. It was as if the composure she'd held on to throughout the ordeal began to crumble. Rain climbed down from the table and went to him, pressing her face against his chest. Trevor closed his arms around her.

"I should've known," she whispered brokenly. "The security system didn't go off when I opened the door. I was distracted and didn't notice…"

"It's okay," he murmured.

He met the detectives' questioning glances over the top of her head. The room fell silent, except for Rain's muffled sobs.

* * *

Trevor stood outside the exam room with McGrath and Thibodeaux while an E.R. physician was inside with Rain. He worked to concentrate on what the detectives had learned so far, but the feel of her trembling in his arms had scattered him into what felt like a dozen pieces.

"All I'm saying is the attack doesn't fit the M.O.," McGrath insisted.

"You mean things like leaving the victim alive? Yeah, I noticed that," Thibodeaux said in his usual caustic manner. "This Dante character is probably ticked as hell the cops interrupted his plans."

Trevor rubbed his forehead. "Was she able to give a description?"

"Caucasian male, wiry build, around five-ten. He was wearing a ski mask." Thibodeaux held up a finger. "And wait for this one. Blood-red eyes. I shit you not."

"Probably Halloween contacts." Trevor had noticed a half-dozen people at the Ascension sporting the gruesome accessory. "Anything else?"

"He had a tattoo around his right forearm that looked like barbed wire," McGrath said. "She scratched his neck pretty good, too. We took a sample from under her nails."

Trevor stared at the closed exam-room door. He was thankful beyond words that Rain had fought her attacker and screamed for help. But something else nagged at him. He couldn't imagine that Dante would have allowed such a mistake. He'd abducted six women without leaving behind a trace. Had he just been supremely unlucky this time?

"The vic indicates her home-security system was engaged when she left earlier this afternoon," Thibodeaux remarked, consulting his notes. "But I spoke with Forensics at the crime scene and they say the wires to the system weren't cut."

"So the assailant knew her pass code?"

"Or she forgot to turn the system on when she left the house and doesn't want to admit it."

"Rain wouldn't lie about that," Trevor said. He didn't miss the look that passed between the two detectives.

There was a pause before McGrath spoke. "If you're staying here, Tibbs and I are going over to the house in the Lower Garden District."

"I'm staying. You guys go ahead."

Thibodeaux stuck the dog-eared notepad in the back pocket of his trousers and glanced at the exam-room window. "She's a little thing. Hard to believe she came out of this in one piece."

His nerves shot, Trevor watched as the men disappeared down the corridor.

Although she didn't look up, Rain felt the weight of Trevor's stare as he entered the room.

"They're going to let me go," she stated softly. "The doctor's working on my discharge papers."

He moved closer, and Rain stared at her hands folded in her lap. Her body was sore, and the significance of what had happened had only begun to sink in.

"Rain…I need to know who has your house's security pass code."

His words caused her to meet his gaze. "You don't think it's someone I know—"

"The system wasn't tampered with. We need to eliminate any possibilities."

She blinked back the ache behind her eyes and tried to think. "There's Alex. And David. There's also a cleaning lady who comes in on Mondays."

And Oliver. Hadn't he used the pilfered pass code less than a week ago to gain access to her home? Rain thought of the barbed-wire tattoo that wrapped around the man's forearm.

She'd have noticed something like that on her patient, she was certain of it. Besides, the height and weight didn't come close to matching Oliver's build.

"Have you given your code to anyone else?"

Rain shook her head. She remained silent as a nurse walked in and handed Trevor several papers, including a prescription for a light sedative, before leaving again. As he helped her slide off the exam table, she was cognizant of her disheveled state. She still wore her yoga clothes, although the halter top was stretched and torn, revealing her lace-edged bra underneath. Her lip throbbed where the man had struck her.

She'd worn a gray zip-up sweatshirt over her top on the way to the hospital. The garment lay across a swivel stool in the corner of the room. Trevor retrieved it and helped her into it, touching her as if she were made of glass. Once the jacket was in place, he carefully zipped it closed. Taking her hands in his, he frowned at her once-manicured nails that were now chipped and broken.

"They took scrapings. They said I probably got his DNA."

Trevor nodded but didn't say anything. When Rain looked into his eyes, she saw guilt reflected there.

"This isn't your fault. You warned me that I should have an officer inside—"

"That doesn't matter now. I'm taking you back to my hotel."

Rain released a shaky breath. "I'm going to the radio station. I'm doing the show tonight."

At first, Trevor appeared stunned into silence. Then he shook his head. "No. Absolutely not."

"I want to talk to that son of a bitch."

"That's not a good idea."

"Why not?"

He raked a hand through his hair, his blue-gray eyes as

dark and turbulent as a stormy sea. "Because he's angry, Rain. The cops messed up his plans, so he's livid right now. You'd only antagonize him by going through with the show."

"You told me before he couldn't reach me through the airwaves—"

"No. Forget it."

"Use me," she urged. "If he's angry, he might let something slip that could lead you to him."

"You've been through too much already."

"I want to go on the air tonight. I need him to know he didn't silence me. What do you have to lose?"

He grasped her arms. The fear in his voice surprised her. "I could lose *you.* Do you have any idea how close you came—"

His words stopped, although she knew what he'd been about to say. Rain was scared, too. But she couldn't stand by and have another female experience the helpless terror she'd felt that afternoon. Dante had to be stopped. She touched Trevor's face and willed him to understand.

"I have to do this," she said. "Unless you plan to physically restrain me, I'm going on the air."

23

Heading down the hallway of the radio station, Rain could see Ella inside the broadcast booth. She lounged in Rain's chair at the console, wearing a set of headphones and adjusting the microphone.

"I was just...doing a sound check," she stammered when Rain appeared in the doorway. Tugging at her short skirt, she rose from the chair. "We didn't think you'd make it in tonight—"

"Well, I'm here."

"But Agent Rivette contacted us from the hospital. He said—"

"Rain?" David strode down the corridor. His eyes swept over her bedraggled appearance, and she self-consciously pushed back the hair that hung limply around her face.

"Jesus, Rain." He whirled on Trevor, who'd walked in from the reception area behind her. "She's got bruises on her throat! Where the hell were you?"

"He isn't my bodyguard," Rain interjected, but David continued his rant.

"Let me get this straight. She nearly gets killed today, and you manage to drag her back in here? Don't tell me you're planning to put her on the air—"

"For the record, I'm against this, D'Alba."

"Sure you are," David scoffed. "Whatever it takes to get your man, right?"

"So I'm *not* going on tonight?" Ella asked. Rain looked at David, unable to hide her surprise. When she'd said he should let Ella do the show, she hadn't expected him to take her seriously.

"Arbitron sweeps start this week," he explained. "A live show does better than a previously aired segment. Ella's a little green, but she's got talent. She's been taking night classes in speech and broadcasting, and I've been training her to act as a backup for a while now. Considering what happened today, I didn't think you'd be here."

"I'm doing the show, David," Rain insisted. "I have to. And I've got less than a half hour to prepare myself."

He studied her face. Then clearing his throat, he said, "Ella."

A pout formed on Ella's mouth. "But you promised—"

"Some other time." Once the woman had stomped away, David released a breath. "Don't disappoint me. I need a solid show tonight."

Rain nodded her understanding. She went into the booth and sat in front of the console. But despite her attempt to focus, she could still hear the two men in the hallway.

"How badly was she hurt?" David asked.

"Some minor cuts and bruises. The cops broke in before it got any worse."

"They get a make on the guy?"

"Nothing beyond race and height. He had on a ski mask."

Rain didn't glance up, but she could sense David's eyes on her through the window. Her chest constricted at his next words.

"No matter what you think, this goes beyond business,

Leslie Tentler

Rivette. I do care about her." He paused. "I wonder if you can say the same."

David's footsteps echoed down the hall. When Rain finally raised her eyes from the monitor, she saw Trevor watching her, his expression tense. He placed his palm on the window in a sign of support and left her to prepare for the show.

The wit and candor that were the hallmarks of *Midnight Confessions* were there, making it sound to the listening audience as if nothing was out of the ordinary. Physically, however, the night was taking its toll on Rain. As she chatted over the air, as minutes of airtime stretched into hours, a single thought repeated itself in her head.

Call me, you bastard.

At a break in the live show, a song played out over the airwaves. Rain briefly covered her face with her hands. Five innocuous callers so far, including a transgender teen who was being bullied at school. She took a sip of water from the glass on the console, relieved her hand didn't shake.

"Rain? We can stop this anytime you want."

Trevor's voice came over her headset, and she met his gaze through the window. Even with his presence, she felt like a lamb tethered to a post, waiting for the wolf to emerge. But it had been her idea to do this and she wasn't backing down now.

"I'm okay," she replied. Overhead, the on-air light began to blink out its thirty-second warning.

"We've got another call queued on line two." This time it was David who spoke. He sat next to Trevor in the production room. "A college coed who's thinking about moonlighting as a stripper to pay tuition. In her own words, 'Mandy's got a rockin' bod and doesn't see why she shouldn't cash in.'"

Rain made her decision in the final seconds before the show returned. This had to come to a head now.

"We're back with *Midnight Confessions*. I'm Dr. Rain Sommers," she announced in a confident tone that belied her unease. "Before we go to our next caller, I have some advice for a special listener."

She pretended not to notice the way Trevor leaned forward in his chair, a look of caution in his eyes.

"Dante, I want you to know you don't have to be ashamed. Erectile dysfunction is a common problem for many men…"

Ella stood behind Trevor and David, and her clipboard clattered to the production room floor. She stared at Rain in open horror as David mouthed the words *holy shit* at her through the glass window.

"Rain, what the hell are you doing?" Trevor wanted to know.

"If you're listening, Dante, why don't you give me a call? We can bone up on your treatment options. No pun intended, of course. I'm waiting to hear from you."

She pressed the button on the interface and put the would-be stripper on the air. "Dr. Sommers, my name's Mandy and I'm a sophomore at NOU. Guys are always telling me I've got a really great body and I've been thinking…"

It was nearly five minutes later when Rain pushed the microphone away with a frustrated shove. She removed her headset and tossed it onto the console. Despite her taunt, Dante hadn't surfaced.

"Want to tell me what that was about?" Trevor leaned against the door frame. She'd seen him leave his post in the production room when the call with the college student ended and David cut to a block of ad spots.

"That was me, pushing the warp-speed button," she admitted miserably.

Trevor appeared calmer than he did earlier, although admonishment still shone in his eyes. He continued standing in the doorway for several seconds, then walked in and pulled up a chair beside her. "I wouldn't have agreed to this if I thought you were going to bait him. What you did was dangerous."

"I want an end to this, Trevor. Before he kills anyone else. I thought if I made him angry enough, he might not take the time to use a voice disguiser or a prepaid cell phone. Maybe he'd call directly from a landline, so you could trace his location."

"So you question his ability to…" Trevor failed to finish his statement. Instead, he shook his head. "Next time, could you let me in on the plan, so I can stop you?"

"I didn't have a plan. I was improvising."

"Why doesn't that surprise me?"

Rain rested her head against his shoulder. She was exhausted, and her body ached from the attack. Her memory of the event slammed into her. When she'd started to lose consciousness on the parlor floor, Rain recalled now that her last thoughts had been about Trevor. He'd have blamed himself for whatever happened to her.

"There's a caller on one of the private lines." David's voice broke in over the intercom, causing Rain to look up.

"Is it him?"

"He won't identify himself, but it sounds like him. He wants to talk to you, but he won't go on the air."

Rain's heart rate accelerated. "Put him through."

"No way. I want this conversation on air—"

"Put him through, D'Alba." Trevor stood as he seconded the demand. "Now."

Rain stared at the flashing light on the console as if it were a ticking clock attached to a bomb. Wasn't this what she'd wanted? She heard Trevor behind her, talking into his cell phone about needing a trace. Rain counted silently backward from ten before putting the call on speakerphone.

"This is Dr. Sommers."

"Apparently you wished to speak with me tonight." Dante's voice was controlled, but anger churned beneath its surface. "I don't appreciate your idea of a joke, my dear. Perhaps you'd like me to prove to you just how wrong your estimation of my ability is?"

"You had that chance this afternoon."

There was a short pause. "I'm sure I don't have the slightest idea what you're talking about."

"You broke into my home and tried to—" She closed her eyes, the words catching in her throat. "But you didn't get to follow through with your plans, did you? When the police showed up, you ran like the coward you are."

He actually laughed, a sound that made the fine hairs on her nape rise.

"Someone's playing a terrible trick on you." There was a dead calm to his demeanor, as oppressive as the slow boil of a Louisiana thunderstorm. "Let's be clear on one thing. If I was interested in cutting your pretty throat, I could've done it a dozen times by now."

Rain swallowed her fear. Dante was draining her courage as easily as he'd drained the blood from his victims.

"I don't plan to kill you, little one," he conceded. "Unless, of course, you force me to."

"And why is that?" Rain asked on a trembling sigh. She looked at Trevor as he closed the cell phone. The hard set of his features offered her little hope. "After you've killed six women, what makes me so special?"

"Because you belong to me, Desiree. You always have."

She was uncertain how long she sat there, but Trevor reached over and pressed the button on the phone's interface, ending the white noise of the disconnected call.

"Please tell me you got something."

He didn't mince words. "The call came from the French Quarter, somewhere on Bourbon Street. There're a string of conventions in town this week. It would be next to impossible to find him in the crowds."

Rain thought of Dante among the throngs of revelers. She tried to imagine him strolling around in a sea of madras shorts and Tipitina's T-shirts, blending in with the tourists and conventioneers sporting cheap plastic-bead necklaces and go-cups filled with beer.

"Did he use a cell phone?"

"It belonged to Rebecca Belknap, the last victim." Trevor's eyes were resolute. "He's probably discarded it by now, but I'll put the uniforms in the area on alert. If we find it, we might be able to lift some prints or at least pinpoint the location of the call. The wireless operator is checking to see if the phone was used any other time during the last forty-eight hours."

She'd been speaking to the killer from her dead patient's phone. Rain pulled her sweatshirt tighter around herself as she came to terms with that piece of information. "He said he didn't do it. Is he lying?"

"If he isn't the one who attacked you, it would explain some things. Like why the perpetrator didn't have a knife."

And why I'm still alive, Rain thought. The events of the day were closing in on her, and she exhaled on a quiet sob. He'd called her Desiree. This ordeal was far from over.

She felt Trevor's hands on her arms as he coaxed her from the chair. Rain stood and leaned against his chest.

"The show's not done yet," she whispered.

"It is for you. I'm getting you out of here."

24

Each time the Taurus passed under a street lamp in the Lower Garden District, its interior was illuminated in a wash of tepid light before being quickly submerged again in shadow. The interspersed light and dark reminded Rain of a camera shutter, its rapid click attempting to capture her emotions. But it simply wasn't possible. She was an empty shell, devoid of feeling. The events of the day had left her numb.

"You okay?"

Trevor watched her from the driver's side of the car. Rain nodded in response to his question, although her eyes didn't falter from the road. She'd insisted on returning to her home before the memory of what had happened there chased her away for good. Sitting mutely, she listened as he used his cell phone to confirm that Forensics was done with the crime scene.

The crime scene.

The phrase rolled around inside her head as the vehicle went past the shadow of trees in Coliseum Square. When they reached the house, Trevor parked against the curb. True to its word, the forensics team appeared to have vacated. There were no vans or jumpsuited technicians anywhere in sight. But as they climbed the steps onto the veranda, Rain could see a uniformed police officer through the window, sitting on the parlor's chintz-covered sofa. He was a large man and he looked out of place against the buttery floral print and striped throw pillows. The officer got up and greeted them at the door. Rain acknowledged him with only a weak smile, her eyes moving to the spot at the foot of the staircase where only a few hours earlier, she'd been certain she was about to die.

She left Trevor talking to the officer and escaped upstairs. In the bedroom, Rain looked at her image in the oval mirror above the antique dresser. Her hair, lifeless and flat, provided a fitting frame for her red-rimmed eyes and pale face. She raised a hand to touch the bluish bruises on her neck.

If I was interested in cutting your pretty throat, I could've done it a dozen times by now.

Rain went into the adjoining bathroom and turned on the shower. Discarding her clothes in a heap on the floor, she stepped into the rising steam. She pressed her forehead against the cool tiles of the stall and allowed the jets to work against her sore muscles.

He'd called her Desiree. A madman obsessed with a singer who'd been dead for thirty years had taken over her life. Rain stayed under the showerhead until the pads of her fingers pruned.

She'd just drawn the sash of a chenille bathrobe around herself when she heard a knock at the bedroom door. Outside, a car started its engine and drove away.

"Rain? It's me."

She called for Trevor to come inside. He'd brought fresh clothes with him, she knew, in a duffel bag he kept on the ready in the sedan's trunk. But she saw he hadn't yet changed. Instead, the tie that had been hanging loosely around his neck had disappeared, and his blue dress shirt was pulled free from the dark suit pants. His service gun, however, remained holstered at his side.

"Officer Dumas was more than happy to go home to his wife," he said quietly. "I told him I'd call his lieu at the precinct, let him know of the change in arrangements."

"Thank you for staying." Rain ran her hands through her damp hair. "I didn't want a stranger here. Not tonight."

He held a glass tumbler filled with water, as well as a plastic vial containing the prescription sedative they'd had filled on their way back from the radio station. He waited while she took one of the pills before giving her the water to wash it down. Once she was done, he took both items and placed them on the nightstand.

"Do you want something to eat? I could make you an omelet."

Rain shook her head, although she was appreciative of the gesture. "Please make yourself something, though. You must be starving."

He didn't answer. Trevor went to the window and stared out through the gap in the gauzy curtains.

"You told me to take more precautions," she reminded somberly.

"I should've *made* you take more precautions."

"What could you have done? Lock me in a tower somewhere?"

He turned toward her, his gaze without rancor. "Knowing my luck, you would've just made a rope out of the bedsheets and shimmied down."

"Probably." Rain slid her hands into the pockets of her robe, pausing before delivering the question weighing on her mind. "How is it possible the person who attacked me might *not* be Dante?"

"He could be lying," Trevor theorized. "Especially since the police foiled him in the act. Something like that would be a blow to his ego. There's also the chance it was a coincidence. A random burglary gone awry, although I doubt that's the case."

He paced the bedroom. "Whatever happened today, it changes everything. You're going to have to take this threat seriously from now on. You were lucky tonight, Rain. You fought him and you screamed, and someone was outside to hear you."

She didn't put up an argument. Their eyes locked for several moments, and then Trevor's shoulders slumped in a sigh. "I'll let you get some sleep. The sedative should help."

Rain touched his shirt as he walked past.

"Where will you be?" She sounded ridiculous, she knew, like a child afraid of monsters lurking under the bed.

"I'm going downstairs to make sure everything's locked up tight."

"What about the front door? The police broke the lock—"

"It's already been repaired. I'm going to change your pass code, too."

He stood there for several moments, the intensity of his eyes pulling at her like a storm tide on sandy beach. She wanted to beg him not to leave the room, but instead she took a weak breath and nodded.

Waiting until he'd closed the door behind him, Rain changed into a short, silk nightgown and turned down the bed's coverlet. Her bones heavy, she climbed underneath the cool touch of sheets and fell almost instantly asleep.

She'd left on the tulip lamp beside the bed. But when Rain awoke, its dusky yellow glow had been extinguished. The bedroom was bathed in shadow, the house quiet and the sky outside still black. Calling softly for Trevor in the darkness, Rain pushed back the covers and got out of bed. She felt the chill of the house's air conditioner on her limbs as she went into the hall.

She found him downstairs, sitting on the cushioned seat of the bay window in the parlor. A contented Dahlia was curled up and purring beside him. Trevor's feet were bare, and he wore jeans and a white T-shirt that stood out against the moonlight pouring through the window. He watched as she approached. Rain wrapped her arms around herself, aware she hadn't taken time to put on a robe over the delicate gown.

"I made coffee." His voice was roughened from several hours of disuse, and he lifted the cup in his hand to show her. Rain noticed his gun tucked into the pillows piled against the back of the window seat. She wondered if he'd slept any, then realized with some guilt that staying up all night was probably an essential part of pulling guard duty.

"What time is it?"

"A little after five." He stroked Dahlia's head as he spoke. "I checked on you earlier. You were out like a light."

He must have turned off the lamp beside her bed. The thought of him watching over her as she slept made her heartbeat quicken. She gazed at him as he sipped from the cup, his lean, masculine fingers curling around the fine bone china.

"I had a bad dream," she admitted softly. "I think it woke me up."

"I'm not surprised." He set the cup on the window ledge. Exhaling, Trevor leaned forward on the seat and bowed his head. Displeased with the change in position, Dahlia rose and stretched, then jumped to the floor and padded off toward the kitchen.

"What you went through in this room," he said finally, making a small, helpless gesture with his hands. "If anything had happened to you—"

She stopped him. "It didn't."

"I'm supposed to keep an emotional distance for this very

reason." Trevor swallowed hard, and his words lowered to a whisper. "But I haven't been able to, Rain…not where you're concerned."

Moved by his confession, she inched closer to him until her legs brushed the coarse denim of his jeans. Trevor looked up at her as the silence deepened around them in the room's shadows. The need built in her to be held by him, feeling almost like a physical ache. Standing, he slowly reached out to run his thumb over her cheek. Rain's fingers encircled his wrist. She wanted him so badly, she realized, needed his mouth and his body to distract her, if only for a little while.

"I need to forget what happened here," she said, her voice shaking. "Help me do that, Trevor. Please."

She turned her head to place a kiss against the palm that cradled her face, causing Trevor to release a ragged, uneven breath. Trevor smoothed her sleep-tousled hair.

"Rain," he whispered. "I've wanted you…I do want you."

"Then make love to me. I don't care about your job or anything else. Not tonight."

He slowly lowered his head, his lips finding hers. His mouth was warm and tasted faintly of the chicory-laced coffee. He hesitated for a few brief seconds before allowing his hands to glide over the gown's silk. She felt their heat as they came to rest at her hips. When the kiss ended, she stared up at him and saw that same internal struggle reflected in his eyes. For a moment, she feared he might put a stop to things now, as he had done in the past. But a sigh escaped him as his mouth took hers again, this time more hungrily than before. For a time, they continued kissing in the darkness, their hands touching and exploring one another as their lips and tongues mingled. Rain's breathing became jagged, matching Trevor's own shallow rasps. She skimmed her fingers under his T-shirt and began lifting it, hungry for the warmth of his skin.

"Not so fast," Trevor murmured. He moved with her, backing her against the parlor wall, until she was trapped there, his body pressing into hers. His lips were hard and firm. Demanding. Rain clutched at his shoulders, melding into him. She shivered as Trevor's hand ran up her bare thigh, leisurely stroking and caressing, moving slowly higher until his fingers slid under the elastic of the lace panties she wore.

"Trevor," she moaned, panting against his ear when he stroked her moist heat. She gasped and arched as he dipped a finger inside her. Rain felt her core tighten, her body go weak.

"God," he uttered, hoarse. "God, Rain."

She was wet for him, wetter than she had ever been in her life.

His mouth took a path along her throat and shoulders, tasting her. He cupped her small breasts through her nightgown, massaged them, teasing her nipples into hard peaks. Rain wanted him to take her now against the wall, drive himself into her for his pleasure. She rubbed against his hardness.

"I need you," she begged again, breathless. "Please, Trevor."

"Not like this." Desire shone in his eyes. "Upstairs."

Wordlessly, he lifted her, making her feel protected and weightless. She wrapped her arms around his neck, pressing her lips against his jaw as he carried her up the staircase to her bedroom. Once they stood in its threshold, he lowered her feet to the floor.

"Are you sure about this?" he asked, voice low. He took care in brushing the silken strands of her hair back from her face, his tenderness making her heart constrict. "After what happened today, maybe—"

Rain covered his lips with her fingers, hushing him. She wanted nothing to come between them, to diminish the craving they both felt. Taking his hand, she led him to the tangle of sheets she'd abandoned earlier in search of him.

Trevor drew the gown's thin straps down her shoulders. She felt herself tremble as the fabric pooled around her waist before dropping to the floor, leaving her naked and exposed to him. He molded his hands to the soft curves of her breasts.

"You're beautiful," he whispered. Trevor lowered her to the bed, and she let go of a quavering breath as his body levered over hers. Breathing in his warm scent, she marveled at the feel of him—his strength, the sheer power of hard muscles under soft skin. Trevor took one of her nipples into his mouth, his hot tongue causing her to writhe underneath him. His teeth raked over the delicate bud, gently biting. Rain moaned as he drew her farther into his mouth. She felt herself implode at the feel of him sucking her, first one breast and then the other.

He worked his way leisurely down her frame—tasting her skin as the rough stubble on his jaw sent erotic chills careening through her. Moving lower still, he dragged the small scrap of lace panties from her, his hands spreading her thighs. She was completely open to him, accessible. Rain's hands tightened in his dark hair as he continued his exploration, savoring her core.

Her climax was almost immediate, and so hard that she was left breathless, repeating his name like a prayer.

After several incredible moments, he raised himself onto his knees. Trevor pulled the T-shirt over his head. His shoulders were broad and toned.

Her eyes heavy-lidded, Rain was vaguely aware of the wallet he took from his back pocket, and the condom he extracted from it. He removed the rest of his clothing and prepared himself for her.

"You're so small. I don't want to hurt you," he murmured.

Rain felt the weight of his body settle over hers again. "You'd tell me?"

She nodded faintly. Her fingers trailed over the fine planes of his face as he pushed slowly into her. There was no pain, only the deep sensation of being filled by him. His mouth slaked across hers, claiming her, as his hands anchored into her hair that spilled across the pillow behind her head. Trevor drove into her over and over, each thrust making her breath catch with sensation. They were joined and for this single moment of time, one. From the window, pale moonlight snaked into the bedroom. It slanted across the bed and their sweat-glistened bodies as their pace quickened, growing more urgent. Rain let herself fall headfirst into the world Trevor created for her, pleasure blotting out every thought but for their lovemaking.

She lay in the circle of Trevor's arms, her fingers stroking the side of his face. A silvery gray had begun to replace the night sky, and a lone bird warbled in the olive tree outside her bedroom.

"You never really told me how this happened," Rain said quietly, touching the healing cut on his forehead.

"I wasn't watching where I was going. Nothing more exotic."

"What about this?" Her fingers moved to the faded scar that ran across his chin. Gently, he captured her hand in his own, bringing it down to his chest. Seconds passed before he spoke.

"I was ten or eleven. My father was drunk. He was going after Brian for spilling milk in the kitchen, and I got between them."

Rain lifted her head. She recalled what Alex had told her, about Trevor's father being an abusive son of a bitch. "He hit you?"

"He shoved me into the counter. I caught the corner of it." His features were impassive as he used his thumb to trace small circles over the back of her hand. Rain felt anger and sympathy for what he'd gone through.

"Where was your mother?"

"There wasn't anything she could do. She was afraid of him herself."

"She could have gone to the police."

He looked into her eyes. "James Rivette *was* the police, Rain. Sixteen years with the NOPD before he was fired for misconduct. My mother called the cops to the house *once*. He made sure she never did it again."

"What happened?"

"She spent the night in jail. When they let her out, my father beat the hell out of her all over again."

Rain fell silent. She pressed her lips against Trevor's shoulder. "I'm sorry. Do you ever see him? Your father?"

He shook his head. "At least not on purpose."

Downstairs, the grandfather clock in the parlor chimed in low tones, announcing the early hour. Trevor slid his fingers through her hair. "As long as we're making confessions, want to tell me why you're unable to drive a car?"

Rain sighed in the darkness, aware it was her turn to share.

"I was fifteen and Aunt Celeste was teaching me to drive. I wanted to get my learner's permit. We were taking practice circles around the block, and the neighbor's dog ran out in front of me. A little blond cocker spaniel named Trixie that I loved. I ran over her. She was stuck underneath the wheels."

She felt a lump form in her throat. "I can still hear her howling in pain while Celeste tried to get her out. We rushed her to the vet, but she died on the way. I was never able to drive again after that. Every time I tried, I'd end up sitting on the side of the road with my heart racing like a freight train, afraid to go farther."

For a moment, she thought he might dismiss her story or try to minimize it in some way. But he lifted her chin and kissed her, as if trying to push away the hurtful memory.

"Thank you," Rain murmured. "For being here tonight."

"I meant what I said, Rain. I don't ever want to hurt you."

Don't think, she wanted to say, aware of the worries mounting again behind his eyes. She needed to cling to this moment a little longer, before reality came crashing back in on them. Tugging the sheet higher, she turned on her side and snuggled against him. Trevor's breath was warm on her skin.

"Close your eyes," he whispered. Their shared body heat enticed her back to sleep.

25

He'd recited the Act of Contrition over and over, as a child.
He recalled the voice speaking right along with his, filling
in the gaps whenever he forgot a word.

O, my God
I am heartily sorry for
having offended Thee
and I detest all my sins.

But now the prayer weakened and died, strangled from his
throat as if by unseen hands. He didn't want this blood-thirst
anymore. It didn't come naturally to him, nor was he able to
easily slough away the guilt.

Despite these feelings, the voice was calling for him again.
It demanded his presence. He left the beads on the cool marble
floor as he rose from his knees and clapped his hands over his
ears. More than anything, he wanted to silence the voice.

For a time, he'd slipped into the raven night, losing himself
in the dim, ancient alleyways and smoke-filled clubs. He'd
become one with the dancers thrashing under pulsing black
lights. *Poseurs, all of them,* he thought darkly, with their dyed

hair and grotesque daydreams of violence and vampires. They had no idea how fucking real it could get.

It would be morning soon. But here, the music still played, the same endless vinyl record, and the smell of perfumed candle wax permeated the room. There was no escape, he realized.

I detest all my sins.

Closing his eyes, he felt lost. He didn't know who he was anymore, except for one of the damned.

26

The phone's insistent ring nudged Rain from sleep. She stretched out her arm and felt for Trevor's presence, but found only an empty mattress. Blinking against the morning light, she picked up the handset.

"Dr. Sommers, this is Art Donovan with the Associated Press. I'd like to talk to you about *Midnight Confessions* and the alleged serial killer you've been speaking with on air—"

Rain slammed down the phone and sat up, pulling the sheets around her naked body. If she had been drowsy when she'd answered, she was wide awake now. No one outside law enforcement was supposed to know about the connection between the serial-murder investigation and her radio show. Retrieving a short silk robe that matched the gown she'd worn the night before, Rain went downstairs in search of Trevor. Rounding the corner into the dining area, however, she nearly ran into the broad back of a uniformed officer who was helping himself to coffee from the French press. He turned, nearly as surprised to see her.

"Morning, ma'am." The bar pin over his shield was inscribed with the name J. Arseneau. A sandy-haired male in his early twenties, he blushed at Rain's state of undress. She tightened the robe's sash around her waist.

"I made fresh coffee. Hope that's okay?"

"Of course." Rain felt cool air on her bare legs and stepped behind one of the chairs, out of his direct line of view. "Where is Agent Rivette?"

The officer poured a shocking amount of sugar into one of the Wedgwood cups.

"Spoons are in the drawer to your right."

"Thanks." He got one out and stirred the cup's contents, awkwardly bumping his holstered gun against the Chippendale sideboard in the process. "Agent Rivette left at seven this morning, soon as I got here to take over his watch. You know, my grandmère always used a French press for coffee. Gives it a richer taste."

Rain hadn't heard Trevor leave, hadn't felt the mattress shift as he left her alone in bed. Glancing into the parlor, she thought of his mouth on hers and the hard feel of his body as he held her.

"They say any publicity's good publicity, right?"

She realized she hadn't been listening to the officer, but his last words made her return her gaze to him. "Excuse me?"

"The paper says this psycho's been stalking you for a while now." He blew on the dark surface of his coffee before taking a sip. "But you've got nothing to worry about with me around. I scored in the top five percent of the academy on marksmanship, top ten percent in hand-to-hand combat. He won't come back around here unless he wants an ass kickin'."

Rain moved her gaze to the table, where the black ink of the headline stood out against the dull gray of the morning newspaper:

Serial Killer Stalks Host of Late-Night Radio Show.

She took the paper upstairs to her bedroom. It was all there in print, from details of the FBI surveillance on *Midnight*

Confessions, to excerpts of her conversations with Dante on the air. Rain rubbed her forehead as she read about the attack in her home, as well as speculation that it was the killer, who'd intended to make her his next victim before being thwarted by police. There was also a sidebar that rehashed her parents' violent murder-suicide thirty years earlier. The piece included a photo of Rain, a publicity shot taken for *Midnight Confessions,* next to a look-alike image of Desiree. The caption read, Déjà Vu: Daughter of Murdered Singer Nearly Becomes a Victim Herself.

Rain jumped when the phone on the nightstand rang for the second time that morning. She viewed it suspiciously—her number was unlisted, but it hadn't kept the AP reporter from locating her.

The Associated Press. The newswire's interest meant the story wasn't just local; it was being picked up for national release. This time, she looked at the caller ID on the handset before answering. The number was one she recognized.

"Rain, I'm sending a car for you. We need you at the studio."

Shoving her hair from her face, Rain glanced out the window. There were two vans parked across the street, the closest of which had WKOL-TV, The News You Need to Know across its side in bold print. Two cameramen and a reporter loitered in the shade of the pecan tree.

"I'm not coming in, David."

"Don't pull this shit, Rain. I've got freaking CNN calling—"

"Did you leak the story?" She closed her eyes, already knowing the answer.

"Who the hell cares? The point is, it's out now. This Dante nutcase is obsessed with you. He tried to kill you yesterday. It's a public-interest story and the media's all over it. I already got a call this morning from *People* magazine. I can't buy publicity like this and I'm not going to let you ruin it for me."

"I'm not talking to anyone. We don't even know for certain if it was Dante who attacked me last night."

"Here's the deal. You're still under contract, the terms of which include promotional appearances for *Midnight Confessions*."

"This is hardly a promotional appearance—"

"Be at the studio in one hour or consider your resignation tendered. Everyone's replaceable. Even you."

The line went dead, and Rain returned the handset to the console. She'd wanted out of her contract, hadn't she? Still, the idea that David had leaked the story in an attempt to gain publicity for *Midnight Confessions* astounded her. Rain thought of Trevor. The story was no doubt causing problems for him. While there had already been media reports about a purported serial killer in New Orleans, the increased publicity would further fuel public attention and increase pressure to find the culprit. Unfortunately, as Desiree Sommers's daughter, her involvement made the story doubly sensational. She retrieved the handset and dialed Trevor's cell phone, but got his voice mail. Rain left a message asking him to call.

By the time she'd showered and dressed, she still hadn't heard from him. She was about to try his cell phone again when a commotion broke out downstairs. Raised voices competed with the high-pitched blare of the security system before the noise was extinguished. Cautiously, Rain opened the door to the bedroom. She peered over the railing to see Officer Arseneau pinning Oliver against the wall despite the younger man's howls of protest.

He was dragging Oliver's hands behind his back and trying to cuff him, when Rain made it down the staircase.

"Let go of him!" she yelled, afraid the officer wouldn't

be able to hear her over Oliver's scathing curses. "He's one of my patients!"

Although Oliver was nearly as tall as the officer, the uniformed man was more muscular and, true to his word, well trained. When the teen tossed off a hostile *fuck you,* the officer kicked the back of his knees. Oliver dropped to the floor with a painful grunt.

"That's enough," Rain pleaded.

"Snotty son of a bitch—sorry, ma'am—came through the back door like he owned the place." The officer replaced the handcuffs on his belt and rested his right hand against the gun on his waist. "He jimmied the lock. I caught him trying to disarm the security system he set off. He's lucky I didn't shoot him."

"You'll be lucky if I don't sue you for police brutality!" Oliver picked himself up. His black hair hung across his eyes and his mouth was a grim line. He pushed the long sleeves of his black T-shirt back up to his elbows, their angular points reddened by carpet burn from the rug.

Rain moved toward him. Although he wasn't physically injured, it was clear his pride was hurt. His face looked even more bloodless and pale than usual. There was also a glassy sheen to his eyes.

"What the hell is *he* doing here?" Oliver demanded.

"Someone broke into my house yesterday." Rain peered at him. "Are you okay?"

"I needed to see you." He yanked at his greasy hair. Glaring at the officer, he added, "Alone."

She stretched out her hand. "Let's go into my office."

"That's not a good idea, ma'am." Officer Arseneau grabbed Oliver by the collar and hauled him backward. "This kid's high as a Georgia pine. Not to mention he just assaulted a police officer. I'll lay you ten to one he's carrying narcotics. Want to empty your pockets for me, son?"

Oliver jerked free. "Screw you! I don't need this!"

"Oliver, please—"

Giving the finger to Officer Arseneau, he stormed out the front door. Rain followed him onto the veranda and called after him as he retreated down the stairs. But the news crew across the street snapped to attention, prohibiting her from going farther. Defeated, she went back inside.

The reporters in the WNOR reception area shouted his name, but Trevor ignored them as he went past. A press conference had been scheduled for noon involving the local FBI, NOPD and the D.A.'s office. The newshounds could wait until then to assail him with their questions.

Ella met him in the hallway outside David's office. "You can't go in there."

He ignored her as well, brushing past and slamming the door closed behind him. David was on the phone, his feet propped up on his desk as he leaned back in the leather executive chair. He didn't seem surprised by Trevor's appearance and continued talking to whoever was on the other end of the line.

Reaching over, Trevor yanked the phone console's cord from the wall. David's loafers dropped from the desk with a thud as he glowered at him.

"Do you have any idea who I was talking to?"

"I don't give a damn. I know you leaked the story, D'Alba. I already talked to the reporter at the *Times-Picayune,* who's claiming an anonymous source. But the guy had dubs from the shows Dante called into. No one else could have given him those."

David raised his shoulders in an innocent shrug. "I give out audio segments all the time. It's good business."

"And the attack on Rain? I guess you're going to say you didn't fill him in on that."

With a smug expression, David rose and walked to the other side of his desk. He sat down on its corner and crossed his arms over his chest. "Let's say I did tip off the media. As a broadcast medium, WNOR is free from prior restraint. I've done nothing wrong. I'm just helping disseminate the news."

"What you're doing is jeopardizing a serial-murder investigation—all for a little publicity," Trevor countered fiercely. "It's practically guaranteed the unsub won't be calling back in here now, shutting down one of the best leads we've had—"

"It's not my fault you haven't been able to do your job and catch this bastard, Rivette."

A knock at the door interrupted them. Ella stuck her head inside the office. "David, I've got the latest draft of the press release. I had Marketing rework my bio like you said."

Sashaying in, she handed him several sheets of paper, then massaged his shoulders as he looked them over. Ella wore a scarf halter top and low-rider slacks paired with metallic thong sandals. She flashed Trevor a barracuda smile.

"I'm taking over for Rain," she announced. "Did you hear? She resigned this morning. The poor thing's too traumatized to continue with the show. It looks like I'll be talking to Dante from now on, Agent Rivette."

Trevor stared at her. "Do you really think he's going to want to talk to you?"

Ella looked perplexed.

"Take the release back to Marketing and tell them it's good to go," David instructed her. "See if they can get it on the wire before lunch."

He waited until she'd left the office before speaking again. "You see, I really do care about Rain. Which is why I'm letting her out of her contract three months early without suing her little ass."

"Let me guess," Trevor said. "You're going to use the media attention to announce Ella as the new host of *Midnight Confessions*."

"I'm a survivor. I won't apologize for that."

Trevor stepped forward. "Listen to me. You've screwed up this investigation all you're going to. If I so much as hear Ella say the name Dante on the air, I'll get an injunction from the municipal judge. You can scream freedom of the press all you want, but it'll take weeks to get the restriction lifted. Time your precious show will be off the air."

He headed toward the door when David's words stopped him. "You're fucking her, aren't you?"

Trevor turned and looked at the other man, who had a razor-thin smile.

"She's sweet, isn't she?" His eyebrows raised. "A bit small for my tastes, but that means she's nice and tight where—"

He barely realized he was moving. Trevor grabbed him by the shirt and pinned him against the wall, bracing his forearm across the other man's throat. David wheezed and attempted to draw in air. Seconds passed before Trevor pushed away, leaving David clutching his throat as he bent his knees and slid down to the floor. Tears squeezed from the corners of his eyes.

And then he started to laugh.

Trevor exhaled sharply, the quick burst of anger leaving him stunned. The room's colors seemed to run together, gunmetal gray and burnt sienna conspiring with the bland oatmeal walls and carpet. Muttering under his breath, he stalked out.

27

Removing the glasses she'd been wearing for computer work, Rain stared out her office window. A wash of lavender sky was visible above the brick wall enclosing the house's rear courtyard, while the intermittent sparks of fireflies dotted the dusk.

Despite the tranquil setting, Rain's mood at the end of the day was anything but calm. Although the news vans outside had disappeared, she still felt as if a reporter or cameraman might jump out at her from any corner of the house. Two of her three patient appointments had also canceled that day due to the media attention. The computer screen on her desk was filled with the partial text of a self-help article she'd agreed to write for a lifestyle magazine, but she couldn't muster another word.

Voices echoed from the foyer. She turned to see Trevor escorting Officer Arseneau to the front door. He'd arrived a short time earlier, his eyes meeting hers for only a moment before he'd disappeared into the kitchen with the policeman. Trevor closed and locked the door once the officer left.

"I saw you at the press conference," she said when he reached her office. "It was on the news."

He smiled faintly, although the act didn't reach his

eyes. "I was hoping you had a chance to witness my public humiliation."

The press conference that afternoon had been brutal, with the media firing questions at Trevor, the local FBI and police heads, and A.D.A. Sawyer Compton. The radio caller and the subsequent attack on Rain had figured prominently in the media's queries. She'd watched with unease as Trevor had been forced to acknowledge his lack of viable suspects in a killing spree that had taken the lives of six women across multiple states.

"I also talked to David," Rain added, her voice soft. "He called after you left the station. He says he's going to file charges against you for battery."

Trevor didn't seem surprised. "Let him."

She pushed away from the desk. "Today must have been a nightmare—"

"How could you have been involved with a man like D'Alba?"

A small breath escaped her at the directness of his question. In truth, it was nearly impossible to rationalize her onetime attraction to David, especially in light of his recent behavior.

"David's in some financial trouble," she said. "You're seeing him at his worst. He's getting desperate."

Trevor walked to the antique terrarium that sat in the corner of Rain's office. Miniature green ferns grew inside it, and he ran his fingers contemplatively over its smooth glass. "He's moved Ella LaRue in as the new host of *Midnight Confessions*. Her first show's tonight. Ella says you were too traumatized to continue."

"That's putting a spin on things," Rain mused. "I refused to come in and do interviews with the media. David gave me an ultimatum—show up or be replaced."

She had to hand it to him. If David could peddle the story

that she'd resigned under duress, it would cast Ella in a better light, making the audience less resistant to accepting her as the new host. With the show on the verge of syndication it was a risky move. But if Ella could win listener support, it might keep the deal from falling apart without Rain's participation. She supposed it didn't matter that Ella wasn't an actual psychologist, as long as she could keep listeners interested. Ella's sex appeal would undoubtedly give David a marketable presence, albeit a less qualified one.

"I'd already told David I didn't plan to renew my contract when it runs out in September. I'd have preferred my exit to be less dramatic, but…"

She left her words hanging, unnerved by the way Trevor studied her. His eyes held a question that went beyond David and Ella and the radio show. She'd thought about Trevor for most of the day, but now Rain ran her hands over her cotton skirt, dreading what she'd been expecting since Officer Arseneau had asked him for a private word in the kitchen.

"Want to tell me about the kid who busted in here today? According to Arseneau, he was trying to enter your old pass code and set off the security system."

Rain moved to the other side of the desk. Turning on the mission-style Tiffany lamp that sat on the table between the two armchairs, she sighed. "His name is Oliver Carteris. He's a patient of mine."

"He knew your pass code?"

Rain nodded. "Yes."

"Last night, when I asked you for the names of anyone who might've been able to get in here, you didn't mention this kid."

"I didn't give you his name because it wasn't him who attacked me."

"That's not the way this works," Trevor argued. "I ask you

a question, and you give me a truthful answer. You don't filter information."

She attempted to brush past him, but he reached out and cupped her elbow. His voice was low. "Christ, Rain. What else aren't you telling me?"

"There's nothing else—"

"And I'm supposed to believe you?"

Rain shrugged free of his grasp and walked from the office.

A minute later, she heard the change in his footsteps as he slowed at the kitchen doorway. She stood in front of the sink with her back to him, filling a glass with water. When it was full, she took a sip and stared at a spot on the tile backsplash.

"It wasn't Oliver who attacked me yesterday," Rain emphasized quietly. "The man's body size, the tattoo. It wasn't Oliver."

Coming up behind her, Trevor placed his hands on her shoulders. "I shouldn't be taking today out on you. But I don't understand why you'd hold out on me."

She turned to face him. "Because I didn't think Oliver could handle an interrogation. I'm a psychologist, Trevor. These kids are my patients—"

"What makes you think there'd be an interrogation?"

"Because I knew if you ran him through the system, his name would come up. He's had some run-ins with the police."

Leaning against the counter, Trevor crossed his arms over his chest as he waited to hear more. The tiny lines of fatigue fanning out from the corners of his eyes reminded Rain of his sleepless night and the long hours he'd already put in that day. She wondered if he'd managed to steal even a few hours of rest. The last thing he needed was to come here and find out she'd been keeping secrets.

"Oliver's only eighteen," she said. "He has a juvenile record for break-ins and petty theft, most of which his father had expunged. But there's a B and E from five months ago that stuck. He was charged as an adult. He's on probation, one of the terms of which is counseling."

"This is the patient you told me about a while back, isn't it? The one who went through your lingerie?"

"I said *maybe* he went through my lingerie. I can't be certain."

"How'd he get your pass code?"

She looked at the kitchen cabinet. "I keep my pass code taped to the inside of that door, in case I forget. He found it—"

"And he's been using it ever since to come and go as he pleases."

Rain needed Trevor to understand. "Oliver's smart. He's brilliant, actually. His IQ's off the charts. But he's very troubled. He lost his mother at an early age, and spent most of his youth in boarding schools in Europe—"

"Rain." He peered into her eyes. "The reality is, I can't afford to overlook any possible angle. The fact that he had your pass code is reason enough for me to bring him in. For all you know, he could've traded it to the killer for a nickel bag of reefer or a Satan decoder ring—I don't know, whatever the hell he's into. I just want to talk to him, that's all."

Lowering his head, Trevor brushed his lips against hers. "Don't worry, I'll go easy on him."

"I should've told you about Oliver. I didn't mean to make things more difficult." She touched his shirt. "This wasn't the way I imagined our first conversation going after last night."

His eyes darkened at the memory of their lovemaking. He tangled his fingers with hers. "I'm staying for a little while, but there's a uniform coming in a couple of hours to relieve me. I've got a meeting in the morning with the SAC of the Violent Crimes Unit. He's flying in tonight and he wants a full briefing on the investigation at 8:00 a.m. I need to get some sleep and be ready. Until New Orleans, this case has been under the radar. It made national news today."

Rain nodded her understanding. Of course Trevor couldn't work all day and keep guard over her until dawn. She didn't expect that. At least he hadn't said the one thing she feared hearing most. That last night had been a mistake.

"I was thinking we could have dinner together," he suggested. "Order something in?"

She forced a smile. "Okay."

"I need to make a few phone calls. Think about what you want and we'll have it delivered." He leaned his forehead briefly against hers and then walked from the kitchen.

They ordered from Nicole's, a popular bistro at the edge of the Garden District. Rain sipped her Merlot as Trevor twirled linguine around his fork before taking a bite. He'd changed into jeans and a T-shirt, his appearance more casual now that the suit and tie were gone. But his gun remained holstered at his side, a reminder of the reality that had drawn them together.

"You're not eating much," he observed, wiping his mouth with his napkin.

"I'm not very hungry. Nerves, I guess."

He poured the remainder of a can of soda into his glass.

"You said at the Ascension that you don't drink, even off duty," Rain recounted. She twisted her napkin in her lap as Trevor looked at her. "Is it because of your father?"

"I get a complimentary psychoanalysis with dinner?" Despite the joke, there was little levity in his words.

"I just want to know you, Trevor."

He took a lackluster jab at his food before setting the fork on the plate's rim. "I tried it a time or two in college. I didn't like the feeling, the loss of control. Besides, my family has a history of substance abuse. You know about Brian."

"I know he's been clean for two years now."

"He's still a recovering addict. That never changes." He paused in reflection. "Our mother had a drinking problem, too. She died a few years ago."

Rain watched his face, aware of the tension in his features. "Alex said you don't see your brother and sister very often."

"It's complicated."

"Do you want to talk about it?" she asked carefully.

When he looked at her again, his eyes appeared shadowed. "I'd rather just have a peaceful dinner with you, Rain."

He sat quietly for the rest of the meal, seemingly lost in his own thoughts. Then he stood and took his empty plate to the sink in the kitchen to rinse. Rain carried her plate into the kitchen, as well. She put the rest of the shrimp and eggplant she'd ordered into a plastic container and placed it inside the fridge. From the corner of her eye, she studied Trevor's profile. He appeared on the point of exhaustion.

"Why don't you lie down in the parlor. Just until the officer arrives to relieve you—"

He shook his head. "I'm fine."

"Trevor." Rain's voice was soft. "You could never be like him, you know. Your father. It's not in you."

Perhaps fatigue had made him vulnerable, but something in his expression made her heart clench. Their eyes met in an unspoken dialogue as a metallic shrill broke the room's quiet. With a sigh, Trevor checked his cell. "It's not me."

Rain searched for the source of the sound. She spotted her own cell phone, nearly hidden beneath the day's mail stacked on the counter. She picked it up as the words *unidentified caller* flashed on its backlit screen.

It could be another journalist, trying to get a quote. But Rain's patients also had her cell number for emergencies. Opening the phone's cover, she spoke into the receiver. A chill danced up her spine as her salutation was returned.

"Good evening, Rain."

"How'd you get this number?"

"I have my ways, where you're concerned."

Trevor put down the dish towel he held and gently pried the phone from Rain's whitened fingers. He pressed the speaker button, then placed it on the counter. Dante's voice flooded the room.

"They just announced your resignation on *Midnight Confessions*," he said. "I'm listening to your replacement at this very moment. She sounds rather...*anemic*."

"Just tell me what you want."

"You don't know that by now? My dear, I thought you were bright."

Trevor steadied her from behind, his hands clasping her upper arms. Rain closed her eyes.

"You called me Desiree last night. I'm not her."

"No, you're certainly not," he agreed. "But I can use my imagination. After all, you look so much like her. You share her blood."

"You're psychotic," she managed to get out.

"If I am, it's entirely your fault. I've been half out of my mind thinking about you. It hardly seems fair that now I'm being denied even the simple pleasure of hearing your voice on the radio."

When Rain didn't respond, he continued, "Am I being punished for my alleged attack on you? The newspapers and television reporters are all accusing me. It's very distressing. So much so that I was forced to find an outlet for my anger. What do they call it in your field of expertise? Oh, yes. *Transferring my aggression*."

Rain covered her mouth as the realization sank in. He'd just confessed to another murder.

"Are you there, Agent Rivette?"

"I'm here."

"I didn't imagine you'd be too far away." Dante sounded amused. "I watched your televised press conference today. You're a very handsome man."

"Why don't you come meet me in person."

He merely chuckled. "I left a gift for you in Coliseum Square. I think you're going to like her very much."

The phone went dead.

"The park's two blocks from here," Rain said. "Trevor—"

She followed as he strode into the foyer. Gun in hand, Trevor threw open the front door. But it was quiet outside. For once, there wasn't even a patrol car on the street.

A sturdy chain with an antique, silver finish lay on the welcome mat. The pendant on the necklace was a small glass vial.

"You know who it belongs to, don't you?" she asked.

Picking up the necklace, Trevor looked around in the darkness. When he turned to her, his eyes were solemn. "So do you."

28

Trevor remained at the crime scene until nearly midnight when the forensics team had completed its job. Now early morning, he stood at a table in the Royal Street police precinct, photos of Marcy Cupich's body spread out in front of him like a losing hand of cards. The images made his chest ache.

She had been dumped in a remote corner of the park, her mutilated, partially nude corpse hidden under a honeysuckle bush. The moment he'd spotted the glass vial with the crimson liquid inside it abandoned on Rain's doorstep, he'd known.

"Hard to believe she was in here a couple of days ago." Holding a coffee mug, Thibodeaux came up to the table and studied the photos. "You think the killer considered her a liability?"

"It's likely he saw me talking to her at the Ascension." Trevor felt a wash of guilt. "He wouldn't know without her glasses she made a poor witness."

"How old was this one?"

"Seventeen."

"Damn." Thibodeaux shook his head. "Did you get what you need?"

"Yeah." Trevor had come by the precinct on his way to

meet SAC Johnston at the FBI field office, to get copies of some of the police files.

He picked up one of the displayed photos, unable to stop punishing himself. The rosary had been wrapped tightly around Marcy's wrists. Like the other victims, she'd suffered slashes on her thighs, stomach and breasts before the final cut that severed the main arteries in her neck. While there were no indications of rape on any of the victims, the FBI profile suggested the killer masturbated during the torture. Trevor wondered how long the madman had drawn out Marcy's torment before ending her life.

Scrubbing a hand over his tired eyes, he focused again on the youth of the victims in New Orleans. Was the age regression coincidental, or did it have some significance he had yet to figure out?

"You talked to the parents?" Thibodeaux broke into Trevor's thoughts.

"A little while ago." He'd felt the need to deliver the bad news himself. "Marcy was a foster kid. She went into the system a year ago when her mother died. She'd been with this latest family for only a few months."

McGrath lumbered into the bullpen. He peeled off his sports coat and draped it over the back of his desk chair before heading for the coffeemaker. "Next time, *you* park the car, Tibbs. The lot out back's full. I had to walk four blocks over."

"A little exercise won't hurt you, Eddie."

"In this heat, it might. Damned if it wasn't ninety by sunrise this morning." McGrath dumped two plastic tubs of nondairy creamer into his coffee, then stirred it with a minuscule red straw until the liquid turned the color of delta sand. "You get any sleep, Rivette? You're looking a little gothlike yourself."

"I got a few hours." *Very few.* Trevor glanced at his

wristwatch. His briefing with Johnston and the local SAC was in a little over a half hour. Johnston wouldn't be pleased another girl had turned up dead, especially one connected to the investigation. He'd probably heard about it already on the early-morning news.

"I've got to go." Gathering the files, Trevor shoved them into his briefcase. "I'll be at the autopsy at noon. I'm also going to want to talk to some of those kids at the Ascension again."

"Good luck with that." McGrath adjusted the window blinds in an attempt to shut out the sunlight. "Anything we can do while you're getting your ass chewed?"

"If you're serious, you can pick up a kid for me." He wrote Oliver Carteris's name and address on a piece of paper and handed it over. "The residence is in the Upper Garden District, right on St. Charles Avenue. He isn't in any trouble as far as I know. But he's a patient of Dr. Sommers and he caused a scene at her place yesterday. I'd like to ask him a few questions."

"Swanky address."

"Give me a call when you bring him in and I'll swing by, okay?"

Trevor left the detectives. Exiting through the back doors to avoid the press out front, he had to agree with McGrath's appraisal. Despite the early hour, the humidity created a sharp contrast to the building's cool interior. It felt as if a steamed towel had been dropped over the Quarter.

"Agent Rivette?" A dark-haired male jogged toward him. He wore jeans and a T-shirt, and a shield hung from a chain around his neck.

"Thought that was you—this will save me a call," he said as he caught up. "I recognized you from the press conference yesterday. I'm Danny Reyes with the DEA. I'm the lead agent over a local drug investigation, and I need to talk to you about the Ascension."

The men shook hands. "I'm headed to a meeting, Reyes. Want to walk me to my car?"

Reyes fell in step beside him. "You're looking at the club in relationship to the Vampire Murders?"

"Who told you that?"

"We've got an agent working undercover. He saw you there a few nights ago. Said you were asking a lot of questions, generally kicking up dirt."

Trevor squinted against the sun. "Two of the three victims frequented the club, including the one who turned up dead in Coliseum Square last night."

"I heard about that. What about the club owner, Armand Baptiste? You been able to link him to any of the homicides?"

"Not so far."

"You should know the DEA has its sights on Baptiste." Reyes tucked his shield under his T-shirt. "We've been following a distribution ring working out of the club for a while now, and we think he's a big part of it. We're conducting a raid tonight, and we also just got matching warrants for his antiques business and warehouse that we plan to enforce at the same time. Our agent says the time is right, so this can't wait. I wanted to check with you first and make sure we didn't get in each other's way."

"I understand. Do the police know about this yet?" Trevor fished in his pocket for the keys as they neared the Taurus.

"Not yet. This has been under pretty deep cover. That's why I'm here—we're going to need some NOPD assistance for crowd control and arrestee processing, among other things."

Trevor considered an opportunity. It wasn't his warrant, but he wondered what the raid might reveal that could be of interest to him. "Do you see a problem with me and a few friends tagging along tonight?"

"A few friends? I don't want the legality of the warrants challenged—"

"Don't worry. I'm not suggesting a league of FBI agents. Just me at the Ascension and a couple of NOPD detectives at the other locations." He shrugged. "We know what we're looking for, so if your agents happen to stumble across anything relevant to our investigation…"

Reyes nodded thoughtfully. "I'm all for interagency cooperation. I'll set up a meeting to coordinate for this afternoon."

Once they'd exchanged business cards, Trevor stared after the agent's retreating figure, then opened the car door. Heat escaped from the interior like a dry sauna. Tossing his briefcase onto the seat, he slid inside and started the engine. He took a small measure of satisfaction in knowing Baptiste was about to get his comeuppance.

Fifteen minutes later, he arrived at the redbrick building housing the FBI field offices near Lake Pontchartrain. Trevor presented his shield and was escorted by a receptionist to a windowed conference room with a long table and swivel chairs. Sweating pitchers of ice water and a row of glasses were in the table's center, although only one other person was already there. SAC Johnston stood with his arms crossed over his barrel-like chest, the fluorescent lights glinting off his smooth, bald head.

"Well, Agent Rivette. I'd say this pimple you've been picking at is coming to a head right here in New Orleans."

"Yes, sir." Trevor laid his briefcase on the table.

"This is beyond a special VCU project now," he said, referring to the task force.

"I'd like to stay here in New Orleans to see this to its

culmination," Trevor emphasized. He had no intention of turning leads over to the local FBI team and walking away. There was too much at stake and he'd followed Dante's trail for too long. "I'm from here, sir, and I'm very familiar with the area. As you know, I've also established a relationship with the unsub—"

"Has he made contact with you about this latest victim?" Johnston asked. He still hadn't sat down at the table, his bearing military straight. Trevor remained standing, as well.

"Last night by cell phone, informing me of the body he'd left in Coliseum Park. He referred to the dead girl as a *gift* for me."

Trevor told him about the planned DEA drug raid on the Ascension that night. He lowered his voice in case anyone was within earshot outside the room. "It's not our warrant and we can't have a dozen FBI agents storming in there, but I can go in informally and see what stands out."

Taking off his wire-rimmed glasses, Johnston used a tissue to wipe the lenses. "This case has become personal to you, Agent Rivette?"

Trevor felt his shoulders tense, but he didn't break his gaze. "I want to get this guy. I've invested eighteen months."

"Agent Fincher won't be able to join you. Another child abduction and murder occurred yesterday near Arlington. We think they're related." He cleared his throat, his gaze remaining stoic. "But you have the local FBI and police."

Footsteps and the murmur of conversation came from down the hallway, letting them know the others attending the meeting were on their way.

"Make no mistake, Agent. I want this case closed before another body turns up."

Just before midnight, revelers poured from the doors of the Ascension like ants escaping a flattened anthill. Inside, DEA and police swarmed the converted sanctuary.

Wearing a Kevlar vest like the other law enforcement roving the club, Trevor worked his way through the chaos and into the shadowed passage that led to the basement. When he reached the bottom of the stone stairwell, his eyes swept over the private playroom of Armand Baptiste and his goth kindred. With the lights on, the gaping room no longer looked eerie, simply bare and dingy. The bar area was deserted except for a half-dozen leather-clad males who were lined up and facing the windowless wall. Their legs were spread and their hands clasped behind their heads as DEA agents and police patted them down.

"How many cows you figure had to die to outfit these losers?" Reyes had come down the stairs, his own Kevlar unstrapped and hanging at his sides. "It looks like the biker convention from hell down here."

"What's the count?" Trevor asked, holstering his gun.

"So far, we've got five for narcotics possession, one for carrying a concealed weapon. There's also an NOPD wagon full of underage drinkers."

Trevor suspected the wagon contained some of the kids he wanted to talk to again, this time about Marcy Cupich's murder. "What about Baptiste?"

Reyes shook his head. "No sign of him here or at the other locales."

Scuffling sounds came from the hallway behind the bar. A stringy-haired male burst through the door with two policemen in pursuit. Blocking the man's exit, Trevor seized him by the shirt and shoved him face-first against the wall.

"I've been looking for you, *Girard*." He pinned the struggling man's arms behind his back.

Girard snarled over his shoulder, flashing pointed teeth. One of the officers stepped in with handcuffs and took over.

"You know this asshole?" Reyes asked Trevor.

"Only socially. He tried to gut me with a six-inch hunting knife."

"Agent Reyes," a muscular African-American in a DEA jacket called from the hallway's threshold. "I think we found something."

Trevor followed Reyes and the agent down the corridor and past the storeroom that had been the site of the knife attack a few days earlier. That room was also now brightly lit, and DEA men were rummaging through the shelving units and cardboard boxes stacked against the walls.

"There's another room at the end of the hallway," the agent commented, pointing ahead. "Some kind of private office."

A second slant of light indicated the other room. As they approached, Trevor noticed the awkward angle of the door, which suggested it had been previously closed and locked until force was applied. It yawned open, hanging gingerly by its top hinge. Trevor and Reyes stepped inside. The room contained only a desk, a chair and a tall metal cabinet, its front padlocked. A bare bulb hung from a cord in the room's center. If this was Baptiste's personal office, it was a far cry from his elegant work space at the antiques firm.

Another agent stood nearby with bolt cutters.

"Do the honors," Reyes told him.

The cabinet's padlock was cut through in seconds. The man swung the doors open.

"Bingo," Reyes intoned under his breath. On the cabinet's shelves sat a half-dozen packages wrapped in brown butcher paper. One was partially ripped open, and pills tumbled from its insides like candy from a piñata.

"This a nightclub or a pharmacy?" the agent with the bolt cutters asked, grinning.

But Trevor wasn't looking at the drugs. His gaze had shifted to the slim rectangular case on the cabinet's lower shelf.

"You want to remove that?" he said to Reyes.

Reyes donned gloves and placed the case on the desk, then opened its lid.

Trevor felt a jolt at what he saw. "Can we get a photographer in here?"

"You bet," Reyes said, calling for one.

Black crystal beads with mother-of-pearl and a Celtic silver cross. His mouth dry, Trevor stared at the pair of identical rosaries inside the velvet-lined case, their glimmering ropes entwined like lovers' arms.

29

Rain had cloistered herself in the upstairs study. She sat on the couch, cradling a cup of herbal tea between her palms as she attempted to distract herself with a late-night television talk show. But the host's opening monologue failed to make much of an impression. Two minutes into his discussion with his first guest, a vapid blonde with collagen-enhanced lips, she clicked off the remote.

She hadn't heard from Trevor since the previous evening when they'd had dinner together. After Dante's taunting phone call, he'd waited in tense silence for an officer to relieve him and then he'd gotten into his car and headed to Coliseum Square. Rain had watched his taillights recede into darkness as the wail of police sirens shattered the neighborhood's quiet. A few hours later, the local news confirmed Dante's vicious claim.

Another girl dead. Rain had to wonder if it was all because of her.

Picking at the fringe on the couch's embroidered pillows, she silently urged Trevor to call and let her know what was going on. The cop downstairs in her kitchen seemed to know little beyond his assignment of keeping guard. Either that or he was being deliberately closemouthed. Despite his run-in with Oliver, Rain much preferred the young and talkative Officer Arseneau over the silver-haired, flat-eyed cop manning the evening shifts.

She set the cup down and walked to the recessed bookshelves that lined the room's far wall. Restless, she ran her fingers over the bound volumes. Academic tomes on psychology mingled with the Victorian novels and books on gardening that had belonged to Celeste. She pulled out *Jane Eyre,* which had been among her aunt's favorites, but paused when she saw the slim paperback tucked behind the others, out of view. Rain stood on tiptoe to reach its worn spine. The lurid illustration on its cover surprised her. Carrying the book to the couch, she opened it at a random spot and began to read.

The content was clearly sadomasochistic in nature, the story about a female submissive engaged in role-playing with a dangerously handsome man.

Will he merely threaten me this time, holding the blade to my throat while he thrusts himself inside me? Or will he take our dark game a step further? I am hot and wet, and nearly come in the knowledge that he is in control...

The rest of the passage was extremely sexually graphic. Rain flipped forward to the front pages and sought out the copyright date. As its yellowed appearance suggested, the paperback was old, printed thirty-five years earlier. Certainly, she knew such S&M erotica existed then. Had it belonged to Desiree?

Twin beams flashed through the room's fan-shaped window. A car made the turn onto Prytania, its headlights creating a sweeping pattern across the beadboard-paneled walls and high ceiling before fading away. Rain felt a twinge of nerves. Dante had been on her doorstep last night, then vanished as quickly as the car's silvered lights. She thought of the *Blue Moon* photos, which had served as inspiration for the twisted fantasy he was bent on repeatedly bringing to life.

She closed the paperback. What things didn't she know about her mother? How much had Celeste protected her?

Returning to the bookcase, Rain replaced the literature in its hiding place, using *Jane Eyre* to seal it back inside its dark tomb.

The Royal Street precinct was as busy as a French Quarter bar on Fat Tuesday. Chalky-faced goths were shuffled through to booking, while surly teens waited in a holding pen until their parents or Juvenile Corrections picked them up. DEA agents and police mingled, trying to sort through the crowd who'd been hauled in from the club on a variety of charges.

Trevor headed to where McGrath and Thibodeaux stood in line at the equipment cage, waiting to turn in their radios and Kevlars. While he'd been at the Ascension with Reyes's team, the detectives had taken part in the synchronized raid of Baptiste's antiques business and warehouse.

"Any sign of Baptiste?" Trevor asked as he approached. "He wasn't at the Ascension, although the undercover DEA agent placed him there just prior to the bust."

"Slippery bastard's in the wind," Thibodeaux remarked. "His residence in the Quarter's staked out, but I doubt he's stupid enough to show up there."

The detectives filled him in on their segment of the raid. Although it was nothing like the find at the Ascension, trace amounts of raw Ecstasy powder and a tablet press had been found at the warehouse.

"Baptiste was using both businesses as channels for his real moneymaker," McGrath theorized. "The antiques firm gave him a way to import drugs into the country without casting too much suspicion, and the club provided a method of distribution."

"Tonight's bust put a stop to that." The statement came from Reyes, who'd joined them after conferring with the station lieutenant. "Sixty kilos of MDMA won't be stimulating the local economy."

He looked at Trevor. "Of course, distribution charges would be nothing compared to seven counts of murder one. That'll get you death row in the great state of Louisiana. Looks like your tagalong paid off, Agent Rivette."

McGrath grunted in agreement. "At the least, the rosaries make Baptiste a person of interest."

"Forget this person-of-interest horseshit. If you ask me, he practically has *killer* stamped on his forehead." Thibodeaux slung his vest onto the counter for check-in. "It all adds up. Two of the vics frequented his club prior to their disappearance, and now we find reproductions of the rosaries in his possession—what more do you want?"

McGrath answered his partner's rhetorical question. "I want Baptiste, sitting in my interrogation room."

"Any way you look at it, Baptiste is knee deep in alligators. We're putting out a fat reward for him. If we don't find him ourselves, some lowlife will turn him in." Reyes walked into the briefing room.

"With that, I'm going outside for a celebratory smoke." Thibodeaux extracted his Marlboro Lights from his shirt pocket. "Buck up, Rivette. Tonight's one of the good ones."

He ambled off in the direction of the precinct's back lot. But McGrath remained rooted in place. He peered at Trevor. "Tibbs is right. You don't look pleased. I thought you liked Baptiste for this."

"I do think he's involved," Trevor said. "But I don't buy that one man is the top dog in a drug-distribution ring *and* a serial killer. The Ascension factors into the murders, but I don't see Baptiste as the unsub."

McGrath shrugged. "Maybe he's a multitasker. He wouldn't be the first drug lord with a kinky sexual sideline. Besides, Tibbs has a point. Baptiste had the rosaries right there in his personal goth hidey-hole, and I'll bet you my next paycheck his prints turn up on the case. Either way, this is gonna get the D.A. off our backs—and your boss at the VCU off yours—now that there's a bona fide suspect. Ever heard about looking a gift horse in the mouth, Rivette?"

"I'll feel better when the horse is in custody."

Their conversation paused as a teen with a ratty T-shirt that read I'm So Goth, I'm Dead was hustled past by a female officer. Trevor forced his mind to shift gears. "What about the kid—Oliver Carteris? I never got a call from you letting me know you'd picked him up."

"That's because we didn't," McGrath replied. "We went to the residence, a big-ass Victorian number. Dr. Carteris claimed his son wasn't home, and he didn't seem too thrilled to see us. In fact, he recommended we go through his attorney prior to any future attempts at conversation."

The detective laid his equipment from the raid on the counter. He pushed it through an opening in the cage to a uniformed sergeant. "Get this, though. The surgeon had himself a shiner, and he wouldn't state how he got it. You sure Junior doesn't have a history of violent behavior?"

Trevor recounted what Rain had told him.

"Call it a cop's instinct," McGrath said, "but I'd warn Dr. Sommers to watch herself around this kid."

"All I see is black eyeliner and black hair. If this goth crap is about expressing your individualism, how come these clowns all look the same?" Thibodeaux made the observation as he stood in front of a cell crowded with detainees. He jerked his head toward a goateed man in a velvet frock coat who was loudly demanding his lawyer.

"At least that one's got style," he said to Trevor. The man yelled again, and Thibodeaux stepped up to the bars. "Calm the fuck down, Lestat. How about taking that right-to-remain-silent speech a little more seriously?"

"Rivette." Trevor saw McGrath walking toward him. "Reyes wants to pull out some of these knuckleheads for questioning. I figured we'd start with your two friends. Since they're facing charges of assaulting a federal officer, we can use that as leverage to see what they know about Baptiste's whereabouts."

"Let's do it." Trevor shifted his gaze to Girard, who glared at him from inside the cage. He reminded Trevor of a rabid dog. They'd also picked up Girard's accomplice in the attack, a hulking giant with a shaved head who sat on one of the cell's benches. Trevor easily recalled him from the shadowed storage room.

McGrath rapped on a Plexiglas window to get the guard's attention. He pointed to the men in question. "Put those two beauty queens in rooms three and four."

As the officer extracted the prisoners, he bumped shoulders with a wiry-looking male who paced nervously within the confined space. Despite the heat generated by the tight press of bodies, he huddled inside a worn denim jacket.

Trevor nudged McGrath. "The tweaker over there. What's the charge?"

McGrath consulted the clipboard. "Collared for drug possession, Class C amphetamines. Not enough for resale, so it's probably for his own use. You recognize him?"

The man turned to pace in the other direction, raking his hands through his unwashed hair. A set of scabbed scratch marks trailed down the right side of his neck before disappearing under the jacket's turned-up collar. Trevor felt a black anger grab hold. Stalking in through the cell door, he dragged the man out.

"Take off your jacket!"

McGrath moved forward. "Rivette—"

"Take it off!" When the man cowered in confusion, Trevor tore the garment from him and slung it to the concrete floor. A thorny barbed-wire tattoo was wrapped around the addict's right forearm.

"Rivette!"

It took both McGrath and Thibodeaux to pull him off.

30

Mallory's was a dive in every sense of the word. The place was shabby, with air that hung heavy with cigarette smoke and smelled like stale beer. James Rivette had a regular perch he used whenever he wasn't tending bar. Tonight was one of his nights off, so he sat on the last vinyl-covered stool near the alcove that held the restrooms. His right hand clutched a whiskey glass. A cloudy oblong mirror ran the length of the wall behind the bar, and in front of it was the usual lineup of bottles in various shapes and sizes.

Looking up, James caught his own reflection. He barely recognized the thick, hunched shoulders and graying hair. The sagging jowls. At one point, he'd been a damn fine-looking man. But all his life he'd gotten the short end of the stick. The disappointments had eventually caught up to him, deepening the lines in his face. He'd given his best years to the NOPD, and for what? The higher-ups had used their first opportunity to cheat him out of his pension.

Coughing, he wiped the back of his hand across his mouth. A man should have a small nest egg, or at least someone to care for him in his advancing years. James hung his head, feeling intensely sorry for himself.

His thoughts settled on his oldest son. He'd been ruminating on him a lot lately, ever since seeing him on the street outside the bar and making the 911 call. Trevor was a man now, a cocky FBI agent who carried a badge and a gun. He'd always hated those federal sons of bitches, with their fancy suits and superior attitude. *But it fit,* James reflected sourly. Trevor always did think he was better than everyone else.

You think I won't do it, Trev?

Go to hell.

He swallowed the remainder of his whiskey. Trevor hadn't wanted to listen to reason. There hadn't been an ounce of forgiveness in his heart.

It wasn't his fault. The boy had antagonized him, forced his hand. He was just a kid—how the fuck did he know what he saw? James rapped the empty glass on the sticky bar top and growled for a refill.

He'd lost everything because of his son.

CNN blared from a TV set hanging over the bar. But the crowd tonight was too boisterous for him to hear much of what the female news anchor said. Instead, he watched the slow crawl of text across the bottom of the screen. Someone started up the jukebox, adding the Neville Brothers to the cacophony.

"Glenlivet, single malt," a man announced to the bartender as he slid onto the stool next to James. "And I'll pay for my friend here. Whatever he's having."

A hundred-dollar bill dropped onto the bar.

James mumbled a gruff thanks. Shifting his eyes to the mirror, he glimpsed the man's dark sunglasses that were out of place at night in the dimly lit establishment. Maybe he was a rich celebrity hiding from those—what did you call them? Paparazzi.

The bartender served them. As the man lifted the scotch to his lips, James noticed his ring. Made of white gold, it resembled a coiled serpent that wrapped halfway up his index finger. Sharp fangs protruded from the snake's open jaws and its eyes were green emeralds. James had never seen anything like it.

"Careful you don't put someone's eye out with that, pal."

The man laughed, a rich melody that fell an octave below the barroom noise. James sipped his whiskey, still not looking directly at the man, and felt slightly unnerved.

"Do I know you?"

"I have a business proposition for you, Mr. Rivette."

He laid a stack of bills in front of him.

A neon sign in the window advertised Budweiser beer. James watched it blink on and off several times. Then he returned his gaze to the proffered cash. Despite the wetness of the whiskey, his mouth had gone dry. He estimated the cash was more than he'd make in two months tending bar.

"A business proposition? You talking about a job?"

"It's quite simple, actually. And if you don't mind me saying so, I think it's something you're going to enjoy."

The man explained what he wanted James to do.

31

Another day had passed, and the messages Rain had left on Trevor's cell phone had all gone unreturned.

Staring out the French doors of her office, her gaze leveled on the officer who sat in her parlor with his nose buried in the evening edition of the *Times-Picayune*. This is what being a shut-in feels like, she realized. She'd become an adult who required babysitting and was forced to rely on others for the smallest of errands—like shopping for groceries or simply walking outdoors to retrieve the mail. With the continued cancellations in her patient sessions, even the distraction of work had been mercilessly removed from her grasp.

Night was falling outside, bringing with it a thickening gray haze. Rain's thoughts dissolved as the doorbell chimed. Laying aside the paper, the officer rose from the sofa and moved to the foyer. He looked out the window before opening the door.

Rain's stomach did a small flip as Trevor entered. He spoke with the officer, but she could hear nothing of their conversation from her location. When he finally reached her office, she already stood at her desk. "I've been calling—"

"I'm sorry. I've been busy."

"The raid on the Ascension's been all over the news. They're calling Armand Baptiste a suspect in the murders."

Trevor slid his hands into his pockets. Up close, the rub of shadow under his eyes and stubble on his jaw told her how deeply he'd been involved in the chain of events.

"We found duplicates of the rosaries in Baptiste's office at the club," he said. "His fingerprints were on the case they were stored inside. It's enough to implicate him."

"But he's disappeared?"

"He's either in hiding here in New Orleans or he's on the run. Law enforcement across four states is looking for him." His shoulders slumped under his dress shirt, and Trevor hesitated before speaking again. "We also caught the guy who attacked you. His DNA matched the scrapings from under your nails."

Her pulse quickened. "He worked for Armand?"

"No, Rain. He worked for D'Alba."

"I don't understand."

He walked over to where she stood in front of the darkening window. "It was a publicity stunt. D'Alba didn't have a choice but to fess up when the junkie he hired to do the job ratted him out."

A weight settled on her lungs that made it hard to breathe. "Why would he do something like that?"

"Because he knew Dante's connection to *Midnight Confessions* could deliver a huge amount of attention, and he wanted to up the ante. The attack on you was the perfect setup for leaking the story about Dante calling in to the show. It heightened the drama and kicked off a media cyclone."

Rain blinked, trying to clear her head. She hadn't forgotten to set the security system when she'd gone out that day. David had given her pass code to the intruder. He'd actually paid someone to assault her, or worse. She closed her eyes, feeling ill. "Has he been charged?"

"With conspiracy to commit assault."

She fell silent for several seconds, giving the shock waves careening through her a chance to subside. When she glanced again at Trevor, he was rubbing his fingers tiredly over his forehead. The knuckles on his right hand were red and abraded.

"Did you hit him?"

"Does it matter?" he asked sharply.

It was there. The ominous look in his eyes that reminded her of the sky graying before a storm. Rain searched his face as worry coiled inside her. "What aren't you telling me?"

He glanced away, studying the sage green of the office wall. "You should know D'Alba claims you were in on it. He said you agreed to and helped stage the attack."

She nearly laughed in disbelief. "And you believed him?"

"No."

But it was clear a seed of doubt, however small, had been planted. Several nights ago, Trevor had asked how she could have ever been involved with David. He'd questioned her about keeping Oliver's possession of her pass code a secret. Whatever trust she'd won from him was now tenuous, if David hadn't managed to destroy it completely.

Rain couldn't keep the defensive edge from her words. "Why on earth would I go along with a plan like that, when I wanted out of my contract?"

"D'Alba had an answer for that, too. He said he offered to release you early without financial repercussions if you went along with the scheme."

The lie was like a slap in the face. Despite everything, it was impossible to comprehend the low David had stooped to this time. His words came back to her. *The show is my last hope. I won't let it go. I'll do whatever I have to.*

"You *do* realize he knows about us?" Rain moved closer to

Trevor. She laid her palm against his chest, no longer caring if the officer in the next room witnessed the intimate gesture. "He'd say anything to come between us, not to mention try to get himself off the hook."

"I know that, Rain." Letting go of a breath, he gently lifted her hand from his shirt, squeezing her fingers before releasing them. But his eyes appeared distant, troubled. "Look, I've got to go. The investigation is changing. We've got police and FBI agents all over the city, looking for Baptiste. I just wanted to come by and update you on the situation."

No, Rain thought wildly. He'd come here to get her reaction. To gauge her face and her words for honesty. Anger tightened her throat, making her voice tremble. "Don't you want to take me in for questioning, Agent?"

"Don't do this," he muttered, looking away.

"Of course, there's no hurry. Anytime you want to interrogate me, you know where I am. Being held like an inmate in my own home."

"It's still not safe. If you need to go out, an officer can accompany you—"

"What I *need* is for you to not shut down on me." Their eyes locked in the room's encroaching shadows.

"I've got to go," Trevor repeated. He turned to leave.

"This is what you wanted, isn't it?"

The question made him pause. His image reflected back to her in the door window.

"If you can doubt me, it's easier to close me out." Rain hugged her arms over her chest. "It's how you deal with anyone who cares about you. Brian, your sister, me. What happened to you, Trevor? This goes beyond your father. What happened that's made it so hard to trust anyone?"

He turned around, and Rain was momentarily frozen by the depth of emotion she saw on his face. Then with a defeated stance, he pivoted on his heel and walked out.

* * *

Rain sat on her bed, watching from the window as the night grew darker. She'd gone upstairs once Trevor's car had pulled away, not wanting the officer to see the tears in her eyes. Tucking her knees under her chin, she wrapped her arms around her legs and tried to quell the heaviness in her heart.

If David could convince the police that the attack on her was a publicity stunt in which she'd willingly participated, the charges against him would have to be dropped. But even more upsetting was the idea that Trevor would ponder her involvement. Did he actually think she had been complicit in David's scheme?

She recalled his troubled expression as he left the house. The accusation she'd hurled at him had hit its mark, causing his soul to bare itself to her for only a moment. He kept a deliberate distance from those he cared for, but why? All Rain knew was that she needed answers if she was ever to have any chance of understanding him.

Reaching a decision, she changed into jeans and sneakers. Then quietly, she went down the staircase of the old house. Rain breathed a sigh of relief when she saw that the officer had moved to the kitchen. She peeped in at him through the doorway. He was devouring a sandwich as he watched an episode of *COPS* on television. His mouth full, he gave encouragement to two on-screen policemen as they chased a potbellied, shirtless man down a hill.

Tiptoeing to the back of the house, Rain hit the bypass button on the alarm system. The noise from the television drowned out its soft beep. She went out through the service entrance. It was a simple matter to open the courtyard gate and slip away unseen.

32

Synapse was closed, its doors locked and the lights in the gallery dimmed to a faint glow. A rap on the front window caused Annabelle Rivette to glance up from her paperwork. Rising from behind the desk in Alex's office, she stole a peek at Haley who was in the next room playing. Then she went cautiously down the hall and into the main exhibit space.

Although she looked different from the alluring female in Alex's photo, Annabelle recognized the petite redhead who stood outside on Julia Street. She disarmed the security system and unlocked the door.

Rain Sommers wore no makeup, and her hair was pulled into a ponytail from which coppery tendrils escaped. Her baby blue T-shirt advertised the New Orleans Jazz Festival. She gazed in surprise at Annabelle from the doorway.

"I'm sorry to bother you, but I was looking for Brian and Alex," she explained. "I went through the lobby and tried their apartment, but no one was home. I thought maybe they were down here?"

"They're out of town on business, but I expect them back later tonight. I'm here catching up on the books." Annabelle could see disappointment etched on the other woman's features, and she looked past her to the darkened sidewalk in front of the gallery. She appeared to be alone. "If you don't mind me asking, are you all right? You seem a little... upset."

"I just needed to talk and I thought..." Her voice trailed away, and she shook her head apologetically. "I should've called first. I'll let you get back to your work."

"I'm Annabelle. Would you like to come in?"

Rain had taken a few steps back, but at the offer she halted her retreat. She hesitated before slowly coming inside. "I'm Rain Sommers."

"I know who you are." Annabelle locked the door behind them. "Does Trevor know you're here? Considering what's going on, I'm surprised he'd let you out at night alone."

"He doesn't know." Rain tucked a few loose strands of hair behind her ear, looking as if she was deciding how much to say. "He thinks I'm at home under guard."

"Should I call and tell him where you are?"

"No, please don't. We sort of had a...disagreement tonight. He left..."

Annabelle studied Rain. When she spoke again, her voice was tentative. "You care about my brother, don't you?"

Although the question seemed to catch her off guard, Rain met her eyes.

"I think I might be falling in love with him." She ran her hands along the front of her jeans, then pressed them against her face. "I shouldn't have said that...I'm a little tired. A lot's happened over the past few days."

Annabelle touched Rain's shoulder. She walked her farther inside the gallery and tried to put her at ease. "I tease Trevor about being my big brother, but he's actually a whopping twenty-eight minutes older than me. Did you know we're fraternal twins?"

"I'm afraid there's a lot about Trevor I don't know," Rain

admitted. "I guess that's why I'm here… I was hoping Brian might shed some light."

"Trevor's had a wall around him for a long time. You look like you just ran into it."

Rain gave a weak laugh. "Something like that."

Annabelle pressed her lips together in contemplation. Rain appeared skittish, as if she might bolt back out through the door at any time. The tell was there in her haunted expression and shimmering eyes; her feelings for Trevor were sincere.

She deserved to know.

"If you still feel like talking, maybe I could be a substitute for Brian? I know we just met, but I've been looking at your photograph over Alex's desk for so long I feel like I already know you. Regardless, you shouldn't be running around by yourself. It's not safe."

Rain stared at the floor. "Thank you for being so nice."

"Let's go into the back, though." She reset the security system using the keypad near the door. "I don't want anyone thinking the gallery's still open."

She led her down the hall, stopping to introduce her to Haley. While Rain chatted with her daughter, Annabelle inserted a movie into the DVD player. Soon, Haley was immersed in a colorful animation featuring a sassy talking fish and sea creatures.

"Why don't we sit in Alex's office." She kept her voice down so she didn't disturb Haley's cartoon. "I know where he keeps the good liquor."

She figured they both deserved a stiff drink before the conversation they were about to have.

He didn't have time for self-recrimination and regret.

Still, Trevor pulled the Taurus over. Its tires spun gravel as it came to a halt on a street at the edge of Audubon Park, near the campuses of Tulane and Loyola universities. He scrubbed his hands over his face and tried to block out the conversation with Rain that kept replaying in his head.

What the hell was wrong with him?

Remorse tore through him like the hot lead of a bullet. He didn't actually think she'd been involved in D'Alba's stunt, did he? Not for a minute, he finally admitted to himself. For one thing, after the attack her fear had been all too real. Trevor recalled the way Rain had broken down in the bay of the E.R. that night. She'd trembled in his arms, her tears making damp spots on his shirt. Guilt spiraled inside him as he thought of the bruises left on her throat by the man's choking grip. That had been no act.

Then why had he reacted the way he did to D'Alba's claim?

If you can doubt me, it's easier to close me out. It's how you deal with anyone who cares about you. Brian, your sister, me.

Rain's accuracy was uncanny.

In many ways, Trevor thought he'd recovered from his past. Moved on. But every day, it still seemed to be claiming a part of him, making him feel distrustful and alone. Before Rain, there'd been other women. Quite a few, in fact. But if any of them made the mistake of falling in love with him, he'd put as much distance between them as he could. His job provided a convenient excuse—too much responsibility, too much travel—for him to forge or maintain any real connection.

Trevor stared at his scraped knuckles, the result of his explosive reaction to seeing the man's barbed-wire tattoo. After he'd been dragged off the perp by McGrath and Thibodeaux, he'd hit the precinct's wall with his fist, desperate to channel his anger. He was lucky he hadn't broken his hand. Had Rain affected him that deeply?

Tugging his lower lip between his fingers, Trevor stared

out the windshield at the park's moss-draped oak trees and lush grass. Below him, a marble-green lagoon reflected moonlight, its surface mirror smooth. The familiar sulfur smell of decomposing plants blew in through the car's air-conditioning vent. This place, this city, was a conduit for broken memories he didn't want to remember.

This goes beyond your father. What happened that's made it so hard to trust anyone?

His cell phone rang. He dug it from his pocket and flipped it open. "Rivette."

Fifteen seconds later, the Taurus made a sharp U-turn as it pulled onto the road. He headed back to the Lower Garden District. The saying "Don't shoot the messenger" crossed his mind, but it didn't keep him from wanting to put some serious hurt on the officer on duty at Rain's house. The man who was supposed to be keeping an eye on her. At least he'd had the guts to call and deliver the news himself.

Somehow, she'd disappeared.

Trevor called Rain's cell phone, but it went straight to voice mail. He left a terse message demanding she call him, then said a silent prayer that she'd left of her own accord.

Whether Armand Baptiste was Dante or not, the killer was still out there somewhere.

33

The vodka was Russian and very cold, taken from the mini-fridge in Alex's office. Although she didn't care for the taste of straight liquor, Rain took a sip and felt the warmth of it unfurl in her stomach, making her feel steadier than she had in hours.

"Alex doesn't keep alcohol in the loft upstairs because of Brian," Annabelle explained as she took a seat in the leather desk chair. "But he keeps a stash down here for the gallery's clients."

Rain looked at Annabelle in the room's soft lighting. Her combination of ivory skin and dark hair was striking. Like her brothers, she was gifted with strong bone structure, but her nose and jawline were delicate and feminine, her mouth sensual and full. *Trevor's twin.* The revelation made his estrangement from his family even more mysterious, considering his connection with Annabelle went beyond mere sibling. They'd shared the same womb.

"So you and Trevor had a fight?"

Rain exhaled. "That would've required Trevor sticking around. Right now, he seems intent on putting distance between us."

"I believe he has feelings for you."

I thought so, too. But Rain said nothing. Instead, she stared into the clear liquid in her glass and realized even twice the amount of vodka wouldn't be able to erase the memory of the distrust she'd seen in his eyes.

"How much do you really know about my brother, Rain? About his childhood?"

"I asked Trevor…about the scar on his chin," she said hesitantly, realizing it was Annabelle's past she was speaking about, too. "He told me how he got it. Alex also mentioned some things Brian's told him."

Annabelle stood and went to gaze out the darkened office window. "You're a psychologist?"

"Yes."

"Then you know in homes where there's abuse, the oldest will sometimes take the worst of it, to deflect it from the others?" She turned to face her. When Rain nodded slowly, she continued.

"Trevor always tried to protect us. Especially Brian, who had a way of setting our father off. Daddy would come home from his shift in a foul mood, just looking for someone to take it out on. Trevor took some terrible beatings."

"Where was your mother?"

"Drinking, mostly." Annabelle set her glass on the desk, her fingers tracing its rim. "She loved us, but she wasn't a strong person. It was her way of dealing with things. She was afraid of her husband, too, and with good reason. In those days, the courts weren't nearly as sympathetic to domestic-abuse victims, especially when the one accused of violence was a police officer. Momma seemed to draw up inside herself whenever Daddy was around."

From down the hall, Rain heard Haley giggling at the cartoon she watched. The little girl's laughter was a sharp contrast to the childhood her mother described.

"Was Trevor the only one of the children your father hurt?"

Absently, Annabelle rubbed the thin line of scar tissue on her left wrist. Rain had noticed it earlier, peeking out from the sleeve of her blouse when she'd started the DVD.

"My father began sexually molesting me when I was thirteen." Her quiet disclosure seemed to echo inside the room, and Rain realized the vodka was as much for Annabelle's fortification as her own.

"Trevor didn't know. No one did. I kept it a secret because I didn't want to cause more problems in our family."

"How long did this go on?"

"For nearly two years… Until Trevor caught him in the act."

Anxiety formed a knot in Rain's stomach. She prepared herself for whatever she was about to hear.

"I was at home alone," Annabelle recounted, her expression tense. "Momma had taken Brian to a doctor's appointment, and Trevor was at junior varsity football practice. I was in my bedroom listening to music when I saw the black and white roll up outside… I knew why he was there, what he would want. I thought about climbing out the window, just running away from it all. If I had, everything would've turned out differently."

Rising from the couch, Rain approached her. "You were barely more than a child. Of course you didn't know what to do."

"He'd always been so careful before." She avoided Rain's gaze. "He'd take me out in the patrol car. We'd go to the levees at the edge of town where there was nothing around but seagulls and muddy river water. Where no one would be able to see."

Bitterness leaked from her soft Southern drawl. "But this

time, he came into my room. He didn't lock the door because no one else was there. He'd been drinking."

"And Trevor came home," Rain whispered.

"Practice let out early. We never heard him come up the stairs. Daddy still had on his uniform. He was making me—" Her words caught, her blue eyes closing and opening again like a fragile china doll's. "Trevor walked in on us."

The vodka bottle sat on the credenza behind Alex's desk. Rain took Annabelle's glass and refilled it, giving her time to pull herself together. Once she'd taken a sip, Rain asked the question weighing on her.

"Annabelle," she urged. "What happened then?"

Her forehead wrinkled, and for a moment she appeared lost in memory. "Daddy backed Trevor to the wall. He slapped him and cursed at him. Then he put the barrel of his service pistol…against his head. He gave him a choice—keep quiet about what he saw, or die. Trevor looked him in the eye and told him to go to hell."

A tear spilled onto her cheek. "Even at fifteen, Trevor was brave to the point of foolishness."

Rain felt her pulse racing. Seconds passed before Annabelle spoke again.

"He hit Trevor with the gun. He swung it hard." She looked at the floor, as if she could still see her brother lying in front of her. "Trevor fell, and Daddy hit him again. I tried to stop him, but I—"

Annabelle put a hand over her lips. Rain touched her back, trying to comfort her.

"Trevor was in a coma for three days…on a ventilator. They had to do surgery. He was bleeding inside his brain."

Rain thought of Trevor in a hospital bed, connected to tubes and wires. The injustice appalled her. "But your father? Surely he was punished for what he did."

"The official story was that Trevor had been hurt during a

robbery attempt on our household, which my father managed to stop when he came home during his break. Since he was a police officer, no one even questioned him. He came off like a hero." Annabelle looked at Rain, her eyes filled with guilt. "At first, we all went along with it because we were afraid of what might happen—what'd he do to us—if we told the truth."

"What about your mother? Brian?"

"They came home right after. Daddy forced Brian to make the 911 call and lie to the operator about what happened. He was ten years old." Her voice thinned, becoming unsteady. "I held Trevor in my arms while we waited for the ambulance, but he wouldn't wake up—"

"Mommy?" Haley stood in the doorway. She gazed at her mother, who hurriedly wiped at her face.

"It's okay, baby." Annabelle smiled sweetly.

"I want something to drink."

"Apple juice?" Annabelle went to the minifridge and removed a small carton. She pulled the tiny straw from the container's side and popped it through the sealed foil top. Bending down, she handed it to her daughter, then wrapped her in a hug. As Rain took in the scene, she tried to process all she'd been told. The night she and Trevor had made love, he'd talked a little about his troubled past, but he hadn't revealed to her the true depth of it. As bad as she'd imagined his childhood to have been, she hadn't expected this.

Once Haley left the room, Annabelle took up the story again, seeming determined to finish despite the toll it was taking.

"When Trevor regained consciousness, he needed help. He was very weak. His speech was slower and he was having trouble with his words. He also had what the doctors called retrograde memory loss—he didn't remember anything leading up to his injury." Picking up a photo in a silver frame on Alex's desk, she ran her fingers over its surface. "Losing Trevor was especially hard on Brian. He looked up to him so much."

"Losing Trevor?"

"Momma sent Trevor to Maryland to live with her sister and her husband. There was an excellent outpatient rehabilitation program there, but mostly it got him away from our father. Trevor couldn't fight him anymore." Her reddened eyes sank into Rain's. "My mother did one brave thing in her whole life, and that was finally telling James Rivette she'd let everyone know the truth if he didn't agree to let Trevor go."

"She could've just gone to the police and told them what really happened from the beginning. I know she was scared, but with you and Brian to back up her story—"

"She didn't want it to come out what my father did to *me*. She was convinced my life would be ruined if anyone knew, and that we had to keep what happened a secret. At first, we lied out of fear, and then we lied to protect me."

Rain stared at Annabelle, who seemed to be waiting for condemnation. When she received none, her hands twisted together briefly.

"My father never touched me again, not after that day. Less than three months later, he moved out. Our parents were devoutly Catholic, but he didn't contest the divorce."

Trevor's traumatic injury had finally broken the fistlike hold James Rivette had on his family. *But it wasn't enough,* Rain thought. There had to be some kind of punishment for such violent, immoral behavior.

"But Trevor *did* get better," she pointed out. The Trevor she knew was strong and healthy, his mind sharp and brimming with intelligence. There was nothing about him that suggested frailties, physical or otherwise. FBI evaluations for agents were rigorous, and he'd obviously passed them all.

"The specialists in Maryland were certain Trevor hadn't

suffered any permanent brain damage," Annabelle said. "It was more like an electrical short circuit. The wires inside his head had gotten crossed, and they needed straightening out. It took several months of therapy, but Trevor was young and very determined. He got completely well."

She replaced the photo on the desk. "But his memory of what happened that day never came back. He asked questions, of course, but he only got lies in return."

"No one ever told him the truth?"

"Sometimes I try to convince myself he was better off that way," she admitted softly. "Aunt Susan and Uncle Frank couldn't have children of their own. They treated Trevor like a son. For the first time, I think he had a peaceful home life. After he recovered, he got an opportunity to attend a private prep school there on scholarship, and he stayed. Trevor's always been so smart. He was thriving without us."

"But he knows now, doesn't he? How did he find out?"

Annabelle gazed at the scar on her wrist. "Aunt Susan finally told him…after I cut myself. She decided it was time for the lying to stop."

She shook her head, causing the dark waves of her hair to move and shimmer under the muted lights. "She brought Trevor home to visit me when I was in the hospital. I was in the psych ward. He tried to be strong for me, but he was very upset. I was pretty drugged, but I remember him holding my hand and asking me why we lied to him."

Her eyes were unflinching despite the emotion they held. "He pulled away from us after that. Trevor's kept in touch over the years, but…"

Rain felt the loss within her own heart. "You and Brian didn't have a choice in any of this. Surely Trevor understands that now. You were victims, too."

"Trevor loved Brian and me more than anything in this world, and we deceived him. He's been through so much, and he has a hard time trusting. If you care for him…I just thought you should know this about him."

It had all happened so long ago, and yet the aftershocks still seemed to reverberate around them. Rain understood what it had taken for Annabelle to lay out the brutal facts for someone who was in essence a complete stranger to her. Even more, she was aware of the courage required for her to move beyond her own tragic childhood—beyond a suicide attempt—to regain her footing and forge ahead. To raise a child on her own. Annabelle Rivette was a true steel magnolia.

"Rain? Brian and I…we're worried about Trevor. We think being in New Orleans might be triggering his memory about what happened that day."

"He's having flashbacks?"

Annabelle looked at her uncertainly. "Is that possible after all these years?"

Rain thought of the stress Trevor was under. Not only was he deeply immersed in a hunt for a violent killer, but he was being forced to run up against painful recollections his mind had worked hard to suppress.

"It's entirely possible," she said.

Trevor. She realized how long she'd been gone—nearly two hours. Pulling her slender cell phone from the pocket of her jeans, Rain cursed silently when she saw it wasn't turned on. Her only hope was that the cop at her house hadn't noticed her absence, and she could slip back inside as easily as she'd gotten out.

"What is it?" Annabelle asked.

Rain pressed the phone against her ear, her heart clenching at the recorded message. Trevor sounded furious and more than a little scared.

Damn it, Rain. If you get this message, call me. Please.

Looking at Annabelle, she dialed his cell phone. He answered instantly.

"Where are you?"

"I'm on my way back home now. Don't worry."

"Don't worry?" Trevor practically barked into the phone. "The cops call and tell me you disappeared. Can you guess what I've been thinking? I've been out of my mind."

She felt Annabelle touch her arm, offering support.

"Just tell me where you are," Trevor said. "I'm coming to get you."

"I'm at the gallery. With Annabelle."

There was a long silence. When he finally spoke, his voice was strained. "I'll be there in fifteen minutes. And for Christ's sake, both of you keep the door locked."

The Taurus's beams threw light into the closed gallery as Trevor pulled up along the curb. As soon as Annabelle let him inside, his eyes zeroed in on Rain. His hard features silenced the apology she'd been about to give. Instead, she stood with her fingers hooked nervously in her jeans and waited for the approaching thunderstorm to let loose.

Trevor stalked toward her. "Want to tell me what was so important you had to ditch the officer assigned to protect you?"

"I wanted to talk to Brian—"

"Then call him on the phone."

"Go easy on her, okay?" Annabelle came over to where they stood. "And lower your voice. Haley's asleep."

Trevor's gaze shifted around the room. His anger receded as he saw his niece sleeping on a bench in a corner of the gallery, and he stepped over for a closer look. Haley's small thumb was poked in her mouth and her dark curls glimmered like a halo under the recessed lighting. Her frayed purple cat lay on the wood floor under the bench.

"Where's Brian?"

"He and Alex went to a client dinner in Pensacola,"

Annabelle said. "They just called from the airport. They're on their way back now."

Trevor ran his hand through his hair, visibly forcing himself to relax. Rain could only imagine the adrenaline that had been coursing through him since he'd learned of her disappearance. She knew the ride back to her house would be a long one.

"Want me to carry her out to the car for you?" Trevor still looked at Haley, who mumbled a few nonsensical words and flipped onto her stomach. The bench's padding gave out a soft *whoosh* as she kicked her sneaker-clad foot and fell back asleep.

"That's okay," Annabelle said. "I've got a few more things I need to do here. Rain and I had a couple of drinks, so I think I'm going to have Brian drive us home. You two go ahead."

She escorted them to the door. Rain didn't miss the long look that passed between the siblings, and she waited while Annabelle hugged her brother. As soon as she'd closed and locked the gallery door behind them, Trevor guided Rain to the sedan. He opened the passenger door and she slid inside. By the time he'd walked around the vehicle, she'd fastened her seat belt and sat with her hands folded on her lap.

"I've had a long day with the investigation. You scared the hell out of me, Rain."

"I didn't mean to," was all she could manage. He slid the keys into the ignition switch and brought the engine to life.

"Do that again and you won't have to worry about Dante," Trevor muttered, although the threat held little steam. He pulled the car out and silence enveloped them. Rain leaned against the headrest, wondering where to go from here. After all she'd learned tonight, she wanted to reach over and touch him, to try to comfort him in some way. But he looked so rigid she feared he might break into pieces next to her.

The car left the Warehouse District and made the path

around Lee Circle. It passed the illuminated bronze-and-marble statue of the Confederate general, then headed toward the Lower Garden District. Within minutes, they were entering the residential area with its Victorian cottages and graceful town houses. Rain cracked the window and let the warm night air inside.

"Annabelle shouldn't have told you," Trevor said finally. His voice was softer than she expected. He shook his head, his grip tightening on the steering wheel. "I didn't want you to know about any of that."

Rain didn't try to feign confusion. She looked at his profile in the shadows. "She thought it was important for me to know."

"None of that matters now."

"I believe it does."

He opened his mouth to say something, but bright lights suddenly swathed the inside of the vehicle. A large pickup truck on oversize wheels had swung from one of the tree-lined side streets and was gaining on them. A double row of hunting lights was mounted on the truck's cab, and its powerful engine roared like a wild animal advancing on its prey.

"Hold on," Trevor advised, accelerating. "I think we've got company."

34

Rain screamed as the truck bumped the Taurus hard from behind. The jolt caused the sedan to fishtail before Trevor regained control and steered it back on course. The monster vehicle revved its engine and cut right, its tires squealing as it raced up along Rain's side of the car. A black-haired male with dark-rimmed eyes sneered down at her from the truck's cab, one hand on the steering wheel and the other around the long neck of a beer bottle. He threw it and laughed as it shattered on the sedan's windshield.

Trevor kept his eyes on the road. "Can you tell how many there are?"

"Three, I think."

The truck veered into their lane, striking the car at the passenger door where Rain sat.

"Son of a bitch!" Trevor yelled as they were forced into the path of an oncoming car. A horn blared and he floored the gas pedal, managing to avoid a collision and get back in front of the truck. Rain turned as much as her seat belt would allow and saw the vehicle pressing up behind them.

"Get ready," Trevor warned, watching in the rearview mirror. He swung the sedan into a wide left-hand turn. It shot down a side street, but the truck seemed magnetized to follow.

Houses whizzed past in Rain's peripheral vision. The truck remained glued to their bumper, swerving dangerously on the narrow, one-way street. Trevor released the snap on his holster, preparing for the worst.

"Do you think they have guns?"

He looked again in the mirror. "I hope we don't have to find out."

They were headed away from the Garden District, the homes becoming more run-down before finally being replaced by cinder-block industrial buildings and metal warehouses. As they neared the freight docks lining the Mississippi, Rain could see large cranes rising up from the ships, looking like dinosaurs against the black night. A short distance ahead, a bridge crossed over one of the canals feeding into the harbor. The truck was bearing down on them again as it gathered speed for another attack.

"Hang on!"

This time, Trevor turned the steering wheel just before impact so that the larger vehicle clipped the corner of the sedan's back instead of landing a full-on hit. Rain closed her eyes as the car spun wildly before he brought it to a stop on the sandy shoulder of the road. But the truck had gained too much velocity. It lurched and flipped, crashing through the guardrail with a sickening noise.

"You okay?" Trevor ran his hands over her, checking for injury.

"I think so."

"Stay inside the car. Use your cell to report the accident." He released his seat belt and got out.

Rain dug her phone from her jeans pocket and called 911 as Trevor climbed over the crumpled guardrail. A second later, he vanished. Once she'd made contact with the emergency dispatcher and been assured help was on the way, she tossed the phone onto the seat. She couldn't just wait. Rain set off in the direction Trevor had taken.

Reaching the guardrail, she scanned the area. Lights from the bridge only partially illuminated a field of kudzu that separated the road from the base of the overpass. The truck had crashed into one of the bridge's steel support columns. Its front was mangled, and its cargo bed hung precariously over the edge of the retaining wall where it had knocked out a portion of chain-link fence. The drop into the canal below would be deadly, assuming any of the passengers were still alive. Trevor was a dozen or so feet from the truck, kneeling over a lifeless form. Even in the dark, Rain could see it was a female.

Picking her way through the knee-high kudzu, she shuddered as a large nutria scurried in front of her. The feeble light from the bridge gleamed off its oily back before it disappeared into the undergrowth. She neared the wreckage just as the driver stumbled out through the front passenger-side door. His hair partially concealed his ghostlike face and a cut above one eyebrow leaked a thin trail of blood. He saw Rain and began to run away.

"You can't leave!" she shouted, her words dying as she glimpsed the handle of the gun sticking out of his pants. But instead of using it, he scrambled past her and faded into the shadows. Rain's pulse thrummed in her ears. The grinding sound of metal against metal caught her attention as the truck shifted slightly, its rear end wobbling over the canal.

"You shouldn't be down here," Trevor said as she reached him. Rain looked at the bloodied woman who appeared to be in her very early twenties. Her black hair was spread out on the ground like ropes. Her eyes were closed, and her face and scalp were badly cut.

"She was thrown from the vehicle. It looks like she went through the windshield." Trevor was using his dress tie as a temporary bandage to stanch the flow of blood from a deep gash on her right arm. Rain's stomach turned.

"She's breathing, but not very well." He stood. "Watch her. There's another male in the backseat of the cab who's not responding to my voice."

"What are you going to do?"

"I may have to get inside to get him out."

"Trevor, that truck could fall!"

Ignoring her, he tried the back door, but it was jammed. He rapped on the window. "Can you hear me? Wake up!"

Finding a large rock on the ground, he covered his eyes with one hand and looked away from the truck as he shattered the window. He reached inside.

"He's got a pulse, but it's weak," Trevor said as Rain caught up to him. She grabbed his arm.

"You can't go in there. The other guy had a gun! The cab's not stable—"

"Go back to the girl, Rain. You may have to do CPR if she stops breathing. Do you know how?"

She nodded. Their eyes held in the darkness. Then she returned to the body that lay in the grass. The female was still unconscious, but her chest moved in and out. Rain watched Trevor climb inside the truck through the open front door. A scream rose inside her throat as it groaned and moved like an awakening beast.

An eternity seemed to pass while he worked inside the cab to free the remaining passenger. Each time the truck shifted on the ledge, Rain said a fervent prayer. In the distance, she heard the wail of emergency sirens. Help couldn't arrive soon enough.

To her relief, Trevor finally emerged dragging the dead weight of the unconscious male as the first maroon streaks of light shot across the sky. But he'd no sooner gotten him out of the vehicle when it gave way with an awful metallic scrape against the concrete barrier. The truck slid over the ledge, followed a few moments later by a thunderous splash. Rain ran to where Trevor knelt next to the victim.

"They're here!" she cried. The first paramedics were already rushing toward them carrying a gurney.

"I think he's stopped breathing." Trevor tilted the male's head back to open his airway. He looked young, the same approximate age as the female. Trevor bent over him, listening for his breath.

"We'll take over now. You folks okay?" an African-American paramedic asked as he dropped down next to Trevor.

"We're fine," Rain answered.

"Were there any occupants still inside the vehicle?"

"They're all out."

She touched Trevor's shoulder, and he stood as another paramedic arrived. He watched them begin resuscitation efforts.

"I took a chance moving him." Trevor pushed his hair from his forehead. "If he has a spinal injury, I could've made it worse."

"You did the right thing. The truck was ready to fall at any second." Rain took his hand, and she felt his fingers curl around hers. She turned to gaze at the injured female who was receiving assistance, as well.

In the canal below them, a boat belonging to the harbor police appeared. Its spotlight lit a section of the canal as it circled the water. Rain peered into the murky depths where the vehicle had already sunk. Anxiety coursed through her as she realized how close Trevor had come to being inside the truck when it went over the wall. She grasped his hand harder.

Along the road, squad cars and ambulances now sat with their lights flashing. A news van had also arrived. One of its crew panned the area with a video camera he held on his shoulder.

"Did you get a good look at the driver who ran past you?"

"Good enough that I'd recognize him again," Rain said. "He was older than the other two. Maybe early thirties. He had a cut over his right eye that could help identify him."

They walked back through the broad-leafed kudzu. An officer approached as they reached what was left of the guardrail. Trevor presented his shield and described the accident, explaining that the truck had been attempting to force them off the road when the crash occurred. He also stated that the driver was armed and had left the scene on foot. As she listened, Rain tried not to think about whose orders the goths had been following, but she couldn't shake the image of Armand Baptiste from her mind.

"The driver took a shot at you?" the officer asked.

Trevor shook his head. "He was more interested in getting away."

"I don't suppose you got the tag number off the truck?"

"The plates were removed."

The cop nodded and spit on the ground. "As soon as we get the vehicle out of the water, we'll be able to track ownership through its VIN number. You think this is related to your investigation into the serial murders, Agent?"

"There's no doubt."

They paused as the injured young woman was rushed past them on a gurney and loaded into one of the ambulances. Paramedics still worked on the male.

"Which hospital are they going to?" Trevor asked.

"All Saints, most likely." The officer stomped off, yelling an order at the news crew to move back. Rain and Trevor were left standing alone. She wanted to get him out of here, before the accident ate at him further, and before the reporters recognized either of them. The car Trevor was driving had been dented and scraped, but to her knowledge it was still operable.

"It's going to be hours before they'll know who the truck belonged to," she said. "You know that."

Trevor looked exhausted.

"I'm sorry about the way I acted tonight, about the whole deal with D'Alba," he admitted quietly. "Sometimes I don't understand myself."

He gazed onto the water as the harbor patrol made another wide arc in the canal. "When the cop called and said you'd disappeared, all I could think about was our last conversation. What if I never had a chance…"

He stopped speaking, and Rain touched his face. "It's late. Just take me home, okay?"

Once they were out of sight of the others, Trevor put his arm around her. Rain felt his lips press against her forehead. She laid her cheek against his chest, shutting her eyes against the madness that seemed to be all around them.

35

Rain avoided the reproachful glare of the officer on duty, aware her escape had probably earned him a dressing-down from his superior at the NOPD. She took to the staircase and headed upstairs, but not before she heard Trevor dismiss the man for the rest of the evening.

Inside the bathroom, she turned on the shower and let it heat while she peeled off her clothes. The canal's brackish scent hung on her skin, just as her mind held tight to the image of motionless bodies lying on the ground. They'd had a close call tonight, with the car chase and the risk Trevor had taken to free the truck's passenger. It occurred to her the driver who'd fled the scene could have shot either of them— Trevor when he was distracted by the injured female, or Rain herself when he'd run past. On edge, she stepped under the sanctuary of the hot spray and tried to shut out the night's events.

She emerged from the bathroom a short time later wrapped in her chenille bathrobe. Trevor stood in the bedroom doorway, his broad shoulders silhouetted by the golden light emanating from the hall behind him. He walked slowly to her. Wordlessly, he laced his fingers in her wet hair, tangling them in the long strands. His mouth covered hers and Rain clung to him through the smooth cotton of his dress shirt. She shivered as his kiss banished all other thought.

Afterward, he continued holding her in his arms.

"I could use a shower, too," he said finally, his breath warm against the top of her head. "I left my bag here, so I should have a change of clothes."

"Go ahead. I'll go down to the kitchen and see if I can find us something to eat." Rain pulled gently from his embrace, but he caught her hand.

"The cop's gone—he won't be back until noon tomorrow when I have to leave," he said quietly. "It's just us."

As he led her back into the bathroom, Rain began to understand what he had in mind. He turned on the showerhead, and she helped him remove his shirt, her hands trembling slightly as she undid the buttons. While she worked, Trevor untied the sash of her robe, easing the garment from her shoulders until it pooled at her feet. She was naked underneath, her skin still flushed and glowing from her shower.

Apparently, she would join him as he took his.

Once he was naked and they'd both stepped under the warm, pummeling jets, Trevor tipped up her chin, his head lowering and his mouth gliding over hers. Rain stood on tiptoe, her arms looped around his shoulders and her breasts pressed against his water-slicked chest as they kissed. The feel of his male hardness was thrilling. Trevor's hands roamed over her, cupping her buttocks, slowly turning her until her back was pressed against the stall's tiles. He'd brought a condom into the shower with them, and he put it on.

Rain's breathing grew shallow as she stared up into his serious, beautiful eyes. The car accident had rocked him as much as it had her, she realized.

"Trevor," she said softly. "I—"

He wasn't interested in talking. His mouth came down on hers again, his lips firm and demanding, his tongue exploring.

Rain's arms tightened around his neck as he lifted her, moving between her legs. She gasped with the shock of it as he entered her, sinking deeply into her core.

"Oh, God," Rain whispered, her eyes closing and her legs wrapping around his hips. Bracing one arm against the wall over Rain's head, Trevor thrust into her, over and over again.

The cloud of steam enveloped them, water pounded on their skin. Head back, mouth open, she felt the spray on her face as Trevor pushed them both to the edge. His teeth nipped at her shoulder, gently biting. It didn't matter if he was using her to block out the car crash, the injured young adults. Their lovemaking attested that they were both still alive.

Their climax came almost in unison. Rain came hard as Trevor gave a last grunting thrust. His mouth silenced her cry of pleasure. Breathless himself, after several long seconds he allowed her feet to touch the tiled shower floor again. She held on to him, her legs shaking from their sensual encounter. His fingers toyed with her breasts.

Their mouths joined. They stayed together, lost in each other's embrace until the water began to run cold.

A short time later, Rain returned from the kitchen, once again in her robe. She carried a tray with dense brown bread, cheese and cold cuts, fruit and two bottles of water. Trevor sat on the edge of the bed, talking on the bedroom phone. Having located his duffel bag, he'd changed into sweatpants and a well-worn Georgetown T-shirt. She waited until he disconnected the call before placing the tray on the coverlet.

"I called the hospital," he told her. "The male had extensive internal injuries. He was confirmed DOA. The female's in ICU on a ventilator. It turns out she's also about eight weeks pregnant."

Seeing his troubled expression, Rain eased down beside him. "Trevor—"

"I talked to the NOPD, too. They got a registration on the truck. It belonged to Armand Baptiste."

Armand was a pied piper in the goth community. It made sense he'd used others to do his bidding instead of chancing capture himself. Rain wondered, had he been trying to exact some revenge against Trevor?

"Do you really think he could be Dante?"

"The evidence from the Ascension is pretty significant, but I still don't know." He looked at her. "Regardless, until we close this case, you're still in danger."

The sheets were turned back and the nearly empty tray of food placed between them on the bed. Rain had changed into pajama bottoms and a lace-edged camisole. She sat cross-legged, slicing an apple with a sharp paring knife. Although she busied herself with the task at hand, she'd been watching Trevor carefully. He'd been contemplative since making the calls to the hospital and police.

"Want to tell me what's on your mind?" she asked, tentative.

He studied the bottled water in his hand. "Your conversation with Annabelle."

Rain put the knife and what was left of the apple on the tray. They'd been on the verge of discussing the things his sister had told her when the truck had raced up behind them. "It's the girl on the ventilator, isn't it? She's making you think about your own…injury."

Trevor set the bottle on the nightstand. Moments passed before he spoke.

"I can remember waking up and being attached to that machine," he confessed. "There was a tube down my throat, forcing air in and out of my lungs. It was the worst thing…"

He shook his head at the recollection. Touched that he'd

opened up to her, Rain reached for his hand and waited for him to continue.

"Even once I was off the ventilator, my mind and my body…they weren't working…right. The things I wanted to say weren't coming out of my mouth." Trevor's eyes darkened. "I hated all of it. The weakness, the loss of control over my life."

"You were young and strong. You *recovered*," Rain reminded gently. "You survived a tragedy that would've destroyed most people."

But she also asked herself, had he really? While Trevor had managed to overcome the most obvious damage, she realized there were deeper emotional scars he'd kept hidden far too long.

"How much do you really remember about that day? About what happened with your father?"

Shrugging, he gazed down at her fingers entwined with his. "I get scenes from time to time. Just random bits and pieces."

"Have the memories been more frequent since you came home?" Rain saw her answer in his face. She moved the tray away and slid closer to him, tracing soft patterns against his back through his T-shirt. He bowed his head.

"Despite what Annabelle told you, I don't blame her and Brian. They did what they had to."

She nodded her understanding. "I know."

"Brian found her in the bathroom, after she cut herself." His voice lowered into a rasp. He swallowed, trying to control his emotions. "Did Anna tell you that? Brian was just twelve. I should've been here—"

"Trevor," Rain murmured. "I'm so sorry, for all of you."

"She tried to kill herself…because of what happened to me."

"You don't know that," she reasoned. "There were other

issues involved. There's a lot of confusion and guilt that goes with sexual abuse, especially when the perpetrator is a family member—"

"What that bastard did to Anna wasn't her fault," he said angrily.

"Of course not." She stroked his forearm. "But it wasn't *yours,* either. Trevor, did Annabelle receive counseling? After the suicide attempt?"

"She's had years of therapy. Brian's been in addiction treatment, too."

"What about you? Have you ever talked to anyone?"

His expression grew shuttered. "I get regular mental-health screenings through the FBI. It's a job requirement."

"It's not the same thing," she countered. "They're only checking to make sure you can handle the pressures of your job. What I mean is, have you ever discussed your childhood or your trauma specifically?"

She felt his near-physical wince beside her. "I told Brian already...I just don't see a reason to dredge things back up. I don't need any couch time. I know you believe in all that—"

"I more than *believe* in it, Trevor. It's what I do."

He fell silent, rubbing his palms over his thighs.

"If you don't feel anything, you don't hurt." Her quiet revelation caused him to look into her eyes. "It's why you've distanced yourself from your brother and sister. From anyone who cares about you. But don't you see? That kind of detachment is no way to live."

He stared at her for a long time, his expression as open as Rain had ever seen it. Then he slowly brushed the still-damp hair back from her face and drew her against him. Rain found comfort in the solidity of his body and the clean, soapy smell of his skin. She could help him, she knew it. If he'd only stop running long enough to allow himself to heal. New

Orleans was the catalyst that had brought back the memories he'd worked so hard to repress. But once the case was closed, what then? Rain suspected he wouldn't be able to leave the city quickly enough. She felt an ache inside her chest.

"What I said earlier...I didn't mean to insult what you do," he tried to explain. "I'm not thinking clearly. I guess I'm just wiped out."

"Then *sleep* with me tonight." She caressed the strong line of his jaw. "The security alarm's set downstairs and you've changed the pass code. You don't have to stay up and keep watch. We'll be fine."

After a moment, he nodded in agreement. Trevor stretched out his free arm to check his gun that he'd laid on the nightstand. Then he reached for the lamp and clicked it off, bathing the room in darkness.

Rain was tired, too. She tugged the covers over their bodies, then settled beside him and shut her eyes. As the last vestiges of consciousness began to abandon her, Trevor pulled her closer.

"I care about you, Rain," he whispered. "God help me, but I do."

Armand Baptiste shoved his hands into the pockets of his wrinkled trousers to hide their tremor. The cocaine he'd snorted earlier was causing him to sweat, making his clothing damp and his palms clammy.

His shoes left indentations in the room's plush carpeting as he paced its considerable length. He walked to the ornately curtained windows, careful to avert his gaze from the massive jowls and sharp teeth of the animal heads mounted on the paneled walls. Oil paintings in gilded frames depicted gory hunting scenes, and an actual coat of medieval armor stood guard in the corner. The room was ostentatious, even by *his* standards.

He bristled at the unfairness. His own assets had been frozen and his comfortable French Quarter home placed under twenty-four-hour surveillance. Two nights ago, he'd barely made it out a back door of the Ascension as law enforcement swarmed the club. Since then, he'd been taking refuge among those in his world who would harbor him. But it was only a matter of time until someone turned him in for the reward. What he needed was money and an escape route, both of which the man behind the desk could easily provide.

"You've gotten yourself into a fair amount of trouble, Armand. What do you want from me?" The voice was distinguished and well-bred, and the green eyes behind spectacles stared at Armand with a slightly bored expression, as if he were a bug that required squashing.

"I need cash." Armand dug out a cigarette and held it between trembling fingers. "Enough to get out of the country and stay out—"

"Do I need to remind you of the artwork in here that won't tolerate smoke? You of all people should know that."

Armand stuffed the cigarette back inside his pocket. He felt his hold on his temper crumbling like old paper. His life had fallen apart and he was being told not to smoke? It was clear he was being toyed with—the room held the fermented aroma of Cuban cigars. A vintage humidor even sat on the desk, its oiled wood top gleaming in the light from the chandelier overhead.

"Are you going to help me or not?"

The green eyes regarded him coolly. "And if I don't?"

Armand gulped. But he didn't look away, the cocaine in his system boosting his nerve.

"Then I'll make a deal with the FBI." His voice rose fractionally. "I'll tell them what your progeny was doing at my club."

The threat hung in the air like smoke from a fire. The other man templed his manicured fingers in front of him, causing the emerald eyes of the serpent-like ring to flash. Sweat rolled down Armand's neck and into his collar, but he continued.

"I saw him, you know. I saw him with the first girl, and then a few days later with the second one. He took them outside and he put them in your fucking Mercedes, Carteris. They suspect *me* of the murders because of what I was importing for *you*. I never asked what you wanted the reproductions for—"

Christian Carteris removed his glasses and laid them on the desk. "You never asked because it was none of your business. I'm your client, and you received a substantial commission for your services. Discretion is key to your trade, is it not?"

Armand exploded. "The rosaries are what linked me to the murders, goddammit! Let me tell you something—they catch me, they catch you! I'll exchange what I know to get out of the drug charges!"

"You're playing a risky game. What if the FBI isn't in the mood to make deals? Especially with a loathsome drug dealer."

"That's why I'm giving you the first option to buy my silence."

After a long pause, Carteris opened a drawer and withdrew a roll of bills. He tossed it onto the desk. Picking up the money, Armand flipped through it. But his bloodshot eyes quickly narrowed into slits.

"Ten thousand dollars? That's not even a down payment." He thumped his chest in self-importance. "*I'm the link*. I'm all the FBI needs to make the connection between those dead girls, the rosaries and you."

Pressing his lips together, Carteris stood to his full height. As he went around to the front of the desk, Armand took an involuntary step backward.

"I'm disheartened you'd use our friendship in this manner, Armand. But I'm going to overlook it since I understand your current distress. I'm also going to fulfill your request, since it's in both our interests for you to disappear. Come with me."

Armand's heart pulsed harder. "Where are we going?"

"To my safe." Irritation laced Carteris's words as he walked toward the wood-carved door that led from his office to the hallway. "Lucky for you, I keep a tidy sum in the house."

Armand fell in step behind his brisk gait, aware of the solid build of his shoulders under the starched dress shirt. It was well after midnight, and yet Carteris had greeted him at the door, fully awake and impeccably dressed. He'd observed the bruise around the socket of his right eye and wondered how the surgeon had gotten it. Subduing one of his victims? The thought gave Armand a chill. The goth community's inner circles had whispered of Carteris's sanguinary activities for some time. But with the murders, it was clear he'd lost control.

"Where's Oliver?" Armand asked.

"He's not home."

His morbid curiosity wanted to know the extent of Oliver's involvement. Did he partake in the goods he spirited from the clubs, or was he merely the delivery boy? Oliver was an overprivileged punk, but Armand didn't see him as a murderer. Carteris's stony silence, however, warned him to keep his questions to himself.

They traveled down a wainscoted corridor lit by porcelain wall sconces. An Oriental carpet runner covered the polished wood floor. Every so often, there was another expensive piece of artwork, a rich oil painting or an antique vase on a mahogany stand. The place practically reeked of money.

"Where's your safe, Bayou St. John?" Armand's joke fell flat. He was growing jumpier by the minute. His high had begun to falter, and he wanted to be gone from this place before it abandoned him completely.

"Patience," Carteris snapped. "Trust me, I want you out of here quickly."

They finally stopped at a set of wide doors. Carteris pushed them open and Armand followed him into a cavernous space with a three-tiered trey ceiling. A built-in bookcase ran the room's perimeter, and a rolling ladder on a brass railing system had been installed to reach the uppermost shelves. But the furniture and carpeting were covered in canvas drop cloths and sheets of white plastic, giving the area a ghostly appearance. Even the chandelier in the room's center was robed in white like some sort of floating apparition. Carteris pointed up to the ceiling, and Armand noticed the crumbling plaster that hung down like globs of cottage cheese.

"One of the responsibilities of fine old houses is their continual upkeep," Carteris lectured. As he walked across the room, bits of fallen plaster crunched under his shoes. "Something's always under renovation."

Ripping down a plastic sheet, he tugged at the edge of a gold-framed painting. It swung outward on hinges, revealing a wall safe. Armand stepped closer as Carteris twirled the dial on its door.

"I want a million."

Carteris laughed. "You'll get one hundred thousand. And I expect you out of New Orleans by daybreak, and out of the country by tomorrow night. I have a connection who can arrange a fake passport for your travel."

The tumblers clicked into place and Carteris pulled open the safe's door. Armand said nothing, deciding to take what he was offered, for now. He'd do his blackmailing from a safe distance, once the money he was given ran out.

"Cardiology must pay well." He gaped at the stacks of bills being extracted.

"My research pays better. I still have ties to a private European firm, you know." Carteris dropped the cash onto a canvas-sheathed table. "Very top-secret stuff."

Probably tax free, too, Armand thought. He'd definitely be getting his full million in the near future.

"I understand you sent some of your minions on an errand tonight?" Carteris's voice was muffled, his head and shoulders back inside the safe as he dug out more cash. For a second, Armand considered scooping up what was already on the table and making a run for it while the surgeon was occupied. But his greed won out and he waited, his nerves sizzling like exposed electrical wire.

"I asked you a question, Armand."

Armand recalled the greasy-haired druggie coming back to him, moaning about the truck being scrap metal. The imbecile had still expected a handful of pills in exchange for his failed attempt. "Oh, yeah. It didn't work out. Look, could we hurry this up? It's going to be light in a few hours."

Carteris placed several more stacks on the table. "What was your intent? To injure Agent Rivette?"

"Why do you care?"

"Rain Sommers was with him in the car."

Armand shrugged, having lost all admiration for Desiree's daughter. She'd started this disaster by bringing her new boyfriend into the club's private sanctum. "What's the saying? You're no better than the company you keep."

"Indeed."

The blade was so sharp, Armand felt nothing as it slid across his throat. Grasping his neck, he stared in horrified surprise at the bright crimson spurting between his fingers and washing down his shirt. Blood splattered onto the sheeting protecting the floor. He tried to speak, but only gurgling noises emerged.

"You could've ruined everything." Carteris ran his thumb

across the wet surface of the knife, then raised the digit to his mouth for a taste.

"I'm very disappointed in you, Armand. I paid you well for your services. I even gave you information on Agent Rivette. And you thank me by threatening to pull me into your mess?"

Armand fell to his knees. He could feel energy rushing out of him, and his vision began to recede. His body hit the floor. His last sensation was of Carteris on top of him, lapping at his throat like a hungry dog.

36

Shallow morning light filtered through the gossamer curtains. Drowsily, Rain opened her eyes as Trevor got out of bed. She watched him pull on his sweatpants and T-shirt, then rummage in his duffel bag that sat on the floor.

"Rain?" His voice was low. "Are you awake?"

"No." With a soft sigh, she rolled onto her stomach. The sheets against her naked skin felt pleasurable. They'd made love again during the night, their bodies still new to one another and the temptation of warm-silk flesh too strong not to give in. Even now, she wanted nothing more than to linger in bed with him, tucked away from the world.

"Will you get up?"

Rain lifted her head from the pillow as Trevor laced up his tennis shoes.

"You can't be serious," she mumbled, looking at the clock. "It's Sunday and barely six-thirty. I don't *do* six-thirty."

"I need to go for a run before it heats up outside. I haven't had the time to go for days and my legs need it. Which means you're going with me. I can't leave you here alone."

Her response was to snuggle in more deeply. She'd just begun to doze when he pulled the sheets away, causing Dahlia to leap from the foot of the bed. Sitting up with a squeak of surprise, Rain made a fruitless grab for the covers that were held just out of her reach. Trevor's lips curved into a soft smile. "Tempting, but we need to get going."

"I *need* coffee."

"Run first, coffee later. C'mon. I have a lot to do."

"It's *Sunday*," she repeated.

"I know, but I need to file some reports before I attend a status meeting this afternoon. My laptop's downstairs, so I can do it from here when we get back."

She blinked at him. "I'm not going to be able to keep up with you."

"I'll take it slow."

With a longing glance at her pillow, Rain climbed out of bed and began to get dressed. She struggled into a sports bra, a blue tank top and running shorts, and secured her hair with an elastic band. Turning, she noticed Trevor sliding a small gun into an ankle holster concealed underneath his sweat-pants. His eyes met hers in the room's retreating shadows, and she tugged self-consciously on her ponytail.

"I must look horrible. I haven't even brushed my teeth yet."

"You look beautiful." He stood and touched her cheek. Rain curled her fingers around his wrist as she gazed at him.

"I'm not a morning person."

"Really? I didn't notice."

He kissed her well enough to lift her mood. Despite the continuing search for Armand Baptiste, despite the grisly accident scene at the canal, Trevor seemed somehow more at peace this morning. If she'd managed to provide a distrac-tion for him, however brief, she was grateful. At least she'd awakened with him next to her, instead of alone, with a uni-formed police officer in her kitchen downstairs. She would be glad for the few hours she had with him before duty called him away.

"You're not sore from last night, are you?" he asked after she came out of the bathroom. Seeing her small grin, he clarified his question. "From playing bumper cars with the truck. Not from...us."

"I feel fine," Rain answered truthfully. Trevor took her hand and led her from the bedroom and down the stairs. He disarmed the security system using the keypad near the front door. Outside, the sun was just beginning to rise over the roofline of the houses across the street, and the scent of gardenias drifted over from a neighboring yard.

"I do yoga in a studio," Rain remarked. "An air-conditioned one."

"There's nothing wrong with a little cross training."

"I expect beignets with my coffee." She stifled a yawn as Trevor braced his hands on the veranda's wrought-iron railing. Stealing a look at her, he bent his head and began to stretch out his calves.

"Sure, but that's going to cost you an extra mile."

The maroon leaves of the Japanese maple concealed the rusted Chevrolet, which sat at the end of the street in the quiet Marigny neighborhood. James Rivette slouched in the driver's seat as he stared at the West Indies-style cottage. He gripped a waxy paper cup filled with coffee, its heat diluted by the whiskey he'd poured into it from a bottle he kept in the glove box.

At one time, the house had been his home. He'd made the down payment and handled the monthly mortgage for more years than he cared to remember. James took a long sip. He'd lost the place in the divorce. It was barely recognizable these days, painted in a god-awful shade that was somewhere between a faggoty pink and a violet.

He rolled down the window and let the warm morning air into the car's stale interior. The aroma of bacon and eggs wafted from one of the brightly hued houses, making his stomach growl. For several seconds, he considered driving to the nearest diner. But he thought of the money he'd been given and decided to stay put.

James sat there until the coffee was gone and he was left drinking straight from the bottle. One thing was certain—whoever his mystery benefactor was, it was clear Trevor had stepped on the wrong toes this time.

He'd been given to reminiscence lately, and for some reason the cold and rainy day of Sarah's funeral popped into his head like a floodlight being turned on. James hadn't seen his elder son in years, but he'd recognized him immediately among the mourners. Trevor had stood with his arm wrapped around Annabelle as she cried, the two of them under the Mercier Brothers Funeral Home tarp that had been hoisted up next to their mother's crypt. Somber-faced and handsome in a black suit and trench coat, Trevor briefly met James's stare. Then he'd callously dismissed him, instead looking out over the aboveground tombs and statuary as if his own father was no more than a ghost. Ostracized, James had been left shivering at the crowd's edge, rain dripping off him like a stray mongrel.

Later that day, he'd followed Trevor to Louis Armstrong Airport in the same beat-up Chevy he sat in right now. The holier-than-thou FBI agent hadn't realized he was being tailed. James had considered confronting his son and reminding him who was the better lawman. Instead, he'd ended up drinking alone in one of the airport bars. He took another gulp from the bottle, upending it and draining it dry.

Who was he to keep someone from bringing Trevor down a peg?

The stranger had been well dressed, with hoity-toity

manners that smacked of money and privilege. Yet despite the dark sunglasses, there was an aura about him that James recalled from his days as a beat cop working the rough streets of Storyville and Treme. The thugs there had the same disingenuous smile, which concealed an innate desire to cut out your heart if you turned your back on them. Similarly, his gut told him the stranger was someone he wouldn't want to cross.

Besides, a deal was a deal. They'd shook hands on it, shared another drink, and James had taken the money.

He belched and tossed the empty bottle out the window. Then he sat up straight as, like clockwork, the house's door creaked open. Still wearing pajamas, the little girl carried a carton of milk against her chest. Taking in the tangle of dark curls, James felt a sense of nostalgia. She looked just like his sweet Annabelle at that age.

He struggled to remember the child's name. What was it? *Haley.*

James put his hand on the Chevy's door handle and heard its soft snick as he opened it. He got out, taking care not to create too much noise. She was on her way to a toolshed in a neighbor's backyard, behind which a litter of kittens waited for their milk. The man told him she came out every morning to make sure the strays got their breakfast. He'd called James late last night, announcing the time to earn his money had arrived.

He wasn't doing any real harm. Didn't he want to get to know his only grandbaby, anyway?

Picking his way past a butterfly bush that hung heavy with cone-shaped flowers, he followed the same path the little girl had taken.

37

Two coffee cups sat on the kitchen counter, and only a dusting of powdered sugar remained from the beignets purchased at the corner bakery. Rain trailed a finger through what was left of the snowy confection. From upstairs came the knock of the old house's pipes, indicating Trevor was in the shower.

As she began clearing away their breakfast dishes, she noticed the blinking light on the phone console that hung on the wall. When had a call come through?

Rain dialed into the message system. A synthesized voice announced there was a single message, with a time stamp of late the previous evening. She entered her access code. Oliver's speech was slurred.

Dr. Sommers? You need to pick up. You're not answering your cell. I've got to talk to you. Fuck. Just pick up the phone…

Her cell phone. As a rule, Rain kept it with her since it was the number she gave to patients for use in case of an emergency. But she now recalled tossing it onto the seat of the Taurus after making the 911 call. Last night she'd forgotten to bring it inside. Oliver's second call, the one made to her home, had gone unnoticed. She wondered if it had been sent straight to voice mail when Trevor was on the phone with the hospital and police.

In her office, she located the number for Oliver's cell. It rang repeatedly but no one answered. A call to the residence on St. Charles Avenue garnered the same response. What should she do? Going to look for Oliver would be pointless, since she had no earthly idea where to find him.

Rain walked into the parlor as Trevor came downstairs. He wore jeans and a fresh T-shirt, his hair damp and his own cell phone gripped in his hand.

"What's wrong?" she asked, seeing his expression.

"Annabelle just called. It's my niece, Haley. She's gone."

Rain thought of the little girl and her heart froze. "Someone took her?"

"Not someone. My father. I need to get over there now."

Still wearing her running clothes, Rain accompanied Trevor to Annabelle's. She found her cell phone in the car and as Trevor drove, she tried to reach Oliver again, but to no avail.

One emergency at a time, she thought as she stuffed the phone into the patchwork denim bag she'd brought with her. It was one of Celeste's favorite sayings, something she'd repeated often when Rain was in the high drama of her teenage years. She only hoped a similar theatrical flair was behind Oliver's call. One thing was for certain—James Rivette had impeccable timing. Rain glanced at Trevor as he drove well above the posted speed limit and wondered how much one man was supposed to take.

Turning onto the street, she saw a squad car in front of a neat raspberry-hued cottage with gingerbread trim and a wide front porch. They parked, and she went with Trevor up the sidewalk as a police officer emerged from the house. Trevor dug his shield from his back pocket and presented it.

The two men walked to a line of green-leafed hosta plants at the yard's edge and spoke in quiet tones.

Going up to the porch, Rain looked inside through the open front door. Annabelle sat huddled on the couch, a tissue wadded in her slender fingers. Alex was next to her, trying to console her, while Brian paced the far side of the room. Rain turned as the officer got into his squad car and drove away.

"They're going to put out an Amber Alert for the Chevy he drives and they're sending a unit to watch his apartment," Trevor said as he came up the porch stairs. Distress filled his eyes. "He left a note on the front door that said he was taking Haley out for breakfast, like it's a perfectly normal activity. I swear, if he does anything—"

He stopped speaking as Annabelle appeared at the door. Rain embraced the other woman.

"It's okay, Anna," Trevor promised. "We'll get her back."

Annabelle met her brother's gaze. Her voice shook. "You were right. I should've gotten a restraining order."

"You had no idea he'd pull something like this."

"Has Dad ever tried to make contact with Haley before?" The question came from Brian, who'd followed Annabelle onto the porch.

"Never," Annabelle said, sniffling. "He'd never even come to the house until a few days ago when—"

"He was looking for me." Trevor finished the statement and Rain touched his arm. She knew that in his mind, he'd already accepted responsibility for his father's stunt, as well as anything that might happen to his niece.

"What can we do?" Alex asked. He'd stepped outside behind Brian.

"Nothing," Brian said. "It's like the old days. We're powerless."

"Like hell." Trevor headed down the stairs. "I can go out looking for the bastard."

Brian caught up to him before he reached the gate. "Where are you even going to start? The police already have an alert out for the car—"

"I can't just sit around here while—"

The phone in the house rang. Annabelle rushed inside with the rest of them on her heels. As soon as she answered the phone, her body went rigid. "Where are you? I want my daughter back!"

Still holding the receiver against her ear, her eyes swung to Trevor. Rain's stomach tightened.

"He wants to talk to you."

Trevor took the phone. He didn't waste time with a greeting. "I want Haley back now. You hear me, old man?"

He listened to whatever his father was saying on the other end of the line. Wearily, he passed a hand over his face and released a frustrated breath.

"We'll be there." Although his voice was low, the threat it held was clear. "If Haley's shed a single tear, I'll kill you."

Trevor disconnected the phone. His eyes were the color of cold gray steel. "He's drunk. He claims he just wanted to get to know his grandchild. They're over at City Park, riding the carousel."

Brian laughed bitterly. "You're kidding."

"He wants us to meet him—you, Annabelle and me," Trevor continued. "He says he made a mistake and if we don't involve the police further, he'll give Haley back without incident."

He looked as though he wanted to throw something through one of the room's paned windows. "He was going on about how unfair life's been to him. How none of what happened to any of us was his fault—"

His words broke off angrily, and Annabelle went to him.

"I just want to get her back, Trevor. Please."

"We're calling the cops and telling them where he is," Brian said as he reached for the phone.

"No." Trevor stopped him. "He says if he sees any cops, he's going to run. I don't want Haley caught in the middle of this. I'll make a call to the police on the way over, tell them to stay on the park's perimeter but not to approach."

Trevor turned to look at Rain, who stood next to Alex.

"Go with your family," she said softly. "You don't need to keep up with me. Besides, a stranger might agitate him."

He appeared hesitant. "When I call the police, I'll ask for the officer who was just here to turn around and come back. It shouldn't be more than five minutes. Until then—"

Alex spoke up. "I'll stay with her. We'll be fine."

Outside, Rain and Alex stood on the porch as the others climbed into Brian's Audi, leaving Trevor's damaged rental sedan behind. The doors slammed closed and Brian started the powerful engine. The car peeled away and disappeared down the street.

"Jesus, Mary and Joseph," Alex intoned, running a hand through his hair. "Can you believe this?"

"Unfortunately, I can." Rain thought of what she'd learned about the family's violent, tragic past. The secrets were bubbling to the surface, and she thanked God that at least Trevor wasn't meeting his father alone. He desperately needed Brian and Annabelle there to ground him, to keep him from losing control.

She sighed worriedly, recalling that Trevor said his father was intoxicated. He'd put Haley in a car and driven away with her, risking her safety.

"Maybe we should go back into the house. Until the police get here," Alex suggested. She followed him inside and locked the front door behind them. As they went into the efficient galley-style kitchen, Rain resigned herself to the fact that she'd have to wait as calmly as she could for the events at City

Park to play out. In the meantime, she could try to contact Oliver again. So far, he hadn't returned either of the messages she'd left him.

"We could have some coffee," Rain said as she searched inside her bag for her cell phone. The coffeemaker on the counter held a carafe full of the dark brew. Not that her nerves needed an added jolt of caffeine, but it could help pass the time.

"Coffee, hell." Alex opened one of the cabinet doors and peered at the rows of canned goods and other staples. He gave Rain a strained smile. "I'm a train wreck, honey. Where do you think Annabelle hides the bourbon?"

38

Although the massive live oaks in City Park provided a canopy against the sun, the midmorning humidity had already grown oppressive. Trevor's T-shirt stuck to his skin as he scanned the children's play area for his father.

True to his claim, James slumped on a wrought-iron bench across from the antique carousel. Haley sat next to him. Still dressed in her striped pajamas, she swung her moccasin-clad feet contentedly and munched on a pink cloud of cotton candy. Lyrical calliope music floated through the trees' low-spread branches.

"Son of a bitch," Trevor fumed. He felt Annabelle touch his wrist.

"Don't scare her," Brian said. "She doesn't understand what's going on."

As they approached, Haley called to them and climbed down from the bench. She ran to Annabelle, who scooped the child up in her arms.

"Haley, you know better than to get in a car with a stranger." Annabelle glared at her father as she wiped sticky sugar from her daughter's face.

"But he isn't a stranger!" Haley waved at James, who

waved back. "That man who came to our house, Mommy? He's my grandfather! He said so!"

"It's about time I got to know my grandbaby." James put his hands on the knees of his trousers and winked conspiratorially. "Ain't that right, sweetheart?"

"Anna, take Haley to get cleaned up," Trevor instructed.

Putting Haley down, Annabelle took her hand. "Let's go to the restroom. Then maybe we'll take a ride on the carousel."

With a concerned glance at Trevor and Brian, she led her away. James leaned back against the bench. Nearby, the miniature train that ran through the park's camellia gardens rumbled past, its bell clanging as children laughed and shouted from its seats.

"If it ain't the saint and the sinner," he mused, his glassy gaze traveling over his sons as they approached.

Trevor kept his voice low and controlled. "Annabelle's taking out a restraining order on Monday. You come within two hundred feet of her or Haley again and you'll land your ass in jail, if what you pulled today doesn't already put you there."

Hauling himself from the bench, James pushed a blunt finger into Trevor's chest. "I got rights to see that little girl—"

"No, you don't. And don't touch me." Trevor shoved his father's hand away. He could smell the alcohol on his breath.

"Thought I'd beat that attitude out of you a long time ago."

Brian gripped Trevor's shoulder. "Don't bring this down to his level. Let's just get Annabelle and Haley and go."

"And what about *you?*" James turned on Brian, sneering. "I've seen you around with your swishy boyfriend. Are you the husband or the wife? You disgust me. You're an embarrassment to the family name!"

"That's rich coming from you, Dad," Brian murmured.

Trevor placed his hand on his holstered gun. "I don't know what this is about, but I don't have time to waste with you. I'm giving you the chance to walk away before this gets ugly."

A drop of perspiration trailed down James's flaccid neck before soaking into his plaid cotton shirt. Sweat had created dark circles under his arms, and he hitched up the belt that was barely visible under his protruding gut. He stared hatefully at Trevor. "I should've finished the job I started on you. That's my regret."

Trevor felt a nerve jump along his jaw, but he didn't look away. His father's eyes held a cruel gleam.

"You gotta ask yourself where your family was when you needed 'em, Trev. They had no problem shipping you off when you woke up with an addled brain—"

"Shut up," Brian said.

"But here you are, making out like the perfect family. Guess you really can forgive. As long as you're in City Park, maybe y'all should have a picnic."

Years of hurt and anger tore at Trevor, but he held his ground.

"You always despised me, Dad, because I stood up to you." He stepped forward, his face directly in front of his father's. "I knew you for what you were. A bully and an on-the-take cop. Now you're just a pathetic drunk who has to stoop to tricks to get his children to even look at him. You're old and alone. You got everything you deserve."

James clenched his fist and pulled it back, but Trevor caught his arm. "I'm telling you one more time to go, before I arrest you myself. Don't come near Annabelle or Haley again."

A charged silence hung between the two men. Then James wrung himself free. His face flushed persimmon.

"To hell with both of you." Staggering away, he halted

when he reached the crushed-shell path. "Oh, yeah. Almost forgot."

He fumbled in his shirt pocket and threw something on the ground at Trevor's feet. White gold glinted against the dewy grass.

"What's that?" Brian asked, looking at his father as Trevor picked up the object.

James shrugged. He wedged a cigarette between his lips and patted his trousers for a lighter. "I'm just the messenger. He said you'd know what it meant."

The delicate serpentine chain pooled in Trevor's palm as he stared at the amethyst pendant. His lungs felt incapable of taking in air. She'd been wearing it the night of Brian's opening, then again when they'd made the trip to the Ascension. The unlit cigarette fell to the ground as Trevor launched forward and grabbed his father's shirt collar. Taken by surprise, James held on to his son's forearms to keep from falling.

"Where'd you get this?"

James sputtered as he tried to dislodge Trevor's hands. "Jesus! A man came by the bar!"

"Trevor!" Brian tried to get between the two men. "He's not worth it—"

"What man?" Trevor gave James a hard shake. "Answer me!"

For the first time, his father looked more nervous than cocky. His face appeared heavily lined in the sunlight that filtered through the tree boughs overhead. "He said you'd been messing with his girlfriend! That you gave her that necklace, and he wanted to send it back to you with a warning—"

"A warning?" Brian repeated, confused. A buzzing built in Trevor's ears that competed with the voice in his head, telling him he'd been a fool. It wasn't a warning, but a subterfuge.

"Use your cell to call Annabelle's house," Trevor ordered Brian. "Right now!"

He dragged James to the bench and shoved him onto it. Cursing, James swung wildly. But his father's inebriated state gave Trevor the advantage. Pulling handcuffs from his pocket, he managed to snap one of the bracelets around James's large-boned wrist. He closed the other over the bench's wrought-iron armrest.

"You can't do this!" The handcuffs clanked loudly, drawing the attention of passersby like a town crier's bell. "I haven't done anything!"

Trevor's knees felt weak. "Try accessory to kidnapping!"

"That little girl's my grandchild!"

"I'm not talking about Haley!"

Brian paced in front of the bench with his phone to his ear. "No one's answering. Trevor, what's going on?"

"Stay with him until I can get the cops to pick him up." Trevor tried not to let the fear show in his face. "Then take a taxi back to the house with Annabelle and Haley. I need your car keys."

Brian didn't ask questions. He handed them over and Trevor took off at a run.

"This is FBI agent Trevor Rivette, badge number JTF0171012. I need a patch to the officer assigned to 1211 Lucerne Street!"

His cell phone pressed against his ear, Trevor reached the parking lot and flung himself into the Audi. He started the ignition and whipped the vehicle onto St. Bernard Avenue heading back to Faubourg Marigny. Within a minute, the radio's crackle came through the phone's receiver.

"Agent Rivette? We've had some trouble at this location. I've got an ambulance here and additional units combing the area."

"How many hurt?"

"Just one. Hispanic male, mid-forties."

"What about the woman?"

There was a brief pause. "Sorry, Agent. There's no one else here."

Trevor disconnected the call and threw the phone onto the seat as he accelerated the car.

Turning onto Annabelle's street minutes later, his heart slammed inside his chest. An ambulance and three NOPD squad cars sat in front of the house with their lights flashing. A gaggle of police officers stood on the porch, and curious neighbors were gathered outside the yard's fence.

Leaving the car in the middle of the street, Trevor flashed his shield at an officer who attempted to block his path on the sidewalk. "This is my sister's house. What can you tell me?"

"Officer Defillo's inside, Agent. He's the one who called for assistance. You should talk to him."

Trevor raced up the porch and into the parlor. The officer was a stocky, Italian-looking man who'd responded to Haley's disappearance earlier that morning. He stood outside the kitchen doorway.

"What the hell happened?" Trevor asked as he approached.

"Looks like the intruder came in through a window in back." Defillo gestured down the hall where Annabelle's bedroom was located. "The screen's been pried off and it was left open. Whatever happened, it went down before I got back here this morning."

"What time was that?"

"Nine twenty-two."

Trevor worked to keep his composure. Barely five minutes had passed between his departure and the officer's arrival, but it had given Dante all the time he needed. He'd been watching and waiting somewhere nearby for his opportunity.

"Has anyone spoken with the neighbors?"

"The lady next door heard a woman screaming," Defillo recounted as he checked the notes he'd scribbled into a writing tablet. "Said she looked outside and saw a black SUV pulling away. She's not sure of the make and she didn't get a license plate, but she noticed the vehicle had some fancy wheels. Probably chrome-aluminum rims."

"I'm going to want to talk to her." Trevor strode into the kitchen, then came to a halt at the scene. Alex lay on the floor. Two paramedics were securing a stabilizing collar around his neck so he could be lifted onto a gurney. Blood oozed through the white gauze on the side of his head.

Trevor knelt next to him. Alex's eyes were closed, and an oxygen mask covered his nose and mouth. Its plastic fogged with his shallow breathing.

"Alex, can you hear me?" When he received no response, he looked at the paramedics. "Is he going to be okay?"

"He took a pretty hard hit," one of them replied. "They'll know more after a cranial CT scan."

Trevor stood as Alex was placed on the gurney. His eyes followed the paramedics' path as they rolled him outside, and then he did his best to take an objective look around the room.

Rain's denim bag and cell phone were on the table. Brown liquid pooled from an overturned coffee mug, soaking into the cloth place mats. One of the chairs was on its side, wedged against the refrigerator. A heavy bookend from the parlor lay on the floor—it was more than likely the object that had been used to strike Alex. Rubbing his closed eyes with his fingertips, Trevor tried to clear his head.

He had to stay focused. It was the only chance Rain had.

The sound of a throat being cleared came from the doorway, and Trevor turned to see McGrath. He had on his standard detective's uniform of trousers, short-sleeved dress shirt and tie. His gold shield hung on a chain around his neck.

"We heard on the scanner," he said as he came into the room, carefully sidestepping the evidence. "They gave the home owner's last name, and Tibbs remembered you had family here. We made the connection."

Trevor looked away from the detective. Through the kitchen window, he could see Thibodeaux standing on the side lawn and leaning against the fence as he spoke to a group of neighbors.

"The woman who was taken. Was it your sister?"

Trevor shook his head. "She was with me."

"Then who?"

He swallowed. "Rain Sommers."

"Shit. What was she doing here?"

"I had a family emergency. I thought she'd be safe until I could get a cop over here to watch her."

With heavy steps, Trevor went to stand in front of the sink. Turning on the faucet, he splashed cold water onto his face and let his head hang down briefly between his shoulders before reaching for a roll of paper towels. Dante's obsession with Rain was the one thing that might keep her alive—at least for a while, he reasoned. He tried not to think about how scared she must be or what might be happening to her right now. Blotting his face with the towel, he dropped the wadded ball next to the basin.

"You sleeping with her, Rivette?" McGrath had walked up beside him. When Trevor didn't respond, he added, "I noticed how close you seemed with her at the hospital. If you ask me—"

"I didn't."

McGrath scratched his mustache with his index finger and lowered the volume of his words. "You're not the first to get emotionally involved in a case. Just make sure it doesn't get

in the way of clear thinking. Otherwise, you need to recus
yourself now before things get any worse."

After a moment, he slid his hands into his pockets an
took a few steps toward the doorway. "Let me know if Tibb
and I can do anything."

"McGrath?" Trevor's voice halted the detective's exit. H
would have to alert the local FBI team about Rain's abduc
tion, get photos of her circulated and updates to the media a
soon as possible. But he needed McGrath and Thibodeaux
as well. "There's a collar being brought into your precinct.
need you to lean on him hard."

"What's the deal?"

"Obstruction of a federal investigation, possible accessor
to kidnapping. He pulled me out to City Park on a prank
giving the killer enough time to move in here and abduct D
Sommers."

"What're you saying? Dante has a partner?"

"More of an unwitting accomplice," Trevor tried to explain
"But he can give us a description, maybe more. At the leas
we should be able to find out if Armand Baptiste and Dant
are the same person."

McGrath peered at him. "You don't want in on this?"

"I'll be watching through the two-way, but I need to kee
my distance."

"Who's the jerkoff?"

Trevor took a measured breath and let it back out. "M
father."

McGrath's eyes bugged before he resumed his cop's heard
it-all demeanor.

"He'll let you know up front he was previously on the job
which is why I want you to question him before I hand hin
over to the Bureau. He equates the FBI with me and he'll shu
down on them. I don't have time for his garbage."

McGrath nodded. "We'll get on it."

A full minute after the detective had left, Trevor still stood at the sink. He studied the bloodstain on the tiled floor where Alex had been lying and realized just how much could have gone wrong with Dante's plan. It was a combination of blind luck and daring that had worked in his favor, enabling him to pull off the abduction in the short space of time Rain had been left without protection. It also wasn't lost on him that Dante had used James Rivette as a pawn in his twisted game. That fact alone pointed back to Baptiste, since he'd already taken pleasure in revealing to Trevor that he knew about his family history.

One thing was certain—whoever Dante was, he had what he wanted now.

Reaching into his pocket, Trevor withdrew Rain's necklace. He stared at the lavender stone and realized he should turn it in to evidence, but at this point it didn't seem to matter. What did matter was how the killer had managed to obtain it. She hadn't been wearing the necklace last night or this morning, which meant it had been taken previously. He thought of Rain's patient, Oliver Carteris. The kid had a history of petty theft and until recently, a revolving door to her house. Rain had been trying to reach him by phone on the drive to Annabelle's that morning. Was there a connection?

Brian's voice broke into Trevor's thoughts. He was outside on the porch, arguing with the police.

"Let him in," he called, feeling a headache pulse behind his eyes. Alex. The only other person who'd seen Dante was unconscious and on his way to the E.R. in an ambulance.

Self-rebuke made it hard for him to breathe. How long did Rain have? Trevor closed his hand around the amethyst pendant, feeling its hard shape against his palm. He should have kept Rain with him. He shouldn't have left her alone, not for a minute.

Brian entered. His face paled when he saw the blood on the floor. Trevor didn't pull any punches.

"Alex is alive, but he's hurt. They've taken him to All Saints. You need to get over there."

"Rain?" Brian managed to ask.

Trevor shook his head.

39

They'd been traveling for over two hours. The Cadillac Escalade had gone through Morgan City a while earlier, then headed west into the quaint town of Jeanerette. From there, they'd driven past fields of young sugarcane before the pastoral setting eventually faded into verdant, isolated marshlands. As the SUV roared over a rusted, two-lane bridge, Rain stared into a sluggish inlet framed by gnarled cypress trees. She had been gagged until a short while ago, when Christian Carteris announced that they should talk. Her lips still stung from the duct tape he'd ripped from her mouth.

"Where are we going?" she asked not for the first time.

"I told you—patience, my dear," he advised from the driver's seat. "Why not enjoy the scenery? We'll be there soon enough."

A peeling billboard loomed next to the rural highway, advertising Saturday-night cockfighting and cold beer at a local venue. Rain tried again to loosen the tape binding her wrists and wondered if Alex was still alive. Carteris had given her a choice—go with him, or watch him slit Alex's throat as he lay unconscious on the floor of Annabelle's kitchen. Her gaze shifted warily to the knife that now rested on the leather armrest between them.

The SUV hurtled past a decaying building choked by kudzu vines. A stoop-shouldered gas pump stood out front and a rusted metal sign under the roofline read LeBlanc's Gas and Bait. Its windows were broken and the screened front door yawned open. The business looked as though it hadn't been operational for years.

"You're a surgeon," Rain choked out, fighting her fear. "You're supposed to save lives."

"I have." Carteris looked at her through fashionable sunglasses. "The lives I've saved far exceed the ones I've taken."

"And that gives you the right?"

He didn't respond. Instead, he asked pleasantly, "Would you care for a bottled water? I've packed refreshments in the cooler in the backseat."

"I don't want any water."

"Suit yourself. You don't want to get dehydrated." He consulted the Rolex on his wrist as if he had an appointment to keep, and Rain's attention was again drawn to the ring on his hand. The serpent's fangs were bared and sharp. She knew what it was—a bloodletting ring. Tears burned behind her eyelids, but she wouldn't allow herself to cry. She had to stay calm. Rain stared out the windshield as up ahead an alligator slithered across the asphalt before disappearing into the foliage on the side of the road.

"Why do you kill?" she asked finally, finding the silence more unnerving than conversation. "If it's blood you need—"

"Then why don't I just get it at the office?" Carteris chuckled. "Really, do you want me to *steal* from the hospital's blood supply?"

She shook her head weakly, failing to understand his sense of humor. "What does any of this have to do with me? Or my mother?"

"I don't expect you to understand yet, but you will soon."

The air conditioner's cold blast caused gooseflesh to rise on her bare arms and legs. She still wore running shorts, a tank top and sneakers.

"I watched you leave your house with Agent Rivette this morning, heading out for a jog," Carteris informed her. "Are you in love with him?"

"No."

"You're lying." He slowed the SUV, taking a left off the highway. "I'd really rather think you're in love with him than just fucking him like a common slut."

The road they'd turned onto was little more than a gravel path. It ran alongside a stagnant pool filled with green algae and islands of water lilies. A trio of egrets fished in the shallow water, but the birds took flight when the SUV approached. As they drove deeper into the wooded bayou, the trees with their hanging garlands of Spanish moss nearly concealed the blue sky. The ground was pitted and rough, and the vehicle bounced over the terrain.

"What about Oliver? Is he part of this?"

"Oliver doesn't have the stomach for it." Carteris's words dripped with disapproval. "But he's been helpful to me, to a certain extent."

"He brings you the girls." Rain felt sick with realization. It was Oliver who'd been seen with Rebecca Belknap at the Ascension that night.

"He's been watching you at my instruction. All this time, you thought he was there for counseling." No longer needing his sunglasses, he tossed them onto the dashboard. Rain saw the bruise shadowing his right eye.

"A gift from my son," he said, noting her gaze. He fished steel-framed spectacles from his shirt pocket and put them on. "Oliver's grown quite fond of you. He could never accept that you were the endgame."

Rain recalled the afternoon in the restaurant when Carteris had invited himself to sit at her table. He'd seemed so concerned about Oliver, even admitting to being intimidated by him. *I was actually a bit fearful of him. My own son.*

All of it had been a lie.

Last night when Oliver called her home, had he been planning to warn her? She wondered what hold Carteris had over him that compelled him to follow his orders. Was it out of fear or some kind of twisted loyalty? Why had Oliver failed to confide in her? Sitting in weary silence, Rain tried not to think about her body being left behind for wild animals to scavenge once Carteris finished with her.

"Did you know I'm an avid sportsman?" His inquiry was as casual as if they were out for an afternoon drive. "I have a cabin I use during hunting season. I think you'll find it rather charming in its simplicity."

They continued bumping along the gravel road for several more minutes, until the trees and shrubs finally began to thin. The SUV emerged into a clearing. What Rain saw stole her breath. The burned-out frame of an antebellum plantation home stood in front of them like a massive gray specter. As was the custom with bayou houses, it had been raised on stone piers to lift it above the floodwaters. But only its chimneys and the sun-faded columns of its wraparound veranda remained intact. The rest had descended into rubble.

"This land was formerly a rice plantation. It's been in my mother's family for generations," Carteris recounted. "Local folklore claims the house was burned years ago by townspeople in one of the nearby parishes. They believed voodoo was being practiced here. Can you imagine?"

The SUV rolled to a stop in front of an overseer's cabin set a few hundred feet back from the remains of the larger house. Although the domicile was likely as old as the ruined manor, it appeared to have benefited from a recent renovation. Its sloping tin roof looked new, and its front porch was built with fresh cypress timbers. Carteris took the knife from the armrest.

"When I returned to the States, I considered rebuilding and residing out here, but I realized I'd miss city life. I'm hardly what one would call a country-gentleman doctor." He smiled at her. "But that doesn't mean I don't require an occasional peaceful getaway."

Carteris climbed from the SUV. After removing a black physician's bag from the backseat, he went around to open Rain's door. She tensed as he reached across her lap to release the seat belt.

"I wanted to share this place with you. It will give us time to be alone." He helped her from the leather seat. As she stepped to the ground, her knees nearly buckled and he caught her against his chest. "Steady now."

The midafternoon sun beat hotly against her skin, which was still clammy from the continual moist jolt of the SUV's air conditioner. She wondered vaguely if she might be in shock.

"Why now?" Rain asked timorously. "You could've taken me at any time—"

"Are you aware of tomorrow's date?"

"It's May twenty-ninth."

"And that holds no significance for you?"

When she didn't reply, Carteris looked disappointed. "It's the thirtieth anniversary of your mother's death. I thought you'd have known that."

With his hand at the small of her back, he propelled her up the slatted stairs to the cabin's porch. The tin roof jutted over the wood-planked flooring. It provided some relief from the sun, but the air was still heated and thick with humidity.

Rain felt as if her lungs were filling with water with each shallow breath. A papery mass the size of a basketball hung under the roof's eaves, and a horde of black wasps hummed around it.

Carteris frowned as he regarded the nest. "That will have to go."

He used a key to unlock the cabin's front door and prodded her to enter in front of him. Stale, hot air met her face.

"The place runs on a generator, but I'll have to start it." He left the door open behind them to allow a little fresh air inside. With a wave of his hand, he indicated a window-box air-conditioning unit. "It might take a few hours to cool off. We also have plumbing and a propane stove. A rustic situation, but I think we'll do just fine."

As her eyes adjusted to the darkened interior, Rain looked at her surroundings. There was a plaid couch with a coffee table and a rough-hewn bookcase. A metal gun safe stood in the corner next to a stacked-stone fireplace. Surprisingly, the cabin's interior appeared…normal.

But she nearly stopped breathing as Carteris came up behind her, standing so close she could feel his warm breath. Sweat trickled down her nape. He released the elastic band that held her hair, causing it to graze her shoulders. Gently, his fingers combed through the strands. Rain bit her lip to keep from crying out.

"That's much better." His mouth next to her ear, he added, "There's something on the bookcase you might want to see."

Rain moved toward the shelving on rubbery legs, grateful for any reason to put some distance between them. There were several framed photos at eye level, and she stepped closer, feeling her stomach plunge. The image in the center was of a young Desiree, wearing flare-legged jeans and a midriff-bar-ing top. A man stood next to her mother. But it wasn't Gavin Firth. The man in the photograph was Christian Carteris.

"Your mother was my first and only love," he explained. "I was a few years older than her and finishing my undergraduate degree when we met. She broke my heart when she chose your father over me."

Rain turned to him. *It couldn't be.* If her mother was still alive, she'd be fifty-eight years old. She looked at Carteris's unlined face and the toned build of his body. He couldn't be more than forty-two or forty-three.

"That's not possible," Rain argued. "Even with plastic surgery—"

"Blood is the elixir of life." He took a step closer, and her eyes darted to the knife he held in his hand. "You asked why I don't steal from the hospital's blood supply. The blood has to be *fresh,* Rain. It must be ingested by one life force directly from another."

She swallowed a scream as he reached for her bound hands. Rain recoiled as he sliced through the duct tape, causing the sharp blade to nick the inside of her right wrist. A thin line of red blood instantly appeared.

"I only meant to release you," he offered apologetically. Peeling away the tape, Carteris looked at the cut. Then he lifted it to his mouth and licked away the small amount of blood. She stood mesmerized, her pulse beating wildly.

"Age is of no relevance to me. Do you understand now, Rain?"

The room tilted as she fought to keep her bearings. Carteris steadied her with his hands around her waist. *This wasn't real.* Rain didn't care what she'd seen in the photo. She had to keep him talking, she realized, delay him from whatever his plans were for her.

"Why do you call yourself Dante?" she asked in a voice made too high by encroaching panic. She placed her hand on his chest and tried to increase the slight space between their bodies.

"You're familiar with Dante Alighieri? The Italian poet who wrote the *Divine Comedy?*"

Rain worked to recall the epic poem, which described Dante's journey through hell, purgatory and paradise. *"Dante's Inferno?"*

He smoothed her hair, his eyes on her mouth. "Desiree was my Beatrice. She was to have been my companion through the journey of life. But none of that really matters now, does it?"

She felt the tremors racking her body grow stronger. To her relief, Carteris dropped his hands from her and walked to the pass-through counter separating the utilitarian kitchen from the main room. He began rummaging through the leather bag he'd brought inside. Rain estimated the distance to the cabin's open door. She prepared to run and take her chances that she was faster than him, but her hope died as Carteris turned toward her again. He held a hypodermic needle.

She skittered backward as he advanced, but the bookcase stopped her retreat. "Please, don't!"

"You're exhausted," he pointed out, closing in on her. "I only want to help you sleep. Things will look better once you're rested."

"Don't stick me with that!"

"Relax." He gave her his best bedside expression. "I'm a doctor, remember?"

Rain tried to wring free of his grasp, but he was far stronger. She screamed and scratched at his wrists, sobbing as the needle pricked her skin. Carteris hushed her, imprisoning her against his chest as he pumped the syringe's contents into her. He held her until her head bobbed and her body began to sag.

"Trevor," Rain heard herself whisper.

She felt his lips against the top of her head. "All in due time."

Her struggling became increasingly weak and uncoordinated. Whatever he'd shot her with was taking rapid effect. He picked her up in his arms.

"I have a room ready for you, little one."

Carter is carried her to the back of the sweltering cabin. The room was windowless and shadowy, and its feminine furnishings looked out of place. But the bed's ironwork headboard seemed strangely familiar to her, as did the antique vanity table with its skirted apron and oval mirror. She recognized the nubbed chenille coverlet, too.

He laid her on the bed and brushed the damp strands of hair from her face. Rain's tongue felt too thick to speak, her limbs too heavy to move. A stuffed animal sat next to her, a pink French poodle with a rhinestone collar and flat button eyes. Her brain was fuzzy, but she knew this place from somewhere deep within her earliest memories. The scent of rose and sandalwood drifted around her, creating a bittersweet nostalgia.

Carter is eased from the room, shutting the door behind him. She heard the metallic slide of a lock being fit into place.

Rain's mind floated like a life preserver on the ocean. As a child, the door in the upstairs hallway had always been closed. But whenever she could, she'd sneak inside the room and play dress-up with her mother's things. She recalled the perfume bottle and the exotic fragrance that emerged from it when she removed its stopper. The scent was ingrained in her memory—was her brain playing tricks?

That room no longer existed. It had been a decade after the murder when Celeste had finally found the courage to redecorate. She'd transformed the bedroom into the upstairs study,

banishing the last of her mother's presence from the house.
But tumbling closer to darkness, Rain was there again.

Somehow, Carteris had re-created Desiree's old room.

40

Looking through the murky glass of the two-way window, Trevor studied the source of the nightmares that had plagued him for most of his life. His father sat hunched behind the scarred, wooden table in the precinct's interrogation room. McGrath was with him, and his voice was a low growl through the intercom.

"You want to spend what's left of your sorry life in prison, Rivette?"

"What do you want from me? I already told you everything I know!"

McGrath leaned over the table. "You expect me to believe a guy you never met just walks into a bar and hands you a wad of cash and an expensive piece of jewelry?"

"I was paid to deliver a package!" James pounded the table with a balled fist. "I didn't do anything illegal!"

"You keep telling yourself that. But you were a cop, you know better. You want to know how it looks to me? Like you were in on it from the beginning. We're talking about kidnapping, maybe murder. You're fucked, Rivette."

The yellowed folder that held James's departmental records lay in front of the detective. Trevor already knew what the file contained—he'd read through it days ago. In addition to a laundry list of civilian complaints that included brutality and extortion, it gave the official reason for his father's dismissal from the NOPD. James Rivette had falsified an insurance claim. He'd turned in items as stolen during a home invasion, then gotten caught fencing the goods at a pawnshop in Treme. But the file contained no mention of the near-fatal beating of his son, which had also supposedly occurred at the hands of the invented thieves. Trevor assumed the NOPD hadn't investigated that far. It hadn't wanted any further bad publicity. Instead, the department had closed the file on the maelstrom and quietly gotten rid of a blight on its force.

James spoke inside the interrogation room. His voice cracked. "I—I want an attorney. A public defender."

"What's the matter, you sobering up?" McGrath shoved a legal pad at him. "Look, I'm tired of hearing the same thing over and over. Why don't you write your crap story down. I'll give you extra credit for proper spelling."

The door opened and McGrath stepped out. A deep line furrowed his forehead. "For what it's worth, I don't think he had any idea of the shit he stepped into when he agreed to deliver the necklace."

"Maybe not," Trevor said quietly. Still, his father was far from innocent.

"I've shown him the photos of Baptiste. He swears up and down he wasn't the guy in the bar. There's a sketch artist coming in and he's agreed to work with him, but the man wore sunglasses, so it's going to be a partial at best." He tugged at the already slackened tie around his neck. "What about the guy who got clubbed at your sister's house? The photographer?"

"I just called the hospital. He hasn't regained consciousness yet."

"Damn." McGrath shook his head. "I read through your father's personnel files, Rivette. He's a real piece of work."

Trevor nodded but didn't say anything. He didn't want to think about the possible charges against James being upgraded to accessory to murder. Dante—*whoever the hell he was*—had made this personal by drawing James into the battle. It was clear he wanted Trevor's wound to be as deep and painful as possible. The vision of Rain's body, brutally slaughtered, made a cold sickness wash over him.

"What're you still doing here?" McGrath asked as Thibodeaux turned the corner into the corridor at a brisk pace. "I thought you were headed to the Carteris residence to see if the son ever turned up."

"He turned up, all right," Thibodeaux announced. "I was getting in the car out back when it came over the scanner. Two uniforms went by the Ascension for a premises check. They found a kid swinging from the rafters by his skinny goth neck. According to the driver's license, the deceased is Oliver Carteris."

Trevor knew the club had been closed down since the night of the raid. "They're sure it was a suicide?"

"The M.E.'s just now on the scene, but all signs point to it." Thibodeaux clicked the top of a ballpoint pen up and down as he spoke. "The kid's cell phone indicates the last number called belonged to Dr. Sommers."

Had the call been a final plea from a despondent patient, or was it something more? Trevor was reaching for anything that might translate to a lead. Rain had been missing for three hours. FBI and police were frantically searching for her—manning roadblocks, distributing flyers—but they were running out of time.

"I'm going to the Ascension." He looked at McGrath. "You'll call me when the sketch is ready?"

"Sure."

"Hold up," Thibodeaux said, following. "I'll go with you."

McGrath called after them, "What do you want me to do with your old man?"

"When you're done with him, call the FBI to pick him up. I don't give a damn what happens to him after that."

Sunlight filtered through the stained-glass windows of the Ascension, casting a prism of colors across the battered dance floor. Trevor watched as two forensics technicians lowered the body of Oliver Carteris to the church's pulpit. A metal folding chair on the platform lay on its side. Evidently, the youth had stood on its seat before stepping off and hanging himself with an electrical cord tossed over one of the iron chandeliers.

He'd been tall, Trevor estimated as the body was laid prone. An inch or two over six feet. Even in death, Oliver appeared handsome in a young–Johnny Depp kind of way—lankily built, with dusky skin and ink-black hair. Had he seen him before? Trevor wasn't sure, but he thought of the kid who'd been standing at the edge of Coliseum Square Park that day as he and Brian drove past.

He held the clear evidence bag that contained the contents of Oliver's pockets. There were the driver's license and cell phone Thibodeaux had mentioned, a small glass pipe for smoking marijuana or crack, and six Ecstasy tablets matching the ones confiscated during the raid. The bag also contained a set of car keys on a pewter fob. It was engraved with a pentagram—the equivalent of a Lacoste alligator for those who ran in Oliver's social circle. One of the keys was undoubtedly to the Mercedes coupe that Forensics was combing over outside. But there was another with a black plastic handle bearing the Cadillac crest.

Trevor lingered on the last item, a tasteful white business card printed in black ink. He felt his emotions splintering like glass.

Rain Sommers, Ph.D., L.C.S.W., Psychotherapy Practice, Evaluation and Counseling for Adolescents

"Body's in full rigor mortis," Thibodeaux announced. He knelt next to the corpse and gripped its stiffened arms. "Kid's been dead for around twelve to fourteen hours. Based on the outgoing time stamp on his cell phone, it looks like he did a felo-de-se right after trying to reach Dr. Sommers."

Trevor walked over for a closer look. Tiny red spots called petechial hemorrhaging dotted Oliver's face and neck. One of the technicians removed the rubberized cord from around the boy's throat, revealing the blackened ligature mark where it had been stretched tight by the victim's body weight.

"What about a suicide note?"

Thibodeaux shook his head. "Nada."

As the flash of the technician's camera started again, Trevor peeled off his latex gloves. The key chain continued to nag at him.

Frowning in thought, he walked to the arched wood doors and exited the church. Outside, a few clouds had entered the vibrant blue sky and heat rose from the concrete like a barbecue grill. A ponytailed Asian male in a Forensics jumpsuit was vacuuming the inside of the Mercedes for even the smallest particles of evidence. He turned off the equipment and emerged from the driver's side as Trevor approached.

"Find anything?"

"An eight-ball of cocaine in the floorboard. There're also a few hairs that don't match the deceased. Long ones that look like they might be female, but it's hard to tell these days." The technician wiped perspiration from his forehead. "One weird thing—the passenger door's scratched up from the inside and the handle doesn't work."

Trevor squinted against the sun. "What about vehicle registration papers?"

"The car's registered to a Christian Carteris."

"Send the hairs to the lab for analysis." Trevor handed the technician his card. "Put a rush on the results and notify me as soon as they're back."

"Yes, Agent."

Walking away from the vehicle, Trevor dug his cell phone from his jeans pocket and made a call. It took less than a minute to run his requested search. The Mercedes was indeed registered to Christian Carteris. But the surgeon also owned a second vehicle. A black 2010 Cadillac Escalade.

There were thousands of black SUVs in Orleans Parish, but as he disconnected the phone, Trevor clung to the feeling in his gut.

"Rivette." Thibodeaux called his name as he jogged toward him. "I just got a call from the uniform sent to the Carteris house to break the news about the son's death. No one answered at the residence, so he went to the hospital to try to locate Dr. Carteris at work. According to his staff, the surgeon was paged for an emergency triple bypass this morning, but he never showed up. You think Junior offed Daddy before killing himself?"

Trevor headed back toward their car. "I think Christian Carteris is Dante."

41

The Victorian mansion's mahogany door took four blows with a battering ram before it gave in, enabling the FBI and police SWAT team to pour inside. Trevor entered after them, his gun raised, with McGrath and Thibodeaux bringing up the rear.

"Clear!" The word echoed along the hallways as rooms were searched for inhabitants. Within minutes, however, the SWAT-team leader returned and shook his head.

"Negative. The place is empty. There's no SUV in the garage, either."

Trevor holstered his gun, disappointment nearly overwhelming him. He scanned the opulence of the two-story entrance, from its glittering chandelier to its Italian-marble floor and French rococo furniture. A curved staircase led to the second floor, and overhead, a stained-glass skylight depicted a Mardi Gras scene in traditional purple, green and gold.

This was the guy, Trevor was certain of it. The black SUV, his unexplained disappearance and connection to Rain through his son—even the description his father had given the sketch artist was a reasonable match. He felt as if an hourglass sat in front of him with sand slowly funneling through to its bottom. If Carteris hadn't brought Rain here, where were they?

"To think we were here a few days ago talking to this asshole," McGrath grumbled, looking around.

"If I was Oliver Carteris, I'd have eighty-sixed myself, too," Thibodeaux observed sarcastically. He stood in front of glass doors that led onto a porte cochere veranda overlooking a lush courtyard and swimming pool. "This place is a real dump—"

He stopped speaking as one of the FBI field agents appeared on the second-floor landing. "Agent Rivette, there's something up here you should see."

Trevor took the stairs two at a time with the detectives behind him. They trailed the agent down the corridor and into the master bedroom. The suite was spacious, with heavy antique furniture and elegant, masculine decor. But it was the tall clothing armoire that captured Trevor's attention. He stepped closer. Its black walnut doors hung open and taped inside were photos. *Rain, her red-gold hair shining in the sun as she weeded the flower garden in her yard. Exiting the radio station in a green top and flowing black slacks. Sitting on a blanket and reading a book in what appeared to be Coliseum Square.* There were dozens of snapshots, their edges overlapping and newer images placed over older ones. Trevor recognized himself in one of the photos. He stood next to Rain, waiting as she unlocked the door to her home.

"Contact Forensics and let them know we're going to need them here. In the meantime, limit who comes into this room," he said, throat tight. The agent who'd escorted them up nodded and went back down the hallway.

Handing Trevor a pair of latex gloves, McGrath studied the collage. "There aren't any of the other females. Why's that?"

"Because Rain's the one he wanted all along."

"If this was about Dr. Sommers, why didn't Carteris just take her from the start? Why all the rest?"

"Maybe the Count's got an appetite," Thibodeaux theorized from the other side of the room as he searched the drawers of an antique writing desk. "The other vics were an appetizer. Dr. Sommers was the main course."

The comment sliced through Trevor. He couldn't allow himself to think of Rain in the past tense. She was still alive, she had to be.

Anxiety pulling at him, he stared out the room's floor-to-ceiling windows that provided a postcard-quality view of St. Charles Avenue with its large antebellum houses and stately trees. Carteris was a top cardiologist and a member of the hospital's board of directors. He had to be exceedingly busy. How did he have time to follow Rain around and take such a large portfolio of photos? Did he have help? Trevor thought of Oliver's body being lowered to the floor of the Ascension.

"The son killed himself because of what he knew about the murders," he said quietly. "Either that, or he was directly involved. He couldn't handle the guilt."

"Yeah?" McGrath pushed tailored suits and shirts around inside the armoire, looking for additional evidence. "How do you figure?"

Trevor didn't respond, still trying to work out the hypothetical scenario in his head. He again contemplated the difference in ages between the victims in New Orleans and in the other cities where the killings had occurred. All the localities had major universities and medical institutions. Was it possible Carteris traveled a lecture circuit? He wondered, What if Carteris had been the sole perpetrator outside New Orleans, but here, he'd been using Oliver to lure the females? It would explain why the local victims were younger, since Oliver was a teenager himself. Not to mention, his height and hair color matched the vague description Marcy Cupich had provided.

If Carteris had forged some type of dominant-subservient relationship with his son, then Oliver might have been forced to do his bidding. Trevor took it a step further—perhaps he was being trained to follow in his footsteps. Even if he was conflicted about his involvement, it was likely Oliver was afraid to refuse.

"When you talked to Carteris, what was your impression of him?"

"Seemed like your typical doctor," McGrath recalled. "Busy, condescending, on his high horse. He acted pissed that we'd interrupted his day—"

"Son of a bitch!" Thibodeaux pried at the desk's fall-front writing slope, but the intricately carved panel wouldn't budge. "Damn thing's locked. Which means there must be something inside it worth seeing."

Pulling a pair of nail clippers from his pocket, he extended the metal file. Then he inserted it into the brass keyhole and began jiggling the blade.

"Didn't grow up in the Lower Nine without learning a few things." He looked up as Trevor walked to the door. "Where are you going?"

"To find the son's room."

He snorted. "Shouldn't be hard to find. Probably looks like an upright coffin."

Trevor headed back down the hallway, his thoughts fractured. He assumed, like most therapists, Rain encouraged her patients to keep journals. Could Oliver have written something that might be of use?

He reached a series of bedrooms as a young police officer rounded the corner.

"Agent? You need to come back downstairs. We found something."

The look on the man's face made his heart plummet. "What?"

"Blood, sir. Under a table. There's a lot of it."

The room appeared to be under renovation, with plastic sheeting and canvas drop cloths protecting the furniture and floor. Bookcases lined the walls, and transom windows let in the flow of bright daylight beneath the crumbling trey ceiling. Conversation halted among the other law enforcement as Trevor entered.

"Did anyone touch anything?"

"What do we look like, rookies?" one of the men on the SWAT team wisecracked.

"This area's sealed off until Forensics gets here." He waited for them to file out, cognizant of the sickening metallic odor in the air. Then Trevor moved to the alcove where a canvas-shrouded table sat under a framed oil painting. Doing the best he could to steel himself, he slowly raised the cloth covering the table. A second tarp stuffed underneath it was saturated in blood. He wiped the back of his hand over his mouth and felt his heart pound.

Had she been killed here? Despite her abduction, despite the blood staining the cloth at his feet, he couldn't accept that conclusion. Squeezing his eyes closed, Trevor fought a rush of dizziness. He stayed like that until he heard the shuffle of feet moving past the open doors.

"What's going on?"

A field agent paused at the threshold. "The cops found a body. It's in a freezer off the kitchen."

Utter blackness washed over him. He walked from the library on wooden legs, following the museum-like corridor until it spilled into a massive gourmet kitchen with stainless-steel appliances and marble counters. Trevor pushed through the men who congregated there. He had to hold it together. He owed it to this investigation, to her.

An elongated butler's pantry led from the kitchen into a work space, the kind used by caterers preparing food for a large number of houseguests. He stopped in the doorway. An industrial-size sink gleamed under copper lights, and double warming ovens took up space in the brick wall. On the far end of the room, a rectangular freezer sat with its lid upraised. Puffs of chilled air rose from inside it.

"I've heard of frozen dinners, but geez," an officer remarked.

A second uniform loitered near the freezer. "Hey, Agent. What do you call this? A Gothsicle?"

Trevor stepped across the checkerboard-tile floor, his heart pounding. Gripping the freezer's rim, he looked down. But among the packages of frozen steaks and king crab legs, it was the face of Armand Baptiste who stared back at him. Ice crystals had formed over the corneas of his eyes, concealing the faded blue irises. Baptiste's mouth hung open in a state of perpetual surprise. A pink slit ran across his neck, and blood spilled in a frozen cascade down his shirtfront like cherry ice.

Relief nearly brought Trevor to his knees. *It wasn't her.* The blood in the library just as likely belonged to Baptiste. Which meant there was still a chance Rain was alive.

"That's the club owner?" the officer next to him asked. "What the hell is he doing—"

The question went unfinished. The officer ducked and swore loudly as the house shook on its foundation. A booming sound like cannon fire faded into eerie silence. Trevor had barely recovered from the discovery in the freezer, but he recognized the blast from his Homeland Security training.

An IED.

He took back off through the kitchen and sprinted toward

the foyer with the others. Behind him, the SWAT-team leader called over his radio for emergency support. The acrid smell from the explosion permeated the air, and thin gray smoke leaked over the upstairs landing. The Mardi Gras skylight had shattered, scattering shards of glass over the marble floor.

"I need a countoff, now!" the team leader yelled.

Along with two of the men, Trevor ran up the staircase and into the haze. An officer lay motionless in their path.

"Help him!" Trevor kept going along the hallway. He neared the master bedroom as McGrath stumbled out, his left arm bloody and dangling against his side. His knees faltered and Trevor kept him upright by wedging his body under the detective's uninjured shoulder. Carrying the bulk of McGrath's weight, he moved him down the staircase toward safety.

"Where's Thibodeaux?" Trevor shouted over the din.

McGrath pointed to his ear, gone temporarily deaf from the discharge. "I can't hear a damn thing!"

In the foyer, Trevor passed McGrath to one of the others, then raced back upstairs and down the hall again. The passage was darkening with smoke, and he pulled his T-shirt over his nose in an effort to block out the fumes. Fuel. Whatever detonation device Carteris had planted, it was designed not only to explode but also to ignite.

Reaching what was left of the bedroom's splintered door frame, he saw flames dancing on the curtains of the broken windows. The armoire lay on its side. It must have protected McGrath from the worst of the explosion. But where was the other detective? He called out for Thibodeaux, but got no response. Coughing, his eyes burning, he searched the rubble.

Dear God. He finally saw him, sitting nearly upright against the far wall.

Scrambling over splintered furniture and chunks of plaster,

Trevor dropped down beside Thibodeaux and felt frantically for a pulse. But he could tell almost instantly the damage was too great. The blast's impact had ripped a large hole in his chest. His face was unrecognizable, the skin peeled away by the intense heat.

Smoke and anger stung Trevor's eyes. But there was no time to mourn. The fire had leaped to the mattress, and it would be seconds before it engulfed the room. Dragging Thibodeaux's body into the hallway, he was met by two officers who helped him carry the fallen detective down the stairs. They laid Thibodeaux on the marble floor. Trevor started up again, but the SWAT leader grabbed his arm.

"You can't go back up there!"

He jerked free and began ascending the stairs. Outside, he could hear the cessation of sirens as emergency vehicles came to a stop in front of the mansion. But he couldn't wait. He'd been headed to Oliver's room when he'd been called downstairs. What if there was a clue, some small piece of evidence that pointed to where Carteris had taken Rain? He couldn't let it be destroyed.

The second blast sent a wave of pressure rolling through the upstairs. It knocked Trevor backward. He landed sprawled on the lower steps with the breath sucked from his lungs. A low flame snaked over the landing and spread quickly down the carpeted runner.

Just before the blaze reached him, strong hands pulled him to his feet and forced him out the mansion's front door. Firefighters in bright yellow protective gear ran past him under the portico, heading into the smoke-filled interior. Trevor coughed and attempted to draw in fresh air as a paramedic led him onto the lawn.

"You need oxygen," the paramedic advised, but Trevor refused. He spotted McGrath hunched on a gurney near one of the ambulances. The grimy sleeve of his dress shirt had been cut away, and a bandage was being wrapped around his bicep by another paramedic. Even from a distance, Trevor could see blood soaking the gauze.

McGrath looked up as he neared. "I found love letters, Rivette. Dozens of them. Ones Carteris wrote to Desiree Sommers—"

He wheezed painfully, and Trevor laid a hand on his shoulder. "Just take it easy."

"The letters were in envelopes stamped Return to Sender. The postmarks were over thirty years old. You tell me how that's possible when—"

Another spasm of coughs racked his body. Trevor exchanged a glance with the paramedic, who tried to place an oxygen mask over McGrath's face. But the detective shoved it away.

"Damn it, all I can hear is ringing! What about Tibbs?"

Trevor shook his head. McGrath winced. He looked around the chaos, and his eyes fell on the body covered by a sheet on the green grass.

"Jesus Christ," he muttered hoarsely. "That desk he was trying to open. It must've been rigged."

This time, when the paramedic tried to push McGrath into a prone position on the gurney, he weakly complied. When he finally spoke again, his eyes were red and his voice was choked with emotion. "You get this bastard, Rivette."

"We need to get him to the E.R.," the paramedic said. Trevor nodded and took a step back. He watched as McGrath was loaded into the waiting ambulance. Around him, members of law enforcement walked around like shell-shocked refugees as firefighters began dousing the structure with hoses. Black clouds billowed from the top floor. Flames shot out through the windows and licked hungrily at the roofline. One thing was certain. The house had been set up to incinerate quickly, as if Carteris intended to obliterate his tracks and take out as many people as he could in the process.

Thibodeaux, a good detective, was dead. Another name to be added to the growing list of victims. Trevor ground his hands against his watering eyes, feeling a cold weight settle inside his chest.

Carteris had vanished, taking Rain with him.

42

Rain stared at the glass that sat untouched on the table in front of her. Outside, thunder rumbled not too far off in the distance. Nightfall was settling over the cabin like a cloak, replacing the bayou's hush with a nocturnal chorus of insects and frogs.

"You haven't tasted your wine," Carteris admonished. He'd changed into pressed slacks and a white shirt he'd left open at the throat, its vee revealing dark chest hair.

"It's a rare Beaujolais." He took a sip from his own glass and blotted his lips with a cloth napkin. "Try it. I think you'll find it enjoyable."

Her head still pounded from the powerful sedative he'd given her earlier. "Why? What did you put in it?"

Carteris smiled. "My dear, if I wanted to sedate you again, I would. I'd hoped we might enjoy a light repast together. Is that too much to ask?"

He leaned forward. His pleasant expression faded and the green eyes behind spectacles transformed into cold stones. "Drink it. Or I'll pour it down your throat."

Rain reached for the glass and brought it to her lips. Swallowing, she felt the liquid drop into the empty pit of her stomach. Perspiration trickled down her spine. Although Carteris had managed to get the generator working, the small air-conditioning unit was hardly a match against the bayou heat. Candlelight danced inside the stifling cabin and created moving shadows on the cypress-paneled walls.

Satisfied she'd at least sampled the wine, he poured himself another glass. A plate sat on the table with cheese, foie gras and crackers. Apparently, the cooler he'd brought with them was well stocked. There was also something that appeared to be caviar, heaped in a small dish that sat in a pool of melting ice. He piled some onto a cracker and popped it into his mouth, chewing with relish. Rain realized she'd had nothing to eat since the beignets she'd shared with Trevor that morning, but the idea of food seemed ludicrous.

A flash of lightning reflected on the windows. The storm was moving closer, and would be upon them soon.

"The gown fits you perfectly."

She pulled the edges of the negligee's low neckline closer together. Carteris had woken her from her drugged sleep only a short while earlier. He'd thrust the gown at her, allowing her to go into the small bathroom to put it on. It was made of pale creamy silk, although its delicate lace trim had yellowed with age.

"I bought it in Europe for your mother and had it tailored for her small frame. It's Chanel. It was quite expensive at the time." He swirled the burgundy liquid in his glass. "I mailed it to her while I was in medical school at Oxford. She sent it back to me unopened."

He rose from the chair and walked to a vintage turntable that resided on a low cabinet next to the wall. Carefully, he placed the needle on the vinyl LP, and Rain tensed as her mother's husky voice filled the room.

"You've heard this before? It's an original issue of the *Sanctity* album." He gazed at the image of Desiree on the album's cardboard sleeve.

Rain felt a tremor pass through her, unable to forget what Carteris had claimed. *He'd been her mother's lover.* Her eyes slid discreetly to the framed photograph on the bookshelf. That image had been doctored. It was the only plausible explanation. She clung to the idea that he was just an insane man whose deluded mind had invented a fantasy world centering around Desiree. It simply wasn't possible to think otherwise.

As if he could read her thoughts, Carteris moved toward her, carrying the album cover. "You still don't believe me, do you? I met your mother when I was a senior at Loyola, Rain. She was singing in bars in the Quarter, mostly for tips. She even worked topless a time or two. My parents thought she was a bad influence. *Nothing but pretty swamp trash,* they'd said. Which was why they sent me to complete my medical education abroad. They knew Desiree was a gold digger, and they wanted to keep us apart."

His eyes met Rain's in the candlelight. "I was what one might call a late bloomer. Your mother was my first sexual experience. Our relationship was very intense, and I was madly in love with her. Obsessed, actually. The things she taught me…"

His words trailed off, and a look of distaste soured his features. He laid the album cover down. "Of course, once I was out of the picture, it didn't take her long to forget me. She took up with Gavin Firth almost immediately. He was already quite famous, and supposedly, he'd come to New Orleans to jam with the blues greats. Desiree saw an ideal opportunity. Firth could help with her career—his connections could make her into a star. Your mother was always a user, Rain."

He reached out, grasping her jaw and tilting her face upward. "You have her delicate features, you know."

"I'm not her," she managed to say, her voice unsteady. "Surely you understand—"

"Get up."

Shaking almost violently, Rain complied. She was once again made aware of Carteris's stature. He stroked the column of her throat, and her pulse fluttered under his fingers as he applied light pressure against the main artery.

"Blood is the key to everything. I'm a wealthy man. How do you imagine I became so?"

"Your family had…money," she stammered. "You're a cardiac surgeon—"

"That's no more than a sideline to me. Have you ever leafed through one of those celebrity magazines and wondered how an actress nearing her fifties could look as young and fresh as a twenty-year-old ingenue?" He paused for several weighted seconds. "There's amazing secret research being done. I'm considered a pioneer, and my work has made me a fortune."

His thumb brushed over her bottom lip. "I could've kept Desiree young and beautiful forever, too."

"How old *are* you?" she whispered.

"How old would your mother be if she was still alive?"

Rain fought every instinct she had not to struggle as Carteris slowly bent his head and kissed her. She remained perfectly still, not resisting but offering no reciprocation. Finally he broke contact and sighed. She jumped as the first fat raindrops smacked the tin roof.

"The storm is here," he announced, picking up his glass. "Bring your wine. We'll finish our drinks on the porch."

She had no choice but to obey. Rain claimed her goblet in trembling fingers, aware her acquiescence might keep her alive a while longer. She walked to the door he held open for her. Carteris, his claims about her mother, the bayou cabin—everything seemed like an unfathomable nightmare. Even her steps were sluggish and weighed down, as if she'd fallen into a terror-induced trance. Moving onto the narrow porch she felt the wind whip under the roof's protective overhang. It brought with it a cool mist that jolted her awake as the shower fell in silvered sheets around them.

A powerful explosion lit the bruised sky. The bolt struck somewhere nearby, lacing the air with a smell like scorched electrical wiring. But Carteris seemed not to notice. He gazed out at the ruined plantation house.

"Desiree loved storms. I suppose that's why she named you what she did." He drained his glass and set it on the railing next to a can of wasp spray. The insects' nest remained tucked under the shadowed eaves, but no buzzing sound emerged. It looked like a dark, abandoned moon.

"Did you know I saw you once, when you were a toddler?" He removed his spectacles and placed them in his shirt pocket. "I was there that night. You were such a tiny thing. I decided to spare your life."

Rain's eyes shot to his face. "What are you saying?"

He chose not to answer. Instead, he smiled wanly. "It's nearly nine o'clock. In a few hours it will be the anniversary of your mother's death, my dear."

Her hold on the glass tightened. She had to know. "Will I die on that day, too?"

Another streak of lightning illuminated her captor's face. "That's entirely up to you."

Carteris moved closer, caressing her bare arms. His weight pressed into her and his palms were hot against her damp skin. He spoke, his voice hard-edged. "I'm going to kiss you again. And this time you're going to kiss me back like you mean it."

His hands sank into her hair. The kiss was rougher, deeper than before, nearly punishing as he forced his tongue inside her mouth. Rain cried out in protest, but the sound was swallowed up inside the cavern of his jaw.

"Desiree," he uttered, sliding his wet lips to her throat.

She dropped the glass and shoved against his chest. The crystal shattered on the wood planks, splattering wine on the hem of her gown. Fumbling backward, she wiped her mouth to remove the taste of him. She couldn't go through with what he wanted. She'd rather die.

"We're going back inside." His fingers clamped over her arm, but Rain grabbed the can of wasp spray. She aimed the stream of chemicals into his eyes. Carteris howled. He clawed at his face as she threw herself down the porch's stairs and into the deluge.

Barefoot, she ran across the clearing and into the foliage, heading toward the road they'd driven in on earlier that day.

His bellows of outrage followed her into the dark.

43

If she kept traveling alongside the gravel road, Rain reasoned it would lead her back to the rural highway where she'd hopefully be able to flag down a passing motorist. She'd been walking for what seemed like an hour, but the going was excruciatingly slow. Her feet were bruised and cut, and the gown's wet silk had molded itself to her body. Overhead, the last residue of light had leaked from the sky. Except for the periodic streaks of lightning, she found herself in darkness that was far different from anything she'd experienced in the city.

Pushing through the downpour, she tried to veer her mind from the menacing swampland with its alligators and other feral creatures. Rain only knew she'd prefer to take her chances with the wildlife than spend another moment with Carteris. His violent curses as she ran from the cabin made it clear that if he recaptured her, she'd pay for her transgression with her life.

I was there that night, you know. You were such a tiny thing. I decided to spare your life.

She couldn't stop thinking about the claims Carteris had made. He'd begun to sound both lucid and convincing.

No, she reminded herself. None of it was possible. Carteris was too young to have ever known her mother—it had to be the ravings of a psychopath. Her mind as muddy as the trail she walked on, Rain's thoughts shifted to Trevor. Sudden tears of longing filled her eyes. Did he know yet it was Carteris who'd abducted her? Was he still looking for her, or had he already accepted the probability she was dead?

The need to get to a phone forced her to move faster. But she'd made it only a few hundred more feet when the glare of headlights cut through the dark. Her heart froze. Rain fled deeper into the brush lining the side of the road. She dropped to a crouch, barely missing the swath of light that sought her.

"Rain!" Carteris had the driver's-side window of the Escalade rolled down. Rocks crunched under its tires as it rolled forward. Had he seen her? The hair on her nape prickled as the vehicle came to a stop a short distance away.

Leaving the headlights glowing, Carteris killed the engine and climbed out. He began searching the foliage with a high-powered flashlight, moving closer to where Rain cowered as if he could smell her scent and her rising fear. She remained motionless, afraid to blink or even breathe.

"I'm already angry with you." His words were clipped. "Come out now. Don't make this harder than it has to be."

His beam landed on her precise location, blinding her. "This is your destiny, Rain. Don't you understand that?"

Rain took off into the woods. She ignored the sting of branches whipping against her face and arms, aware only of her pursuer's shouts and the wet slap of his shoes behind her. Adrenaline catalyzed her flight. She slid down a moss-slick embankment, trying to put as much distance as she could between them.

For a time, it seemed as though she'd lost him. The flashlight's shaft no longer followed her trail, and all she could hear was the sound of her own labored breathing. But Rain

ontinued running until she tripped over what must have been
e upraised roots of a swamp cypress. She fell several feet
efore landing on her hands and knees in shallow water. A
arp pain jolted up her right wrist, and she bit back a cry as
mething slithered over her ankle.

"Rain!"

He must have heard the splash. Carteris's yell caused her
scramble up. Her wrist throbbing, she slogged her way
the stagnant pool's muddy bank. The odor of fermenting
egetation filled her nostrils and mosquitoes buzzed in her
ars. Grasping at spindly roots, she worked frantically to pull
erself up the slick incline.

Reaching the top, her fingers closed around something
ard and smooth sticking up from the bayou silt. In the sec-
nd-long flash of lightning, she saw that it was the bone of a
uman limb, the flesh picked clean from it by wild animals.
ain made a guttural moaning sound. The rounded cap of a
kull peeped out from the wet ground nearby. A few clumps
f long matted hair still clung to it.

Bile rose in her throat. She staggered to her feet just as the
orceful blow came from behind. Rain tumbled onto her stom-
ch, her hands sinking in mud. Dizzy, she turned her head
nd saw grime-covered shoes. Carteris trained the yellow
ircle of light on her face.

"Running from me is a stupid thing to do."

She screamed as he grabbed her hair and yanked her
ughly to her knees. Her efforts to fight him were futile.
e hauled her up and began half dragging, half carrying her
the waiting SUV.

Returning to the house on Prytania felt like a mortal
ound. Trevor stared at the kitchen counter, which still held
eir breakfast plates from early that morning. Exhausted, he
bbed a hand over his face. He'd let his guard down, allowed

his father and his past to distract him long enough for Carter
to make his move. God only knew what was happening
Rain right now, or if she was even still alive. They had nothi
working in their favor except an APB on Carteris's vehicl
Feeling as if he was drowning, Trevor closed his eyes.

Eventually he became aware of Dahlia's purr. She'd spru
onto the counter, and he stroked the cat's silky head befo
getting out a can of food from the pantry and feeding he
For a time, he stared out the window over the sink, lost i
his own helplessness as raindrops trailed down its darkene
pane. Then he dialed into Rain's voice mail system, usir
the pass code he'd gotten from her service. He listened to th
message left by Oliver Carteris shortly before his death.

I've gotta talk to you...fuck. Just pick up the phone...
Had he been trying to warn her?

Carteris's travel records had confirmed Trevor's suspicion
The surgeon's lecture circuit over the past eighteen montl
meshed with the time line of killings in the other cities. N
to mention, one of the hair strands found in the Mercede
was a match to Cara Seagreen. He envisioned Oliver in Ne
Orleans, scanning the goth clubs and hangouts, searching f
prey to take home to his father. With his exotic good lool
and Carteris's pricey sports car, it probably hadn't been a di
ficult task.

His cell phone rang. He withdrew it from his pocket an
answered.

"Agent Rivette? This is Sandra Bellamy, a research assi
tant at the FBI field office. I thought you'd want to know w
had another sighting of a black Cadillac Escalade. This tim
near Vermilion Parish in the southwest part of the state."

Trevor shifted the phone to his other ear, hopeful this on
had more significance than the twenty others reported sinc
an alert had been issued statewide on the news. "The plate
matched?"

"The caller didn't get a look at the numbers. But he says the vehicle was a late model, with halogen fog lamps and aluminum wheels. The total package."

"Did he see the occupants?"

"Only the driver, sir. A white male. He wasn't sure if there was anyone on the passenger side. The caller was a farmer parked on the side of the road where he'd gone to check crawfish traps. When he saw the news tonight, he thought he should call."

Trevor released a breath, knowing the sighting was a long shot. "Any idea where the vehicle was headed?"

"Just into the bayous. Geographically, there's not much beyond that point except wetlands."

"Sandra, can you run a check to see if the Carteris name is linked to any property in that part of the state? Check the suspect's mother's maiden name, too. It's Benoit." He spelled the surname and heard the rapid click of a keyboard through the phone.

"I'll have to access the tax-assessor records for each of the parishes in that area," she said. "It might take a while."

"Just do it as fast as you can." Disconnecting the phone, Trevor walked through the parlor and into Rain's office. He turned on the mission-style lamp and thought about what McGrath had told him outside the burning mansion. Just before the bomb had detonated, the detective found love letters Carteris had supposedly written to Desiree Sommers. But the math didn't add up. The correspondence all bore postmarks from the seventies. According to the hospital's personnel records, Carteris was forty-three years old. Which meant at the time the letters were written, he couldn't have been much more than a child.

None of it made sense. To make matters worse, those letters were gone now, destroyed along with whatever else might have been inside the residence.

Dropping into the chair behind Rain's desk, he turned o
the computer. It didn't take long to locate the notes from he
sessions with Oliver Carteris. Ten minutes later, however, he
found no clues and certainly nothing to indicate that Olive
might have been involved in anything as serious as murde
His mind reeling, Trevor lowered his head into his hands.

A short time later, a soft knock caused him to look u
Brian stood in the office doorway. His dark hair and stripe
polo shirt were damp from the downpour outside. He held
set of house keys in his hand. "You left them in the door."

"They're Rain's," Trevor said quietly. "I took them fro
Annabelle's this morning."

"Alex has a set, too. He thought I should check o
Dahlia."

And on you, Brian's blue eyes seemed to say. Trevo
shook off the concern he saw on his brother's face. "Alex
awake?"

"He's got one mother of a headache and he's worried sic
about Rain, but the doctors think he'll be fine. They're keep
ing him a couple of days for observation." Pausing, he steppe
farther inside the room. "The explosion at the surgeon's hous
was on the news tonight. They're calling him the prime sus
pect in the murders. You were there, weren't you?"

When he didn't answer, Brian continued, "They said peop
were hurt, and a detective was killed. Are you okay?"

"Yeah," Trevor said. But after a moment, he admitted, "
don't know."

He ran a hand through his hair, unable to hide his fear an
frustration. Getting up from behind the desk, he walked t
the window and stood with his arms crossed over his ches
After a moment, he felt Brian squeeze his shoulder. The sup
portive gesture was almost more than he could bear.

"This isn't your fault—"

"The hell it isn't," Trevor replied, his throat tight. "Th

whole thing with Dad this morning was a setup. I walked right into it."

"What were you going to do? He had Haley. You had no reason to think—"

The digital shrill of Trevor's cell phone halted Brian's words. Trevor looked at the number on the screen and flipped open the device. What Sandra Bellamy told him gave him a flare of hope.

"What is it?" Brian wanted to know once he'd completed the call.

"There're several hundred acres of rural property near Vermilion Parish registered to Myrna Benoit, Carteris's mother. She died several years back, but Carteris has been paying taxes on it since. Someone called into the hotline earlier today, claiming to have seen a vehicle matching Carteris's headed in that direction."

"Do they know where the property is?"

"Somewhere in east Jesus, out in the bayous."

"That's *west* Jesus, actually," Brian murmured.

"Either way, there's not even a postal address. They're trying to pinpoint a location."

The cell phone rang again. Trevor answered it quickly, expecting it to be the research assistant calling back with additional information. But the voice he heard was distinctly male. Electricity snaked up his spine.

"Good evening, Agent Rivette. I apologize for the poor reception, but I'm in a rather remote location. Did you have a pleasant visit with your father this morning?"

Trevor gripped the phone. "Just tell me if she's still alive, Carteris."

"She's very much alive. For now."

He turned his back on Brian and strained to hear the surgeon through the phone's crackling static.

"I've been listening to the radio. I understand the FBI and

police made an uninvited visit to my house today. Your intru
sion cost the life of a detective. Shame."

"Did the news tell you about your son? He committed su
cide. He hanged himself at the Ascension."

The airwaves between them sizzled, and for several sec
onds Trevor feared he'd lost the connection. But then Carteri
spoke again, his words sounding almost resigned.

"I'm aware of Oliver's death."

"It's time to end this."

"Indeed," he agreed solemnly. "I have a proposition fo
you. I'm going to give you my exact location. If you come t
me tonight, perhaps we can make some kind of arrangemen
Are you willing to do that?"

Trevor went to Rain's desk. He wrote down the direction
as Carteris gave them.

"One thing, Agent. Come alone. No SWAT team or assist
ing agents. I promise you, if I so much as see another huma
being I'll cut her throat without hesitation."

"I want to speak to her," Trevor said.

"You're in no position to make demands."

"If you want me to come out there, I need proof she's stil
alive."

A second passed and he heard Rain cry out, her scream
fading into sobs. He felt something break inside him.

"You should hurry, Agent," Carteris said. "Before I ge
bored and start finding ways to amuse myself."

The phone went silent. Trevor bowed his head, desperat
to slow the pumping of his heart. He wanted her back. He
had to find a way to get Rain out of this mess alive.

Brian spoke from behind him, reminding him of his pres
ence. "Tell me you're not planning to go out there alone."

"I have to." Tearing the directions from the notepad he'
written them on, he folded the paper and shoved it into hi

jeans pocket. He began to walk from the office, but Brian blocked him.

"Listen to me. You need to alert the authorities out there. Hell, take the entire FBI and the National Guard with you—"

"He'll kill her if he sees anyone else."

"He's going to kill you!"

Trevor brushed past, but Brian caught up to him in the foyer and grabbed his arm. "Stop it, Brian—"

"Let me come with you," he offered. "I'll take you out there in the Cessna. You can make it in half the time than if you drive, especially with the way it's raining. I'm an instrument-rated pilot trained to fly in these conditions—"

Trevor threw off Brian's grasp. "No."

"Damn it, Trevor!" He looked both angry and terrified. "You take me or I'm calling the FBI and letting them know what's going on!"

His face conveyed the seriousness of his threat. "I'm not bluffing. I'll call them the minute you leave."

"You do that and you're going to get Rain killed," Trevor warned.

"If I let you go out there alone, you'll both be dead."

The house's front door stood open. Water danced on the sidewalk and dripped from the roof's gutter. Why did Carteris want him out there? Trevor didn't know. But Brian had a point—getting there by car would take hours, and he wasn't sure how long Carteris's patience would hold out. He stepped onto the veranda and put his hands on the railing.

"When Dad hurt you, I was too young and scared to do anything about it," Brian said, standing next to him. "Annabelle and I stayed silent, and we've regretted it our entire lives."

Trevor looked at him. "I don't want you getting mixed up in this."

Brian's expression was grave under the porch lamplight. "I just got you back, Trev. I can't lose you again. Let me help you. The Cessna has a GPS system. All I need is a two-lane highway and I can put the plane down."

His brother was right. Alone he was most certainly walking into a death trap. Not only for himself, but for Rain. He was fully aware Carteris had no intention of letting her go. But with the plane, Brian could be Rain's ticket back to safety, if only Trevor could distract Carteris long enough for her to get away.

If she could somehow make it to Brian, he could fly her out of there.

44

"Your lover wants you back." Carteris closed the phone with a hard snap as the Escalade bounced along the rutted, nearly washed-out road. He glared at Rain. Even in the darkened cab his eyes looked irritated from the wasp spray.

Pressing herself against the passenger door, she cradled her swollen wrist. He'd twisted it viciously, until she screamed and begged him to stop. *His proof to Trevor she was still alive.*

"I suppose you heard Oliver's dead."

She managed a weak whisper. "How?"

"I'd say his therapist failed him in his time of need."

They continued in silence until the SUV's headlights broke into the clearing. Carteris wrenched the vehicle into park in front of the cabin, then turned off the engine and opened his door. "Get out."

Rain hesitated a second too long. Reaching into the SUV, he seized her again by her wrist. Fresh pain seared up her arm as he propelled her across the leather captain's chair. She spilled out through the open door, landing on the ground at his feet. Snatching her up, he pushed her in front of him up the stairs.

She limped inside the cabin. The candles still burned,

although Desiree's husky voice no longer emerged from the turntable. Instead, the needle scratched where it had fallen off the record's vinyl groove.

"Take off your clothes."

Rain whipped her eyes to his. Every ounce of the gentlemanly facade Carteris had hidden behind earlier was gone.

"I said, take off those filthy clothes," he repeated through gritted teeth.

The gown's wet silk was nearly transparent in the candlelight. She hugged her arms over her breasts, her eyes falling to her muddy and bleeding bare feet. Her mind threatened to shut down. Carteris clutched her shoulders, his fingers digging into her skin. Her head jerked back as he gave her a hard shake.

"You're not supposed to look like this!" Perspiration covered his face, and the sockets around his reddened eyes were purple shadows. "I've planned carefully for this! I won't let you ruin it for me!"

Dragging her into the small bathroom, he reached into the stall and turned on the shower. A thin stream of water spurted out. He left the room and then came back, throwing her shorts and tank top onto the floor.

"Clean yourself up. You have five minutes to get back out here. I guarantee you'll regret it if I have to haul you out."

The door slammed closed. Rain was left alone in the cramped, windowless space. She caught her reflection in the hazy mirror that hung over the sink. Dirt smeared her forehead, and there was a large scratch on her cheek from her flight through the brush. She thought of the human remains she'd stumbled on. Tears filled her eyes as she peeled off the gown and stepped under the weak spray.

Carteris was bringing Trevor here to kill him. There was no way he'd allow either of them to leave this place alive.

* * *

Numbly, Rain emerged from the bathroom a short time later. She'd redressed in her own clothes, although her hair was still wet and uncombed. Desiree sang again, her haunting voice backed by a moody orchestral arrangement.

You didn't want me, but I swear to God you'll pay.

Her mother crooned about rejection and revenge. Tremors racked her body as Rain slowly stepped into the candlelight.

The leather physician's bag was overturned on the table. Pill bottles, vials and syringes were scattered around it. Carteris stood with a black tube secured tightly around his upper arm. He injected himself with something, although Rain didn't know what. His eyes closed, his expression growing slack as the drug took effect. When he finally looked at her, he made no mention of what he'd just done. Calmly, he laid the empty syringe on the table and held out his hand.

"Come here," he demanded. Too frightened not to obey, Rain put her hand in his. "Your fingers are like ice, little one."

He'd changed from his own mud-streaked attire into clean slacks and a fresh shirt. Wrapping his arm around her, Carteris guided her to the couch and eased her down next to him on its cushions.

"He'll be here soon. You'll have to make a decision. You'll have to choose between him or me. I gave your mother the same choice thirty years ago."

She inhaled sharply as he extracted a surgical scalpel from his shirt pocket, although he made no threatening move with it. Turning it over, he examined the glinting blade.

"Desiree's death was the most sexually exciting experience of my life," he murmured. "I dream about it to this day."

"But you weren't…there. You're confused. You couldn't have been—"

"Are you certain?" He tilted his head to look at her, and she worked to process his taunt against everything she knew about that fateful event. Her parents' deaths had been a murder-suicide, an open-and-shut case.

"They were fighting…they both had speed in their bloodstream," she stammered. "It was in the toxicology report. Gavin—my father—stabbed my mother and then—"

"Cut his own throat?" Carteris finished her statement, his lips twitching into a chilling smile. "Your parents were amoral rock stars. They'd already had a child out of wedlock, quite scandalous in those days. Of course they'd be drug abusers. It made perfect sense."

He coiled a strand of her damp hair around his finger. "Amphetamines ensured the police would ask few questions. It was a simple matter to administer the drug to the bodies, then plant more around the house. I was completing my medical residency at the time. I had access. I got away with the perfect crime."

"I don't believe you." She cried out as he grabbed her throat and forced her to look into his eyes. What she saw there was both evil and dead.

"I've waited a long time to relive that night. Your mother begged for her lover's life. Will you?" Releasing her with a small shove, he glanced at the clock on the fireplace mantel. "It's already after ten. The time is nearly at hand."

She understood with terrifying clarity. It was a play Carteris had already written, the actors already cast. He intended to re-create her parents' deaths. Trevor would take the role of Gavin, and she would be Desiree.

"What if I choose you? We can leave together now, before he gets here—"

"Listen to you. Already scheming to save his life." He shook his head in rebuke. "You've caused me to expend a great deal of energy. All that pointless running around outside."

Using his index finger, he dragged the strap of her tank top down her shoulder, exposing her skin. Rain's heart pounded.

"In many ways, I owe everything to Desiree. She was my first taste. I felt my body taking in her energy, my own strength being amplified as hers was diminished. I drank her *essence* that night. It was the sweetest revenge." Carteris stroked the curve of her neck, causing her to shudder violently.

"It was then I realized blood held the secret. That discovery has been the basis for my research." He leaned closer, his lips tracing her jaw. "I could use a taste of *you* now, Rain."

With the last of her strength, she pushed away and ran to the cabin's door. But he caught her again in two quick strides, ripping her hands from the door frame. His size enabled him to easily overpower her. She screamed as he carted her back to the couch and shoved her down roughly, pinning her onto the cushions with his weight. He held the scalpel in front of her face as a warning.

"Shh. Don't move."

"Please," she begged.

"You act as though I'm going to bite you. You've seen too many horror movies." He pressed his nose against her skin, breathing in her scent. "In reality, unless one wishes to kill, a controlled cutting technique is much more desirable."

Rain gulped air as her eyes trained on the weapon in his hand.

"There's a saying in ancient Sanskrit. One life feeds on another."

The scalpel sliced into her shoulder. Rain sobbed as a rivulet of her own red blood appeared and trailed down her skin. Carteris lowered his mouth to it, and she felt herself spiraling into the black hole Dante had dug.

The waning candlelight caused the shadows around her to shift and deepen. Rain lay across the couch. How long had she been out? Briefly, she wondered if it had been some horrible nightmare. But her rustic surroundings came slowly back into focus.

"It's time for you to wake, my dear."

Carteris's cultured voice brought her fully back to reality. She sat up and pressed her fingers against her forehead as the room dipped slightly. He lounged next to her, a look of charmed amusement on his face.

"Feeling weak? You needn't worry. I didn't take enough to harm you. Not too much more than if you'd donated at a clinic, really. But I'm afraid I don't have any cookies or juice to offer you."

Despite her unsteadiness, Rain stood. She touched the smooth plane of skin near her clavicle, her pulse quickening as she felt a sting. The cut still oozed blood.

"What did you do to me?" she croaked.

"The instrument was sterilized. The risk to you is minimal."

She took a step backward as she realized what Carteris held. He toyed with a strand of black prayer beads, winding it around his wrist as he spoke.

"I've been watching you sleep." He rose from the couch.

Rain nearly toppled as her calves came flush with the coffee table. Hysteria threatened to claim her. "If you take a step closer I swear I'll—"

Carteris made a grab for her, then stopped. His features hardened and he raised a hand to silence her. "Quiet! Do you hear that? I believe our guest has arrived."

There was no discernible sound. Even the downpour had

topped its racket on the cabin's roof. The hush echoed around
ler like a death knell. If Trevor was out there, she had to
varn him.

She shouted his name, but Carteris was on her immedi-
tely, sealing her mouth with his hand. She clawed at his fin-
;ers as he towed her with him to the gun safe. The door of
he metal cabinet was already open, and he took a powerful-
ooking handgun from its shelf.

"Keep your mouth shut or this all ends now." He loosened
lis grip over her aching jaw and pressed the gun's barrel into
ler side. Keeping a tight hold on her, they walked across the
:abin floor and onto the porch.

"I know you're out there, Agent Rivette!" Carteris
velled. He held Rain in front of him, a human shield. "Show
vourself!"

Her knees nearly gave out as a lone figure stepped from
he brush at the edge of the clearing. The navy windbreaker
vas nearly invisible in the darkness if not for the gold FBI
nsignia on its front.

"Drop your firearm," Carteris ordered.

No, Trevor. Rain shook her head, trying to communicate
an unspoken plea for him to refuse. But he laid his gun in the
ow grass.

"Kick it into the bushes!"

He did as instructed, then raised his hands as he took several cautious steps closer. "I'm here to talk, Carteris. I came
ilone. Just like you wanted."

Carteris lifted the gun and fired. Rain screamed as Trevor
'ell to the wet ground.

45

"Relax," Carteris scolded as Rain twisted in his arms. "He's wearing a vest. Don't believe me? I'll let you take a look for yourself."

He released her. Rain clambered down the stairs and dropped to her knees beside Trevor. Repeating his name, she felt the vest's padding under his windbreaker. To her relief, he moved and opened his eyes, although he appeared dazed. Tearing open the jacket, she saw where the bullet had embedded.

"You see? Kevlar, standard issue." Carteris traveled across the grass and stood over them. "Completely predictable."

She worked her hand under the vest and felt the dry fabric of Trevor's T-shirt. No blood. But she'd heard of policemen being severely injured from the bullet's impact, even if it didn't penetrate.

"Nice of you to join us, Agent Rivette." Carteris motioned with his gun. "Now get up. Inside, both of you."

Grimacing, Trevor slowly raised himself to a sitting position and Rain helped him to his feet. As they climbed the porch stairs with their captor behind them, she was aware of the way he used the stair railing for support. Hope leeched from her. He'd come here on a suicide mission. He had to know that.

Reaching the doorstep, Carteris gave Trevor a shove. She gasped as he turned to find the gun pointed in his face.

"I'm here to negotiate. I followed your instructions—"

"There will be negotiations," Carteris remarked. "Only not between you and me. Move to the bookcase, away from the door."

As they complied, Carteris walked to the turntable to replace the needle on Desiree's record. Trevor's words to Rain were hushed. "No matter what happens, if you get the chance, go."

She shook her head, touching his face. "Not without you."

He clasped her shoulders. "Listen to me. There's help on the way, but I needed a chance to get you out first. Brian's waiting at the highway—"

He stopped speaking as Carteris approached.

"Did you see my son, Agent?"

Trevor looked him in the eye. "Do you mean hanging from the ceiling of the Ascension, or on a slab at the morgue? Either way, the answer is yes."

"Did he leave a note?"

"To explain why he killed himself? That's obvious. He couldn't live with what you were doing. With what you were forcing him to do." He lowered his voice. "Respect his memory. This has to stop now."

Carteris smiled coldly. "But we're only getting started. We have a long night ahead of us."

"Your son cared about Rain. He tried to contact her before he died, and I believe he was going to warn her. At least let her go. Do it for him."

"Oliver was a weak, disobedient child. Perhaps if I'd been

a harsher disciplinarian, he'd have turned out differently."
Carteris's eyes gleamed behind his spectacles. "But you'd
know something about that, wouldn't you, Agent? Spare the
rod and spoil the child? I've perused your medical records.
You had a very unfortunate childhood. A litany of bruises
and broken bones."

"You told Baptiste what my father did to me. That's how
he knew," Trevor murmured in realization.

"Armand felt threatened by your interest in the Ascension.
He needed something he could use to shake you up a bit. Your
medical files were a wealth of information, especially relating to your traumatic injury in your teen years."

"And you figured out my father was responsible?"

Carteris caressed the gun's barrel, obviously enjoying the
control he held over them. "You're not the only one with in-
vestigative skills, Agent. I did some sleuthing of my own.
Given your medical history, the treating physician on your
case had suspicions about how your head injury was sus-
tained. Your family's story seemed off to him. He recorded
his doubts in your files—files to which I have access. The
doctor's retired now, but I gave him a call. He remembered
your case clearly. In fact, he said he contacted the police with
his theory, but Officer Rivette paid him a visit and threatened
him. He let the matter drop."

Rain's head buzzed with fear and exhaustion as the two
men glared at one another in the shadowed room. Over the
fireplace, the mantel clock struck midnight in deep baritone
chords.

"I wasn't certain you'd come out here," Carteris said. "Is
she worth that much to you? You're willing to die to see her
one last time?"

"Just let her go. She apparently means something to you,
too."

He cut his stony gaze to Rain. "Help him take off that est."

Trevor shrugged free of the windbreaker and let it fall to 1e floor. He slowly raised his arms out from his sides. Hesiintly, Rain did as she was told. She released the Velcro straps 1at held the vest in place. Wincing with the effort, Trevor 1lled it over his head, and she thought again of the bullet 1at had nearly pierced his chest. He dropped the heavy garient on top of the discarded jacket.

"Keep your arms out." Carteris kept the gun pointed. Startig at Trevor's ankles, he patted him for weapons but found one.

"I figured you for a man who carries a backup." He tossed 1e handcuffs he took from Trevor's jeans pocket to Rain. Cuff his hands behind his back, and don't play games. I ant to hear a snap when they close."

When she wavered, he swung the gun toward her. "Do it ow!"

"Do what he says, Rain." Trevor looked at her, his eyes lled with compassion. Then he placed his wrists behind is back. Her hands trembling, it took several tries for her to uccessfully close the cuffs. When she was done, he briefly aught her fingers within his and squeezed. Emotion broke 1rough the terror enveloping her, making her eyes mist.

"So what happens now?" he asked.

"That's up to your lover." Carteris took a step toward Rain nd roughly cupped her jaw. He chuckled as she tried to rench from his grasp.

"He dies either way," he said, no longer speaking to Trevor. You decide how much pain he endures."

Carteris let go of her. Confident Trevor no longer posed threat, he slid the handgun into the back waistband of his rousers. But he was only trading one weapon for another,

Rain soon realized. He walked to the physician's bag and re
turned brandishing the knife he'd had earlier that day.

"How much do you love him? Shall I make it a quick death
or a lingering, painful one? If you really do care for him, yo
won't want him to suffer overly."

An icy dread swept through her. Rain's mind raced fo
some way to placate him, to buy a few more moments of pre
cious time. Stepping in front of Trevor, she placed her han
on Carteris's chest.

"You don't have to do this! I swear I'll do anything yo
want." If it would keep Trevor alive, she meant it. She'd se
her soul to keep him breathing. "Let me make up for Desiree'
betrayal. We'll leave the country. Just the two of us."

Carteris stared at her. In the fading candlelight, he n
longer looked distinguished, but monstrous and horrific. "
asked you a question. What will it be? A quick and easy death
or a slow one? It's time to make your choice."

"But I choose you!" she cried, her face ashen. "What els
do you want?"

"I want you to prove it. I want you to tell me how to ki
him."

Rain's mouth opened soundlessly. She felt her sanity slip
ping by degrees.

"Your vacillation is sealing your fate! I want a de
cision!"

"Don't do this to her," Trevor demanded. "Finish this wit
me, not her!"

"Very well." Carteris's soulless eyes remained on Rair
"I'll have to make the choice for you. Just as I made it fo
Desiree—"

She grabbed Carteris's arm. "No, please!"

"I've regretted I didn't make Gavin Firth suffer more fo
taking what belonged to me. He died quickly. *Too quickly.*
won't make that mistake again."

He broke her hold, his intent made clear by the knife gripped in his fist. But Trevor was one step ahead. He barreled into Carteris, taking him off balance and falling with him. The coffee table cracked loudly under the men's combined weight. It splintered in half and deposited them both on the floor.

"Rain, get out of here!"

Using the couch, Trevor leveraged to a standing position. But Carteris was halfway up, as well. Trevor landed a blow with his foot, toppling him back down. The knife fell from Carteris's hand, but he quickly scrambled on top of it. He swung the weapon in a wild arc, forcing Trevor to back away.

"Go!" he yelled again.

She wouldn't leave him, As Carteris got to his feet, Rain threw herself into the chaos. She latched onto him, but he flung her off like a child discarding a toy. Landing on the floor, her injured wrist radiated pain that made stars explode in front of her eyes. She forced herself up just as Carteris slammed Trevor against the wall. With his hands cuffed behind him, he was defenseless. Carteris thrust the knife low into Trevor's rib cage. He gave the weapon a vicious turn and plunged it in again.

Rain's scream turned into a ravaged sob. "Trevor!"

Carteris stepped back. Trevor released a ragged breath as a dark stain appeared on the gray cotton of his T-shirt.

No. Please, God, no.

He slowly collapsed to the floor. Rain dashed to him, falling to her knees and cradling him in her arms. Trevor's jaw clenched, his eyes squeezing closed in pain.

"I know what I'm doing with a knife," Carteris stated dully. "Death might take a while, Agent Rivette."

Seizing Rain's arm, he jerked her up. She reached out frantically, calling for Trevor as Carteris dragged her away like a dog on a leash. He stopped to snatch the rosary from the wooden shards of the broken coffee table. Its beads glittered like tiny black orbs, and the knife in his hand held the red tinge of Trevor's blood. Carteris's eyes were glazed with the darkest kind of lust.

"Come, little one. It's time for us to finally be together."

46

revor's instructions to Brian were explicit. Stay with the
essna, and leave with Rain if she made it back without
m. He'd also given Brian the small handgun he carried in
ankle holster, in the event Carteris managed to follow her
ck to the plane. Then Trevor had hugged him as if he ex-
cted to never see him again.

Despite their father being a cop, Brian had never held a
n, let alone fired one. But the shot that echoed across the
ampland had brought him to a quick decision. He'd taken
f at a run on the mud-and-gravel road, traveling in the same
rection as his brother. To hell with what Trevor told him to
—he wasn't going to let him die out here.

Cautiously, Brian peered into the dimly lit interior from the
bin's open doorway. Trevor was on the floor on the far side
the room—he was hurt, but how badly Brian didn't know.
ould he wait? Trevor had radioed the FBI field office not
ng after they'd taken off from Lakefront Airport in New
leans. Backup couldn't be too far behind. He hesitated,
raid of making a fatal mistake. But Rain's screams tore at
m as the man hauled her across the room.

When they neared the door, Brian took a breath and
pped inside, pointing the gun.

Surprise registered in Christian Carteris's eyes. He pul[l]
Rain in front of him, holding the knife against her throat. [H]
face was pale and streaked with tears.

"You lied about coming alone, Rivette. I'm impresse[d]
Carteris called over his shoulder. He looked amused as [he]
gave Brian the once-over. "And who are you?"

Brian tightened his grip on the gun. "I'm the man wh[o's]
going to blow you the fuck away if you don't let go of he[r.]"

His grin widened. "You're the brother, aren't you? T[he]
artist?"

"Drop the knife! I'm not kidding!"

He responded by increasing the blade's pressure. Ra[in]
made an agonized sound as a line of crimson appeared [on]
her skin. Fear flashed in her eyes.

"Would you like to watch me bleed her, Brian? May[be]
you'd like a taste yourself? It's quite addictive."

"You're sick—"

"I promise, drugs don't compare. Not liquid cocaine [or]
heroin—it's like no high you've experienced." He swip[ed]
his index finger across the blood on Rain's neck. Then [he]
brought it to his mouth and licked. Brian swallowed ha[rd,]
his stomach twisting.

"Your brother's dying—quite painfully, actually," Carte[ris]
goaded. "If he's still breathing when I finish with this who[re,]
I might show him some mercy and slit his throat."

For a fraction of a second, Brian's gaze darted to Trevo[r's]
slumped form. The distraction gave Carteris opportuni[ty.]
Shoving Rain aside, he sprung. Brian squeezed the gu[n's]
trigger, but Carteris struck his arm, knocking the bulle[t's]
trajectory off course. It shattered the paneled wall as no[ise]
exploded and the acrid odor of gunpowder filled the air. Bri[an]
fell with Carteris on top of him.

The knife skittered under the couch as they fought for co[n-]
trol of the gun. Brian held on to it, but Carteris had a visel[ike]

rip on his forearm. He slammed Brian's hand repeatedly
gainst the wood floor. Brian felt his tenuous grasp on the
eapon weakening with each hard whack. He yelled a curse
s it finally slipped from his fingers.

Carteris intercepted the gun and shuffled backward like a
and crab, his expression victorious. He hoisted himself up.
till panting from the scuffle, he raised the gun.

From the corner of his eye, Brian glimpsed Trevor strug-
ling to stand. Realization settled over him like a woolen
lanket.

He was about to die.

Instinctively, Brian shielded his face with his arm, but not
efore seeing the faint movement behind Carteris. Rain.

Another deafening explosion shook the room. A second
ater, Carteris dropped his arm and let go of the weapon. His
nees buckled and he fell face-first to the floor. Rain stood
vhere Carteris had been just moments before, smoke curl-
ng from the barrel of the gun gripped in her hands. Blood
pread from a fist-size hole in the center of Carteris's back.
A last rattling breath escaped his lungs and then the monster
ay still.

Brian got up. "Jesus, Rain!"

"The gun was in the waistband of his pants." Her voice
hook. "I...pulled it out and I..."

His heart thrummed. He looked at Trevor, and even in the
andlelight he could see blood staining his shirt. He'd slipped
ack down to the floor. His head leaned against the wall, his
yes closed. Appearing stunned, Rain continued staring at
Carteris's body, and Brian gave her a small shake.

"We've got to get Trevor out of here. To a hospital." He
hought of the small clinics in the outlying bayou parishes,
ll equipped to handle a life-threatening emergency. "A real
ne, with a trauma center."

"The FBI's on its way. They can help—"

"We can't wait. Get your shoes and find the keys to th SUV outside. We can use it to get him back to the plane. W landed on the highway."

She started toward Trevor, but Brian grabbed her arn "Find the keys, Rain. There's not a lot of time."

Nodding jerkily, she went in search of them.

"Trevor." Brian crossed the room and sank to his knee. His brother's skin where he touched it was clammy.

"I told you to stay with the Cessna," Trevor said, his wor threaded with pain.

"Yeah? Good thing for you I don't listen." Brian tried n to appear alarmed by the amount of blood. Anger ripple through him when he saw that Trevor's hands were cuffe behind his back. It hadn't even been a fair fight. "How do get these off you?"

"The keys are in my pocket." With some effort, Trevo leaned sideways so Brian could reach inside his jeans. Onc he removed the handcuffs, Brian got up and headed int the kitchen, returning with a stack of clean dish towels. H pressed them against Trevor's wounds, working to stay cal as his brother flinched.

"Sorry about that," Brian said softly.

"Carteris is dead?"

"One hundred percent. Rain shot him right through th heart."

"That's my girl," he whispered.

"Trevor, you've got to help us get you to the plane. Thin you can do that?"

"Yeah." But his nod was weak.

Rain returned wearing sneakers and clutching the keys t the Escalade. Her frightened gaze met Brian's over the top o Trevor's head.

"I'll carry most of his weight," Brian told her. "But you'r

going to have to keep pressure on the wound. The moveme.
might make the bleeding worse."

She knelt next to Trevor, placing her hand over the towels
as Brian removed his. Trevor looked into her face. "You all
right?"

Her eyes sparkled with tears. "I'm fine."

"Did he hurt you? I need to know—"

"I'm okay," Rain repeated. She smoothed his damp hair
back from his forehead with her free hand.

"What you said to Carteris, about making up for Desiree's
betrayal…" Trevor paused, his brow furrowing in pain. "Who
the hell was this guy? McGrath found letters he wrote to your
mother thirty years ago—"

She hushed him. "Save your strength. None of it matters
now."

"Let's do this," Brian said. With Rain's help, he got Trevor
to his feet. He put his shoulder under his brother's and Rain
did her best to support him on the other side. They moved
forward, stepping around Carteris's body and the blood that
bloomed around it. Leaving the cabin's interior, they slowly
navigated the porch stairs. Brian looked at the silhouetted
frame of the burned-down plantation manor and felt a chill
go up his spine.

At the SUV, he got into the backseat first, pulling Trevor
in after him so he was lying on his back. Once they had him
situated, Rain removed her hand from the towels. Her face
paled at the crimson already soaking through them. Trevor's
head rested in Brian's lap, his chest rising and falling with
his shallow breathing.

"How're you doing?" Brian asked.

"My chest hurts," Trevor murmured. His eyes closed, but
Brian tapped his cheek until they flickered back open.

"Hey. No sleeping on the job, Agent." He attempted a

smile, but it faltered as Trevor coughed. He looked at Rain. "We need to go."

The keys to the Escalade were in her hand. Backing out of the vehicle, she ran to the driver's side and got in. Rain put the keys into the ignition and the engine roared to life. The SUV's headlights cut into the darkness, illuminating the boughs of ancient trees.

"Drive slowly," Brian instructed from the backseat. "We don't need to get stuck."

It was only after the mud-splattered SUV reached the rural highway that he remembered. Rain was terrified of driving— always had been, according to Alex. In his concern for Trevor he'd completely forgotten her phobia. Rain hadn't mentioned it, instead climbing behind the wheel as if it was the most natural thing in the world. She hadn't wanted to waste the precious seconds it would have taken for them to switch positions, he realized. She'd driven admirably well, maintaining control of the vehicle and slipping only once on the makeshift road.

By the time the SUV came to a stop, Trevor's breathing had grown increasingly labored. Brian dragged him from the vehicle into the waiting plane.

"I'm afraid he's going into shock." Rain huddled in the nearly nonexistent space between the cockpit and the first row of passenger seats next to where Trevor was lying. She pressed her hands over the saturated towels covering his wound. Brian threw himself into the pilot's chair and prepared for a daredevil takeoff on the isolated stretch of road.

"Damn it, Trev!" Brian swiveled in his seat as the plane's propellers started. He felt the sting of tears behind his eyelids. "You stay with us, you hear me?"

"Just go," Rain pleaded. Her fingers, rusty with blood, stood out against the towels.

A few moments later, they were headed up into the starless

ight. Brian contacted emergency services on the plane's
dio, requesting that an ambulance be waiting for them at
e airport in New Orleans.

47

Rain flung open the Audi's door and raced through the entrance of All Saints Hospital. Brian was close behind her. There hadn't been room for either of them in the ambulance, so they'd been forced to follow in its wake from Lakefront Airport. As Brian went to the admitting desk and began tersely asking questions, Rain felt the blatant stares of others inside the E.R. She was aware of her appearance, including the blood staining her clothes. But she didn't care. All she wanted was to know Trevor would be all right.

He'd stopped breathing as the plane made its descent. Rain had performed mouth-to-mouth while Brian brought them down on the tarmac next to the glistening black waters of Lake Pontchartrain.

So much blood. She thought of Trevor's fading pulse under her fingers and covered her face with her hands. How anyone could survive such a trauma seemed out of the realm of possibility.

When she looked up again, she saw Annabelle coming toward them.

"What's happening?" Brian asked, meeting his sister. "I can't get the Nazi at the front desk to tell me a damn thing—"

"They've got him stabilized. He just went up to surgery." s soon as the plane was back in the range of cell towers, rian had called Annabelle and alerted her to what had happened. She must have been waiting at the hospital when the nbulance carrying Trevor arrived.

She laid her hand on Brian's face, her eyes soft. "Go see lex, okay? He's lying upstairs in bed, crazy with worry."

Reluctantly, he nodded and walked down the corridor to le elevators. As soon as he'd gone, Annabelle's gaze traved over Rain's cuts and bruises. "Rain? Shouldn't you see omeone? You look like you could use a doctor, honey."

"I'm okay." But she winced when Annabelle touched her. Ier wrist was stiff and throbbed dully.

"Oh, God! Your arm is black and blue—"

"I just need a shower and some coffee." She refused to aste time sitting for an X-ray while Trevor was fighting for is life. "Did they tell you anything?"

Emotion darkened Annabelle's eyes. "Not really. I heard lem mention a pneumothorax?"

"A collapsed lung," Rain said softly.

"Dr. Sommers?" A tall, muscularly built man with wheatolored hair approached. Despite the time of night, he was ressed in khaki trousers and a crisp button-down shirt. Somerly, Annabelle made the introductions.

"Rain, this is Sawyer Compton. He's with the D.A.'s ffice."

Rain knew who he was. She'd seen him on television, being lterviewed on the parish courthouse steps on numerous ocasions. Most recently, he'd taken part in the news conference eld by the joint FBI and police task force relating to the serial lurders. Sawyer Compton was known for his tough stance n crime, his disregard for the good ol' boys' network, and is reputation as one of the city's most eligible bachelors.

"I grew up in the same neighborhood with the Rivette

family," Sawyer explained. "Trevor and I are old friend
Don't let him tell you otherwise."

Annabelle's reddened eyes hadn't escaped him. He turne
to her. "You okay, chère? The doctor hasn't been back dow
here?"

"Nothing like that," she replied. "I'm just feeling a b
weepy."

Sawyer's hand lingered at Annabelle's waist. He looke
at Rain apologetically. "I came down here to give Annabel
moral support, not to conduct official business. But we'
got an NOPD detective dead and an FBI agent wounded, s
I need to ask you a few questions."

"I understand."

"I got a call from the FBI. A SWAT team went out t
Vermilion Parish at Agent Rivette's request. They said D
Carteris is dead. Agent Rivette shot him?"

Rain's eyes were unwavering. "No. I did."

She told him everything she knew about Carteris.

Rain took a shower in Alex's hospital room while A
nabelle went in search of clean clothes for her to wear. A
the hot spray kneaded her exhausted body, she stared dow
at the drain. Brownish water—a mixture of bayou dirt an
Trevor's blood—swirled at her feet and disappeared. Hold
ing her stomach, Rain doubled over in the stall and retche
But there was nothing inside her to come out. She sank t
her knees, hoping the noise of the running water muffle
her quiet sobs. He had to live. Trevor had been in surgery fo
nearly two hours, and they'd been told next to nothing.

Several minutes later, Rain turned off the shower. Sh
stood in the collected steam and tried to regain control ove
herself. A knock sounded at the door.

"Rain?" It was Annabelle. "I found some clothes. They'r
medical scrubs, but at least they're clean."

"Thanks," she replied weakly, unsure if the other woman could even hear her. But the door opened a few inches and Annabelle placed the garments on the edge of the sink before closing it again.

When she came out, Annabelle handed her a wax-paper cup filled with coffee and covered with a plastic lid.

"Any word?" Rain asked, but Annabelle shook her head. Rain glanced at Brian, who sat in a chair next to Alex's bed. But he looked away from her and focused his gaze on the television set bracketed to the wall.

"We're all praying for him," Alex said as he grasped Brian's hand.

Nodding, she cupped her palms around the coffee's warmth for a few moments. Then she placed it on a shelf, leaving it untouched.

"I'm going back to the waiting room," she murmured and walked out.

She had to leave, before she fell apart in front of them. Rain kept on her path down the brightly lit corridor, despite Annabelle calling after her. She pushed the button in the elevator bay and looked out the plate-glass window. The darkness outside had never seemed more formidable, although she knew daybreak was only a short time away. Fear whispered to her that she might never see Trevor again.

Annabelle caught up to her as the elevator doors opened. She stepped on beside her. "I'm coming with you."

Rain looked at the floor, unable to hide her tears.

"No one blames you," Annabelle said. "Brian's just upset. He's second-guessing himself about not taking Trevor to one of the parish clinics."

"It's my fault he's in surgery. He was trying to save *me*."

"You didn't cause this," Annabelle reasoned as the elevator began moving down. "Trevor has a dangerous job. We're all aware of that."

Rain rubbed a hand over her eyes, unwilling to absolve herself of responsibility. "If it hadn't been me who Carteris abducted, Trevor would never have done something as reckless as go out there alone."

"He couldn't have lived with himself if anything happened to you. Call it a twin's intuition, but I think Trevor loves you, Rain. He'd risk anything to protect the people he cares about. I'm proof of that."

Trevor loves you. Annabelle's quiet assertion was more than Rain could handle. She fought another wave of tears. "Oliver was my patient. I should've known—"

"Should've known what?" Annabelle asked gently. "That his father was some deranged vampire freak obsessed with your mother? You had no reason to think anything except that Oliver Carteris was a troubled young man who'd been given too much money and too many freedoms. He never said anything to you that hinted at what he was involved in, did he?"

"No." The elevator doors opened again. Rain knew Annabelle had heard her conversation with Sawyer Compton. She released a breath. "The assistant D.A. probably thinks I'm insane."

"Sawyer's having his staff dig into Carteris's background. But he's heard pretty much everything in his line of work."

They walked into an alcove near double doors marked Surgical Staff Only. The waiting area was lit by ceramic table lamps and the silvery glow of an aquarium, and couches were arranged around the room. Brian joined them a short time later. He sat next to Rain, pulling her to him as he whispered an apology.

Holding her injured wrist, Rain fell into an uneasy sleep against him. But it wasn't long before Brian's movement brought her back to consciousness. She rose to her feet with

e others as a fatherly-looking man walked into the wait-
g area.

"Rivette family?"

His scrubs bore the telltale stains of blood.

48

She couldn't take her eyes off him. Rain held Trevor's hand which felt cold and still within her own.

The surgeon forewarned he'd been placed on a ventilator to allow his injured lung to heal more easily. But she now realized she hadn't been prepared for the reality. A tube ran into his mouth, connecting him to the equipment next to the bed. Its rhythmic whooshing accompanied the beep of the heart monitor. Rain thought of Trevor's confession to her about his terror when he'd awoken with a machine controlling him all those years ago.

His chest was bare, and another tube had been inserted between his ribs to drain fluid that had collected in the space around his lungs. She brushed her fingers over the ugly bruise where the vest had stopped the bullet. *The first time she thought Carteris had killed him.*

More tubes went into his forearm, channels for IV drip that hung from poles, and still more traveled under the blue hospital blanket and into bags draped along the bed's frame. The surgery had repaired his nicked spleen, as well as the tear in the paper-thin tissue of his lung. But the biggest threat was the hypovolemic shock that had set in from the severe blood loss. Even with transfusions, Trevor's blood pressure remained low, and medication was necessary to increase it.

Sitting in a chair at his bedside, Rain lowered her head to the sheets. She wanted to fall asleep next to him and let sweet oblivion drown out the hospital noise and antiseptic smells. But the ICU had a visitation policy of fifteen minutes every two hours, limited to family. She wasn't even supposed to be here, but Annabelle and Brian had insisted she go in first.

Rain stayed a few more minutes. Then she reluctantly rose to leave. Placing a kiss on Trevor's forehead, she turned to see Brian standing outside the door of the ICU bay. He touched her shoulder as she walked past.

In the waiting room, Annabelle and Sawyer sat together in quiet conversation. Sawyer's arm rested intimately on the back of the couch behind Annabelle's head. Cognizant they were no longer alone, Sawyer stood and offered to get a round of coffee from the vending machine, then excused himself.

"How does he look?" Annabelle asked as Rain sat down.

"Not good. I know they told us to expect that, but…"

"He's going to get through this." Annabelle spoke with conviction. "I'm sending Brian home to get some sleep. You should go, too. If anything changes, I'll call."

Rain shook her head. "I'm staying."

"You've had a horrible experience yourself. Now that Trevor's out of surgery, don't you think you should see an E.R. doctor?"

Her wrist was swollen and painful, but that seemed trivial compared to what Trevor was going through.

"Rain," Annabelle said quietly. "Did that man hurt you?"

She focused her gaze on the carpet. Carteris hadn't raped her, although what he'd done had made her feel violated. Her stomach clenched at the recollection of his scalpel cutting

into her. He'd held her down and lapped at the blood flow
ing over her skin. Had he been reenergizing himself for th
night ahead? She'd pushed those memories aside, but no
everything was beginning to resurface. Carteris had planne
to re-create the night of Desiree's death, and Rain was awan
of just how close he'd come to succeeding.

"There was a room…in back of the cabin," she said, nee
ing to give voice to the nightmare. "Carteris made it loc
like my mother's old bedroom. I remembered it from m
childhood—it had the same furniture, the same bedsprea
Even the stuffed animal on the bed was identical."

Rain ran her hands over the thighs of the hospital scrul
she wore, avoiding Annabelle's eyes. "Carteris was goin
to kill me in that room. He was only waiting for Trevor 1
arrive. He wanted him to die knowing what was happenin
to me, but being unable to stop it. If Brian hadn't shown u
when he did, that's exactly what would've happened."

"How could he have known what your mother's bedroo
looked like? You don't really think it's possible he was ii
volved with her?"

"I don't know."

Annabelle leaned forward and lowered her tone, althoug
the waiting room was otherwise unoccupied. "Christian Ca
teris was on the board of directors at *this* hospital. I've see
him—his photo's in the lobby. That man couldn't have bee
more than forty or so, could he?"

Rain sighed. A rational answer eluded her. Not even plast
surgery could have turned back the clock for Carteris to th
degree. And it went beyond his face—he'd been strong an
quick, able to manhandle her as if she was a child. She thoug
of the human remains in the swamp. She'd told Sawyer abo
that, too.

"There was something about him that seemed…" But Rai
couldn't find the right word. *Superhuman?* Unwilling to sa

aloud, she let the thought slip away as Sawyer returned balancing two coffees. He gave one to Annabelle and the other to her. He was a handsome man, with even features and thick, blond hair cut military short.

"As soon as you finish that, Annabelle says I'm taking you home."

Annabelle sipped from her cup. "She needs to go to the E.R. first to get herself examined. Her wrist needs X-raying, and some of those cuts look pretty bad."

"We'll take care of that, too," he agreed. Annabelle gave her a look that dared her to argue, and Rain relented. The pain in her wrist was persistent, and her body shook with fatigue. She'd be no good to any of them if she collapsed on the waiting-room floor.

"You promise you'll call?"

"He won't be awake for hours. Go home and sleep. Have something to eat. You can come back in the afternoon."

A little over an hour later, Sawyer held the door open for Rain as they walked outside. She carried a filled antibiotic prescription and wore a brace on her fractured wrist. Above them, darkness was giving way to the glow of early morning.

Television-news crews had set up in the hospital parking lot. Sawyer maneuvered her through the crowd, stopping only long enough to make it clear there was no official comment at this time. He shielded Rain with his arm, propelling her toward his green Ford Explorer as reporters called after them.

"This is big news—it's not every day a top cardiac surgeon turns out to be a serial killer," Sawyer said as he helped her climb into the vehicle. Once he'd gotten in on the driver's side, he continued, "The D.A.'s office is conducting a press conference with the FBI and police this afternoon. The Bureau's BCU director is also flying in from D.C. Trevor should be

getting the glory—instead, he's probably going to get h
ass handed to him for breaking protocol and going out the
without proper backup, not to mention taking a civilian wi
him to assist in the rescue."

He gave her a serious glance. "Things could've gone ve
wrong out there, Dr. Sommers."

Rain fastened her seat belt. Her heart ached for Trevor.
just want him to be okay."

"Don't worry. Trev will pull through." He smiled faint
and started the engine. "He's too stubborn not to."

"How long have you been seeing Annabelle?" Rai
asked.

"I've been seeing her for a long time." Sawyer appeare
thoughtful as he pulled from the parking lot. "Thing is, i
only lately she's started to see me."

At home, after she'd had dry toast and a cup of tea, Ra
wandered into her office. Dahlia rubbed against her ankl
as she stood at the window overlooking the small courtya
garden. Celeste's delicate tea roses were in bloom, and a pa
of mourning doves perched on the birdbath at the edge of t
brick patio. Purple wisteria hung from the tree boughs.
would have been a peaceful scene, if not for the worry clutcl
ing her heart. Annabelle had been right to send her home, sl
admitted. But she'd nap for only an hour or two and then g
right back to the hospital.

Turning, she noticed her computer was on. Its screen he
notes from her sessions with Oliver Carteris. Trevor mu
have gone through them, looking for clues to her whereabout
Searching her memory of her conversations with Oliver, sl
wondered if there'd been some sign she'd missed. Regardles
she had an inescapable feeling that she'd somehow failed
do her job.

Rain tried to will away her anxiety. She'd told the E.F

doctor what Carteris had done to her, but he'd assured her any risk of HIV transmission through saliva was low. Thankfully, she'd been inoculated against hepatitis B as a precaution during her doctoral program, when she'd spent time working in a facility for troubled adolescents. Still, he'd given her a booster shot to put her mind at ease.

She took the ice pack she'd made in the kitchen and went upstairs to her bedroom. Sunlight slanted across the unmade bed, which was just as she and Trevor had left it the previous morning. Skimming her fingers over the rumpled sheets evoked vivid images of their lovemaking. She needed to think of that, and not Trevor lying bleeding and unconscious on the plane's floor.

The lack of sleep had caught up to her. Rain's limbs were sore and her eyes burned with fatigue. Too tired to even locate a nightgown, she shrugged out of the oversize medical scrubs and slid naked under the sheets. Pressing her face against the pillow where Trevor's head had rested, she hoped to catch some lingering scent of him. But there was only the light floral fragrance of the laundry detergent. Disappointed, she closed her eyes.

The slow fall of footsteps interrupted her drowse. Rain sat up, drawing the sheets over her breasts. She called out, fearing a response, and was relieved when she heard only silence in return. After a short while she brushed her hair from her face and lay back down, chalking it up to her clattering nerves.

Rain was just falling asleep when she heard the strains of music coming from downstairs. Desiree's husky voice floated up to her on the rich melody. Fear tingled along her skin. She wasn't alone.

She dashed to the door with the intent of slamming it closed and locking it, but a towering frame filled the threshold. Carteris's green eyes behind his spectacles held a mocking glint.

"You thought you could kill me that easily?"

He carried her backward in one swift movement and fell with her onto the bed. Rain tried to scream, but his weight crushed the air from her lungs.

"We have unfinished business, little one." Grabbing her hair, he forced her head back and bared her throat. Rain's eyes widened as his mouth opened to reveal long, pointed incisors. His head drove down, his teeth sinking painfully deep into her neck. Carteris's grunting sounds of pleasure echoed in the room as he fed.

Paralyzed, Rain felt herself dying. The warm, sticky wetness of her blood poured over her throat and chest, soaking the mattress under her.

She awoke to the phone's ringing. The sheets twisted around her were soaked with perspiration, and her voice when she answered came out breathless and unsteady.

"Rain?" Annabelle was on the other end of the line. The clock on the nightstand indicated it was nearly three in the afternoon. The ice pack she'd brought from the kitchen had melted into a mess beside her on the bed.

"I overslept," she said, instantly panicked. "What's happened?"

"He's awake." Annabelle's words held a tremor. "He tried to pull out his breathing tube. They're trying to calm him down, but it's not working."

Rain phoned for a taxi and left the house.

The nurse at the monitoring station called after her, but Rain kept going until she reached the windowed ICU bay. Two orderlies were exiting the area. She inhaled sharply at the sight of Trevor's wrists enclosed in padded restraints against the bed rails. Annabelle bent over the bed, talking to him in a soothing tone. Although his eyes were closed, tears leaked from under his dark lashes. Rain could see anxiety etched on every millimeter of his face.

"Trevor," she whispered, moving closer.

He opened his eyes at the sound of her voice and Rain offered him a gentle smile. His pupils were dilated, overpowering the stormy blue-gray of his irises, and his gaze appeared glassy and fevered.

She ran her fingers through his sweat-dampened hair and spoke to him softly. "I know you don't like the ventilator, but you have an injured lung and it needs time to heal. That's all it is, a tiny little tear in your lung. Everything else is fine, I swear."

She wasn't sure if he understood her. But when she slid her hand into his, Trevor's fingers clutched hers tightly, as if she was his lifeline. Moisture welled in her eyes.

"This is just for a few days, until your lung is stronger," Rain urged. "Just rest. Let the machine do the work for you."

She continued stroking his hair until his eyes closed again. The rapid beep of the heart monitor slowed to a steadier pace. After a minute or so, she felt his grasp loosen. He'd drifted back to sleep, but she didn't dare move. Rain looked at Annabelle. She stood at the foot of the bed, her arms wrapped around her stomach.

"They sedated him through his IV line, but it hasn't had much effect," she said quietly. "They don't understand it. The doctors don't want to put him all the way under because his blood pressure is so low already. But they said if they had to, they'd medically induce a coma."

Her voice broke on the last word. "I don't know how he has the strength to fight."

"He has a strong will," Rain murmured.

"He's remembering the last time he woke up on a ventilator, isn't he?"

Rain hoped Trevor hadn't done any damage when he'd attempted to extubate himself. The surgical tape that held the breathing tube in place concealed the scar that ran along the base of his chin. *War wounds. Trevor had a lifetime of them.* Even in his weakened condition, it was possible he was having a flashback of emerging from his coma years ago. Rain thought of the difficulties Trevor had gone through then, trying to rebuild his strength and regain his verbal skills. What if he feared the same thing had happened to him again?

Annabelle must have sensed her thoughts, because she added, "I think seeing me is upsetting him."

"He's disoriented. He's just confused about what's happening," Rain reassured her. But in that moment, the courage and faith Annabelle had shown throughout the past evening appeared to be slipping. It was clear how much she loved her brother.

"Have you checked on Haley yet?" Rain asked. She knew a neighbor of Annabelle's was watching the little girl. "You've been here since last night."

She wiped her cheeks. "Brian's coming in another hour. I'll go then."

"Go ahead and go now. I'll stay with him."

When she saw the worry in Annabelle's eyes, Rain promised, "I won't let them throw me out. To hell with the ICU rules. I've already dealt with a serial-killer vampire. I can handle a bossy nurse."

Annabelle's vision lingered on the rise and fall of Trevor's chest.

"He responded to you," she said. "As soon as he saw you, he was able to let go. He needs you, Rain."

She picked up her purse and put its strap over her shoulder. "The ICU is supposed to be family only. Just so you know, I gave your name at the desk this morning as Trevor's fiancée."

They shared a long look and then Annabelle left the room. Shifting her gaze back to Trevor, Rain took in the paleness of his features and the shadows under his eyes. He looked fragile to her, immersed in a labyrinth of tubes and wires. She was achingly aware that he stood on the edge of a dark abyss. Holding his hand, she vowed not to let him fall.

49

"I hope we're not talking shop in here."

Trevor looked up from the hospital bed to see Annabelle in the doorway. Considering the guilty looks being exchanged between Sawyer Compton and Eddie McGrath, who were also in the room, he figured there was little point in denying a briefing was taking place.

"Your sister's gonna have my hide if you don't say something," Sawyer muttered. "She warned me to go easy on you."

"I asked them to come, Anna." Trevor's voice was raspy from the tube that had only recently been removed from his throat. "I needed details on the case."

"You *need* to rest." Taking the chair beside the bed, her expression reflected concern. "You've only been out of ICU for two days."

"I'm okay." Nearly a week had passed since the surgery. Although Trevor still felt like hell, his desire for information currently overrode his need to recuperate. He'd called both men and asked them to come by and fill him in on what had been pieced together on Carteris so far. As he already knew, the surgeon's lecture circuit matched the time line of the killings in other cities. But his DNA had also now been linked to

e victims, indisputably establishing him as the killer of all
even women. Not to mention, the remains of two additional,
nidentified bodies had been located in the swamps near the
ayou cabin.

What was less clear, however, was Carteris's past. The
arther the story went back on him the murkier it got, begin-
ing with a discrepancy about the year of his graduation from
xford Medical School. The date supplied by the university
nd the one in Carteris's personnel records at All Saints dif-
ered by nearly two decades. As for a birth certificate, there
as none on file. The Louisiana Office of Public Health listed
as *officially misplaced.*

Trevor thought of the man who'd been at the center of
is manhunt for well over a year and a half. The same man
who'd abducted Rain and stabbed him. He'd seen Carteris
ith his own eyes and he was damn sure he'd been nowhere
ear eligible for a senior citizen's discount.

"We're trying to get access to Carteris's records prior to
is return to the States two years ago," Sawyer said, picking
ack up on the discussion. "But since his research took place
t private institutions in Europe and Asia, they've been less
an forthcoming about what he was working on."

"What about the autopsy report?" Trevor asked.

"Based on the condition of the internal organs, the M.E.
stimates Carteris was in his early forties. And despite his
ondness for ingesting human blood, he was amazingly dis-
ase free. But he'd definitely had some cosmetic work done.
. rhytidectomy, which is a fancy word for a face-lift. I have
) admit that kind of plastic surgery seems out of the ordinary
or a man that young."

"But it's not unheard of."

"Did you tell him about the wife?" McGrath interjected.

Trevor shifted his attention to the detective. "Carteris's?
/hat about her?"

"There was no car accident," McGrath said. "The medical file says she died of a massive hemorrhage. Apparently she *fell* from a balcony nine years ago and was impaled on a garden stake. The Thai authorities ruled it an accident, but who knows for sure."

Sawyer leaned against the robin's egg–blue wall of the private room. "If I had to guess, I'd say Carteris was bedbug crazy and not some kind of superfreak."

Still, Trevor knew about the things Carteris had claimed to Rain during the time he'd held her captive. Although he concurred with Sawyer's assessment, Carteris's boasts had to be unsettling to her.

"Have the labs come back on the drugs found in Carteris's bag at the cabin?"

"They're still running analyses," Sawyer said. "But the preliminary report indicates high-dosage antioxidants, steroids and injectable HGH, or human growth hormone. There were also two compounds they've been unable to identify that might be part of Carteris's research. Trace amounts of them showed up in his bloodstream. Which again points to crazy, not immortal."

"So how do you account for the graduation date from Oxford?" McGrath asked.

Sawyer shrugged. "Maybe the university got the dates messed up, or there was another Christian Carteris who graduated years earlier. Maybe our guy assumed the original Carteris's identity. There're still a lot of questions."

"All I know is what I saw at the surgeon's house." McGrath adjusted the sling that held his injured arm. "The letters were addressed to Desiree Sommers, and they were postmarked over thirty years ago. They were *love letters,* signed by Carteris."

"Letters that no longer exist," Sawyer reminded. "The

burned with the rest of the house. There's no way to test their authenticity."

"Okay, then what about the photo from the cabin? The lab can't find any indication of it being doctored."

Sawyer crossed his arms over his chest. "Don't tell me you're buying this ageless-vampire thing, Detective McGrath? Because you sound like you are."

"All I'm saying is maybe there're things we're not supposed to know. Things that defy explanation. This *is* New Orleans, Counselor. Weirder stuff has happened here. Tibbs would've chalked it up to some bad juju. He'd remind us Carteris is dead—case closed—and that we've got plenty of live dirtbags to focus on."

"Thibodeaux was a good cop," Trevor said.

"Damn straight." McGrath's expression was somber. "And he's probably pissed right now Carteris got the jump on him."

One thing was for certain, Trevor thought. Whoever or whatever Carteris was, he'd taken too many innocent lives.

"One more issue." Sawyer switched topics. "You should know D'Alba's out on bail. He's been arraigned on conspiracy to commit assault."

Trevor's jaw tightened. "I hope the D.A.'s going after him."

"Like flies on…" Sawyer's words faded as he glanced at Annabelle. "You know."

Coughing, Trevor grimaced at the flare of pain in his chest.

"We should let you get some rest." McGrath moved to the door. "I've got somewhere I need to be, anyway. Tibbs's funeral is still going on. It's one hell of a party, Rivette. Shame you're missing it."

Trevor was aware New Orleans funerals could last a week, particularly in the African-American community. He

imagined a parade being led by a full jazz band and boisterous memorial events taking place at the French Quarter bars.
There was no doubt it would be a proper send-off.

Sawyer followed McGrath's exit, his fingers subtly brushing Annabelle's as he went past. In the doorway, he turned
and said to Trevor, "Don't forget what we talked about."

Trevor nodded.

"You look terrible," Annabelle observed once the men had
left. She waited while he pushed the button that administered
pain medication from the electronic console and laid his head
back on the pillow. "I'm serious, Trevor."

"When were you going to tell me about you and Sawyer?"

"He told you?"

"He didn't have to. I might be in a medicated cloud, but
all the staring and touching has been hard to miss. He spent
the last five minutes making cow eyes at you."

"Sawyer doesn't make *cow eyes*." She sighed as she folded
her hands over her denim skirt. "I wasn't sure I was ready
to tell anyone. I've just made so many mistakes in the past.
Sometimes it's hard to trust myself."

"What does Haley think about him?"

"She likes him. Even though she told him he has porcupine
hair."

The comment made Trevor chuckle. He winced as his su-
tures pulled again.

"Has Brian been here?" Annabelle asked once he'd settled
back down.

"He came by. Early this morning."

"Then he told you a gallery from Chicago called about
a showing. Alex is teasing him that he's going to leave the
South behind for big-city life."

"I'm proud of him." Trevor thought of Brian's skilled landing on the rural highway, and the way he'd trailed him into

e bayou instead of following orders to wait at the plane.
rian had saved Rain's life, as well as his own.

A space of silence filled the room. Standing, Annabelle
ussed with an arrangement of flowers on the nightstand.
They're not going to be able to charge Dad with anything
·lated to taking Haley since they were only a few miles away
nd he called to tell us where they were. To a jury, it would
·ook like a grandfather making an innocent mistake. Saw-
·r's still pushing for aiding and abetting Rain's abduction,
ut he's doubtful on that, too, since he appears to be an un-
·itting accomplice. I asked him to let me tell you instead."

Although it seemed clear their father was merely a pawn
· Carteris's game, it didn't keep Trevor from wishing they'd
ave found a way to put him in jail where he belonged. If
nyone deserved retribution for the unspeakable acts he'd
ommitted, it was James Rivette.

Annabelle appeared to weigh her next words before speak-
ıg. "They're considering removing the statute of limitations
n forcible rape in Louisiana. I know it's something they've
ılked about in the legislature before and it probably won't
appen...but if it did, I'd consider pressing charges."

When he peered at her silently, she added, "I want him
o pay for what he did. To both of us. I should've been brave
nough to do it years ago."

"Anna," Trevor said softly. His eyes held hers.

"I've never forgiven myself for lying about what hap-
ened to you, Trevor. If I'd only told the truth about what
e'd done—"

"You were scared. You and Brian were trying to survive.
understand that."

"Understanding isn't the same thing as forgiving," she
ıurmured.

Trevor studied her face. What he was about to say wasn't
asy for him, but he knew it was time.

"My staying away from here…it hasn't been about ange
It's about me not wanting to remember." He slowly shook h
head. "I've tried like hell to forget about our childhood ar
every bad thing that happened to us. But every time I cam
back here…every time I saw you and Brian…the truth is,
all became real again."

Trevor took a steadying breath. All the decisions he'd mac
over the course of his life now seemed questionable to hin
and he fought a wave of regret. "I thought if I stayed away…
could have some kind of peace. But I realize now that all I'v
done is isolate myself from the people who matter most.
punished you and Brian because I wasn't strong enough 1
deal with the past. I'm sorry for that."

She squeezed his hand. "Trevor, you're the strongest perso
I know."

He stared at the plastic hospital-ID bracelet around hi
wrist. *Rivette*. It was a name he was tied to by blood, a cor
nection that had proved hard to break. When he looked at h
sister again, he saw the anguish in her eyes. Annabelle's su
cide attempt. Brian's drug use and their mother's alcoholism
Family secrets had wound their roots around each of then
threatening to drag them down into darkness. Trevor had ru
from those powerful tendrils even as they clutched at him.

"Rain believes the memories you're having…she think
therapy could help you." Annabelle looked at him uncertainl
"Would you consider talking to her? If you're not comfor
able with that, she can refer you to a different psychoanalys
Even one in D.C."

Rain. She'd been a constant presence during Trevor's tim
in ICU, soothing him each time the panic had seized hin
Much of the events of the past week were foggy, but th
care he'd seen in her amber eyes remained vivid. Rain ha
managed to pull him through the worst of it, despite wh

she'd been dealing with herself. He'd held on to her when everything else was spinning out of control.

"I'll talk to her about it," he promised quietly.

Their intimacy was broken by the arrival of an orderly with a lunch tray.

"Can you believe me?" Annabelle chided herself. "I chased off your visitors and now I'm the one tiring you out."

Once the orderly was gone, she pushed the mobile table to the bed, then lifted the tray's cover to reveal a bowl of yellow noodle soup, lime gelatin, a roll with a pat of butter in foil wrapping and an ice-cream cup. "The soft-food diet. How does your throat feel?"

"Like I swallowed razor blades." He glanced at the tray's contents with disdain. "I'll take the ice cream. You can roll the rest back into the hall."

Annabelle helped him raise the bed higher. As she did, her eyes lingered on the greenish bruise under his collarbone, visible in the gap of the cotton hospital gown.

"I can't believe that man shot you before he stabbed you," she said worriedly as he peeled the lid off the ice-cream cup. "You're like a cat with nine lives, Trevor. And I'm afraid you've lost count of how many of those lives you've already run through."

Thoughtfully, he scraped the wooden spoon across the ice cream's surface before speaking. "Sawyer offered me a job."

Annabelle looked stunned. "Here? In New Orleans?"

Despite the positive press the FBI had gotten for closing the case on the serial murders, Trevor had been notified that he was being brought before the Bureau's Board of Professional Review. There was nothing SAC Johnston could do about it—his superior had told him as much by phone, even as he'd congratulated him for his hard work. Trevor had broken protocol going after Carteris alone in a hostage situation. While that was a forgivable offense considering the outcome, he'd also endangered Brian, a civilian. But if he had handled it any differently, Rain would be dead now. He was certain of it.

While Trevor didn't think the infraction would end his career, it was possible he'd be placed on suspension, or even busted down from VCU to a field agent position. What Sawyer was offering was a chance to move forward, not take a step back.

He was also presenting a way to come home.

"Sawyer thinks my background in criminal investigation would be an asset to the D.A.'s office," Trevor said. "I'd have to pass the state bar here, of course. And I went straight to Quantico after law school, so I haven't had much trial experience. But it's a good offer. It could be a new challenge for me."

"I never thought you'd consider coming back here." Annabelle couldn't hide the hope that infused her features. Sunlight filtered through the blinds behind her, framing her against a brilliant blue sky that was like the backdrop for a studio photograph.

"A few weeks ago, I wouldn't have," Trevor replied honestly. He met her gaze. "But I'm thinking of giving it a try."

He must have fallen asleep sometime after lunch. When Trevor opened his eyes, the light in the room had softened and Annabelle was no longer there. Rain sat in the chair next to his bed. She was looking at a get-well card Haley had made out of construction paper.

"How long have you been here?" he asked, groggy.

"A little while." She stood the card upright on the night stand. "I had a couple of therapy sessions scheduled this morning."

"You're back to work?"

"It keeps my mind off things." Rain shrugged her slender ulders. She wore her hair loose, and she pushed a curtain coppery waves behind one ear. Although her scratches and s were healing, a brace still encircled her right wrist. Her isive expression gave him pause.

"You okay?"

She nodded and changed the subject. "I met your aunt san and uncle Frank in the lobby last night. They seem e nice people."

"They are." Still studying her, Trevor shifted his weight efully. He patted the mattress. "Come here."

"I don't want to hurt you."

"You won't. It's not like you take up much room, any- y."

She got up from the chair. Smoothing down her linen cks, she sat on the edge of Trevor's bed, careful to avoid the line attached to his arm. Her fingers stroked his temple.

"I guess we haven't had much time to talk," he said.

"No, we haven't."

There had been a steady stream of visitors since Trevor had en moved from ICU to a private room: Annabelle, Brian d Alex, Sawyer and Eddie McGrath. Even Danny Reyes th the DEA had come by. Nate was still on assignment, but had called twice and sent a ridiculously large fruit basket. s aunt and uncle had also driven over from their retirement mmunity in Florida. Rain had been there as well, but there d been little opportunity for a private conversation between em.

"Want to tell me what you're thinking about?"

She stared at the floral arrangements around the room. ust that all these flowers…they could've been for your neral."

"I'm right here, Rain. I'm going to be okay."

"You don't understand." Her lovely hazel eyes held a

shimmer of tears. "You stopped breathing as we were land
ing in New Orleans. Did you know that?"

"Brian told me. He said you gave me mouth-to-mouth unt
the paramedics could take over."

When she didn't respond, he touched her cheek. "He als
said you drove Carteris's SUV back to the plane."

Rain shook her head. She seemed in disbelief herself.
don't know how I did it. All I could think about was gettii
you out of there. Nothing else mattered."

"You shot Carteris."

"I had to." She pressed her lips together, obviously reca
ing the things that had transpired during her time alone wi
the surgeon.

"Who was he?" she whispered.

"They're still working to figure that out."

"He said he killed my parents. That it was never a murde
suicide at all."

Trevor fell silent, wanting to give her the answers she de
perately needed but being unable to do so. Sawyer had tc
him the D.A.'s office was considering reopening the investig
tion into her parents' deaths, but he didn't think now was t
time to discuss it. Regardless, it was unlikely there would
much evidence left to support or invalidate Carteris's clain
The more probable outcome would be a new firestorm
tabloid articles on Desiree and her violent murder—anotl
event Rain would be forced to endure. This latest chap
in Desiree's legacy only deepened the mystery surroundi
her.

"Who were the other women in the swamp?" Rain aske

"They don't know yet. They're trying to match them
missing persons cases in the area. It's possible they we
prostitutes from New Orleans. Or runaways. Women w
wouldn't be easily missed."

"Do you think Carteris was as old as he claimed?"

"No," Trevor stated. "Although I think *he* believed it. But he's gone now. It's over. We need to focus on that."

"I'll try." Her hand skimmed his forearm. In the room's light, he could see the faint spray of golden freckles across her small nose, and her porcelain skin appeared luminous. Trevor slipped a hand through her hair, marveling at its silken feel. He was unbelievably fortunate to have gotten her back.

"You shouldn't have come out there, Trevor. You knew he'd never let you leave alive."

He looked into her eyes. "If he'd killed you, I wouldn't have survived anyway."

She lowered her head and pressed her lips to his. The sweetness of their mouths joining was something Trevor felt in his soul. Rain offered a calmness to his intensity. Her lightness balanced his dark. For the longest time, he'd felt as if something inside him was broken and unfixable. But Rain gave him hope that he could somehow defeat the ghosts that still haunted him. He realized he'd do whatever he had to in order to heal. Trevor needed his heart to be open to his family, and to her. He cupped her delicate jawline.

"We haven't known each other for very long," he said, his voice soft. "But there're a couple of things I already know about you."

"Like what?"

"I know I love you."

A tear slipped down her cheek. "What's the other thing?"

He wanted to see her smile. "You seriously need to learn to drive. And I mean more than in emergency-only situations. Couldn't you see a therapist about this phobia thing?"

"Therapists?" Rain rolled her eyes. "Don't you know? They're all a bunch of New Age quacks."

"Then I guess I'll have to get used to driving you around the rest of my life." His expression had turned serious and she

gazed at him, confused. Slowly, he tugged her mouth ba
to his for another kiss.

Returning to New Orleans would require coming to ter
with his past. He'd have to live in the same delta city whe
James Rivette existed. Could he do it? Become a part of t
place again? If he could overcome the obstacles, he believ
it would be worth every effort. He belonged here with A
nabelle and Brian, and with Rain. His history and his futu
were undeniably intertwined.

Settling against him, Rain laid her head in the crook of
neck and exhaled lightly, her breath warm against his ski

"I love you, too," she murmured.

It was time to confront the shadows and bury them de
in the fertile earth of the Mississippi riverbanks forever. T
desire for family and friends—*for real connection*—was u
familiar, but it was there inside him just the same. All Trev
knew was that he wanted to start living his life.

He was ready to stop running.

REQUEST YOUR FREE BOOKS!

2 FREE NOVELS
FROM THE SUSPENSE COLLECTION
PLUS 2 FREE GIFTS!

MSUS

Start your Best Body today with these top 3 nutrition tips!

1. SHOP THE PERIMETER OF THE GROCERY STORE: The good stuff—fruits, veggies, lean proteins and dairy—always line the outer edges of the store. When you veer into the center aisles, you enter the temptation zone, where the unhealthy foods live.

2. WATCH PORTION SIZES: Most portion sizes in restaurants are nearly twice the size of a true serving and at home, it's easy to "clean your plate." Use these easy serving guidelines:
- Protein: the palm of your hand
- Grains or Fruit: a cup of your hand
- Veggies: the palm of two open hands

3. USE THE RAINBOW RULE FOR PRODUCE: Your produce drawers should be filled with every color of fruits and vegetables. The greater the variety, the more vitamins and other nutrients you add to your diet.

Find these and many more helpful tips in

PRESENTING...THE SEVENTH ANNUAL
MORE THAN WORDS™ ANTHOLOGY

Five bestselling authors
Five real-life heroines

This year's Harlequin
More Than Words award
recipients have changed lives,
one good deed at a time. To
celebrate these real-life heroines,
some of Harlequin's most
acclaimed authors have honored
the winners by writing stories
inspired by these dedicated
women. Within the pages
of *More Than Words Volume 7*,
you will find novellas written
by Carly Phillips, Donna Hill
and Jill Shalvis—and online at
www.HarlequinMoreThanWords.com
you can also access stories by
Pamela Morsi and Meryl Sawyer.

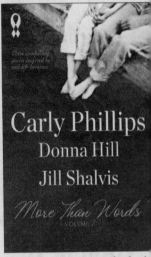

Carly Phillips
Donna Hill
Jill Shalvis

More Than Words
VOLUME 7

Coming soon in print and online!

Visit
www.HarlequinMoreThanWords.com
to access your FREE ebooks and to nominate
a real-life heroine in your community.

Proceeds from the sale of this book will be
reinvested in Harlequin's charitable initiatives.

MTWV7763